A MAGICAL KISS

"You're probably the most beautiful woman I've ever seen," Travers said.

And you're the best-looking man, Zoe thought, but didn't say.

Travers leaned toward her. He was going to kiss her, and she should use the better part of valor to move away. Not that it would be easy to move in this small bathroom. And not that she wanted to move.

Travers's lips touched hers and hers parted. Somehow her arms found their way around his neck, and his found their way around her waist, and she was pressed against him, her body fitting his as if they had been made for each other.

She willed her brain into silence, not that it took much work, and surrendered to the kiss. It was slow, and leisurely, as if their mouths were getting to know each other as a prelude to them getting to know each other. . . .

Books by Kristine Grayson

UTTERLY CHARMING

THOROUGHLY KISSED

COMPLETELY SMITTEN

SIMPLY IRRESISTIBLE

ABSOLUTELY CAPTIVATED

Published by Zebra Books

ABSOLUTELY
CAPTIVATED

Kristine Grayson

ZEBRA BOOKS
KENSINGTON PUBLISHING CORP.
http://www.kensingtonbooks.com

ZEBRA BOOKS are published by

Kensington Publishing Corp.
850 Third Avenue
New York, NY 10022

All Kensington titles, imprints and distributed lines are available at special quantity discounts for bulk purchases for sales promotion, premiums, fund-raising, educational or institutional use.

Special book excerpts or customized printings can also be created to fit specific needs. For details, write or phone the office of the Kensington Special Sales Manager: Kensington Publishing Corp., 850 Third Avenue, New York, NY 10022. Attn. Special Sales Department. Phone: 1-800-221-2647.

Zebra and the Z logo Reg. U.S. Pat. & TM Off.

First Printing: January 2004
10 9 8 7 6 5 4 3 2 1

Printed in the United States of America

*For KW and Geri Jeter,
in honor of their new home*

Acknowledgments

Many thanks to John Scognamiglio for all his input on my work, and to Merrilée Heifetz for believing in me. Kudos also have to go to my husband for his support on these books, and his willingness to live with someone who names her cats as oddly as the familiars in these novels.

One

Zoe Sinclair carried three overflowing beer steins toward the darkened corner of the bar, ignoring the catcalls and cries of "Hey, baby, bring 'em over here!" coming from the men at tables around the room. The calls came in perfect counterpoint to the beep-beep of the video poker machines lined up against the wall by the door. The cigarette smoke was thick and blue in the low-ceilinged room, and Zoe wouldn't have it any other way.

She was emphatically not a waitress—never had been, never would be, no matter how tight her money got—but she had perfected the three-stein carry in the nineteenth century, when she spent way too much time in German beer gardens, trying to find a secret doorway to Faerie that she'd heard about in Munich. She never found that German doorway, but she had come away with some practical skills, most of them having to do with beer.

O'Hasie's Pub was crowded tonight, which meant that one of the downtown casinos was hosting a major poker tournament. O'Hasie's was on the wrong side of Fremont Street, as far from the Fremont Street Experience as a walker could get.

O'Hasie's catered mainly to the locals, but during major downtown tournaments, the poker players—usually the losing ones—made their way through the drug dealers and hookers who found refuge in this last unDisneyfied section of Vegas, and stopped at O'Hasie's for some refreshment.

If Zoe had remembered that this was the big event, she would have suggested a different bar. But there were so many casinos in Las Vegas now, each with its own round of tournaments and concerts and special events, that she couldn't keep track of any of them.

Whenever Zoe went to a tourist venue, she wore the traditional costume of the traveling American: blue jeans, logo t-shirt, and sneakers. What she usually liked about O'Hasie's was that no tourists ventured close to it (except during major tournaments), and she could dress however she pleased.

Tonight she wore a black skirt with a slit along the side, and a see-through blouse over a black t-shirt. She topped it all with a small black fedora on her chin-length black hair. Certainly not camouflage clothes. The tourists looked at her as if she were a member of Vegas's exotic nightlife.

Zoe managed to make it all the way to the back without spilling a drop—not a mean trick, considering how wobbly her stiletto heels were on the pilled carpet. She skirted around two bulky women in green Fitzgerald's t-shirts, and headed for the booth next to the restrooms.

The booth had the benefit of privacy. It had tall sides made of the original mahogany wood that had once graced O'Hasie's. In the many remodels this bar had undergone since 1955, the mahogany mostly disappeared, except in a few surprising places—this booth, the corridor leading to the restrooms, and an old-fashioned, glass-doored phone cubicle just past the men's room door.

A small, red-shaded lamp glued to the wall above the table gave the booth an even greater air of privacy. From the bar, the patrons sitting in the booth were impossible to see.

But as she stepped across a rip in the carpet that had been there since 1983, the booth came into view. Its red upholstery looked particularly seedy, and the plastic oak-veneer tabletop, which someone had replaced the old wooden tables with four decades ago, had dried water stains that looked orange in the weird light.

Her friends, Herschel and Gaylord, were using two straws to slap a wadded-up straw wrapper back and forth as if it were a hockey puck. They were bent across the table, the game obviously serious, as games always were with the two of them.

They looked enough alike to be brothers, even though they weren't. They both had thick black hair, slightly pointed ears, and slender forms that they tried to hide under heavy leather jackets covered with lots of chains and metal. Lately Herschel had tried to toughen up his pretty face with piercings, but the studs in his nose emphasized its small, perfect shape, and the rings in the eyebrows only served to accent their upswept arch, which made them look like wings. Nothing these two guys could do—not even Gaylord's bruised right eye—could take away from their unearthly beauty.

Zoe set the steins down, then slid one to Herschel and the other to Gaylord. She took the third stein for herself and sat down next to Herschel, adjusting her skirt so the slit didn't show quite as much thigh to the drunk and disappointed poker players.

"You screwed up the arena," Gaylord said, raising his straw as if it were a lance. "You got water all over the playing surface."

Zoe picked up the crumpled wrapper, rolled it into a perfect ball between her manicured fingertips, and then tossed it into the wastebasket halfway across the room. She hit the basket, but didn't shout *Two points!* like she normally would have.

Instead, she leaned back in the booth and said, "We've had enough table hockey for the night."

"You know, Zo," Herschel said, tugging on a ring at the corner of his delicate mouth, "there are times you are no fun at all."

Zoe sipped the foam on her beer, wishing this bar had something more exotic than Heineken on tap. "I've got two divorces, one insurance fraud case, and one missing dachshund to find, so if you two—"

"Missing dachsund?" Gaylord giggled. The sound was high-pitched and infectious, and caught the attention of the poker players at a nearby table. They looked at Gaylord in shock, probably trying to decide how old he was. When Gaylord giggled like that, he sounded like he was three.

"Zo," Gaylord said, "you're better than finding missing dogs."

"It's my job," Zoe said. "I take the work that interests me."

"Since when did you become a pet detective?" Herschel asked.

Zoe felt a thread of irritation. "Since the client came to my office. Which is where I'm going to go if you two don't tell me why I'm here."

"Zo, Zo, Zo," Gaylord said. "You should get your money the old-fashioned way. You should conjure it."

He clapped his hands together and stacks of neatly wrapped, hundred-dollar bills littered the tabletop.

"I don't do that," Zoe said. "You know that."

She believed in earning her way through hard work, not magic. Besides, she was a mage, subject to the judgement of the Fates, and the rule of the Powers That Be. Herschel and Gaylord were faeries, who lived under different rules. The

Faerie Kings—the Faerie equivalent of the Fates—didn't seem to mind a lot of magic use, where the Fates punished mages for using too much.

Gaylord picked up a stack of bills and waved it under Zoe's nose. The stack smelled faintly of clover. "C'mon, Zo," he said. "Live a little. Party up, girl. You work too hard."

Zoe slapped the money away. "I don't cheat people."

"This isn't cheating," Gaylord said. "People are always so happy to get cash."

"It's Faerie money," she whispered. "It'll fade away in twenty-four hours."

"Long after you're gone, sweetheart," Gaylord said. "The humans'll just think they've lost it or spent it or counted it wrong when they were drunk."

Zoe crossed her arms. The poker players from the next table were watching, their eyes big.

"Get it out of here," she said very quietly, "or I'm leaving."

"By the solstice, Zo," Herschel snapped, "when did you get to be such a pain?"

Zoe gave him a cold smile. "I always have been, Hersch. I just usually pain in your favor."

Herschel tugged harder on the ring on the side of his mouth. "You make it sound like I take sides. I don't. Usually."

"Neither do I," said Zoe. "Now get rid of this stuff."

"If you promise to stop using real names," Herschel said. "You're making me nervous."

She had intended to make him nervous. The real name of a magical person—be he faerie or mage—had a lot of power. With the right spell, someone magical could control another magical person, just by using their real name.

"Well," Zoe said, nodding toward the Faerie money, "you're making me nervous, not to mention attracting a lot of attention."

Gaylord cursed in Gaelic which, from his accent, was not his native language. He clapped his hands together, and the money disappeared.

Zoe stretched one long leg toward the seat on the other side of the booth, then crossed the other leg over it. The slit in her skirt fell open, revealing a lot of skin.

She hoped the poker players noticed, so that they didn't search for the missing cash.

"You boys called me," she said softly. "Tell me what's going on or I'm taking your beers back to the bar."

Both Herschel and Gaylord grabbed their steins as if she had already tried to take them. She had taken their drinks away before. She felt she had that right.

She always bought when the three of them met because she didn't want to risk her reputation around town. Contrary to what Gaylord said, mortals did remember who gave them Faerie money. And even though they might not understand what happened, and eventually came to think of it as some kind of cheap parlor trick, they did resent it.

"Word on the street, Zo, is that the magic is gathering around you," Gaylord said.

"Which street?" Zoe asked. "Are we talking about the Strip or that avenue in Faerie you boys coated with pyrite?"

Herschel rolled his eyes. "It's not fool's gold, love. It's pixie dust, and you know we weren't supposed to tell you about that."

"I don't remember ever telling her about that," Gaylord said, giving Herschel a sideways look. "Did you?"

"We had to," Herschel said. "Zoe's never going to Faerie, are you, Zo?"

Zoe didn't answer that, at least not directly. She was afraid of Faerie. The prophecy that each mage got when her magical career started warned Zoe against Faerie, while promising her great rewards if she lived near it.

She could still hear the words as if they were being spoken for the first time: *You shall find your true love near Faerie, if you don't lose yourself inside its ever-changing walls.*

For the first few decades of her magical life, she had sought out Faerie, trying to find an entrance. She wanted to find her true love. She actually hoped that she would.

In those early years, she found two entrances to Faerie — and had two disastrous relationships while she lived nearby. Finally, she gave up on finding her true love. She wandered all over the world, settling in Los Angeles and becoming a private detective.

In the end, though, Faerie's siren song lured her to Las Vegas, the center of the faerie universe. She loved it here, with its combination of glitz and seediness. She loved the people who came through, the cases that she got, and the mortals that she met. She even had a lot of faerie friends.

But she refused to go anywhere near the entrance to Faerie, and tried hard to forget about the prophecy that had once guided her entire existence.

So she didn't answer Herschel's question directly. Instead, she said, "Why should I go to Faerie when it comes to me with rumors?"

"I been hearing them all over, doll," Herschel said, sipping on his beer. "Sages, prophets, the glamour-eyed. They are all talking about you."

"Me?" Zoe felt unsettled. The people Herschel mentioned were human with touches of magic, not part of the magical universe at all (although some of them eventually would become part of it). But these people saw corners of things, and it did the magical well to pay attention to what these people said.

"You, love," Gaylord said. "Everyone's saying the magic is gathering around you. Your time has come."

Zoe's mouth felt dry. "My time for what?"

"For whatever your destiny is," Herschel said. "Magic doesn't gather unless a destiny is about to be fulfilled."

"That's Faerie belief," Zoe said. "We don't believe that."

Herschel shrugged. "We all dip into the same magical well, Zo. Believe or don't believe. We just thought we'd warn you. Your prophecy is about to come true."

Gaylord stuck the straw he'd been using as a hockey stick into his beer. Then he stirred the amber liquid, ostensibly watching bubbles rise. But, Zoe could tell, he was looking at her out of the corner of his black-and-blue eye.

"It's not a bad one, is it?" Gaylord asked.

"What?" Zoe asked, a little too quickly.

"Your prophecy. It's not bad, right?"

Depended on whether you looked at the true love part or the warning part. But again, Zoe didn't answer him directly. Her prophecy was none of his business.

"All the mage prophecies are about love," Zoe said.

"Oh, yeah." Herschel giggled. His giggle wasn't as infectious as Gaylord's but it ran a close second. "Hearts, flowers, happily ever after. Soulmates. All sweetness and light, just like our Zoe here."

"Don't make fun," Zoe said. "Some people take this really seriously."

The smile left Herschel's metal-covered face. "You one of them, Zo?"

She used to be. Before her heart got broken, shattered, stomped on, and flattened.

"You know me," Zoe said. "Give me an Elvis Chapel, a bouquet of black hearts, and a million dollars, and I'll be happily married until the money's gone."

"I can give you a million dollars, babe," Herschel said.

Zoe narrowed her eyes. "Real money, Hersch. Real money."

"Liar." Gaylord slurped the beer through his straw. He'd

done that as long as Zoe had known him, and every time it creeped her out. Especially the sucking sound, as if he were pulling hops off the bottom of the stein with his lungs.

"I'm not lying," Zoe said. "I hate your money."

"You're lying about your dream, there, Zo." Gaylord stirred the beer with the soggy end of his straw. It had teeth marks in it, pointy holes from Gaylord's extra-sharp canines. Or, as he liked to call them, his fangs.

"I am not," Zoe said, clutching her own beer stein tightly. Except for one sip, she hadn't had any beer. And now she didn't want any more. But she held the stein in front of her as if it were a shield.

"Hon, you can have black hearts and Elvis, if you really want that. I'm not disputing that part. I'm disputing the money part. You've got enough to last you and with a snap of your fingers, you can conjure more." He stirred hard enough to make more bubbles rise.

Herschel tugged at a diamond pierced into the side of his nose, then realized what he was doing, stopped, and wiped his hand on his leather pants.

Gaylord continued, "You're an idealist, Zo. It's clear in all you do. You hide it, you pretend you're as cynical as they come, but you like the mortals and you like helping them, and you're not in it for the money."

Zoe gripped her beer stein tighter. She didn't think Gaylord was smart enough to see through her—not that it was hard. Anyone looking at her actions would know that she wasn't as cynical as she pretended to be.

She just hadn't thought anyone else was paying attention.

"So I betcha you believe in all this true love hogwash, and are secretly hoping some Prince Charming'll knock you off your feet and ride off into the sunset with you."

"Talk about mixed metaphors," Herschel muttered.

"And such a lovely image, too," Zoe said.

"So," Gaylord said, undeterred by the criticism, "if the magic is gathering, your Prince Charming is on the horizon."

Zoe set her beer stein down. "First of all, I don't believe in Prince Charmings. I don't believe in Prince anythings, having met several of them, and realizing that just because they're royalty doesn't mean their ears don't stick out."

"Hey!" Herschel put his hands over his severely pierced, jeweled, and pointed ears.

"She was referring to the British royalty, bud," Gaylord said.

Zoe pretended she hadn't heard the interchange. "Secondly, I don't believe in Charming. Charming means liar. Charming means a man who'll do anything to get what he wants. Thirdly—"

"We get it," Gaylord said. "You're not into this love thing. Which is why we warned you."

"Actually," Herschel said, "we warned you because gathering magic isn't always a good thing. Just because your destiny lurks doesn't mean that you'll get it. I mean, each prophecy has a dark side. Right? Ours do, anyway. Things can go good or they can go bad. Same with yours, right?"

"I didn't know you had prophecies," Zoe said with surprise.

"Um." Herschel looked at Gaylord, who looked back. They had equal expressions of panic on their handsome faces. "We don't."

"That's right," Gaylord said. "We don't. Of course not. Why would we befriend a mage if we had prophecies?"

Herschel kicked him under the table. Zoe saw Herschel's leg move, and heard the thud as his steel-toed boot connected with Gaylord's knee.

Zoe pushed her stein into the center of the table, and

leaned forward. She felt cold. "You befriended me because of a prophecy?" she asked.

"No," they said in unison. Herschel actually shook his head repeatedly, a clear sign that he was lying.

"Why would we do that?" Gaylord asked.

"You tell me," Zoe said.

They looked at each other again, wide-eyed, guilty looks.

"You may as well," Zoe said. "You aren't doing a good job of covering up. All I have to do is go to one of the seedy casinos on the Boulder Highway and ask around. They'll tell me who gets prophecies, and then I'll tell them who spilled the—"

"All right!" Herschel said, holding up his hands as if she were robbing him. "All right."

Gaylord watched him in stunned fascination. Or maybe it was fear. Zoe couldn't really tell, not at this angle and in the dim light.

"We have prophecies," Herschel said, "and they're not individual like yours. They all have to do with power, and right now, you're the power center, Zo."

Whatever she had expected him to say, it wasn't that. "Me?" she asked, not trying to cover her surprise.

He nodded. "I mean, we've always known, me and Gaylord, that you'd have something to do with the power shift in Faerie, but we didn't know how, especially after we got to know you—"

"And like you," Gaylord added, as if he were afraid she would be mad.

She wasn't sure if she was mad or not. She'd always known her friendship with two faeries was unusual, but she'd prided herself on her open-mindedness. She figured they had prided themselves on theirs as well.

"—and after we found out that you didn't ever want to

go into Faerie. We just figured, you know, that you'd hold the key to the entire regime change."

"Regime change?" Zoe asked.

Herschel shrugged. "It's not as bad as it sounds, not really. The Kings've been in power for a long time now, and they're getting real stale. Not to mention power-hungry. So we figured if the power floats around you, then we're safe near you. If you know what I mean."

Zoe didn't know what he meant. "I thought you said this had to do with my prophecy."

"Well, technically, it does and it doesn't." Gaylord grabbed her beer and shoved his straw into it. Zoe grimaced. He stirred the beer, ignoring her reaction.

"Magic gathers whenever a destiny is about to be met," Herschel said.

"It doesn't matter whose destiny." Gaylord was studying the swirling straw. "It could be yours, it could be Faerie's, it could be someone else's."

"So you didn't really want to warn me at all." Zoe folded her hands together, mostly so she couldn't shake these little men like she wanted to. "You came here to find out what I knew."

Herschel set his empty beer stein next to Gaylord's, then moved them to the edge of the table, probably hoping the bar's lone cocktail waitress would see them and interrupt the conversation.

"Well, you know," Herschel said, "we figured if we mentioned the rumor, then you might just enlighten us."

"You've done that before," Gaylord said as he kept stirring.

Zoe grabbed the straw, and pulled it out of her beer. She moved the dripping thing into Gaylord's stein, and pulled hers back in front of her.

She didn't want to drink from it—not anymore, especially

not after the straw incident—but she felt like she needed it as her shield again.

"I've told you things I shouldn't have?" Zoe asked.

"You know, when you've asked us for information," Herschel said. "We've traded."

Apparently they traded a little more than she knew. She used to go to them for any information that had to do with faerie-owned casinos—and there were a lot of them in Vegas, mostly on the outskirts. Ancient, seedy casinos, with long-enchanted customers who sat in front of slot machines and pulled and pulled and pulled until they got carpal tunnel or died.

"You guys have been using me," Zoe said.

"No more than you've been using us," Herschel said.

"It's not like that," Gaylord said, almost at the same time. "We like you, Zo."

The thing of it was, she knew Gaylord was telling the truth. For all the times they had traded information, there were other times where they'd simply sat around a non-faerie-owned bar, like this one, and talked. They liked her stories, and she liked theirs. They had all lived long lives, and they loved to share parts of the past.

She wasn't as angry as she should have been. She never fully trusted them anyway, and she doubted they fully trusted her.

And they had called her here to do her a favor.

Zoe sighed. "What should I be looking out for?"

Gaylord and Herschel exchanged glances again. Those looks were beginning to make her nervous.

"Anything unusual," Herschel said.

"More unusual than usual," Gaylord said.

"More unusual than usual how?" Zoe asked.

"Like power stuff or love stuff might be a tip you're in difficult waters," Herschel said.

"Or stuff that isn't quite what it seems," Gaylord said.

"Like you guys." Zoe couldn't resist jabbing at them.

"No!" Herschel said.

"Yes!" Gaylord said at the same time.

"Okay, maybe a little like us," Herschel said. "But not right now. You've known us, like, forever."

"At least since you've moved to Vegas," Gaylord said.

"But we're talking about in the next few days," Herschel said. "Watch out for strange stuff."

"Realize it's part of a prophecy," Gaylord said.

"Whose?" Zoe asked.

"If we knew, we wouldn't be so cryptic," Herschel said. "We're not privileged, Zo. You know that."

Zoe felt her head beginning to spin. She hated dealing with magic. It had been a burden her entire life, and now, it seemed, the burden was going to get worse.

"Oh, and watch out for the blond guy," Herschel said.

"What blond guy?" Zoe asked.

"The one with the kid," Gaylord said.

"I know a lot of blond guys with kids," Zoe said.

"The new one," Herschel said.

"The new kid?" Zoe asked.

"The new blond guy. He'll be tall and—"

"Really good-looking," Gaylord said with a wink.

"—and he's got this really powerful kid who hasn't come into his magic yet," Herschel said.

A shiver ran down Zoe's back. "Why should I watch out for him?" she asked.

Herschel and Gaylord exchanged yet another glance. And this one was filled with worry.

"Because," Gaylord said, "he's going to get you to go into Faerie, and you'll get trapped in the Circle."

"The Circle?" Zoe asked.

Herschel waved his hands, as if to say that an explanation of the Circle wasn't important.

"Stay away from the Circle, Zo," he said. He was more serious than she had ever seen him. "Everyone who gets trapped by the Circle dies."

"In case you've forgotten," Zoe said, "I'm immortal."

Gaylord shook his head. "Not in Faerie, you're not."

"Just like we aren't in Mount Olympics," Herschel said.

"Olympus," Zoe said, absently. Was that what her prophecy had meant? Trapped by narrow walls of a Faerie Circle? For eternity?

But they had said "died," not "trapped."

"What should I do?" she asked.

"How should we know?" Herschel asked. "We just came to let you know that the magic had gathered. We did that."

He slid out of the booth, tossed a few bills onto the table, and looked at Gaylord.

"C'mon, Gaylord," Herschel said. "We've done enough."

And then he walked out of the bar. No one seemed to see him go—one of the many magicks that the faeries always used to great advantage.

Gaylord was trapped in the booth by Zoe. He put a hand on hers. His skin was warm and dry. She wasn't sure she'd ever touched anyone from Faerie before.

"Zoe," he said, "do what you always do. What we're taught about prophecies is that you can't fight them. You just have to be yourself. The ending is determined not by the Kings or some divine energy, but by your uniqueness, and how you've developed it over time."

"Great," Zoe said. She hadn't done so very well over her time. If she had, she wouldn't be living in a seedy town that had more glitz than it should have and more magic per square acre than any other place on the planet.

Gaylord squeezed her hand. "You'll do fine," he said, and vanished.

She let out a small sigh and leaned back. No one else in the bar saw him disappear—and if they had, they wouldn't remember it. The faerie often used mind trickery forbidden to mages.

She wished she had someone she could turn to. Her mentor had moved on a long time ago. They hadn't been in touch in more than a hundred years.

Zoe had very few magical friends. Most of them were scattered across the globe. She supposed she could call or just pop in on them, the way that Gaylord was popping in on someone right now, but she wasn't sure they knew any more than she did.

And she knew better than to go to the Fates. Those three women, in charge of prophecy and magical justice, would just talk in circles, never letting her know what to do. They relished their superior place in the scheme of things, and weren't about to sacrifice it to give someone like her advice.

She was on her own, the magic was gathering, and she had no idea what she was going to do.

Two

At that moment, the blond guy with the powerful kid was in a motel one step below Motel Six in Ashland, Oregon, wondering how his older sister always managed to talk him into something he would never normally do.

The blond guy's name was Travers Kineally. He was a Certified Public Accountant who owned his own firm, handling investments and financial advice for a group of very well-to-do and well-connected people in Los Angeles, all of whom would be quite appalled if they knew he was sprawled on a double bed with his clothes and shoes on, hands behind his head because the two paper-thin pillows the motel provided didn't give him enough support, staring at a TV that was bolted to the dresser.

His son, Kyle, was lying on the other bed in the exact same position, except that his shoes were off, and his Superman socks glowed kryptonite green in the half-light.

Normally, Kyle was not allowed to be up this late, so he was treating *The Tonight Show* as if it were a filthy movie broadcast on Pay-Per-View. Every time Jay Leno cracked a remotely risqué joke, Kyle looked sideways at his father, either hoping that Travers wouldn't notice or that he wouldn't shut the television off.

Kyle was precocious for an eleven-year-old, but he was also naïve, something Travers wanted to maintain as long as possible. The other children at Kyle's private school seemed to know everything there was to know about sex and drugs and even rock and roll, but Kyle didn't seem to care.

He lived for his comic books and his computer and his books, just like Travers's sister Vivian used to do. She had turned out pretty darned good, except for her strange friends and somewhat mysterious new husband.

Travers and Kyle had been in Portland attending Vivian's wedding when this entire odyssey got started. And Travers had been feeling so good, so magnanimous, that he had agreed to Vivian's outrageous proposition.

At the time, it had seemed like the brotherly thing to do.

"Dad," Kyle whispered, "do you think they can hear us?"

Travers started. His son was oddly prescient at times. Travers hadn't really been thinking about the three strange women in the next room, but he was moving there. After all, they were traveling with him and Kyle at the behest of Vivian, who seemed to think that Travers wouldn't mind some company on the way to Los Angeles.

"Does it matter, Kyle?" Travers asked. One of the pillows slipped from his grasp, and his head thudded against the headboard—which, for some unknown reason, was made of real, hard and painful wood.

"Dunno." Kyle sat up, and wrapped his pillow around his waist. His round glasses slid to the edge of his nose, giving his face an owlish cast. "It's just that. . . ."

He shook his head, like he didn't want to finish the sentence. Kyle often didn't like to discuss what was on his mind, particularly with his father. He and Travers were about as different as two people could get.

That was one reason why Travers was sorry to see Vivian stay in Portland. She, at least, could talk to Kyle. Travers usually found himself starting sentences with *If you only listened . . .* and *Maybe if you tried to be like the other kids . . .* sentences his youngest sister, Megan, a child psychologist, said were guaranteed to alienate any child.

"It's just that *what*?" Travers asked.

"Well, don't you think they're a little weird?" Kyle turned to face him. Even though they'd been driving all day, Kyle had somehow managed to get ink smudges on his cheeks. The boy spent most of his time drawing his own comic books, even though Travers wanted him to learn some outdoor activities, maybe even join a league, although what kind of league, Travers didn't know. Kyle wasn't the most coordinated kid in the world, and most teams seemed to know that just by looking at him.

Then Travers realized what his son had said to him. Kyle was calling someone "weird." Kyle hated that word, having had it thrown at him too many times.

Travers sat up.

"I thought you didn't like to call people weird," Travers said, and then immediately wished he hadn't. Megan would have called that one of his manipulative moments.

Let the boy be himself, Travers, Megan had said to him during the wedding reception. *You try so hard to have Kyle be the perfect L.A. kid that you fail to realize how very special he is.*

Travers did realize how special Kyle was. Travers also saw how much pain being special caused his son—through teasing, taunting, and general bullying. Megan may have been quick with the advice, but she wasn't the one who had to clean

Kyle up when he came home with his clothing torn and his nose bloodied.

Travers wanted his son to have a normal childhood, just not the normal childhood of a nerd.

Now Kyle shrugged. He shoved his glasses up his nose in a movement reminiscent of Vivian.

"Dunno," he mumbled. "Just kinda seemed like the right word."

Then he lay back down, put his hands behind his head, and stared at Jay Leno, who was doing his usual Jay-walking segment at Universal City. Travers had always thought Kyle would find this part of *The Tonight Show* appalling and funny at the same time, but the boy wasn't laughing. He was watching, but he clearly wasn't paying attention.

Travers suppressed a sigh. He had been a single father since Kyle was six months old, when Kyle's nineteen-year-old mother had fled the tiny apartment filled with dirty diapers, squalling baby, and sleepless husband.

I'm too young for this, Trav, Cheryl had said just before she left. *I need to live a little before I settle down.*

Travers hadn't even pretended to understand. He was the same age. They had been high school sweethearts, and they had always talked about spending the rest of their lives together, having a passel of kids, and living the American Dream.

Apparently, for Cheryl, the American Dream didn't include a happy baby who believed that nighttime was for playing, an apartment without cable television, and a bathroom that constantly looked like it was the center of a war zone. Not to mention a skinny husband who couldn't seem to get a better job than bag boy at the nearby grocery store.

There wasn't a lot of Cheryl in Kyle. There wasn't a lot of Travers, either, except in the looks department. Kyle was just as thin and gawky as Travers had been at eleven.

Only Travers had turned his attention to sports, become not just the best player on the basketball team, but the resident statistician for all the sports at both his junior high school and his high school. Travers had always loved numbers, and they had always loved him.

Numbers, he liked to say, were the only constant in his life.

Which wasn't exactly true. He had his family—his parents and his two sisters and Kyle—and he loved all of them more than anything else.

This time, he sighed and got up, crossing the narrow space between the two beds, and sitting down next to Kyle.

"How come you think those women are weird?" Travers asked quietly.

Kyle shrugged and continued to stare at the TV. Travers could see the colors on the screen—the fleshy tones of Leno's skin, the green neon that seemed to dominate Universal City, the blue of the jeans everyone wore—reflected in Kyle's glasses.

Travers grabbed the remote or tried to. It was bolted to the nightstand. Why would anyone bolt a remote to a nightstand? Or, more importantly, why would anyone think an old hotel remote was worth stealing?

He didn't have time to ponder those questions. Instead, he leaned toward the nightstand, looked at the multi-colored buttons, and pushed the red one.

The television winked off.

"Hey!" Kyle said. "I was watching that."

"Tell me why you think they're weird," Travers said.

Kyle glared at him, rolled over, and hit the red button. The television winked back on, but instead of Jay Leno, the picture showed the movie choices the hotel had thoughtfully provided. A good fifty percent of them were labeled Adult, and required going to another screen.

Kyle was about to press the channel changer buttons when Travers caught his hand.

"We don't need to watch any more," Travers said.

"I think they can hear us," Kyle said. "But if the TV's on . . ."

He didn't have to say any more. Travers hit the button for the NBC affiliate, and left the volume up.

"So you'll tell me?" Travers asked, feeling a bit like a supplicant. He had felt out of control with his son since Kyle started school. The outside influences severed a bond between them, one that had seemed so tight that it almost felt as if they knew what each other was thinking. At times, Travers wanted that bond back. At others, he simply wanted to know how come he no longer understood his own son.

"Weird," Kyle said, sitting up and crossing his legs, "is one of those cool words that people don't use right."

Travers bit his lower lip. He didn't want to say anything, but at the same time, he didn't want a lecture. And Kyle was good at lectures.

"It means 'mysterious' or, you know like 'ghostly' or something. It comes from the Old English word 'wyrd' with a 'y' which means, literally, fate."

Kyle put his elbows on his knees and leaned forward, his hands expressing his thoughts as if he couldn't speak without them.

"In Norse mythology, there's these three women. They're called the Wyrd Sisters—with a 'y'—and they control fate, literally. Their real name is the Norn, and one of the sisters—I think the one who controls the past—is called Wyrd, which is kinda confusing, I know, but kinda cool, too—"

"Kyle," Travers said. He already had too much information.

Kyle nodded, as if he realized he was telling his father too much. "Okay, so when I asked you if you thought they were weird, I meant strange, but not in the way that people mean when they call *me* weird. When they call *me* weird, they don't mean weird, they mean dork. When I called *them* weird, I meant it in the coolest possible way. Like they were bound by tree limbs, you know?"

"Bound by tree limbs?" Travers couldn't help but ask.

"Like the Wyrd sisters. They guard the root of this tree, Yggdrasill, which is in the middle of the world. The Wyrd sisters guard the root that extends into the earth, which the Norse called Midgard. There are two other roots. One goes to the underworld, and the third goes to the home of the frost giants. Which isn't important, but is cool."

"Yeah," Travers said. "Cool."

"But all day, as we've been riding with these women, I kept thinking of the Wyrd Sisters. I wrote a comic book for Vivian called *Defender of the Fates,* and it dealt with the Fates, remember, Dad?"

Travers nodded, although he didn't. All of Kyle's comic book plots and drawings seemed the same to Travers, which, his sister Vivian said, had a lot more to do with Travers than with Kyle.

"Well, if you look at the pictures, you see all three women. They look just like those ladies next door. And they talk like them, too, all jumbled up, and interrupty, and everything." Kyle's cheeks were flushed. He was excited to be talking about this. "And if you look at the Defender, she looks kinda like Aunt Viv, and she falls in love with this guy who looks like Uncle Dex, only I wrote it before I met him. And when we were coming up to the wedding, I started a new comic book called *Fates' Clues,* and in it, there's these same three women—only I was going to look up the Wyrd sisters, and kinda use them as the basis, and then there's this other woman who's a detective and she looks like that movie actress, that chocolate one?"

It took Travers a minute to follow that. "You mean Juliette Binoche."

"Yeah, her. Only tall, with a dancer's legs, and a longer face, but just as pretty—maybe prettier—"

"I get it," Travers said.

"And I keep thinking that maybe I'm not making this stuff up. Maybe I'm, like, channeling it from the future, you know? Like Aunt Viv."

"Your Aunt Vivian can't see the future." Travers knew that for certain. Sometimes she knew—in a very uncanny way— what someone else was thinking. And she could figure out all sorts of odd things, like who was going to call the moment before the phone rang, but she almost never saw the future.

Although every once in a while, she would pass out— which used to scare the whole family when Vivian started the practice in high school—and she would come to with the most amazing stories of things she'd seen. She called them visions. Their mother called them dreams, and Aunt Eugenia, who, before her death, used to pamper Viv, called them normal.

There was nothing normal about those visions, and watching Viv go through them was the only time in Travers's life that he was glad he and his siblings weren't related by blood. They were all adopted, which anyone could tell by looking at them—Viv with her dark skin, dark eyes, and dark hair; him, all tall and blond and Nordic; and round, chubby little red-haired Megan, who wasn't quite so little anymore.

"Sometimes she can see the future," Kyle said, and he sounded defensive.

Travers had mentally moved so far away from the original remark that it took him a moment to realize that Kyle was referring to Vivian, not Megan.

"But mostly, she kinda sees the present—especially if it's happening somewhere else." Kyle had an expression on his face that Travers hadn't seen before. The expression was a combination of defiance and hope. Kyle truly believed this. "She saw Aunt Eugenia's murder when it happened."

"Kyle!"

"It's true."

"Vivian told you that?" Travers asked, thinking honeymoon or no honeymoon, he'd have a talk with his sister about the stories she told his son.

"Nope." Kyle's voice was soft. "I saw it, too."

Travers folded his hands together, looking at them and counting to ten, just like Megan told him to do when his son said something he didn't believe.

"You're psychic," Travers said as calmly as he could.

"I think so." Kyle's voice was barely above a whisper.

"You hear people's thoughts," Travers said.

"Sometimes," Kyle said.

"And you see the future," Travers said.

"Yeah," Kyle said. "I draw it. If you look at my comic books, you'll see a lot of stuff that I knew before it happened. Like I knew all about Uncle Dex and Aunt Viv when they met and stuff. I didn't know I knew it, but I made a comic book out of it and gave it to Aunt Viv before we left Portland that first time."

Travers raised his head. Behind Kyle, some rock group was playing in the middle of *The Tonight Show* soundstage. "You believe that?"

Kyle's look of anticipation faded. His entire face closed down. "No, of course not," he said in a perfectly normal tone of voice. "Why would I?"

"But you told me about the comic book," Travers said.

"And it's a good story, isn't it?" Kyle uncrossed his legs. His socks looked even greener in the light from the TV.

"I thought you said this has something to do with those women." Travers was confused. He wasn't quite sure what Kyle had been trying to tell him.

"It does," Kyle said. "They make me think of the Wyrd Sisters, which is what made me think of the comic book, and Aunt Viv, and stuff. I'm sorry, Dad. You know me. I just get carried away."

He did, too. He got caught in his own imagination. Travers nodded. His stomach twisted, and he felt, once again, as if he had lost control of the conversation.

"I shouldn't have agreed to bring those women along with us," Travers said. "I should have told them to take the train or something."

Kyle snorted. "Like they would've done good on the train. They'd've been arguing in the station and missed it."

Travers nodded, in spite of himself. The only reason the five of them were in this seedy hotel was because the Wyrd Sisters, as his son called them, had argued about the best place to stay for so long all the other hotels from Medford to Ashland were full.

Travers had been tempted to drive all night, but everyone, including Kyle, managed to talk him out of that.

Kyle lay back down and tucked his hands under his head. He watched Leno for a moment, then as a Lexus commercial came on, he said, "You know, Dad, there's just one thing."

Travers stood. He headed back to his own bed. He was tired, more tired than he cared to admit. And this conversation, like the day, had taken something out of him.

"What's that?"

"I have this feeling that the Wyrd Sisters—they're not supposed to go to L.A."

"Yes, they are," Travers said. "They told me. Vivian told me. And they even offered me a free kitten if I took them there."

Kyle giggled. He'd seen the kitten exchange, as had everyone else at the wedding. The Wyrd Sisters had given a group of kittens—well-trained kittens, or so they claimed—to anyone whom they trusted.

They claimed they trusted Travers.

"Seriously, Dad, I don't think they're supposed to go to L.A.," Kyle said as his giggles faded.

"Where are they supposed to go?" Travers asked, knowing he would regret the question later.

"Las Vegas." Kyle sounded very serious. "I keep seeing them escorting me through the *Star Trek Experience.*"

Travers grabbed his paper-thin pillow and pummeled Kyle with it. Kyle laughed again, grabbed his pillow, and whapped Travers with it. They had a good, old-fashioned pillow fight as *The Tonight Show* theme song faded into the jazzy opener for *Conan O'Brien.*

Then he and Kyle collapsed on their respective beds, sweaty and laughing, and very tired.

They agreed to go to sleep, and Kyle went through his routine first, using the bathroom, brushing his teeth, and putting on his pajamas. Travers shut off the television and lay on his bed, thinking about the conversation.

It left him unsettled, although he couldn't say why. Perhaps it was the belief in Kyle's voice as he discussed his own psychic ability. Perhaps it was the long day with the three chattering, oblivious women. Or perhaps it was the mention of Las Vegas.

Travers had been avoiding Las Vegas his entire life. He had no logical reason for doing so. It was a number-man's Mecca, a place where a CPA could meet a game theorist could meet a statistician, and all of them would have enough math to keep them happy for the rest of their lives. He could watch the average person in a controlled gambling environment and see his pet theories proven again and again.

Normally, most accountants and mathematics fiends loved places like Vegas where odds were a way of life.

But Travers didn't trust odds. They never worked quite right for him. And he hadn't discussed that with anyone—especially not his superstitious family.

Fortunately, they had never asked him how he paid for college after Kyle was born. He didn't want to tell them that he had done so with his lottery winnings. Not that he had won the big Powerball Jackpots or anything that spectacular. No. It was quite simple. He would stand in front of the scratch-off counter in a convenience store and know, somehow *know,* that the third ticket from the bottom was worth fifty dollars. That was the only time he would then do the math. If he made a profit after buying all the tickets to that one, he'd buy them. If not, he'd tell the clerk that the third ticket from the bottom was worth the fifty dollars. Later, the clerk would always tell him he was right.

The weirder ones were Powerball. He never hit the automatic number-choosing button. He always closed his eyes and imagined the little Ping-Pong balls in their little blower. He would see them come up—not the way they did on TV—but with big red numbers above the rotating Ping-Pong balls, as if someone, somewhere were trying to tell him which numbers would win.

He never put in all of the numbers. He just couldn't. It wasn't fair. So he'd see how low the pay-out was, and put in three or four, and take home his $20,000 or his $150,000. He never told anyone, and his name was never printed in the paper. Only the people who ordered the names of the weekly winners ever saw his. And they apparently never made the connection.

Not even Kyle knew. Travers kept that strange ability to himself, and lived as comfortably as he dared without calling attention to his wealth. CPAs made good money. They just didn't make great money. So he made sure he looked like he was worth good money and nothing more.

But Travers knew that as tempting as Powerball was for him—and he had trouble walking past one of the kiosks without seeing the damn red numbers—that Vegas would be worse. He always imagined himself watching the numbers come up correctly on the roulette table or in craps or even at the blackjack table, where math and luck lived together in an uneasy alliance.

It was—in Kyle's word—Fate, and Travers didn't want to tempt it.

If Kyle was right, and those women needed to go on to Las Vegas, Travers would help them find the right public transportation to get there. He was never going into that city.

His life would change once he did.

It was an irrational fear, he knew. But everyone, even the most normal person on the planet, was entitled to one irrational fear.

Entering Las Vegas was his.

And he clung to it, just like Kyle clung to the illusion that he was psychic. Because it made him feel safe.

Because it made him feel like he was in control.

Even when he wasn't.

Three

It took nearly an hour for Kyle's dad to go to sleep.

Kyle lay in his bed closest to the window, listening to the traffic zoom by on I-5. Headlights constantly illuminated the flowered wallpaper, and the occasional horn would startle him, even though he wasn't asleep.

His dad had this big block about magic. Aunt Viv had warned Kyle about that, even as she told him about her magic, and her discoveries in Portland this last year. His new Uncle Dex, who was a dead ringer for the 1940s comic book *Superman* (which kinda fit, considering Aunt Viv used to say that the original Superman was the handsomest guy on the planet), could do all sorts of magical things. He just wasn't willing to.

Only Dad would never believe it. Dad hated all this mystical talk. Somewhere along the way, Dad had convinced himself that he was really practical and a non-believer in anything that he couldn't see—from God to magic to psychic abilities.

But Dad had to have seen the weird stuff at Aunt Viv's

wedding. Like the way all those people popped into the hotel. Most of them arrived without luggage (it had popped in, too) and without obvious transportation.

After a day of suspicious arrivals, Kyle had actually planted himself in the lobby, and watched person after person appear on the front sidewalk out of nowhere. Not that anyone else seemed to notice or even care.

Then the Wyrd Sisters had shown up. That wasn't their name, of course. Their names were strange enough, though. Clotho, Lachesis, and Atropos. They were model-pretty and they did carry kittens with them everywhere, and they glowed like they had magic, even though they didn't.

Aunt Viv and Uncle Dex had the first argument of their marriage over those women. Aunt Viv said they still needed protection, and Uncle Dex agreed, but said it wasn't his responsibility anymore, and then the Wyrd Sisters got involved and said that they would get their protection from Zanthia in Los Angeles, because she walked the mean streets.

The Wyrd Sisters were going to fly to Los Angeles until they realized that meant on an airplane (what else could it have meant? That had really intrigued Kyle), and then they saw Dad, and said that he was perfect; they'd travel with him.

Aunt Viv tried to talk them out of it, saying that Dad was pretty straightforward and not real imaginative, but they didn't care, and then Aunt Viv told Uncle Dex, who laughed and said he wasn't responsible for the women anymore, and that their instincts seemed to be good. Which was when Aunt Viv started disagreeing with him, and Uncle Dex held up his hands, not wanting to fight at the reception, and Kyle snuck off to talk to Dad, who at that point didn't know he was going to be stuck in an SUV for two days with three of the strangest people he'd ever met.

Kyle counted his dad's soft snores. When the count reached

fifty, Kyle slid his covers back and eased out of bed. Then he tiptoed across the floor until he reached the door.

Kyle slowly brought his arm up to the chain lock. Sound—or the lack of it—was really critical to sneaking out of the room. He slid the chain across its little track, then out of the track, catching the chain as it fell away. He set it against the door, very gently, so that there was no sound at all.

Then he turned the knob, and felt it click rather than heard it. He pulled the door open slowly, and the hinges creaked. Kyle bit his lower lip and looked at his dad. His dad didn't wake up.

Kyle slipped out of the door. He pulled it closed, and stood for a moment on the concrete balcony that overlooked the parking lot and, beyond it, the interstate.

Lots of trucks went by. The parking lot was full of cars and trucks and a few trailers. Kyle's bare feet were cold. In fact, his whole body was cold. He shivered, rubbing his hands over his arms. His pajamas were a lot thinner than his regular clothes. And it had gotten a lot colder out here than it had been a little while before.

Maybe this wasn't such a good idea after all. Maybe he should've waited until morning to talk to the Wyrd Sisters. But he wanted to give them the heads-up that their advice hadn't worked and that magic—or at least psychic abilities—weren't something they should even try to talk to his dad about.

No sense in having Dad mad all the way to L.A.

The concrete was scratchy. Kyle hopped across it, using the iron railing as a brace.

He got to the next room, only to discover a handwritten sign on the door.

K.

At the pool—

Kyle sighed, looked down at his bare feet, then at the stairs several feet away. He'd be an ice cube by the time he got to that pool.

But he sucked it up, and walked—not hopped—to the stairway. The concrete there was smooth, and the railing wobbly. He hurried down, his feet making a slapping sound. The stairway turned toward the center of the complex, into a little breezeway with a Coke machine, an ice machine, and a pay phone. Just beyond it, in a fenced-off alcove, was the tiny, square-shaped thing the manager called a pool.

He hobbled across the breezeway, avoiding bits of glass and gravel, until he got to the open gate door. As he got close, he could hear laughter floating across the breeze.

". . . so much better than being in that cave." Clotho's rich voice had a touch of laughter in it. "I do like seeing the sun now and then."

"It was better than a cave," Lachesis said. Kyle knew it was Lachesis, not because he recognized her voice, but because these women always spoke in order: Clotho first, Lachesis second, and Atropos last. In the three days Kyle had known them, they hadn't varied the pattern once.

"Caves aren't that plush," Atropos said.

"Whatever," Clotho said. "It's just nice to see the stars."

Kyle pushed the gate open and stepped into the pool area. Lawn chairs that had once been white but were now a kind of dingy gray surrounded the pool. An umbrella teetered over a glass-topped table. Tiny hotel towels sat on the concrete near the square pool.

"Come on in, Kyle," Lachesis said. "The water's nice."

All three women were swimming back and forth in the tiny pool. And, Kyle blushed to realize, they weren't wearing anything. Or at least, it didn't seem like they were.

He immediately covered his eyes.

"Oh, dear," Atropos said. "This New World puritanism is something I really do not understand."

"It's pretty simple," Clotho said. "It comes down to up-bringing. The children simply do not understand that the body is a natural thing, that there is no shame involved in naked-ness and—"

"You could get arrested, you know," Kyle said as he pushed the gate open, careful to keep one hand over his eyes.

"Really?" Lachesis asked. "How delightfully medieval."

Kyle stepped through the gate.

"Where are you going, Kyle?" Atropos asked.

"Back to the room." He stopped, though. He was pretty angry. He didn't realize it until now. He had listened to these women this afternoon, when they told him to have a heart-to-heart with his dad, and then they said he could talk to them. And now that he wanted to, they were—well, nude.

"I thought you wanted us to be available for conversation," Clotho said.

"I did," Kyle snapped, his anger finally coming out. "But I can't talk to you like this."

"Like what?" Lachesis asked.

"When you're—naked." Just saying the word made him blush even more. He was glad it was dark.

"Oh, child," Atropos said. "We didn't mean to make you uncomfortable. We'll get out."

"No!" Kyle said, and sprinted toward the stairs.

"With our clothes on." Clotho's voice floated after him.

He stopped in front of the Coke machine. It hummed. He swallowed hard, hoped his dad hadn't heard him yell, and said, "You will?"

"Certainly." As Lachesis spoke, water splashed. The women were getting out of the pool.

Kyle didn't turn around. He stared into the parking lot, and the passing trucks beyond, wondering how these women got away with all the things they did. They pretended they didn't know money—Kyle had to explain the difference between coins and cash to them at the Quickie Mart outside of Salem; they seemed to know some things about the culture, like HBO, but other things, like laws, eluded them.

Dad simply said they were nuts, but that was a blanket description which really didn't get to the heart of the problem. They might have been nuts, but they were nuts in a really odd and consistent way.

"All right," Atropos said. "We are—what is your word?— decent."

"Which, if you think about it," Clotho said, "goes right to the heart of the point. 'Decent' would only be used in this context if nakedness were somehow indecent."

"Which is why I made the point," Lachesis said.

Kyle turned around. Slowly he let his hands drop from his eyes. The women, wrapped in big, fluffy robes, were sitting in the ancient lounge chairs.

Lachesis was bent at the waist, drying her red hair. She was built like a plus-sized model—his dad had called her zaftig at the wedding and Aunt Viv had punched him—and yet she looked the best in the robe.

Atropos had her robe wrapped around her knees. She was as thin as Calista Flockhart, only prettier, with black hair that fell to her shoulders. But the thinness probably made her as cold as Kyle was. His feet felt like little blocks of ice.

Clotho stood up. She was the blonde, and looked kinda like pictures of Kyle's mom (whom he couldn't remember). Clotho pushed the gate open and held it for him.

"We're sorry," Atropos said. "If we had realized you would have been uncomfortable, we wouldn't have gone swimming."

"It's not just me," Kyle said as he walked back to the pool. "I wasn't kidding when I said you could get arrested."

"Why?" Clotho asked as she closed the gate behind him.

"Because you're in a public place. You can't be nude in public."

"See?" Lachesis said. "It seems to me that was a plot point in one of the movies we watched."

"Probably several, but Henri—" The women always insisted on calling Uncle Dex "Henri" for reasons Kyle didn't understand—"said that we shouldn't learn everything we know about modern culture from the television."

Atropos seemed puzzled by the statement even though she was the one repeating it.

"You guys are really weird," Kyle said, as he sank into one of the lounge chairs.

"I thought you didn't like that word," Clotho said.

"So I was right," Kyle said. "You could overhear us."

"Just that part." Lachesis sat up, the towel wrapped turban-like around her hair. "Then we decided we'd better come down here so you could have a private talk."

"How did it go?" Atropos asked.

Kyle shook his head. "Not good. That's what I came to tell you. My dad doesn't believe in magic. He never will, so stop trying to convince him, okay?"

"We never said you *had* magic." Clotho sat down beside him. The plastic lounge chair squeaked under her weight. "We said you would develop magic at twenty-one."

"And then you'd be exceedingly powerful," Lachesis said, "so you really should begin your training now."

"Well, my dad's not going to pay for any training." Kyle couldn't quite fight the feeling of disappointment. "He thinks I'm just goofy, that there's a logical explanation for everything, and he doesn't believe in predicting the future."

"What about *his* magic?" Atropos asked.

"Shush," Clotho said. "We've done enough."

Kyle shrugged. "My dad doesn't have magic."

"Certainly he does," Lachesis said. "Or we wouldn't be here."

"I thought you needed a ride to L.A.," Kyle said.

"I'm sure there would have been others to take us," Atropos said.

"Now I understand why Vivian was worried about our safety." Clotho leaned back in her chair. "We are becoming too impulsive."

"That's for another discussion." Lachesis put her hand on Kyle's arm. He jumped. "No one ever taught your father the rules of magic?"

"Why would they?" Kyle asked.

"Oh, dear," Atropos said quietly. "And here we are, taking him to his soulmate."

"Huh?" Kyle asked.

"It's all right, dear," Clotho said. "We do need Zanthia's help as well."

"Dad's soulmate is named Zanthia?" Kyle asked, feeling confused.

"Shh!" All three women said in unison.

"You should never discuss someone else's soulmate before the souls mate," Lachesis said.

"Who *are* you guys?" Kyle asked.

"Well," Atropos said, wrapping her robe tighter around herself. Kyle had guessed right; she was just as cold as he was. "You weren't that far off with the Wyrd Sisters."

"You heard *that,* too?" Kyle felt his cheeks heat up. He didn't like calling people names because they might overhear—heaven knew he always did at school, even though he pretended like he hadn't—but he was talking to his *dad,* for heaven's sake. And that was private.

Clotho shrugged. "It was part of the same discussion."

"It was what made Clotho decide we needed to come down

here." Lachesis's towel turban was slipping slightly, giving her face a pirate-like air.

"She's not real fond of that nickname," Atropos said.

"I didn't give it to her," Kyle said, his voice rising with the denial. He kinda had, but he wasn't going to admit it, at least not in this way. "I mean, it's Norse. You know, the myths."

"We know the myths." Clotho stretched her bare legs out. She had goose pimples running along her calves. "We're the Fates, child."

"Or at least, we used to be." Lachesis sounded sad.

"Used to be?" Kyle asked.

Atropos waved her hand. "Long story, and one I'm sure you'll hear when we meet up with Zanthia."

"Names!" Clotho and Lachesis said in unison, as if they were reminding Atropos of something.

Atropos clapped her hands over her mouth. "Sorry."

"Fates?" Kyle said again. "The ones who determine life and death?"

"Yes, child," Clotho said.

"You're not making this up?" Kyle asked, feeling his neck get warm, too, as his blush moved down. "Like using the names as a test or something, like for school?"

"What do you mean?" Lachesis asked.

"You know, like I was supposed to notice that you were named after the Fates or something." Kyle put his feet on his chair and rubbed his cold toes. His hands weren't much warmer. But it gave him an excuse to keep his head down. "I don't remember ever learning your names. We had to memorize the Muses. There's Erato and Terpsichore and Polyhymnia and—"

"Oh, please don't confuse us with those bores," Atropos said.

"Besides," Clotho said. "They stopped working as a unit centuries ago."

"Millennia," Lachesis said.

"Three women can get along," Atropos said. "Nine, however—"

"It does make things dicey," Clotho said.

"And you *would* have to mention Polyhymnia," Lachesis said. "Religious poetry is one thing, but religious music—"

"That's not fair," Atropos said. "There was a lovely Golden Age—what, a few years ago? That Bach fellow—"

"Like Johann?" Kyle asked.

The three women—Fates?—nodded.

"That was centuries ago," Kyle said, feeling shocked.

Clotho waved a hand in dismissal. "I'm still not certain of the ways that mortals tell time. A century, a year, what's the difference?"

"Decades," Kyle said.

"Still, we're not to the central point," Lachesis said. "Which is helping you."

"If your father won't acknowledge his magic, then there's not much we can do," Atropos said.

"Don't you have magic?" Kyle asked.

"We used to," Clotho said, and all three women looked very sad.

"It's part of that long story," Lachesis said.

"Oh," Kyle said. "Well, look, my dad might wake up and find me missing, and if he does I'm in a heck of a lot of trouble, so I'm going to go to bed. Just don't talk to him about this, okay? And all the magic stuff? Tomorrow, let's just drive. Really, it's for the best."

The Fates nodded. Kyle nodded back, like a grown-up would, and then he stalked away from the pool, not caring that the concrete seemed even colder than it had a moment ago, and that he was hitting rocks with his bare feet.

Served him right for listening to other people. It didn't matter that Aunt Viv had found someone who appreciated her psychic powers. It didn't matter that Uncle Dex believed in (and maybe even had) magic.

All that mattered was that Kyle's father didn't believe in psychic powers or magic, no matter how much psychic ability Kyle had.

And he had to remember that, instead of getting carried away because someone else found the secret to happiness.

Kyle hurried up the stairs, ripped the note off the Fates' door, and let himself into his own hotel room. His dad was still asleep, only he'd rolled away from the door. His even breathing reassured Kyle, as Kyle pushed the door closed.

It was the two of them. It had always been the two of them.

And it always would be.

Four

A few days later, Travers found himself sitting on a Las Vegas freeway, wondering when his life had spiraled out of control.

He was hot. The air conditioner in his SUV was running at full blast, but it didn't seem to matter. He was sitting in the sun, his hands pasted to the steering wheel, trying to negotiate all the traffic on Interstate 15 heading into Las Vegas.

Kyle was buckled in beside him, staring gape-mouthed at the conglomeration of hotels and goofy architecture that made Vegas a place out of nightmares. The SUV was paralleling the Strip and to the right were some of the architecturally strangest buildings Travers had ever seen.

A large, green hotel that went for stories. A replica of the Statue of Liberty, almost hidden by all the buildings, a replica of the Eiffel Tower (who would go to that thing? Why not go to the real one?), and a volcano that spewed fake lava into the overheated air. There were pools and marble statues and big, big, big signs advertising names Travers had never heard of and a whole bunch that he had.

In the back seat, the three Wyrd Sisters, as Kyle had once called them, were arguing quietly about their next course of action. At least, Travers thought they were being quiet. He wasn't sure. He had the radio on full blast, letting Travis Tritt and Alan Jackson and Oak Ridge Mountain Boys speak for him.

Travers wasn't about to get into a conversation with those three women again, if he could help it.

He wasn't even sure how he ended up in Las Vegas with his son at his side, and three of the craziest women he'd ever met in the back seat. Sure, he knew the sequence of events. Those were easy.

First, he had driven the women to L.A., and asked where they wanted to be dropped off. They had no idea, so he had taken them to his house (mistake number one), where they examined the phonebook and let Kyle look on the Internet for this woman they were supposed to see.

Her name, apparently, was Zanthia, but she answered to Zoe as well. (Everyone the Wyrd Sisters seemed to know had more than one name. Even the guy that Vivian had married had a different name, at least according to the three women.) This Zanthia was a private detective, according to the Wyrd Sisters, and should have been fairly easy to find.

Of course, she wasn't easy to find. There wasn't a Zanthia as a private detective anywhere in L.A. Nor was there a Zoe as a private detective. Not in the phone book, not on the Internet, and not at any of the big firms that the Wyrd Sisters had convinced Travers to call.

Then, it turned out, this Zanthia/Zoe woman had been a private detective since the 1930s which, in Travers's book, meant she was either dead or retired, although the Wyrd Sisters didn't think so. Kyle, bless him, didn't do the math, so he didn't think the history was strange either.

He just continued his Internet search, going through old

databases that the libraries had set up until he found her. Zoe Sinclair, Private Detective. With an address from the 1940s.

Of course, the Wyrd Sisters were convinced that was their woman, and they insisted that Kyle do a broader search. Any private detective anywhere in the nation with the name Zoe Sinclair.

Because, one of the Wyrds (Clotho?) had said to Travers, *she would probably have moved on by now. It's quite a problem when you don't age properly.*

Kyle had nodded, as if that statement had been logical, and at that moment, Kyle had discovered a Zoe Sinclair who worked out of Las Vegas.

This was where the sequence of events got strange.

The next group of events was one long blur consisting of Kyle begging Travers to take care of the Wyrd Sisters and get them to Vegas, Travers calling Viv to ask her what she had gotten him into, Viv refusing to answer the phone (it was her honeymoon, after all), and Kyle throwing a temper tantrum right around bedtime.

So the Wyrd Sisters had spent the night in Travers's house in the Hollywood Hills, and the next morning, he awoke to find them sitting at his table, counting pennies, hoping that $3.56 would be enough for bus fare.

Event Six was the clearest, though. Kyle pulling Travers aside and saying, *Dad, look. They're just not like normal people. You can't let them get on a bus by themselves. That's what Uncle Dex was worried about. You need to hand them off to someone.*

Like the Olympic Torch? Travers asked, too exhausted to worry about his sarcasm.

Exactly! Kyle had said, and clapped his hands together.

And somehow Event Six had led to Event Seven, which was Travers pouring everyone into the SUV all over again, and heading out across the desert to Las Vegas.

Eight hours, six traffic jams, and one mistaken casino lunch stop later, they were pulling into Sin City proper, with no real idea of where they were going, and no plan on how to get there. Kyle had downloaded maps for this Zoe Sinclair's office, which happened to be somewhere called Fremont Street, which looked like it was just past the downtown.

Drivers zoomed in and out of the lanes as if they were playing bumper cars. The traffic in Las Vegas was heavy, but not nearly as heavy as L.A. traffic. At least in Vegas, the traffic kept moving.

The problem was the distractions. The glittery signs advertising Celine Dion at Caesar's Palace, Siegfried and Roy at the Mirage, and the Blue Man Group at the Luxor fairly screamed for attention from the side of the road. More hotels, some looking like European palaces, rose up to the right, and to the left, shops and hotels, and houses that shimmered like a heat mirage in the desert air.

A neon sign for a bank Travers had never heard of kindly informed him that it was 105 degrees—not normally a problem for him (he was a native Angelino, after all)—but in this condition, with these women in his car, his quiet son beside him, and in this city where he didn't know anyone, it was simply one more irritation.

And he was sitting in the sun, unable to turn until I-15 became I-515 in a few more miles.

Not to mention the fact that his plans were shot. He had planned to leave early enough to make the drive—both ways—in one day. That way, Travers wouldn't miss any more work, and Kyle would be home in time to register for the month-long summer session at his school.

Travers wondered if this weren't all a plot. After all, Kyle had mentioned the Wyrd Sisters and the *Star Trek Experience* nearly a week ago. All the way here, he was reading travel guides like they were the Bible.

The approach to 515 came up faster than Travers expected. Somehow he had gotten it into his head that Las Vegas was the same size as L.A. Nothing in North America was the same size as L.A. Maybe in population, but not in sheer sprawl.

He whipped the SUV into the correct lane, making his passengers gasp, and then, on two wheels, somehow managed to slide in front of a very large truck without anyone hitting the brakes.

Travers turned on 515, and told Kyle to watch for Las Vegas Boulevard South, which would take them to Fremont Street. The signs were telling Travers that he was heading toward downtown Vegas and the Fremont Street Experience, whatever that was. Apparently everything in Vegas was an experience.

The women were chattering behind him, but thanks to Charlie Pride (Wow! A station that played Charlie Pride couldn't be all bad), Travers couldn't hear what they were saying. He didn't really want to know, anyway.

His plans were pretty simple. He would escort them into the private detective agency, make sure this Zanthia/Zoe Sinclair actually existed, and then walk back out, leaving her with the most naïve group of women Travers had ever met in his life.

Then he would find a hotel for him and Kyle, maybe one close to this *Star Trek* thing—if it was for kids and not for adults. (Travers had his doubts.) They would do whatever an eleven-year-old and a grown-up could do on a weeknight in Las Vegas, and then, in the morning, they would drive home and return to their normal, everyday Wyrd-Sisters-free life.

The turn onto Las Vegas Boulevard put the sun directly in Travers's eyes. He swerved slightly to avoid something shiny in the road, then made the relative quick turn onto Fremont.

At that moment, his complacency ended.

Everything he had imagined about Las Vegas—everything he had feared—was right here in front of him. Women in short skirts, fishnets (how clichéd was that?), and teased hair walked the streets, eyeing the cars. A drug deal was clearly going down on the corner, and a group of young men walked in a pack toward a parked car.

"Oh, Dad," Kyle said. "This isn't good."

"No kidding," Travers said. Maybe the neighborhood would clean up closer to the detective's agency.

In L.A., neighborhoods sometimes changed quality from block to block.

"How much farther we got to go, Kyle?" Travers asked.

"Not much," Kyle said, squeezing the Internet map so hard that the paper he'd printed it on made rustly sounds of protest.

Well, this was a twist. And once he reached the address, Travers would have to determine the best course of action besides the one he really wanted to take.

He really wanted to dump the Wyrd Sisters onto the sidewalk and run.

But he wasn't that kind of guy, as Kyle kept reminding him. And Travers had already brought them this far.

He might as well finish the trip.

Five

Zoe Sinclair took a washcloth from the cupboard above the sink in the extremely small private bathroom next to her office. She turned the water on cold, and listened as it clanged through the rusty pipes.

Never again. Never again would she try to find someone's familiar. That damn dachshund had led her around all of Vegas before Zoe finally figured out how to trap the obnoxious little creature.

Sausages. She bought lots and lots of sausages, created a trail from the dachshund's last known site, and baited a trap. Only she couldn't use a real trap on a familiar (rules, rules, rules—Zoe was nothing if not diligent about following the Fates' rules), so she had to catch the thing herself.

That little dog snapped and snarled and bit, its teeth as sharp as any real dog's teeth—not that a familiar wasn't a real dog. It was a real dog with a little something extra—the ability to enhance magic, to make it purer, better, stronger.

Zoe ran the cloth under the ice-cold water, letting the chill run through her fingers and up her arms. The sensation—

cold hands and sweat-covered, exhausted body—was becoming her Vegas norm, particularly this summer with her air conditioning working at half-capacity.

She'd already tried to fix it herself—she had even used a spell—but the magical fix only lasted so long. The building's manager had already called to complain that the other tenants were getting upset.

Zoe was the building's secret owner, and the only reason she wasn't fixing the air was a simple one: it required redoing the entire system. She would have to put in a modern air conditioning unit, which meant redoing the duct work, which meant knocking out a few walls, which meant having a mold inspection, which meant having an inspection—and this building was not up to any outside investigation.

Zoe had owned the place (under a corporate name) since 1953, and while she had made upgrades, she knew that the building itself was probably only one step above condemned. The way Vegas property values were going, she was better off tearing the place down and building new than going through the hassles of inspections, repairs, and remodeling.

She wiped the cloth on her face, then wrapped the cold wetness against the back of her neck. A shudder ran through her. A delicious shudder, brought on by the chill.

She shut off the tap, staggered back into the main part of her office, and closed the blinds against the sun, which was beginning its descent in the western sky.

Normally, she would have a long night ahead of her—she still needed some surveillance photographs on that divorce case—but she deserved an evening off. Anyone would, after cradling that smelly, rebellious little dachshund in her arms for the better part of an hour.

The dog had been living in garbage cans and rolling in whatever horrible smell it could find. The dachshund had clearly reveled in just being a dog, rather than in being a familiar. She probably would, too, considering that the dog belonged to a minor entertainer on the Strip, known for his shady business practices and his willingness to look the other way whenever something illegal happened nearby.

Zoe had compromised. She'd found the dachshund, but it was clear the dog didn't want to return to its familiar duties. So, after the entertainer had paid her for her time, she had sent both of them to the Fates to have the Fates decide if the poor dog had to continue in its servitude to a magician who wasn't really worth anyone's time.

Zoe took the cloth off the back of her neck, wiped down her arms, then tossed the cloth into the bathroom. She turned back toward the main part of her office.

It looked like every gumshoe's office in every bad detective movie. Walls that needed painting forty years ago. A trenchcoat hanging off a coat tree beside the door. Rows and rows of filing cabinets filled with long-closed cases. A ratty couch against one wall, two ancient chairs in front of an old oak desk that had once belonged to a successful mob lawyer.

She even had a black rotary phone on the desktop, although the phone wasn't her primary source of communication anymore. For that, she used her cell, just like everyone else in America.

And she ruined the good-old-fashioned detective look by having three computers in the main room. One, a modern iMac, sat on her desktop. Another, a Dell, sat on the shelf she had built in front of the window. She used that Dell as her Internet computer, figuring she wanted to keep her P.I. files separate.

Then she had a laptop in a carrying case on the floor beside her desk. The laptop was only for travel and reports, and she never kept her files on it, knowing how easy it was for someone to break in, get the machine, and compromise it.

Of course, she was old-fashioned enough to prefer hard

copy. And she had piles of that, also on her desk top. Three stacks of half-completed cases lined the far left, like a barrier against the light from the shuttered window.

Sometimes she thought Herschel and Gaylord were right; sometimes she thought she should just live off her magic. Make a few dollars off the tourists and retire to her home near the university. The impulse that had brought her to this job, at this time, faded when she was doing glamour work like leaving sausages out for on-the-lam dogs, and hiding in her car outside cheap motels, taking pictures of two people who should never be anywhere near an open window when naked.

When she'd first started as a detective eighty years ago, it hadn't been a glamour job, but it had been a necessary one. In those days, she had only taken female clients, and had helped them with all the things that their husbands got easily. Then the divorce cases had had meaning because in those days, without proof, the judgement always favored the man.

Women often got accused of crimes when they hadn't committed any, and got the shaft in court cases because they didn't have as many rights as men. Zoe had been on fire then, and it had carried her through her Los Angeles days.

She had come to Vegas in the heyday of the mob, figuring there'd be a lot of underdogs here, too, and she found them. She was one of the few private detectives who wasn't afraid to take on gangsters, mostly because she knew she could win.

But gradually Vegas changed and so did she. Not only had the mob left, but the magical moved in, and one by one, they found her. She was doing all kinds of jobs like finding familiars, recouping losses created by the faeries, and hiding magical misdemeanors so that the Fates wouldn't find out and imprison some poor sap for two centuries for a simple act of kindness toward a mortal.

Zoe walked over to her desk, opened the bottom drawer, and pulled out her purse and her car keys. She would order take-out from P.F. Chang's, pick it up on the way home, and watch some trashy movie while she soaked the dog bite on her arm.

Then she'd read the latest Nora Roberts—the only writer she bought in hardback (and yet she felt the urge to hide the novels, because reading about romance hurt her own tough mental image of herself. But she felt if she couldn't have the real thing, then the fictional form would have to do). A book, some ice cream—and oh, yes, a long, hot bath.

The perfect evening for the working woman, alone with her thoughts.

She had stepped around the desk, looking for the sneakers she had pulled off, when she had returned to the office, when someone knocked on the door.

She glanced up. Behind the frosted glass, she saw several shapes. She also got a sense of magic—faint, but present. Her heart pounded. Usually the magical called first. In fact, most of her clients came by e-mail or by phone these days.

Zoe considered not saying a word, but even as she did, the doorknob turned. A man poked his head in and smiled at her.

He had the most gorgeous smile she had ever seen.

"Excuse me," he said, "but where can I find Zoe Sinclair?"

It took Zoe a moment to process the words. She wasn't usually susceptible to male beauty but this guy was incredible. He had wheat-blond hair—a color most people usually lost when they left childhood. His eyes were the deep blue of topaz neon. His tanned face had classic features—an aquiline nose, high cheekbones, square jaw—and just to make things interesting, he had a smile line on his right cheek, but not his left.

The asymmetry saved him from perfection and made him arresting.

"I'm Zoe Sinclair," she said.

He shook his head.

"You may be *a* Zoe Sinclair," he said, "but you're not the one we're looking for. She's a detective. Has to be in her—gosh, I don't know—eighties by now?"

Zoe felt cold. Mages weren't supposed to use the same name from place to place, unless they thought they were untraceable. She had been using Zoe Sinclair since 1900, and no one had ever connected the Zoe Sinclair of those early days to her.

In fact, no one in Vegas had ever asked why her detective agency had been in business under the name of Zoe Sinclair since the mid-1950s. Vegas was such a transient town that no one had ever noticed before.

"Perhaps you'd better come in, Mr.—?"

"Kineally," he said, stepping inside the door. He had a long, lanky build—a basketball player's frame—with broad shoulders and just the right amount of height. He accented that with a white polo shirt over khaki pants. No shorts for this man, even though the temperature outside had to be 115 on the concrete. His only concession to the weather were sandals, and they revealed bony, square, sexy feet.

Zoe had never found feet sexy before.

She put a hand to her cheek to cool herself off.

As Mr. Kineally stepped inside, four other people followed him. Three women, beautiful enough to be actresses, and a young boy who wasn't more than twelve. The women looked familiar, but they didn't give off the hint of magic.

That came from Kineally himself, and from the boy. The boy's magical vibe was a strong one that suggested he had already come into some of his powers, even though mages generally didn't manifest until the hormone surges were mostly passed—twenty-one for males and after menopause for women.

Zoe had been lucky in that; she went through menopause in her mid-thirties, a long, long time ago.

Kineally stayed by the door, snicking it shut after his companions entered.

"She is lying," said the blonde woman. "This is Zoe Sinclair."

Zoe frowned slightly. She had met this woman, but she couldn't place her. And that was unusual for Zoe, who usually recalled everyone she had come across.

The woman had delicate features. She wore a diaphanous pink sundress that fell to her knees, and she looked as cool as a woman at an ice hockey game.

The other two women also looked comfortable. The one in the middle was a redhead without the freckled skin. She was big-boned and solid, like the Greek sculptures of the gods on display at the Louvre. Her dress was a solid emerald green that made her skin glow.

The third woman was tall and so slender that she looked like she might break in half if grabbed wrong. Her black hair had brown highlights, and her strong features made her look exotic. Her dress was white, showing off her dark skin, and reminded Zoe of a toga.

A sense of the women's identity rose, and then faded as the second woman said, "See? She does not deny it."

"Deny what?" Zoe said, wondering how she had already lost the thread of the conversation.

"That you are Zoe Sinclair," said the third woman.

"I *am* Zoe Sinclair," Zoe said, wondering whether *Candid Camera* had been revived for the fourth time. "I never denied that."

"I said she couldn't be," Kineally said from his post near the door. "She's too young."

"Posh," the first woman said, grabbing the nearest chair and sitting down. "Ignore him. He knows nothing."

The woman acted as if she and Zoe were old friends. The redhead took the other chair, and the black-haired woman stood behind them.

The three of them were clearly a set.

The boy stood near Kineally. They looked like brothers. When he got contacts and lost some of his baby fat, the boy would look just like the man beside him.

"What's this about?" Zoe asked, trying to regain control of her office.

"Dear, I don't suppose you've been tied into the politics at Mount Olympus lately," the redhead said.

Zoe blinked, looked at Kineally, and then back at the women. There were a hundred ways she could play this and none of them made sense. Technically, she was supposed to deny the existence of the mage ruling council, but Mount Olympus did have some meaning to mortals as well.

And for all Zoe knew, Mount Olympus could be a new casino concept from the desk of the ubiquitous Steve Wynn, who had come up with the Mirage and half the other "wonders" of Las Vegas Boulevard.

"Um, no, I haven't," Zoe said, deciding that letting her visitors talk was the best policy.

"Oh, by the Powers, where do we start?" the brunette asked.

But as she said "Powers," all three women bowed their heads and spread their arms out in obeisance.

Zoe hadn't seen anyone do that since the last time she visited the Fates, nearly a hundred years ago.

Then she leaned back in her chair, so shocked that she gasped. These women looked like the Fates. Only they couldn't be. The Fates had more magical ability than all the other mages combined. And these women had none.

They had walked in. They looked like normal people and they weren't toying with their appearance all the time the way they used to.

And *they had walked in*. To Zoe's office. In Las Vegas. In Modern America. On Earth.

The Fates never appeared outside the magical realm. Hell, Zoe wasn't even sure they left their little judicial post near Mount Olympus. Sure, they changed its appearance all the time, but they had stayed in the same place—somewhere near Greece, but not *in* Greece or anywhere else in the mortal realm—since the heyday of Athens, thousands of years ago.

"No," Zoe whispered.

"No?" Kineally asked. He had been watching her. She had felt that blue gaze as if it were fingers on her shoulder. "No what?"

"Is this some kind of joke?" Zoe asked.

The blonde smiled. "Finally, some recognition."

"We were beginning to think we looked too normal," the redhead said.

"Yes," said the brunette, "like Real People."

She said that with just enough of a mixture of contempt and amusement that Zoe felt the sense of recognition grow even more. Still, she held her breath.

"I think," said the blonde.

"We were all worried," continued the redhead.

"That you had forgotten us," finished the brunette.

Zoe shook her head. No one forgot the Fates. Especially not when the Fates had treated that person with a mixture of fondness *(Really, darling, you are such an iconoclast—even for a mage)* and fury *(We make rules for a reason, child. Order must be kept)*.

"It's not possible," Zoe said.

"What's not?" Kineally asked. She met that startling blue gaze. He truly seemed confused—not just by her, but by everything. She hadn't noticed before how he hung back, stayed away from the three women, and simply observed.

And what had he said? *You're not the one we're looking for. She's a detective. Has to be in her—gosh, I don't know— eighties by now.*

He had come into his magic within the last few years, judging by the look of him. How could he not know that mages were long-lived?

Zoe crossed her arms and looked away from him, studying the three women. Zoe wasn't going to say whom she thought they were. They would have to admit it. If this was some sort of magical scam, she wanted them to get it under way.

She wasn't going to be an easy mark, someone who gave away too much information just by making assumptions.

"Ma'am?" The little boy stepped forward.

His fair skin was sunburned on the right side only—obviously he'd been in a car too long, under the sun—and his round glasses had slid to the edge of his nose, making him look much more bookish than his athletic brother.

"I know you don't trust us," the boy said, "but these ladies, they need your help. My dad doesn't know how much trouble they're in. They haven't told any of us except my Aunt Vivian, who never told us either, but I know. This is pretty serious, and these ladies, they're scared."

All three women turned in unison and stared at the child. If they had stared at Zoe like that, she would have been afraid of turning into stone.

But the child seemed unfazed.

Then Zoe realized that she wasn't unfazed. She was fazed. That kid had called the man next to him his dad.

"You're this boy's father?" Zoe asked Kineally.

The man raised his eyebrows. "Is that a problem?"

"Yes," Zoe said. "No. I mean, I thought you were brothers."

Kineally smiled. It was a devastating, brighten-the-room-with-a-thousand-suns kind of smile, and Zoe felt herself melt.

"He's my son," Kineally said. "His name is Kyle, and I'm Travers."

Zoe had to concentrate again to hear his words. She'd often read about women who were so overwhelmed by the men they met that they couldn't concentrate, but she'd never had it happen to her. She'd always believed it to be a fictional contrivance, just like she felt love at first sight was the same thing, and happily-ever-after came from children's stories.

"Travers," Zoe found herself saying before she could stop herself. The name was unusual, just like he was, and it suited him. "Travers Kineally."

He nodded. "You know it?"

She had to shake her head, which made her feel like a dork. And she hadn't felt like a dork since she had gone through puberty too many years ago to count. She wasn't even sure if there had been such a word back then. Dork. Imbecile, maybe, but not dork.

"Ma'am?" the boy said again in that tentative voice. "I know you think my dad's cute and all, but can we focus on the problem here?"

Zoe blushed. Her cheeks grew so hot she was sure steam was rising from the top of her head.

She hadn't blushed since she was a child—at least that she could remember.

"Kyle!" Travers said. He sounded shocked and embarrassed.

"Yes, dear," said the blonde, turning around in her chair so that she faced Zoe.

The redhead turned, too. "We have a problem."

The brunette's turn was perfectly orchestrated to make the entire maneuver look like a schtick from a Broadway musical. "And we believe you're the only one who can solve it."

Six

Travers put his hands on Kyle's shoulders and pulled his son back toward the door. Travers was going to tell Kyle that this was no longer their concern, that his son was getting too personal and that it was time to leave, but the shock on Zoe Sinclair's face was too much.

Travers couldn't tell if the shock came from Kyle's comment about Zoe's attraction to Travers or if it came from the weird way the Wyrd Sisters were speaking to her.

Kyle dipped his knees and slipped out of Travers's grasp. That kid always seemed to know what Travers was going to do. Kyle moved far enough along the unpainted wall that Travers would have to leave the door to reach him. And for some reason, Travers wanted to keep the door at his back.

Part of that reason was Zoe Sinclair herself. She was stunning. She had chocolate brown hair, stylishly cut so that it brushed her cheeks. Her skin was ivory, but those cheeks had a reddish tinge even when she wasn't blushing.

She had kissable lips (he hadn't been able to stop thinking about them since he walked into the room), and the most startling eyes he had ever seen. They were large, with heavily fringed lashes that made them seem even more dramatic than they already were. Her brows, arched along the perfect bone above her stunning eyes, also added to the drama.

But the thing about her eyes that he liked best was that their color perfectly matched her hair. Right down to the highlights. Her hair had golden highlights and her chocolate brown eyes had golden flecks.

Flecks he couldn't stop staring at.

Good thing Kyle hadn't mentioned Travers's attraction to Zoe. Although hearing that Zoe was attracted to Travers did make his heart rise, just a little. It rose even more when Zoe blushed.

She didn't look like the kind of woman who blushed. Although she had a blusher's skin—that soft, luminescent color—her body language, her black skirt and t-shirt (worn despite the day's heat), and that hard glint in her eyes made it obvious that she didn't like the softer emotions in her or in anyone else.

He wondered about her past. Obviously, she came from a long line of female detectives. Had her grandmother opened this place? Then had her mother followed or had the Sinclair Detective Agency skipped a generation?

And why did he care? He wasn't ever going to see her again, no matter how beautiful she was.

"We should go," Travers said to Kyle.

Kyle looked at Travers as if Travers had committed the social gaffe of the century. It took a moment for Travers to realize he had interrupted one of the Wyrd Sisters.

"I mean," Travers said to his son, "we've done what we came to do. We should let them get on to their private business."

"Da-ad," Kyle said, stretching the word out. "We can't leave. Not now."

"I'm confused," Zoe said. Her voice was husky and low, a smoky alto—the kind that always sent a shiver down Travers's spine. Like a blues singer, only richer, with a little less cigarette-and-alcohol rasp and a bit more warmth. "Aren't you part of this group?"

"I'm just the delivery boy," Travers said.

"Daaad!" Kyle stepped farther away from Travers's grasp.

"Come on, Kyle," Travers said. "Meetings with private detectives are confidential."

Travers didn't know that for certain, but he assumed it. Besides, in his own business, he didn't let strangers in the same room as his clients. Certified Public Accounting wasn't psychotherapy, but it did have its own sets of rules. He was sure detecting was the same.

Zoe's gaze met his. There was a question in those interesting eyes, and a challenge. He wasn't sure what the question or the challenge was, and he doubted he would ever get the chance to find out.

His fingers found the doorknob. He needed to leave before his interest in this woman got the better of him.

"You must stay, Travers," said Clotho.

"This concerns you, young man," said Lachesis.

"After all, you're years behind in your studies," said Atropos in a voice that sounded so much like his mother's that Travers actually let go of the doorknob before he realized what he had done.

"I have no studies," Travers said, "and all I'm behind in is a few days' work. Kyle and I have to find a hotel room, so we'll leave you to your business. It's been a pleasure, ladies."

"Stop him!" Clotho said to Zoe.

"Use a spell, something," Lachesis said.

"He cannot leave this room!" Atropos said.

Zoe's face had gone ashen. In fact, it changed color the moment Lachesis said the word "spell."

Zoe looked from him to the women and back to him again. "Tell me what's going on here," she said to him, "and this time, don't hold anything back."

Seven

Zoe had no idea why she had commanded Travers Kineally to tell her what was going on. After all, he seemed almost as confused as she felt. He looked from his son (son! Travers must have been a child himself when he fathered that boy) to the possible Fates and, when it was clear none of them was going to say anything, he looked at Zoe.

And shrugged.

The movement was elegant, boyish, and somehow charming. She had to resist the urge to smile.

"All I can do is tell you why I'm here," he said.

"Shoot." She crossed her arms and leaned back, her chair squeaking as she did so.

But the blonde spoke first. "I do believe it would be better if we told you—"

"Shh!" the redhead said.

"Have you, of all people, forgotten the main objective?" the brunette asked.

The blonde put a hand over her mouth. "The situation is getting serious. We are losing touch."

"Shh!" the redhead said again.

"Let the boy answer her," the brunette said.

"Me?" Kyle squeaked.

"No, child," the blonde said. "The other boy."

"Your father," the redhead said.

"After all," the brunette said without a trace of sarcasm, "he's the one who wants to abandon us."

"I do not!" Travers said, looking surprised. Then he shrugged again, and Zoe found that she liked that boyish mannerism. "I mean, I do want to leave, but you're adults. You're not my responsibility. Kyle is, and we have to get home."

Zoe frowned. She looked from the man to the boy. Kyle's cheeks had reddened, and it seemed like he was angry.

"You promised, Dad," Kyle said.

"I promised you I would bring them here," Travers said. "I've done that."

"But you don't know if she's the right Zoe Sinclair!" Kyle said.

"What's this about the right Zoe Sinclair?" Zoe asked.

"She is," said the blonde.

Zoe shook her head. "Someone please tell me what's going on."

And again, she looked at Travers

He held out his hands in a helpless, who-knows gesture. "My sister, at her wedding, asked me to drive these three women down to Los Angeles. I did that. Then it turns out that they want to find a woman who used to work there named Zoe Sinclair. My kindhearted son—"

Kyle's flush grew even deeper.

"—begged me to help them find this woman, saying that these three ladies shouldn't be on their own. Kyle's pretty astute for a kid his age, so I agreed."

Zoe folded her hands on the desktop, not wanting Travers to see how unnerved she was. These women had to have something to do with the Fates. This was some sort of complicated scam. Zoe wondered if the real Fates knew about it—nonmagical women doing a fairly excellent impersonation of the most powerful beings in mage history (excepting the Powers That Be, of course).

Travers sighed and shook his head. "Long story short, there hasn't been a detective named Zoe Sinclair in Los Angeles since—"

"The 1950s," Zoe said. "You can stop pretending you don't understand this now. You found me. What do you all want?"

Her voice was harsher than she had intended but she was getting annoyed. She was finally able to see past Travers's beauty, which had stunned her for a while. She hadn't thought clearly.

If she had, she would have realized that the magical always knew other mages. And they knew about long life spans and the way that the magical aged slowly.

So Travers, for all his protestations, knew that she was who she said she was. And the women, who should have been magical and were not, did not, apparently, know that Zoe could suss out their lack of magical abilities.

The only real mystery here was Kyle. The kid seemed sincere. But Zoe had seen a lot of Vegas scams built on children. Children could be the absolute best at sincerity, partly because they didn't have to try as hard.

"Excuse me?" Travers said. He looked like she had thrown cold water on him. "You can't be that Zoe Sinclair."

"And why not?" Zoe asked.

"Because you're—what? Thirty? And to be that woman, you'd have to be eighty, like I said."

"And you can stop playing dumb, Mr. Kineally," Zoe said. "I'm not some wilting mortal woman who is unwilling to admit her piddly age. I'm going to be one hundred and seventy-four in August, more than old enough to be your Miss Sinclair from Los Angeles and from Vegas fifty years ago. I'm not a grandmother, I never will be, and I'm not about to start now."

He stared at her. She could have sworn that the shock he was pretending to have was real. It felt real. It resounded through her as if she were the one who was shocked.

"I'm not a fool, Ms. Sinclair," he said.

"Good," she snapped. "Then let's get down to business."

"I mean," he said, as if she hadn't spoken, "no one lives one hundred and seventy-four years. I don't know what you're trying to pull, but this isn't working."

"Me?" Zoe's voice rose. "You're the one who comes marching in here, decides that I can't be who I say I am, pretends not to have magic when it's clear you do, tries to pass off three non-magical women as the Fates, and somehow managed to rope your poor son into all of this."

"What?" Travers pushed off the door. His blue eyes seemed even brighter than they had a minute before. "I'm not conducting a scam."

Zoe silently cursed herself for using the word "Fate" before anyone else had, but she was committed now.

"You clearly are. Anyone with a hint of magic could tell that you and your boy are about as magical as they come. That kid's going to be something, with the abilities he already has. I sure hope his training is better than yours, because it's clear that you're not smart enough to scam anyone. First of all, you have to know that—"

"Wait a minute." Travers's voice got lower when he was angry. And softer. Which made it seem more menacing, somehow, than a yell. "I am not involving my son in anything illegal."

"Not by human laws, no," Zoe said, "although I haven't heard the pitch yet. Is it to steal something?"

All three women nodded their heads.

"Well, then, I'm not your man, metaphorically speaking," Zoe said. "Because I don't break laws—mortal or mage. It's just not good for me, my reputation, or my business."

"We haven't asked you to break any laws," Travers said.

"Um, Dad," Kyle said, so softly that he might have hoped Zoe couldn't hear him. "The Fates just did."

"The Fates." Travers put his hands on his hips. "I believe that they're the Fates as much as I believe that you, Ms. Sinclair, are one hundred and seventy-four years old. I have had enough of this craziness. Kyle, we're leaving."

"No." The boy flopped onto Zoe's couch. A cloud of dust rose off the cushions, and Zoe almost smiled despite her annoyance. Her housekeeping skills did leave something to be desired. "We're not leaving until someone promises to take care of the Fates."

Now the boy was calling them the Fates, but Zoe didn't know if that was because she had done so first. She silently cursed herself again for making that mistake, and made a mental promise that she would never again berate clients who made the same one. It was startlingly easy to fall into that kind of trap.

"Travers," said the redhead, "you really must stay."

"We will need you on this mission," said the brunette.

"Mission?" Now his voice went up. And it moved from baritone to Irish tenor. Which Zoe still found attractive, even though she was annoyed. And the fact that she found him attractive when she was annoyed annoyed her even further.

"Look, ladies," he said, "I've done all I'm going to do. Get Miss Sinclair to baby-sit you for a few days. Maybe she can find someone new to pass you off on. I'm outta here."

He took steps toward the couch, looking forever like an angry father about to grab his son and take him out of a dangerous place. Kyle ran to Zoe and hid behind her chair.

"You've got to hear this out," Kyle said, all in a rush. "Because we're not scamming you and no one's lying to you and my dad really is clueless—he has been since I was a baby. He always says it's coincidence that I know stuff, not that I'm psychic, even though my Aunt Viv is psychic and my new Uncle Dexter used to be Superman."

That last caught Zoe by surprise. "Dexter?" She turned toward the boy, and saw him only partially out of her left eye. He had ducked behind the chair, and was holding its back with his hands, as if it were a shield that he could move to block his father.

"We're leaving, Kyle," Travers said. "Enough games."

"Superman?" Zoe asked, a memory playing in her mind. Something about Canada and—

"Henri Barou," the blonde said. "In the 1930s, he went afoul with some children, let them see him fly, and they wrote a comic book? Do you recall the scandal?"

Zoe looked at the blonde. Zoe did recall the scandal. She had met Henri Barou, who was calling himself Dexter Grant. He wanted to know if she would help him with a case. He didn't dare use his magic, since the Fates had forbidden it, but he knew of a purebred puppy mill in which the animals were being mistreated. He just didn't know what to do about it. His old method would have been to fly in and rescue the animals, but he couldn't anymore. The Fates had forbidden his interference in mortal affairs. So he had come to Zoe, asking for help.

She had taken photographs, documented proof of the abuse, and had reported the mill's owners to the state. The state shut the mill down, and Zoe had used her own magic to heal a lot of the injured and sick animals, just so they could be adopted by caring people.

Travers was watching her. "You believe this Superman crap?"

"Honest," Kyle said. "My dad doesn't know about any of it. I wish you could feel what I know . . ."

His voice was barely above a whisper, and this time, Zoe knew that Travers couldn't hear his son.

Zoe raised a hand and sealed her door shut. Then she boosted the air conditioning because the room had gotten stiflingly warm.

"Mr. Kineally," she said, "you have been out-voted by your son and his friends. You're staying until I understand exactly what's going on here."

"Sorry," Travers said. "Kyle and I are going. And if Kyle doesn't want to leave, then I guess he can stay here without me."

The parental bluff. Only Travers Kineally gave it enough of an edge to make it seem real. He walked to the door and turned the knob. But of course the door didn't move. The knob didn't even make its normal clicking sound.

"I wasn't kidding," Zoe said. "You're staying."

"Open this door." He grabbed the doorknob with both hands and pulled. The muscles in his well-shaped arms strained, but the door didn't budge.

"Dad," Kyle said.

"Open it!" Travers braced a foot against the doorjamb and pulled. Still nothing happened.

Zoe raised her eyebrows and leaned back in her chair. This man was putting on an excellent performance.

"Travers," said the redhead with a bit of a sigh, "the door won't open."

"Open the door, dammit, or I will come over to your desk, find the remote locking mechanism, and smash it." As he said that last, he turned toward Zoe. His hands were still on the knob, one foot still rested against the doorjamb, and Zoe was tempted—ever so tempted—to release the binding spell she had put on the door.

Then Travers would have tumbled backwards and maybe

even fallen into the so-called Fates. But then, of course, he'd leave, and Zoe wouldn't find out exactly what was going on.

"I didn't use a mechanism," Zoe said. "I spelled the door. It's blocked until I open it."

Travers let go of the knob, turned, and put his hands on his hips. He looked exasperated. His cheeks were red, and perspiration dotted his forehead.

"Spelled," he said.

Zoe nodded.

"That's impossible."

Zoe sighed. She didn't like games. She was about to say so when Kyle touched her arm.

"Really," the boy said. "He doesn't get this."

"He was abominably trained," the brunette said.

"If we were still in charge," said the blonde, "we would take his mentor—"

"— and punish him for dereliction of duties," finished the redhead, just like the Fates used to do. They always finished each other's thoughts.

Travers glared at the women, but for once, Zoe ignored him.

"What do you mean, still in charge?" Zoe asked, wishing that she hadn't. She didn't want to get involved, she didn't want to be sucked deeper into this scam, and yet something compelled her. The honesty of the kid and, if she were truthful, the beauty of the man before her.

And the strangeness of the three women.

"That's why we asked you if you were aware of the politics of Mount Olympus," the brunette asked.

"Things have gotten worse in the last—decade? Century? I'm never sure how mortals tell time." The blonde looked to her friends.

"Suffice to say, we've been—what is that term? Laid off?" the redhead looked at the brunette.

"The Powers That Be imposed term limits on our position," the brunette said without answering any of her friends' questions.

"We had to resign," said the blonde.

"While the Powers reexamine our job," said the redhead.

"The qualifications have changed," the brunette said.

"And if we want the job back," said the blonde.

"We have to reapply," said the redhead.

"But only if we meet some new qualifications," said the brunette.

"Which is why we're here," said the blonde.

"To reapply?" Zoe asked, feeling confused. It was that confused sensation, more than anything, that was beginning to convince her that the women in front of her were the Fates.

"No," the redhead said. "We're here in this office to get your help finding something of ours. We're here on this mortal plane to meet the new qualifications."

"Or we were originally," said the brunette, "before we realized it was all a big power play by Zeus."

"Zeus?" Zoe asked.

"Zeus?" Travers asked at the same time, only his tone was a lot more skeptical than Zoe's. Zoe had met Zeus. He was a short, bullish man with a strange charisma and a self-confidence that bordered on the ridiculous.

"This is getting completely out of hand," Travers said. "Unblock this door so that Kyle and I can leave."

"I want to hear about Zeus," Kyle said from behind Zoe. "I didn't know he was still alive."

Zoe started at that, until she remembered that mortals learned about many mages through myth and legend. Some of the younger mages, like Dexter Grant, had found their way into popular culture. But the older ones had a lot of myths written about them.

"Zeus is not still alive," Travers snapped. "He never existed. He's a made-up god for a culture that's long dead, and these women are living in a fantasy world that Miss Sinclair is somehow buying into. I don't think this is a healthy place, Kyle, and I don't think we should stay."

Zoe's eyes narrowed. "Who are you?" she asked Travers.

"I told you," he said. "My name is—"

"I caught your name," she said. "But I was wondering who you are—what you do—that makes you so very judgemental. Zeus is still alive—"

She caught herself before she could add the word "unfortunately." No sense in having someone report that slip back to the randy old man.

"—and still wields a great deal of power. If he's somehow messed up in this, I want to know about it."

Travers was staring at her with his mouth open.

Zoe ignored him, and focused on the women.

"Did Zeus remove your magical powers?" she asked.

"Of course not, child," the blonde said. And the use of all those endearments should have been a tip-off. How many women Zoe's age—or apparent age—called her "child" and "darling" and "dear"? Those were patronizing terms, old lady terms, and if anyone qualified as the old lady in the room, it was Zoe.

Unless these three women really were the Fates. Then Zoe was just a babe in arms.

"Zeus didn't take our powers away," the redhead said.

"We gave them up voluntarily," said the brunette.

"What?" Zoe asked.

"In order to reapply," the blonde said, "we had to expand our knowledge in three areas."

"We had to learn about other cultures," said the redhead.

"We had to improve our diplomatic skills," said the brunette.

"And we had to understand powerlessness," said the blonde.

"So we gave up our magic to come here to learn about powerlessness, and another culture," said the redhead.

"We're still struggling with diplomacy," said the brunette.

"Obviously," Travers said dryly. Then he raised his eyebrows at Zoe. "You believe all this?"

"Parts of it sound plausible," she said. "But parts of it seem quite unlikely. I mean, if there are no Fates, who's in charge of judicial review and law enforcement?"

"Well," the blonde said, looking at her friends, "that's the problem."

"They're not very competent," said the redhead.

"Who isn't?" Zoe asked.

"The children Zeus installed in our place," the brunette said.

"In fact," the blonde said, "that's why we're here. This entire thing is a mess."

Zoe felt a shiver run through her. It was indeed a mess, and there was only one real way she could get to the truth.

She waved a hand in a relocation spell, and commanded, "To the Fates!"

Eight

And then she disappeared. Right in front of him. As if she had never been there at all.

Travers took one step forward and almost collided with Lachesis's chair. Zoe Sinclair was really and truly gone.

Kyle leaned on the chair and waved his hands in the space where Zoe had been. He looked pleased and confused, and Travers didn't have to be psychic to know what his son was thinking: Kyle thought Zoe's disappearance meant that magic really happened, but he was confused as to how she did it.

The Fates—or whomever they were—seemed calm. They weren't upset or talking among themselves. In fact, Clotho and Lachesis had leaned back in their chairs as if they were expecting a long wait.

Travers had had enough. He stomped around to the back of the desk and wished, for the very first time in his life, that he knew something about illusionists. Because someone—maybe this Zoe Sinclair—was playing him for a fool.

He crouched and looked for a trapdoor. When he found

none, he reached for the desk, wondering what he would find around it.

Kyle grabbed his hand. "Hey, Dad. You always said desks were private."

"I don't like what's going on here." Travers stood up and shook his son's hand off his arm. He placed his own hands on Zoe Sinclair's paper-covered desk and leaned forward. "Would you ladies kindly tell me the point of this adventure?"

He used polite words, but his tone wasn't polite. If his mother had heard him, she would have rapped his knuckles. Travers tried not to use that tone in front of his son, either, not wanting Kyle to pick up bad habits, but now was not the time for that kind of caution.

Something strange was going on here, and Travers had to know exactly what it was.

"Unfortunately," Lachesis said, "the magical streams no longer consider us the Fates."

Travers glanced at Clotho. She was twirling a strand of blond hair around one finger.

Was all of this some great, big practical joke designed by Vivian and Kyle to get Travers to knock off his criticism of comic books? Was Vivian doing this because she could afford to, now that she had inherited their Great Aunt Eugenia's money?

"I don't care about 'magic streams,'" Travers said. "I care about whatever it is you four are trying to do to me and Kyle."

"Four?" Atropos asked.

"You and the woman who just 'vanished.' Zoe, or whatever your name is, you can come out now." Travers directed that last toward the open bathroom door, knowing that Zoe had to be somewhere nearby where she could hear him.

"She will not come out," Clotho said, probably giving Zoe a signal. Somewhere along the way, around the time Zoe had accepted the magic ideals as easily as she had, Travers realized all of these women were working together.

It didn't matter how attractive he found Zoe. He didn't like being played for a fool.

"She won't return until she has a few answers," Lachesis said.

"As if she can get answers from those children," Atropos said. Then, oddly, all three women giggled in unison.

"Dad—"

"And you," Travers turned halfway, raising one hand and pointing a finger at the sky. He wanted badly to shake that finger in Kyle's face, but that would be wrong. His son was trying something, and he clearly had help. The worst thing Travers could do was overreact.

But he was getting a little freaked out, locked in this office with three strange women, a disappearing detective, and a child who didn't belong here at all. If Zoe didn't return soon—if things didn't return to normal soon—Travers was going out the window and taking Kyle with him.

"Me?" Kyle asked.

"What is this all about?"

Kyle shoved his glasses up the bridge of his nose with the knuckle of his forefinger. "How come you think I know something?"

"Because we're here at the behest of your Aunt Vivian, who always conspires with you, and her three friends, whom you championed once we got to L.A. I figure you all did this as a ruse to get me to Las Vegas. Did you think that I needed to meet someone now that Vivian's married? Or is this about your so-called magical abilities?"

To his surprise, Kyle's eyes filled with tears. "I didn't do anything, Dad. Honest. Aunt Viv and I didn't plan anything. I don't know anything about anything, and I just like Clotho and Lachesis and Atropos, and I worry about them because they clearly don't know anything about our world, which you would notice if you just paid attention. You never really pay attention, Dad. Haven't you ever wondered how come I know so much stuff about other people? Haven't you wondered why Aunt Vivian once owned the only accurate psychic hotline in the nation? Haven't you wondered why you can win the lottery *every single time*?"

Travers flushed. Kyle wasn't supposed to know about the lottery. Travers thought no one did.

"You don't know what's going on," Travers said.

"No!" The tears were gone without a single one falling. Kyle looked defiant now.

"But you wanted to come here," Travers said.

"Of course. I wanted someone else to take care of the Fates. Dad, they don't know anything. They barely understand how money works. Haven't you wondered why?"

He hadn't wondered why. He hadn't thought about it in quite that way. He had simply assumed the women were eccentric, and perhaps had once been pampered by their husbands. Women like that often didn't know how money worked. He had a lot of elderly, rich widows on his client list who had to learn how to write a check when their husbands died.

"But the Fates aren't elderly, Dad," Kyle said.

Travers started. He hadn't spoken aloud, had he?

"No, you haven't said a single word," Kyle said. "You always think that when I respond to your thoughts, and I never correct you. You're not mumbling, you're not talking aloud. You're having thoughts that broadcast. I can hear them."

Travers clamped his lips together. Hearing thoughts wasn't possible, and he would prove it. He would think of—Liberace. Kyle was so young he probably never heard of Liberace, but Vegas was Liberace's town. There was even a Liberace Museum, according to the signs on the way into the city. What would it have, a white feather—

"—boa and a million candelabras?" Kyle asked. "And I do too know who Liberace is."

Travers sank into Zoe's chair. She clearly wasn't there. The chair wasn't even warm any longer. His heart was pounding. Maybe he was dreaming.

That was it. He had heard the alarm, rolled over, and fallen back to sleep. This entire day had been one long, crazy dream.

"Get real, Dad," Kyle said. "If you'd overslept the alarm, I would've woke you up because we had to get out of town before the traffic got bad."

The Fates were watching this interchange as if it were a tennis match, their heads swinging back and forth in unison from Travers's face to Kyle's. They didn't even seem confused that they were only hearing half of the conversation. In fact, it seemed to amuse them.

"This isn't possible," Travers whispered.

"Of course it is, Dad." Kyle grimaced at the Fates, then turned his back on them. He leaned against the desk, facing Travers. "I tried to tell you about it a number of times, remember? I told you I could read minds when I was three, but you laughed and told me I watched too much television."

Travers raised his head. He felt slightly dizzy, probably because he hadn't been breathing. "You remember that?"

"Of course I remember it, Dad. I was so confused. I thought everybody could hear thoughts, and then I realized only I could. But I figured you're my dad, so you can, too, and then I told you and you laughed. You laughed, Dad, and I was really scared."

Travers frowned. He remembered laughing, and telling Kyle he watched too much television. Then he grabbed his small son, pulled him into a hug, and cuddled with him on the couch, joking that they'd watch even more television.

But he couldn't remember Kyle's expression, and he wasn't sure why he remembered the incident. It was eight years ago, and seemed like nothing out of the ordinary.

"Perhaps, Travers," Clotho said, "it is time you stop questioning what happens around you and start believing."

Kyle was still studying him with that same expression of hope and concern that he had every time this topic had come up.

And it had come up dozens of times every year. Kyle tried to convince Travers that psychic powers existed and Kyle had them, and Travers laughed or dismissed them or found some other explanation.

But Kyle often knew what people were going to say or what they were going to do, and a few times, he even kept Travers away from danger. Twice in the last year, Kyle had told his father to slow down on the Ventura, and both times a wreck happened right in front of them not five minutes later.

If Kyle hadn't issued the warning in both cases, their car would have been in the middle of those wrecks.

But psychic abilities didn't exist. Magic didn't exist. Any more than miracles existed.

Everything of value in this world could be proven by science or mathematics.

Everything.

"Except your ability to win the lottery," Kyle said, his expression grim. "No matter how you run the statistics, your ability with lottery tickets is mathematically impossible, and you know it."

"Kyle—"

"I'm not going to shut up about it, Dad. How many other people in the history of the world have gotten rich winning the lottery—not one big lottery, but hundreds of small ones? Hmmm? I'm going to wager no one. That's like my ability to hear thoughts, Dad. You can make numbers work for you."

Travers swallowed. He wasn't sure what unnerved him more; Kyle's proclaimed ability to read minds (which Travers was finally starting to believe) or the fact that Kyle had just revealed that Travers can manipulate numbers.

He didn't believe he could manipulate numbers. He just thought he had an incredible lucky streak going. One that would end someday.

Even though it had been going on since he was twenty-one, broke, and alone with a young boy.

"No, it's not me, Dad," Kyle said even as Travers looked at him, just beginning to make that speculation. "Your ability with numbers is your own. I have to cheat on half my math quizzes just to get the right answers."

"Cheat?" Travers asked, more as a stall. He wasn't really concentrating on what Kyle was saying. He was thinking, and worrying, and wondering what happened to the woman who owned this chair, the woman who had been here not a few moments before. Was that why he was here? So that he would admit his ability with numbers? Did this have something to do with the National Lottery Commission? (Was there a National Lottery Commission? He didn't even know.)

Kyle was looking sheepish. "I have to read other people's thoughts sometimes. Then I take the answer most people have. It's kinda cheating and kinda not. Sometimes I have the right answer before I double-check."

Psychic cheating. Travers shook his head. If this were true, any of it were true, then he would have to rethink everything, including his parenting.

"It's all true, Dad," Kyle said.

"You can hear thoughts," Travers said.

Kyle nodded.

"All thoughts?" Travers tried not to be afraid of this answer, but there were some thoughts—many thoughts—most thoughts—that should just remain private. Jeez, what if his kid overheard what he thought about Sandra Bullock the other night when they were watching *Speed*?

"Ick, Dad. I don't want to know that you can even think like that." Kyle put up his hands, palms out, as if he were pushing the information away from him. "I only hear big, important thoughts. The ones that are filled with emotion. That you broadcast."

"But you seem to have heard all of my thoughts here," Travers said, willing his voice to remain even. He was afraid it would shake, afraid that everything he had ever believed— about privacy, about parenting, about himself and his son— was about to change.

"That's because you're really upset, Dad," Kyle said. "It's like you're thinking with a megaphone. Usually you're just a quiet little hum and not emotional at all. It's kinda good you're like a robot. Aunt Viv can zoom in on you any time, but I only get you when you broadcast."

"Vivian can hear my thoughts?"

Kyle bit his lower lip. Obviously he wasn't supposed to say anything about that. "She tries not to. She doesn't like to eavesdrop, and besides, she hates country music."

"What does country music—?" Travers started to ask the question, then stopped himself. Country music had something to do with it because he listened all the time. Either the radio was on or he was playing his 100-disk changer or he was listening to one of the XM broadcasts on his computer.

His privacy saved by his love of music.

Then he shook his head. "Okay," he said, trying to get this straight. "You and Vivian got me here so this illusionist could get my attention long enough to have me talk to you about psychic powers—"

"Dad!" Kyle put his hands over his face. Dramatic, but effective. He should have starred in silent movies.

"Zoe Sinclair is not an illusionist," Lachesis said quietly.

Still, Travers jumped. He had forgotten the Wyrd Sisters were in the room.

"Fates, Dad," Kyle whispered. "They hate being called the Wyrd Sisters. They think it's an insult."

"Have you ever read those Norse myths?" Atropos asked, crossing her arms.

Travers shook his head, but Kyle nodded. Then Travers bit back irritation. "This is a discussion between me and my son. You don't belong in it."

"Don't belong." Clotho pursed her lips. "Of course we belong. If we had known that your mentor was screwing up, we would have interfered long ago. It's our job to deal with the magical."

"Or it used to be," Lachesis said.

"It doesn't matter," Atropos said. "What matters is that you must believe in yourself, Travers. Your magic will become dangerous if you don't."

"My magic?" Travers laughed. "I have as much magic as—"

He had been about to say *Kyle,* but he was beginning to realize that Kyle had some kind of magic.

"Well, as you do," Travers finished lamely. He had heard the women confess (confess? lie?) that their magical powers were gone. That would help—a little.

All three women looked sad.

"Actually," Clotho said, "at the moment, you have more."

"Considerably more," Lachesis said.

"And you have no idea what to do with it," Atropos said.

"So?" Travers asked.

"So?" Clotho rose out of her seat. She was clearly shocked.

Lachesis put a hand on her arm and eased her back down. "So," Lachesis said. "In our world, that's a crisis."

"Well, we're not in your world," Travers said. "We're in mine."

"Yes." Atropos stepped around the chairs, moving in front of the other two Fates. "We're in yours and you have just met your—well, you have just met your match, so to speak."

"What?" Travers asked.

Clotho made a face and shook her head. Lachesis rolled her eyes. Atropos shrugged.

"You have a slight magic, fortunately," Clotho said. "If it were larger, your problems would have shown up earlier."

"I don't have magical problems," Travers said.

"Besides me," Kyle said.

Travers ruffled Kyle's hair. "You're not a problem, kiddo. You never have been."

And Kyle smiled. Maybe there was something good about broadcasting thoughts after all. At least, Kyle knew that Travers wasn't lying.

"Your magical problems are about to be compounded," Lachesis said.

"And unfortunately," Atropos added, "there's nothing we can do to stop it."

Nine

Zoe materialized in a library that smelled ever so faintly of pee. She had been here before, a long time ago. She recognized the bookshelves that rose as far as the eye could see. The tomes beside her were thick and dust-covered, which she did not remember. The library she had been to in the past had beautifully bound, well-cared-for volumes in a multitude of languages.

The multitude of languages remained, but the volumes were no longer well cared for. Many of them had fallen onto the floor, and were open to various pages. Others were stacked on tables, the books open and the spines bent.

In addition to the pee odor, the air smelled musty and like something else, something sweet and childlike. The scent was what Zoe always thought of when she had to imagine what pink smelled like.

It was the smell of—

Bubblegum.

Zoe blinked, and tilted her head, wondering if she hadn't spoken correctly when she completed her transport spell.

Maybe that delicious man in her office had distracted her enough . . .

But that was ludicrous. She had recited the spell, and she had been irritated at the time, not drowning in lust. (Well, she'd actually still felt the lust—it hadn't gone away—but the irritation simply overrode it.)

She had done the spell correctly. She just wasn't where she expected to be.

Zoe stepped over a pile of books, putting one hand on a shelf to brace herself. The lighting was dim and flickery, as if she were in candlelight. Far away, from a direction she couldn't quite locate, she heard voices.

In the past, whenever she had done a "To-the-Fates" spell, she had ended up right in front of all three women. The first time, she had appeared in what looked like a Greek temple, complete with columns and fountains and that wonderful Greek sunshine.

The Fates themselves had looked like something out of a Greek myth (which, she knew, they were—only, of course, they were the basis for the myth, rather than the other way around). They were wearing long white gowns that fastened on one shoulder, and they had their hair swept up, a single curl falling on their bare skin. They wore sandals and gold jewelry and looked beautiful.

That was the other thing. Even though the women in her office had been lovely, they weren't astonishingly beautiful— not breathtakingly, amazingly, astoundingly gorgeous, the kind that took the breath away, no matter what your gender. If those women had been the Fates, then even the outstanding Travers Kineally would have faded in comparison.

But he most certainly dominated that room.

Zoe stepped over another pile of books, and then another. Finally she had no choice but to walk on several, wincing as she took each step. Dust motes rose in the weird light, and she sneezed several times.

Then she heard a bark. It was more of a yip. More, actually, a sound of irritation.

And she recognized it.

The dachshund had made that sound after he had found out who was at the end of the trail of sausages.

To the Fates, she had said, pointing at the dachshund and waving her arm. *And his master, too.*

The dachshund had disappeared and somewhere else in Las Vegas, that horrible little magician had disappeared as well.

Apparently they had come here.

Zoe bit her lower lip so hard that she could taste blood. What if something in her spell-making abilities had gone awry? What if they were all trapped in this place?

She walked in the direction of the yip. She had to step over more books, and push aside a table. As she did so, a stack of yellow legal pads fell over.

Each stack was covered in writing—most of it Greek (literally), although some of it was English. One of the pads had doodles on top of the Greek—little smiley faces, a few flowers, and one *Crystal ♥ Dudley.* That was followed by *Crystal and Dudley 4-Ever,* and *Dudley Rocks!* In a different handwriting, someone had written **Dudley The Dull Dude.** And in yet a third handwriting, in a different ink, someone else had written: *Wait Till Daddy Finds Out And Guess Who's Gonna Tell Him? HA! HA!*

Zoe straightened the legal pads as best she could, trying not to read any more, worrying that she was seeing something important that she didn't understand.

She continued toward a wall of bookshelves. The voices were growing closer.

"I don't get it," a young female voice whined. "How come you can't do this?"

"It's not my turn," said another young female voice. "Besides, I always have to look things up."

"It's better than calling Daddy," said a third female voice.

"No, it's not," a man said.

Zoe walked past yet another stack of yellow legal pads (Tiffany Eats Toads! was written across the top of one), and nearly tripped on a librarian's stool half buried on a pile of magazines. The bookshelves opened to the right, and through them, she could see an even light flowing across the dirt-covered hardwood floor.

"It's stupid," said the first female voice.

"Yeah, like who cares about a dumb dog?" asked the second female voice.

Zoe's stomach clenched. Where had she sent that poor dachshund?

"You guys, we're supposed to care about all this stuff," said the third female voice.

Zoe stepped over a mound of dirty laundry, then peered at it. Blue jeans, tank tops, and bras, twisted together along with girl's underwear with the days of the week written across the butt in pink. The laundry gave off a stale odor that mixed with the smell of bubblegum that somehow reminded Zoe of a girl's camp she investigated one summer.

"Look," said the male voice. "You ladies think about this and I'll just take Bartholomew home."

Bartholomew was the name of the dachshund. A name that poor dog hated.

Zoe hurried toward the voices now, nearly slipping in something wet near the door.

"Did you hear something?" one of the girls asked.

"I always hear something and you always say it's nothing," said a second girl.

"No," said the third girl.

Zoe checked her shoes, sniffed, and sighed. Pee. Dog pee, to be more precise. How long had that poor dachshund been here? And why hadn't anyone paid attention to his needs?

"Hey, you ladies didn't answer me," the man said. "How's about I just skedaddle, and you figure this out and call me?"

Skedaddle? Only Morton the Magnificent would use a word like "skedaddle." Only Morton wasn't Magnificent at all. He wasn't even Adequate. Morton had long ago sold out and was performing his magic—real magic—as tricks in front of a live audience every night at one of the marginal casinos just off the strip.

Zoe hated that, and she figured once the Fates found out, they'd punish him for violating a major rule: Mortals Should Never See The Magic . . . or if they do, They Shouldn't Think It's Real.

Since most mortals figured the shows in Vegas were faked somehow, Morton thought he was getting by on a technicality, which he probably was. But that didn't stop his behavior from being, at the very least, unethical.

Zoe peered around the door frame as if she were on the job. Inside a big room with floor-to-ceiling windows were couches, chairs, and a large table. On top of the table sat three teenage girls. The one farthest from Zoe was skinny and blond, in that shapeless way that teenagers who didn't eat enough had. She wore what looked like a decorated bra and a pair of low-rider jeans. A pair of slides hung off her toes, revealing very dirty feet.

Next to her sat a redhead with hair so short it looked like a crewcut. There was no mistaking her femininity, though. Her green eyelet blouse and Capri pants accented her lush figure. She would have looked exotic if she were older, but at her age, which Zoe guessed to be about fifteen, she simply managed to look rebellious.

The third girl had cornrows decorated with beads made out of real ivory. Even though she was wearing a sleeveless dress, cut slim for someone without hips, she sat with her legs crossed.

Morton the Magician looked as scummy as always. He wore a gold lamé sports jacket worthy of Elvis, and tight brown polyester pants. His shoes were shiny tux pumps that he had forgotten to polish. His hair was thinning on the top, and he had circle combed it—apparently magic didn't work with bald spots.

Zoe had to look around to find the dachshund. He sat under the table, his tail wrapped around his plump body, his head down as if he were embarrassed to be in such company.

Or maybe he was hungry. Or sick from all those sausages. She felt a pang of guilt.

"How come every time someone comes here, they have a new problem?" the blond girl asked.

"Just lucky," said the redhead, and blew a bright pink bubble. It grew until it was the size of her face. The girl with cornrows looked like she was about to pop the bubble when the redhead sucked it back into her mouth.

Zoe had no idea what she was looking at. So she stepped into the room.

"Excuse me," she said. "I'm looking for the Fates."

"There she is." Morton the Magnificent pointed at her. His finger was stubby and the nail was black and yellow, not with polish, either. "She's the one who magicked me here. That has to be against the rules."

The cornrow girl rolled her eyes. "I'm not looking up another rule."

"We can't find the ones we're supposed to find already." The blonde really was a whiner.

"Can't you all just leave and solve stuff on your own?" asked the redhead.

"I'd be happy to," Zoe said, "if you point me in the direction of the Fates."

"Gawd!" the cornrow girl said.

"How come nobody thinks *we're* the Fates?" the blonde asked.

"Because we're too young," said the redhead. "Even *I'm* beginning to think we're too young."

"That's because you don't want to do any of the work," the cornrow girl snapped.

"Excuse me," Zoe said again. "Um, I know the Fates and believe me, you're not them."

"We are them," said the blonde with more anger than self-pity. "We're just not the them that you were expecting."

Morton was shaking his head. The dachshund lay down, put his head on his paws, and whined. Or moaned.

"Has anyone given Bartholomew water?" Zoe asked.

"What do you care?" Morton asked.

"He's been outside for three days, he ate too many sausages, and I sent him here at his request. I notice that no one let him out when he needed to go—" Zoe wrinkled her nose. The pee smell on her shoes had trailed into the room with her. "—and frankly, he doesn't look all that well."

The dachshund raised his eyebrows at her. His brown eyes were very intelligent, and if she wanted, she could give him the power to speak English. She had done that earlier, and had learned about all of his grievances. Then she had sent him here. As far as she could tell, her spell had worn off, but the Fates—wherever they were—would have known to spell him for language.

Or maybe they could just understand him without it.

"See, now, look." Morton stood up and hiked his pants up by the belt. The pants rose to the middle of his bulky stomach, and were tight enough to reveal more of Morton than anyone should actually be able to see. "She talks a good game, but when push comes to shove, she don't deliver. I mean, I paid her good money to find the dog and what does she do? Sends me away from my work to come here to meet you kids, and pretends like the dog has a complaint. Has he said anything? I mean, really."

"Has anyone given him a chance?" Zoe asked.

The girls were watching Zoe with frowns on their faces.

"What kind of chance?" the redhead asked.

"To tell you what happened," Zoe said.

"Well, we asked him, but all he did was bark," the corn-row girl said.

"Oh, for heaven's sake," Zoe said, hating that expression be-cause it showed she had been among the mortals too long. She wished she could take it back. "Did one of you give him the power of speech? Or did you forget that little magic lesson?"

"What power of speech?" the blonde asked.

Zoe shook her head. "Morton?"

He shrugged. "It was your idea to send us here. I wasn't going to falicitate it."

"Facilitate," Zoe said, "and I didn't send you here, at least not on purpose. I sent you to the Fates."

"We are the Fates," the girls said in unison.

"You are not," Zoe said. "Unless someone cast a really nasty spell on Clotho, Lachesis, and Atropos."

"I told you," said the redhead. "We're not the them you were expecting."

"Actually, you didn't tell me," Zoe said. "She did."

And even as she nodded to the blonde, Zoe felt the rest of her argument die in her throat. These girls were speaking in a certain order. Just like the other Fates. And they spoke in unison. Just like the other Fates.

And they were in the right place, only it was a mess. In a way that the other Fates would never, ever have allowed.

"We're Brittany, Tiffany, and Crystal," said the cornrow girl, "and we're the new Fates."

"Kinda," the blonde added.

Zoe blinked and looked at Morton. He shrugged.

"Listen, I already been through this. What I get is that these little chickies are the Interim Fates because their Daddy don't want the old Fates to be interfering with his lifestyle no more. If these kids can do the job, they get it for good. But they gotta apply, just like everybody else."

The women in Zoe's office had said they were the Fates. They had said they were laid off from their jobs because Zeus was making a power play, and they would have to reapply for those jobs, after they learned a few new skills.

Zoe felt cold.

"Is Zeus your daddy?" Zoe asked the girls.

"Well, *duh*!" they said in unison.

Morton grinned. "They *are* kinda cute."

"Cute my butt," Zoe said, putting her hands on her hips. "How old are you girls?"

"A hundred, maybe," said the redhead, obviously lying.

"Which one are you?" Zoe asked.

"She's Crystal," the cornrowed girl said, and Zoe felt that dizziness she always got with the original Fates. The rotating conversation was maddening.

"And you are?" Zoe asked.

"She's Tiffany," said the blonde.

"And the pretty one who just talked to you is Brittany," said Morton, earning a glare from the other two.

"Figures," Zoe said.

She took a step closer to the table, and realized as she did so that her left foot was wet. The pee must have soaked through her shoe. She suppressed a sigh.

"You girls aren't a hundred," she said. "You haven't gone

through puberty yet, let alone menopause. How many rules did your dad break here?"

"Daddy never breaks rules," Crystal said.

"He's grandfathered in," said Tiffany.

"Actually, he made most of the rules so he knows what he can and can't do," Brittany said.

"In other words, he broke the cardinal rule," Zoe said. "He gave you girls magic before your hormones settled down."

Morton shot Zoe a frightened look. She tried to ignore him. Zeus had already caused enough trouble for mages. It was his arguments that allowed men to gain their magic at twenty-one and women to wait until after menopause. And he was the one who exempted all the Powers That Be from all of the rules, although Zoe had never heard that the children of the Powers That Be were exempt.

"Hormones aren't an issue for us," said Crystal.

"Like we ever get out of here to hormone over anyone anyway," said Tiffany.

"Then who is Dudley?" Zoe asked.

Crystal's face turned as red as her hair.

"He's such a dweeb," said Brittany.

"Is not," said Crystal.

"Is too," said Tiffany.

"Look," said Morton, "I already lived through this argument once which, I gotta tell you, was one time too many. Can we move on to important things like you sending me back to the Sands?"

"The Sands was torn down," Zoe said.

"That's the name of the new nightclub I'm headlining, baby," Morton said with a wink.

"Have you told these girls—Fates—Interim Fates—what you're doing?" Zoe asked. As if the girls would care.

"He already told us enough stuff," said Brittany.

"Yeah, we got at least two new rules to look up," said Crystal.

"And they never do the looking up. I do." Tiffany pulled on a single cornrow and chewed the end. "I'm beginning to think they can't read."

"We can read," Brittany said.

"We just don't like to," said Crystal.

"Hey!" Morton said. "Can we stop the bickering and get back to sending me home?"

Zoe glared at him. Then she glared at the girls. How selfish *were* these people? "Would one of you get the dog some water?" she asked.

"He'll just pee again," Tiffany said.

"Yeah, that's just plain gross," said Brittany.

"Well," said Zoe, trying to keep her temper in check. It wouldn't do to get mad at these girls if they had Zeus's power behind them. "You could have let him outside or cleaned up after him."

"Ew," said Crystal. "We don't clean."

"That's obvious," said Zoe and Morton in unison. They looked at each other. Morton looked as appalled as Zoe felt.

"Maybe it's time you start," Zoe said.

"Um, like, no," said Brittany.

"A simple snap of the fingers would do," Zoe said.

"We don't waste our magic that way," said Crystal.

"Besides, the non-magical need some kind of purpose," said Tiffany.

"You have non-magical people clean up after you?" Zoe asked, unable to hide her shock. It was against the rules to enslave or employ the non-magical in roles that made them clean up after the magical.

All three girls blushed.

"Not here," said Brittany. "At home."

"In your father's house," Zoe said.

Crystal nodded. "It's much cleaner there."

"Figures," Zoe said.

"We keep waiting for someone to show up here, but no one has," Tiffany said.

"But you're the acting Fates," Zoe said.

"Interim," Brittany said.

"Couldn't you just get someone to clean up?" Zoe asked.

"What a great idea!" Crystal looked at the other two girls. "Isn't that a great idea?"

"Maybe the next person who comes in wanting rules should just clean the place," Tiffany said.

"Or look up the rule." Brittany clapped her hands together.

"Excuse me," Zoe said. "But the dog?"

"Oh, ick," Crystal said.

"Like anyone cares about the damn dog," Tiffany said. The dachshund whined.

"What did you want us to do about him?" Brittany asked.

Zoe snapped her fingers and a water bowl appeared in front of the dachshund. His tail thumped once in appreciation, then he stood and drank.

"If he pees, you're cleaning up this place," Crystal said.

"I don't think so," Zoe said.

"We'll call our dad," Tiffany said.

That was a real threat, but Zoe didn't let the girls see that it intimidated her.

"I think your dad is probably real tired of you girls asking him for help." Zoe was guessing, but from the way the girls flinched, she knew her guess was right. "So you all should leave me alone, and concentrate on what you're supposed to do."

"What're we supposed to do again?" Brittany asked.

"You're supposed to make all sorts of rules and decisions

and legal judgements," Zoe said. "In this case, you're making a decision about a dissatisfied familiar."

And as she said that, she finally understood why she hadn't been able to find a new familiar. Her lovely Seraphina, a cat, had died three weeks ago. Zoe had a substitute familiar, on loan from a friend, but she hadn't found her regular familiar yet.

"You do know that you're all in charge of familiars, don't you?" Zoe asked.

"No." Crystal pulled the gum out of her mouth in a long, pink string which she proceeded to wrap around her little finger.

"Does that mean all cats and dogs or is it other stuff, too?" Tiffany asked.

"I thought only people with no talent had familiars," Brittany said.

"Oh, jeez." Morton put his hands in his thinning hair. "I'm getting queasy."

So was Zoe. And her foot was beginning to stick to her shoe. The dachshund kept drinking, as if he had been about to die of dehydration.

"Everyone has a familiar," Zoe said. "Or should. Our magic doesn't work right if we don't have one."

"We don't have one," Crystal said.

"We don't need one," Tiffany said.

"Yeah," Morton said, "like I don't need a new head of hair."

"Shut up, Vegas Boy," Brittany said, pointing her finger at him. "We have the power to make you completely hairless."

"Give me a *real* threat, baby," Morton said.

The girls raised their hands, and Zoe stepped between them and Morton, although she wasn't sure why.

"The problem here," Zoe said, "isn't Morton's baldness or the fact that you girls lack familiars."

Although that probably was a major part of the problem. Zoe silently cursed Zeus, and wished she had never come here.

"The problem is," Zoe continued, "that Bartholomew here—"

"There ain't no Bartholomew here," Crystal said.

"It's the dumb dog," Tiffany whispered.

"Oh," Brittany said.

"—Bartholomew and Morton aren't really a good match," Zoe said, pretending she hadn't heard the interchange. "Bartholomew's not happy and he's acting out, as you can tell from the um—urine—in the other room. He ran away how many times in the past month, Morton?"

Morton bowed his head. "Five."

"And that's the sign of an unhappy dog," Zoe said, "which makes for bad magic."

"My magic is fine," Morton said.

"Maybe at the moment," Zoe said. "But I think you should give Morton a familiar that he deserves, and let Bartholomew come with me. I'll find him a new home. How's that for solving your problem?"

The girls brightened.

"You'll take the smelly dog?" Crystal asked, shoving her gum back in her mouth.

Bartholomew whined and lay down again. Zoe could almost feel his thoughts. He didn't think he was smelly.

Although she had had the same thought about him not two hours ago.

"I'll take the dog," Zoe said.

"And what should we do with this guy here?" Tiffany asked.

Take his magic away, assign him to a hundred years of making change for folks sitting at slot machines, and make sure he never, ever gets a full head of hair, Zoe thought but didn't say. Instead, she said, "That's your decision."

"You said a familiar he deserves, though," Brittany said. All three girls were leaning forward as if Zoe had the answers to a particularly hard test on the day before the test was scheduled.

"Yeah," Crystal said. "What'd you mean by that?"

Caught. Zoe gave Morton a sideways look.

He raised his hands. "Hey," he said, "I paid you. I sent you out looking for the dog, and you brought him back."

"Three times," Zoe said. "Four was too many. I had to ask him why he wanted to leave."

"He just don't like Vegas," Morton said. "He'll get over it."

"He doesn't like the way you treat mortals," Zoe said. "And he thinks you're misusing your magic, which he's afraid he'll have to pay for."

The dog whined again, almost as if he were telling her to shut up.

"Although I doubt in this climate that that's an issue," Zoe added.

"What does *that* mean?" Tiffany asked.

"You're a bright girl," Zoe said. "You figure it out."

"Do you know how many cases we're behind?" Brittany asked.

"How many rules there are to learn?" Crystal said.

"How many people want answers now, now, now?" Tiffany asked.

"It'd be better if you just tell us what to do with the familiars," Brittany said.

"Well—" Morton started, but Zoe interrupted him.

"You should give Morton a new familiar. Let me take Bartholomew, and then you should start researching familiar laws, because you are way behind on your duties in that area," Zoe said.

"How do you know?" Crystal asked.

"Because I lost my familiar a month ago," Zoe said, feeling a pang, "and I haven't been able to find one. Now I know why."

"Why?" Tiffany asked.

"Because, you little brainless moron," Morton snapped, "you're supposed to provide new familiars to people who lose theirs."

The room was quiet. Zoe had to work to keep a smile off her face. All three girls stared at Morton, and for the first time, they looked menacing. Bartholomew slunk as far under the table as he could go.

"What can be a familiar?" Brittany asked Zoe.

"Anything so long as it's alive," Zoe said. "A snake, a bumblebee, a rat."

"A dog," Morton said.

"That dog don't like you," Crystal said.

"So it can't be a dog," Tiffany said.

Zoe wasn't sure she wanted to see how this worked out. "Would you mind if I took Bartholomew?"

"For you?" Brittany asked.

"Um, no," Zoe said, not sure she could stand the dog either. "I'm sure I'll find someone."

"Okay," Crystal said.

"You know," Tiffany said, still looking at Morton, "maybe a gerbil'd be nice."

"Gerbils don't have a lot of power," Morton said.

"So?" Brittany asked.

Zoe crouched, opened her arms, and beckoned Bartholomew toward her.

"I'd like to keep my dog," said Morton.

"Well, you big brainless moron," Crystal said, "that ain't gonna happen."

You go, girl, Zoe thought.

Bartholomew crawled toward her on his stomach. When he reached her, he whined again. He really was smelly. Sausages and urine and a bit of garbage, plus doggy sweat. Poor thing. He just needed someone to love him.

"Maybe a spider," said Tiffany.

"Yeah," said Brittany, "one of those little ugly ones."

"I'm an arachnophobe," Morton said. "Can we think of something else?"

Zoe silently recited a spell to take her and Bartholomew back to the office.

"An arachnophobe?" Crystal asked. "What's that?"

"He's afraid of spiders," Tiffany said.

All three girls laughed. It was a terrifying sound.

The dog shivered, and Zoe finished the spell. They both disappeared.

Only to materialize in her office—in the middle of a mountain of money.

Ten

Travers hadn't meant to do it, and he still wasn't sure how he had. Atropos had asked him to think of a five-dollar bill, and the next thing he knew, he was holding one. He assumed the Fates had shoved one in his hand, but he hadn't seen them do it.

Then Clotho asked him to think of a thousand five-dollar bills, and the desk got covered with them. Then the Fates wanted him to think of a million five-dollar bills, and a mountain of money appeared on the floor.

Kyle squealed and dove in it as if it were a pile of leaves. The Fates were watching Travers with glittering eyes, and then Zoe reappeared right in the middle of the money mountain.

Holding an obese dachshund that smelled of grease, urine, and overripe bananas.

She looked frazzled and angry—Travers wasn't sure how he knew she was angry, but he sensed it—and then she blinked. Her expression changed, as if she had done so on purpose, and then she surveyed the room.

Including the mountain of money that hid her legs all the way to the middle of her thighs.

"Is this my fee?" she asked. "If so, the answer's yes."

Travers flushed. Kyle rolled out of the money pile and sat on the floor, his arms wrapped around his legs. He was staring at the dog with a look of longing that Travers immediately wanted to squelch.

The Fates glanced at each other as if considering Zoe's question.

"No," Travers said. "This is all fake money."

"It doesn't look fake." Zoe shifted the dog slightly so that she could pick up one of the five-dollar bills. She held it up to her face, then crumpled it. "Feels right. Looks right. Smells right, if Bartholomew here hasn't ruined my sense of smell. It's real money. Where did it come from?"

She looked at Kyle first, as if he could do this. Kyle gave his dad a frightened glance. Perhaps he was wondering if he could.

Then she looked at the Fates. "I thought your powers were lost."

"We gave them up," Clotho said.

"Voluntarily," Lachesis added.

"Even though it was a mistake," Atropos said.

"Which, of course," Clotho said.

"We realized in hindsight," Lachesis finished.

Zoe sighed, and finally turned to him. Her gaze met his. Her eyes caught him again—that brown mixed with the gold flecks. At the outside corner of her eyes, her lashes curled, giving her a naturally festive look.

His flush deepened. "I don't get it," he said, even though he did. He felt a whoosh, like a breath leaving him, each time he imagined more money. He wondered what it would be like to imagine a billion fives—if that whoosh would be even worse—and then he felt it, just the same as before.

For a half second, he closed his eyes, not wanting to see.

"That's impressive," Zoe said. "But I was happy with the first pile."

Travers opened his eyes. The room was filled with cash. Everywhere. Even the Fates were covered with money, as if someone had thrown a ticker tape parade with five-dollar bills.

"Dad?" Kyle whispered.

"Okay," Travers said, happy that his voice was level. "I'm freaking out. Can we stop this?"

"You're the only one doing anything," Atropos said.

"Our magic is long gone," Clotho said.

"And young Kyle here hasn't come into his," Lachesis said.

"Except for his psychic abilities." Zoe's timing put her in the middle of the Fates' usual one-two-three routine. Atropos looked at her in amazement.

Zoe shrugged. "What were you doing, pretending to be a giant slot payout?"

Travers shook his head. He felt slightly dizzy. The room had the smell of cash, that sharpish Magic Marker scent, mixed with the odor of old paper, and a faint hint of sweat.

"How do I make it go away?" he asked.

"Zoe would like it as a fee," Atropos said.

Travers shook his head. He had no idea where the money came from.

"If I wanted magically generated cash, I could do it myself. Besides, I haven't agreed to take your case yet." Zoe pushed some of the money aside, like a swimmer trying to brush aside water in a pool. "Can you move your newfound wealth to your SUV or maybe your hotel room? I need to set the dog down and get to my desk."

Travers started, and the very first thing that came to mind came out of his mouth. "How did you know I have an SUV?"

"Oh, please," Zoe said. "Look at yourself. I didn't even have to peek through the window to double-check the assumption."

Travers opened his hands in confusion.

"You have some kind of professional job, corporate maybe, or working near corporations. Very stuffy. Very Keeping-up-with-the-Joneses—whom I've met, by the way, the original ones? And they're really not worth keeping up with at all. When was the last time you had fun?"

Travers frowned. His sister's wedding had been fun. Kinda. He hadn't danced, even though Kyle urged him to, and he hadn't had more to drink than soda, but he had a good time.

"I bet you were always like this. Very buttoned up. Even when you were in your jock phase. What were you, anyway? Baseball? Basketball—maybe second string college?"

"No," Travers said, beginning to feel angry. Who was she to judge him? "I never went to college."

Zoe raised her eyebrows. Kyle opened his mouth, then closed it again.

"I went to night school for a few years before I got enough credits to get into a real school. And that took a lot of juggling for a single father." His words had bite to them, but he wasn't going to say what he was thinking.

He hadn't had fun—not the kind she was talking about—because he'd had responsibilities from a young age. She looked like a woman who had never had responsibilities.

At that moment, the dog whined. Zoe absently petted him, her long fingers toying with his ears. Travers had never envied a dog before.

"Sorry," she said, but the word was brusque and didn't sound sorry at all. "Now, will you get back to my original question and clear out the office?"

Travers looked at the Fates with great concern. "Do I just say—?"

"Wait!" Clotho said, holding up her hand.

"Don't think!" Lachesis said, holding up her hand as well.

"You have to be very careful with this one," Atropos said, amazingly not imitating the posture of the other two women. "It's a delicate spell."

"What is?" Zoe asked.

"He's a baby wizard," Clotho said.

"He's at least thirty," Zoe said. "He's been doing it for a while, protestations to the contrary."

"No," Travers said, trying hard to understand what "don't think" meant and how anyone could pull that off. "I haven't been doing anything."

"Except winning the lottery," Kyle muttered, "and having the best record with the IRS of any CPA in California history. You know what people say about my dad?"

"Kyle!" Travers breathed.

Zoe got that curious half-smile that made her seem even more attractive. "What do they say about your dad?"

"That if you want to do well with money, he's the go-to guy." Kyle spoke with obvious pride.

Travers felt his cheeks heat even more. He had always hated that recommendation. It made him sound sleazy, even though he wasn't. Could he be blamed for having a talent for picking successful clients? Not that they were all successful when they came to him, but within a year, he got their numbers to improve—if, of course, the client listened to him. What was wrong with that?

"Really?" Zoe asked and looked at the Fates, as if they knew something he didn't.

(Well, of course they knew something he didn't. They seemed to know a lot that he didn't, but those things weren't really things he wanted to know. At least, he thought he didn't want to know them.)

Then Travers shook his head, trying to keep the parenthetical thoughts to a minimum. He needed to pay attention, not get sidetracked by the nitpickiness of his own mind.

"This man has a limited magic, dealing only with numbers?" Zoe was asking. "Is that possible?"

"Of course it's possible," Lachesis said. "You're seeing it in front of you."

"And, to be honest," Atropos added, "he's lucky his magic is limited."

Clotho nodded, her fingers on the bridge of her nose as if she were getting a headache. "We had one case, just a few years ago—"

"Or maybe a few decades," Lachesis said.

"We really do have trouble with time," Atropos said, as if no one else had noticed.

"Anyway," Clotho said, "there was a young woman—"

"Well, she wasn't *that* young," Lachesis said.

"She was a thousand if she was a day," Atropos said.

"A thousand!" Kyle said, only because he managed to get the words out before Travers. Travers felt the same shock that he heard in his son's tones. "Magic people live to be a thousand?"

"Several thousand," Clotho said.

Travers felt as if he had been hit in the stomach. He had magic and he would live to be several thousand years old? He let out a small breath. If this was *Candid Camera,* he wanted Alan Funt or Alan Funt, Jr., or whoever was in charge of the tricks these days to appear mighty soon, because Travers wasn't sure he could take much more.

"Is this rambling tale really necessary?" Zoe asked, joggling the dog just a little. "I really want to sit down."

"Anyway," Lachesis said, putting emphasis on the word, probably to discourage more interruptions, "this girl—"

"Woman," Atropos corrected. "Remember your political correctness lessons."

"Oh, geez," Zoe said and rolled her eyes.

"This *woman*," Clotho said, as she had been the one to make the mistake, "her name was Emma Lost, and she had powerful magic."

"Frighteningly powerful magic," Lachesis said.

"And no training at all," Atropos said, "because everyone believed she was only thirty when she'd been—"

"Get to the point," Zoe said, only because she, too, was quicker than Travers.

"Well," Clotho said, managing to sound offended, "Emma's magic was so powerful and out of control that she was turning cats into lions—"

"In nice suburban neighborhoods where apparently the changes didn't go over well," Lachesis added.

"—raining furniture on unsuspecting secretaries," Atropos said.

"Nearly killing one," Clotho added.

"—and exasperating college professors," Lachesis said.

"Which, by far, caused the most trouble," Atropos said.

"And this is relevant how?" Travers asked. Some fives fell from the ceiling, but he couldn't tell if they remained from his last *whoosh* or if they were from some new random thought he hadn't acknowledged.

"Her magic was out of control," Clotho said.

"And it was very, very powerful," Lachesis said.

"Making her quite dangerous," Atropos said.

"Fortunately," Clotho said, "you don't have to worry about that."

"What?" Travers asked, wishing these women didn't confuse him so. "I don't have to worry about what? The dangerous part or the out-of-control magic part?"

"The dangerous part, Dad," Kyle said. He, apparently, was having no trouble following the Fates' twisted syntax. "You don't have enough power. They were saying you were lucky that you didn't."

"Oh," Travers said, and sank into a nearby chair. Money crunched beneath his weight. "Nice to know there's no worries."

"We didn't say there were no worries," Lachesis said.

"After all, now that you've discovered the talent, it will manifest even more," Atropos said.

Travers frowned. "So what do I do?"

"You get trained immediately, of course," Clotho said.

"After you get rid of this money in my office." Zoe pushed at it again. "Or I will."

"Perhaps you should, dear," Lachesis said. "I'm afraid if he does it, all the money in the vicinity will vanish."

"Good point." Zoe leaned over the pile of money and shoved the dog into Travers's arms.

The dog reeked. It had some white, flaky garbage on its back, and part of a banana peel between one of its toes. A Snickers wrapper stuck to the pad of one foot, and its tail was slightly wet—giving off that pee odor Travers had noticed first.

"Thanks," he muttered. The dog licked his face, adding the spicy scent of Italian sausage to the other odors.

But Zoe didn't notice. She snapped her fingers, and the money piles all disappeared, down to the last five-dollar bill.

Travers stood up and looked at the chair. No money on the seat cushion. No money on his backside, either, so far as he could tell.

"Wow," Kyle breathed. "How did you do that?"

"You'll learn it eventually," Zoe said. "Explaining it now will simply confuse you."

"How about explaining it to me?" Travers asked.

Zoe gave him a sideways look. She studied him for a

moment, making his cheeks grow even warmer. He hated blushing like a child. He felt naked before her, and not in a good way. At least, not in the way he would have liked.

Then he felt his neck and chest flush as well. The heat was overwhelming.

"You can't read my thoughts, can you?" he asked, hoping that none of them could. What if the Fates could? Did they know how he had felt about them on the entire trip? How embarrassing.

Zoe grinned. "Why? Was that blush for me?"

The blush went even deeper. His entire body felt like one giant heat rash.

"No," he lied.

"They can't read you, Dad." Kyle was still sitting on the floor, only now, instead of sifting through money, he was leaning against the desk. "Only I can do that, and it's because you're broadcasting. And really, I don't need to have thoughts like that in my head. Sandra Bullock was bad enough, but—"

"Kyle," Travers cautioned.

Zoe laughed. "I know how men think, Mr. Kineally. That was an education I got a long, long time ago."

"I wasn't, really," he lied. "I was just—"

"Worrying about your magic, right?" Zoe walked behind her desk without grabbing the dog. The poor thing just lay in Travers's arms as if it were the most tired dog in the universe.

"Right," Travers lied. Or maybe that wasn't a lie. He was worried about this so-called magic of his—

"Stop it, Dad," Kyle said. "It's not 'so-called.' It exists. Or do we have to do more experiments to prove it to you?"

"No," Travers said a bit too quickly. "No more experiments."

"Good," Zoe said, "because I now have several problems to deal with."

She leaned her chair back and put her high heels on her desk.

"Like the dog?" Travers asked. "He needs a bath."

"No kidding," Zoe said.

The dog whined softly.

"Maybe a magical bath?" Travers asked.

The Fates frowned.

"Technically," Zoe said, "and you'll learn this as you learn the rules, we're not supposed to use magic for simple tasks unless the situation demands it."

"My nose demands it," Travers said.

The dog whined again.

"You kinda get used to it." Zoe put her hands behind her head. "As I was saying, I have several problems now. I have the dog, whose name is Bartholomew, by the way, even though he wants it changed."

The dog yipped and his tail thumped. Travers made the mistake of looking at the dog's face, and he saw eagerness and agreement, and way too much intelligence for a lesser mammal.

Travers made himself look away.

"Then," Zoe said, "I have the rather horrible discovery that children are running the legal and judicial branch of our government—"

"Oh, you met them," Atropos said.

"I met them," Zoe said, "and they are absolutely terrifying. How could you leave them alone like that? They have no idea what they're doing."

"It's not our fault," Clotho said. "We were forced out. Term limits, remember?"

The dog squirmed again. Travers wondered if the pee smell was growing stronger. "You need to get down, little guy?"

To Travers's great consternation, the dog nodded.

Travers set him down a bit too quickly.

"Oh, yes, term limits," Zoe said. "You started the conversation that way several days ago."

"Was it days?" Atropos asked. "I would have thought it's only been hours—"

"But that does explain why we're so hungry," Clotho said.

"She's exaggerating," Travers snapped.

"About what?" Lachesis asked.

"About the time," Kyle said. "It only feels like days."

Zoe grinned at him. Travers's breath still left his body when she grinned, even when she grinned at someone else.

"Thank you," Zoe said. "And now, after seeing them, and realizing that this conflict in government could become permanent, I have the unfortunate feeling I need to ask you ladies something."

"What?" the Fates asked in unison.

"Before you do," Travers said, "do you mind if Kyle and I leave? After all, we've done our part—"

"No, you have not," Atropos said. "You have to stay."

"Your part is just beginning," Clotho said.

Travers's heart was pounding.

"Besides," Atropos said, "you need a new mentor."

"Your old one obviously wasn't up to snuff," Clotho said.

"So we're assigning you one," Lachesis said.

Travers held his breath. He couldn't help it. Bartholomew waddled away from him, heading toward the bathroom. Kyle followed, as if the conflict in front of him didn't interest him.

But Travers felt like everything was about to change.

"The only person who can teach you now is Zoe," Atropos said.

"Because, after all," Clotho said, throwing an impish look at Zoe, "you are the closest mage."

Travers looked at Zoe, who stared at him. Her mouth was slightly open, in a seductive, kissable way. How could he learn anything from her? He would never be able to concentrate. He wouldn't be able to think of anything at all when he saw how her dark hair curled ever so slightly against her high cheekbones, how her shapely legs rested so comfortably on the desktop, how long those shapely legs were, and—

"No," Zoe said.

"No?" Travers asked. He hadn't even propositioned her yet. Not that he would with his son in the room. His son and three strange women. His son, three strange women, and the smelliest dog he had ever encountered.

"No," Zoe said, but it soon became clear she wasn't talking to him. "Las Vegas is lousy with mages. Get one of them."

"Do I get a vote?" Travers asked.

"No," all four women said to him in unison.

That annoyed him, and made him stop thinking of Zoe as a beautiful woman for a moment. His concentration returned and as he turned to the Fates —who really were becoming a single unit in his mind, which was also unnerving him—he asked, "I thought you guys weren't in charge anymore."

"We will be," Lachesis said.

"If Zoe helps us," Atropos said.

"It's only a matter of time," Clotho said.

"But for now," Travers said, "you have no power at all."

"Oh," Zoe said. "I see where you're going with this."

He nodded at her and she sat up, swinging those luscious legs off the desk.

"You can't make me his mentor," Zoe said, "because you have no authority for that."

"But he needs one," Lachesis said.

"And do you really want those children to assign him one?" Atropos asked.

Zoe gritted her teeth. "You're going to guilt me into this, aren't you?"

"Well, no," Clotho said. "You don't have to do it if you don't want to."

"But," Lachesis said, and she was not smiling, "if we do get our power back, we will remember this and—"

"I don't want her," Travers said. He was astonished at himself. He was doing his share of lying this day. Maybe enough to last him an entire decade.

He did want her. He just didn't want her as a teacher. Well, not a teacher of magic. She could teach him other things.

Which she'd probably slap him for even thinking about in her presence.

Good thing she couldn't hear those thoughts.

"I can, Dad!" Kyle yelled from the bathroom. "Will you knock it off?"

Travers felt his cheeks heat again. He hadn't even realized the earlier heat had faded until the new heat appeared. He had to get out of this office before he went completely insane.

"It doesn't matter what you want," Atropos said.

"You need to be trained," Clotho said.

"Zoe needs an assistant," Lachesis said.

"I do not," Zoe said, sounding very indignant. "I have worked alone my entire life."

"Of course you have, dear," Atropos said. "But our case is brand new."

"All cases are new at one point or another," Zoe said.

"No," Clotho said. "New for you."

Zoe seemed confused. Travers certainly was. All he wanted was to go home and pretend this last week hadn't happened.

But Kyle wouldn't allow that.

And besides, pretending this last week hadn't happened would mean Travers would have to forget about Zoe, which was something he wasn't willing to do.

At least on the fantasy level.

"Da-ad!"

"Sorry!" Travers yelled.

The women ignored the interchange, just like they were ignoring the sound of water running. Travers wasn't ignoring it. He just felt he was better served staying in the main office than finding out what his son was doing in the back.

"I'm going to regret asking this," Zoe said, "but in what way will the case be new for me?"

"Well, my dear," Lachesis said, "unless your life has changed dramatically while we've been in exile, you've never ventured into the places this case will take you."

"Yeah, right," Zoe said, and somehow Travers believed her. He had a hunch she had seen more mean streets than he ever knew existed. Dark corners, dark alleyways. Zoe Sinclair gave off the sense of knowing more about the shady side of humanity and inhumanity? What were these people called?

"Mages, Dad," Kyle yelled.

"What?" Atropos asked.

Travers shook his head. "Seems I'm broadcasting again."

"Yeah!" Kyle yelled. "Quit it."

"Would if I could," Travers said. But he had no idea how. Just like he had no idea how the money—

Whoosh!

—fell from the sky.

Like it was doing now. It was literally raining five-dollar bills in the tiny office.

"Cut it out," Zoe said.

"Now is not the time, Travers," Clotho said.

"I don't know what I'm doing," he said.

"No kidding," Zoe said.

"Say 'Reverse!'" Lachesis said.

"Reverse!" Travers said as Zoe said, "No, I don't think that'll . . ."

But she let her voice trail off. For a moment, the money

stopped raining. Then it slowly rose back to the ceiling, one bill at a time. The problem was the bills just floated up there, not raining, not disappearing either.

"Wow," Atropos said. "Paper currency is very real to you, isn't it?"

"Economics is the foundation to everything," Travers said. "If you look at all human motivation, you'll find economics behind each and every action."

"Bull-pucky," all three Fates said in unison.

"He has a point," Zoe said.

The Fates looked at her.

"When did you become so cynical?" Clotho asked.

"I'm not cynical," Zoe said, "and this isn't about me. It's about him."

She pointed at Travers. He felt like a ten-year-old who had been bad.

"How do I make it disappear?" he asked.

"I'll do it," she said. "Just let me finish this conversation, okay?"

"Okay." He rested his hands on his knees and tried not to think. He also tried not to look at the five-dollar bills, moving back and forth across the ceiling, like clouds building on a stormy day.

"All right," Zoe said, giving him a harsh look. Even that was attractive.

Travers tried to block those thoughts as well. He almost gave himself permission to think of pink elephants, but the problem with those would be—

Whoosh!

—a single pink elephant, the size of a small horse, appeared in the middle of the room. The elephant was stuffed, with a trunk that curled upwards like an upside-down question mark, and it was Barbie pink.

It looked vaguely like an elephant he'd won for Kyle at the fair when Kyle was five.

"Stop it!" Zoe said again.

"Sorry," Travers said.

"You promised," Zoe said.

"Sorry," Travers repeated.

"So just stop thinking," Zoe said.

"I did," Travers said.

"No," Zoe said, "you were quite obviously thinking of something else. Try white noise. Try a hum. Try concentrating on this conversation for a change."

"Yes, ma'am," Travers said as meekly as he could. He'd never created anything out of thin air before, and here he was, creating pink elephants and money and broadcasting his thoughts. The next thing you knew—

"Dad! Stop that!" Kyle yelled from the back.

Travers took a deep breath. "If you want me to concentrate on this conversation," he said, "you have to converse."

"Okay." Zoe leaned forward, eyeing the Fates. "You said that this case would take me somewhere I've never been before."

"Someplace you're afraid of," Lachesis said.

"Someplace you've avoided your entire life," Atropos said.

"Cut the dramatics," Zoe said. "If you want my help, you'll have to be clear and precise."

"Faerie," Clotho said. "You'll have to go to Faerie."

Eleven

Zoe felt cold, even though the office was stifling. The air conditioning was running so hard she could hear the hum, but the cool draft wasn't keeping up with the stress, the body heat, and the outdoor temperatures beating against the walls.

Besides, this rather small room was filled with too many people and a giant pink elephant that was grinning beneath its obscene pink trunk.

The Fates were staring at her expectantly. They thought she was going to be angry about their case—about Faerie— and she was. She was angry at the intrusions, she was angry that she had a shoe soaked in dog pee, and she was angry that she wasn't home, reading a romance novel and trying to forget the world.

But she would be soon. Because there was no way, no matter what had happened, no matter who wanted her help, that she would ever, ever, ever go into Faerie.

These Fates knew she wouldn't go. It was their fault, after all. It was because of the prophecy they had given her, the prophecy that said she might get lost in Faerie.

Forever.

"You're testing me," Zoe said.

The Fates looked startled.

"This was all one big test to see how far you could push me," Zoe said.

Travers frowned at her. He didn't know what was going on.

Well, of course he didn't know what was going on. He didn't even know that magic had existed until two hours ago. Now he was creating stuffed animals from thin air.

She had to turn slightly so she couldn't see his face. She had never known a man's face had that much power to distract. Even when she wasn't looking at it, she was thinking about it.

She clenched her fists, and made sure she was making eye contact with at least one Fate. This time, she chose Atropos.

"You decided to give me everything, right?" Zoe asked. "A cause—saving you from those children—a heroic young boy, and the best-looking man you could find. Then you send me into Faerie, thinking you can reform me, make me into someone who follows all of your rules—"

"You don't?" Lachesis asked.

It apparently didn't matter anymore. These Fates weren't in charge. They might never be in charge again, if Zeus got his way. And if Clotho, Lachesis, and Atropos did get back to positions of power, they'd have so much to deal with, they wouldn't even think of Zoe.

"Of course I don't follow your rules!" Zoe stood. "Your rules are petty and stupid and impractical in the real world. Because of your silly rules, I can't take three seconds to magically clean a dog who badly needs it. I have to throw the poor creature into a bathtub—"

At that moment, a long, drawn-out howl echoed throughout the office. The Fates cringed.

Zoe looked toward the bathroom. She had heard splashing water, and had guessed that Kyle was giving Bartholomew a bath, but she hadn't really thought about it until now.

"It's okay, really!" Kyle yelled from the back. "Just keep arguing."

Zoe almost smiled. That kid was one in a thousand.

"Our rules are sane," Atropos said.

"Really?" Zoe asked. "You brought up Henri Barou. Let me point out how dumb your treatment of him was."

Travers had turned his attention back to Zoe, who had obviously forgotten to keep him out of her line of vision. Handsome, handsome man. Henri Barou was supposed to be handsome in that traditional American way (he looked like Christopher Reeve crossed with Tom Welling, plus one chin dimple and the blue-black hair usually only found in comic strips) but Zoe had never found him particularly striking.

Unlike Travers, whose blue eyes had a clarity that—

"We did not treat him poorly," Clotho said, bringing Zoe back to herself.

For a moment, she thought Clotho was referring to Travers, and then she remembered: they were talking about Henri Barou.

"Yes, you did," Zoe said. "The poor guy has a bad mentor, and so he strikes out on his own. He goes from town to town *helping* people, and you punish him when two kids confuse what he does and write him up as a comic book superhero."

"Not just any superhero," Lachesis said.

"He became a legend," Atropos said.

"A cultural icon," Clotho said.

"Super Agent Man," Lachesis said.

"You mean Secret Agent Man?" Travers asked. "As in, what? The Green Hornet or Maxwell Smart or—"

"Superman," Zoe said between her teeth, not because Travers interrupted (truth be told, she'd rather talk to him than all the Fates in the world—and there seemed to be an abundance of those lately) but because the Fates were nearly impossible to have a conversation with. All of the Fates. All six of them. "He became the prototype for Superman."

"Oh, yes," Atropos said. "We saw those movies. With Margot Kidder. She's quite the spunky girl."

"Dumb as a post," Clotho said. "Who knew that mortals could be fooled by glasses?"

"Stop." Zoe almost clapped her hands together, and she caught herself just in time. The Fates, if they ever got their power back, might forget that she had challenged them, but they wouldn't forget if she spelled them. "Just stop talking for a moment."

All three women looked at her with identical expressions on their non-identical faces. Blue, green, and brown eyes were open the exact same width, as were their mouths. Even their chins were at the same angle.

Travers, fortunately, didn't share the expression. He was watching Zoe with a bemused smile.

"Henri Barou," Zoe said, "was helping people. You shut him down because of something out of his control. You said he was leaking information to the mortals when he was not. He was simply doing what mages have done from the beginning of time. He was becoming a myth. And you stopped that."

"Mortals no longer have myths," Lachesis said.

Zoe held up the index finger on her right hand, like a schoolmarm about to discipline unruly children. "I said, stop talking."

Lachesis bit her lower lip. The other Fates did the same.

Zoe said, "You forbade Henri from interfering in mortal affairs because of his little infraction, so he had to come to me when he saw some trouble that he didn't know how to deal with. In the meantime, you let people like Ealhswith—"

"You know Ealhswith?" Atropos asked.

"Oh, please," Zoe said. "She tried to hire me years ago to find Sleeping Beauty."

"Sleeping Beauty?" Travers asked.

"Long story," Clotho said.

"And besides," Lachesis whispered, "we're not supposed to talk."

"Oh, yeah," Atropos said, putting her hands over her mouth. "Sorry."

Zoe sighed. Even she had gotten distracted by these women. How crazy was that?

"Anyway," Zoe said, "you let people like Ealhswith and Eris and Cupid—"

"Cupid?" Travers asked. "The God of Love?"

"He was never the God of Love," the Fates said in unison.

"It's a misnomer we're not fond of," Clotho said.

"But we'll discuss it later," Lachesis whispered to Travers, as if they were co-conspirators.

"You let all of them run free," Zoe said, "wreaking havoc on the mortals, and they caused a lot more destruction than Henri Barou or any of the good mages ever could."

"May we speak now?" Atropos said.

"Oh, why not?" Zoe sat down. She was getting tired of arguing.

"All three of the people you mentioned are imprisoned now. Ealhswith for life," Clotho said.

"And Cupid for a goodly long time," Lachesis said, still speaking in a near-whisper.

"We, of course, don't know about Eris," Atropos said.

"I doubt those children punished her at all," Clotho said.

Zoe had heard that Eris got a long and particularly ugly sentence for the things she had done in Oregon last summer, but Zoe wasn't about to admit that. She didn't want to think of the Interim Fates of doing anything approaching a good job.

"We punish violations when we can," Lachesis said, "but it's hard to monitor everyone, which was what we were supposed to do."

"We realize now that it was more of Zeus' undermining. He gave us too much work, and not enough time to do it. He wants us to go away, you know," Atropos said.

"You mentioned that." Travers spoke up. He didn't look at Zoe. In fact, he seemed to be deliberately avoiding eye contact. "Why would a god like Zeus try to hurt the three of you?"

"Good question, Dad!" Kyle yelled from the next room. Then there was a splash, another yip, and a *dang it!* followed by the sound of skin against porcelain, and more splashes.

"Do you need help?" Travers asked.

"Nope!" Kyle's voice sounded strangled. "I got it just fine."

"Zeus is not a god," the Fates said, with as much vehemence as they had used about Cupid.

"I was raised that he was—a mythological god, but a god nonetheless," Travers said.

"See how they corrupt?" Clotho said to Zoe. "See why we don't like myths?"

"If he's not a god, what is he?" Travers asked.

"A Power That Is," Lachesis said. "One of the ruling body of the magical, so old that he has a lot more magic than he should."

"And too many privileges with which to indulge that magic," Atropos said.

"The others in Mount Olympus don't take this kind of advantage," Clotho said.

"Strictly speaking," Lachesis said, "some of them do."

"Ladies," Zoe said. "I'm tired of the digressions. I've made my point, and you've probably already forgotten it. Heck, I've even forgotten it, and I was the one making it. So let's just call it a day. You can go back to wherever it was that Mr. Kineally found you and I can continue in my nice, quiet little life in my not-so-nice, not-so-quiet hometown. Okay?"

"No," the Fates said.

For a group that no longer had magic, they were doing an excellent job of speaking in unison. Were they linked to each other's thoughts? Zoe wasn't sure she wanted to know.

"Well, I say so, and it's my office, so you're going to leave." Zoe stood again and nodded toward Travers. "It looks like you'll need to find someone else to take these ladies off your hands."

"Nope." He stood, too. "I'm leaving them here. C'mon, Kyle."

"Just a minute, Dad."

"Now, Kyle."

"Okay."

There was a squishing sound, followed by the *swoosh* of a drain. Kyle Kineally came back into the office, looking like he'd been swimming with his clothes on. He carried Bartholomew under one arm. The dog didn't even look wet. But he didn't smell as bad, either. His ears had perked up and his tail was wagging.

Zoe had never seen him look so happy.

"Can we keep the dog, Dad?" Kyle asked.

Travers looked at his son, and his shoulders sagged. "What would we do with a dog, Kyle?"

"He likes us," Kyle said. "He told me."

"You talk to animals now, too?" Travers asked.

Kyle ducked his head so he couldn't make eye contact with his father. Obviously, he still wasn't comfortable talking about his powers with Travers.

"Only *some* animals," Kyle said.

Bartholomew's tail kept wagging. Little drops of water were spraying all over the office.

Zoe could only hope that the water was from the sink.

Travers had his hands on his hips. He sighed heavily.

"So, Dad," Kyle said, raising his head, "can we keep him?"

"Kyle—"

"He really likes you, and he says you need help, and he's willing to help in any way a familiar can." Kyle finally took a breath. Travers looked like he was about to say something, when Kyle continued. "But you have to give him a new name. He wants to be called Fang."

Everyone in the room looked at the obese dachshund in Kyle's arms. The dog squirmed happily, resembling nothing more than a happy sausage with a tail and a head.

"Fang?" Travers somehow managed to speak with a straight face. "He wants to be called Fang?"

"Well, he would have insisted on Bruiser, but people might have thought that was a joke." Kyle spoke with complete seriousness. "So he's settling for Fang."

"You want me to own a dachshund named Fang." Travers still had a straight face, but his tone had become a little deeper, as if he were trying to hold in his emotions.

"You can't really own him, Dad," Kyle said. "He's a familiar. But he'd be a good one, provided you don't rip people off."

"Rip people off doing what?" Travers asked.

"Accounting, I guess," Kyle said. "His previous owner— familiar guy—whatever—"

"Mage," Atropos whispered.

"Yeah, him," Kyle said. "I guess he ripped people off, and Bartho—I mean, Fang—doesn't want to do it anymore."

"Good for him," Travers said. "But I don't need a familiar."

"Yes, you do!" Kyle spoke in unison with the Fates this time. Both Travers and Zoe jumped. Then they looked at each other, and Zoe could tell that Travers liked Kyle speaking with the Fates even less than she did.

"I don't want a pet," Travers said.

"He wouldn't be a pet, Dad," Kyle said. "I keep telling you that. He's a familiar."

"Tell you what." Zoe was ready to have this day over with. "You take the Fates, I'll take the dog. I'm in between familiars, too."

The dachshund's tail sagged and his round little body wilted. Even his head went down.

You didn't have to be psychic to know that Bartholomew, a.k.a. Fang, didn't want to go home with Zoe.

"No deal," Travers said.

"Besides," Clotho said, "he needs a familiar."

"As well as a mentor," Lachesis said rather pointedly.

"His magic, now that he has acknowledged it, will really go awry," Atropos said.

Zoe looked from them to the boy and back to Travers. "I'm supposed to feel guilty about this?" she asked, not because they wanted her to, but because she already did.

Feel guilty, that is. She felt like she wasn't doing her part, whatever her part was supposed to be.

"No," the Fates said.

"Yes," Kyle said.

The dog added a little yip.

"You must help us," Clotho said. "You're the only person we can turn to."

That turned Zoe's guilt into anger. She hated being bullied. "As I said, there are a great number of mages in Las Vegas alone. I'm sure you'll find someone to help you."

"But Zanthia," Lachesis said, deliberately taking power by using Zoe's very real, very impractical name, "you are the only detective among our people. You are the only person who can find our wheel without resorting to excessive magic."

"Wheel?" Zoe asked before she could stop herself.

"Yes," Atropos said. "That's why we're here."

"We really don't need a babysitter," Clotho said, but behind her, Kyle mouthed *Yes, they do.*

Travers rolled his eyes. Bartholomew—Fang—the dang dachshund—kicked his squat little legs, and forced Kyle to set him down. The dog ran to Travers, sat in front of him, and rose on his hind legs into a begging position.

It was the only cute thing Zoe had ever seen the dachshund do.

"I don't have food," Travers said, rather plaintively.

"He can't be hungry," Zoe said. "He ate more meat than Tony Roma's serves in a month."

The dog looked up at Travers with soulful eyes. His long ears trailed down his back and his snout was pointed directly at Travers's face. The dog now looked like a pillar with a dachshund head.

"Oh, for heaven's sake," Travers said, and crouched. The dog got down, and his tail wagged. He licked Travers's hands and then put his paws on Travers's knees, and went for his face. Travers shook his head.

"Can we keep him, Dad?" Kyle asked again.

"I'm not taking care of the Fates," Zoe said.

"We can't split up now," Lachesis said.

"I was thinking that the three of you go on your merry way," Zoe said to the Fates. "I'll stay here, and Kyle, his dad, and the dog can go on their way."

"How do you convince people without magic?" Atropos asked the other Fates.

"Everyone here has magic," Clotho said. "Or will."

"No, goofy," Lachesis said. "She means how do you convince without magic?"

"Like she knows," Atropos said. She sank into her chair.

Zoe felt the guilt return. She sighed. "You do it," she said, "by presenting a coherent argument."

Travers picked up the dog, then wiped his face with the back of his hand. "You're not helping yourself here," he said to her.

She grinned at him. "Neither are you."

For a moment, they were the only two people in the room. No boy, no dog, no Fates. Just her and Travers, grinning at each other like teenagers.

And they shouldn't grin. Not with what they were both thinking.

They were both thinking of giving in.

Zoe sighed, and so did Travers. They sighed in unison, as if they were as closely connected as the Fates.

A little shiver ran through Zoe. But it wasn't an unpleasant sensation. If she wanted to connect with anyone, it was Travers Kineally.

There was a certain inevitability to the day. Zoe wouldn't get her bath and her romance novel, but she might get something else—a memorable few days, if nothing else.

But there was no way Zoe would go into Faerie. Not for the Fates, not for the sexiest man she'd ever met.

Not for anything.

Twelve

Parenting had taught Travers many skills he never thought he would gain. Patience was one. Enjoyment of someone else's company was another.

And the third, which in some ways was the most important, was knowing when and where to pick your battles.

Travers had picked this small, badly air-conditioned office for his battle, and he had lost long before the first five-dollar bill had fallen from the ceiling. He had probably lost when his sister Vivian had batted her dark brown eyes at him and asked him to take her friends to Los Angeles. He had certainly lost when his son had fallen in love with an overweight dachshund who thought he was a rottweiler.

So Travers gave in. The worst he would get was a dachshund. It looked like Zoe might get custody of the Fates.

Which was not a—fate—he would wish on anyone.

At his suggestion, they left the office and went to the Strip. He and Kyle—and the Fates, apparently—needed a hotel room, and Zoe knew some people who knew some people who might give him a package for the week to take the sting out of the price.

They finally picked a no-name hotel just off the Strip, one that only had video poker machines and a few slots, nothing that was really considered gambling, at least not in a town like Las Vegas.

Zoe had come with them, squeezing into Travers's SUV rather than taking her own car. She said that going to the Strip made the trip easy for her, because if she wanted to leave, she could just take a cab.

But from what he was learning, if she wanted to leave, she could just snap her fingers, wiggle her nose, or mutter some magic charm and vanish.

He could probably do that, too, which gave him the shivers.

Just like that pink elephant had. The pink elephant that Zoe made disappear before she unspelled the front door of her office, before she conjured up a leash for Bartholomew Fang.

Bartholomew Fang. That name rather suited the dog. Travers couldn't think of the poor creature as Bartholomew, and he certainly wasn't your average Fang.

Or even your below-average Fang. The poor dog would simply have to understand that being called Fang all by itself was as much of a joke as being called Bruiser.

Zoe gave Bartholomew Fang and his leash to Kyle, which surprised Travers, since he thought the dog was supposed to be his. But Travers really didn't mind, and Kyle liked the animal. Kyle seemed focused on him, while Travers was focused on the next few hours.

He had surprised himself by deciding to stay.

Travers had stepped out of the humid, smelly, moldy climes of that small office into the Vegas heat and had wilted, glad he had decided to end the standoff, and not as sorry that he had lost as he had expected to be.

Part of that was Zoe. For the first time since his marriage, Travers let the idea of being around a woman dictate his actions.

And he tried to keep that thought to himself. He didn't want Kyle to know.

He certainly didn't want to think about it. Nor did he want to think about the lighter feeling he'd had since the magic stopped *whooshing* out of him. Not because he'd used it—no. He'd been using it for years just like everyone said, only he'd been coming up with other explanations.

Rationales that seemed to work for his logical brain, sort of. Part of his mind, the subconscious, maybe the truly logical part, had known that even with each rationale, the statistical anomaly of his luck with numbers was so extreme that something else had to be causing it.

And if Travers admitted that his son had psychic powers, then he would be admitting that magic—or things beyond his ken—actually existed. Then he would have to admit that his skill with numbers, his older sister's psychic hotline, his Great Aunt Eugenia's ability to appear at just the right moments, all of those things had an explanation other than the surface one.

Of course, it had taken three women out of Greek mythology, an overweight dog, and the most beautiful woman he'd ever seen in his life to convince him. Oh, yeah, and a storm of money as well as one stuffed, obscenely pink elephant.

Because of the stress, because of the changes, Travers had decided to get his own room. He had rented two suites in the no-name hotel—one suite for him and Kyle, and the other for the Fates—and Zoe had done the negotiating with the people who owned the place.

While she had done that, Travers had tried not to hyperventilate. As well off as he was, he never spent a lot of money. He wasn't going to change that habit—he had learned as a CPA that frugality kept the rich rich—but he would be comfortable, at least for the next few days while four women reorganized his life.

For a no-name hotel, the suite was pretty impressive. Two large rooms in the center had a kitchen and a living room big enough to seat the Fates, the pink elephant, and all of their friends. Travers's own bedroom had another sitting area walled off from the bed with stained glass. He could hibernate if he wanted to, and not even see Kyle.

Kyle's room was a little smaller, but not much. He also had his own television, which Travers had restricted when he checked in so that Kyle couldn't get Pay-Per-View movies, HBO, or any other channel that wasn't child-friendly.

Travers might be reorganizing his life, but he wasn't going to overlook his kid. Not even in the small details.

The hotel didn't mind the dog, either. In fact, the woman at the desk had food and water dishes, as well as a doggie bed, delivered to the room.

The suite he had gotten for the Fates was like his, only with three bedrooms. He had inspected it briefly, but the women declared it fine, so he didn't worry about it much.

Zoe had remained downstairs, finishing the negotiations, and he hoped she would stay. She had looked shell-shocked on the drive. Shell-shocked, exhausted, and slightly defeated. Something more than the Fates disturbed her, and Travers wanted to know what it was.

He wanted to know everything he could about her, which scared him. He had vowed, when Cheryl left, that he wouldn't get involved with another woman until Kyle was grown. But Kyle wasn't near adulthood yet, and here was Zoe—exotic, intriguing, and obviously dangerous.

Travers sat on the edge of the bed. It felt odd to be in a hotel room and not have anything to unpack. He would have to get clothes for himself and for Kyle, as well as toothbrushes and all the other essentials.

Travers felt overwhelmed by that, too. He'd never been impulsive before. He'd never changed his plans in the middle of an afternoon, not once in his entire life.

Someone knocked at the door. In the other room, Bartholomew Fang yipped and Kyle shushed him. Travers pulled open his bedroom door as Kyle opened the door to the suite.

Zoe walked in as if she were the one staying here. Her stride was confident, but when Travers saw her face, he realized that she didn't seem confident at all. Her skin was paler than it had been, and she had frown lines beside her mouth. She dropped her purse beside the couch and leaned on it as if she needed something to hold her up.

"Everything work out at the desk?" Travers asked.

She nodded. "You're getting off-season rates, with a corporate discount and complimentary breakfast. It was the best they could do."

By Travers's quick math, that meant she had saved him nearly five hundred dollars over seven days. And she was apologizing.

"Sounds good to me," he said.

"Is it room service?" Kyle asked.

Zoe bent down to pat Bartholomew Fang. The dog wiggled his entire body in excitement, looking like a brown balloon animal that was about to explode.

"I have a hunch the complimentary breakfast is in the buffet," Travers said to his son.

Kyle frowned at him, obviously expecting Zoe to answer. But Zoe seemed preoccupied.

She stood and gave Travers a distant smile. He didn't like the distance. That connection he had felt to her earlier, when

she had finally given in and asked the Fates to give her a coherent argument, was gone.

He missed it.

"I suppose we should round up the Fates," she said.

He didn't want to round up the Fates. He was tired of
those three women. Their constant conversation, their ability
to find the heart of a matter and expose it, their strange way
of viewing the world, made them seem like forty women instead of three.

Before he saw them, he wanted to talk to Zoe Sinclair, see
if he really liked her. Even though there had been that connection in her office, he wasn't sure if it had been because
they were both stressed and pushing against similar things
(read: the Fates) or if they truly had something in common.

And he wanted to see past her beauty, to see if the woman
behind it was someone he would enjoy as much as parts of
him seemed to think he would.

He certainly hoped he wasn't broadcasting his thoughts
this time, but Kyle wasn't complaining. He also didn't seem
to be blushing. Instead, he had bent down, picked up Bartholomew Fang, and held him so that Zoe could keep petting
him.

"Don't you think?" she asked Travers.

For a moment, he thought he had lost the thread of the
conversation. Then he realized that he had been silent too
long and she had simply reminded him that she had asked
him to go with her to get the Fates.

"Before we go," Travers said, "I need to apologize."

"For what?" she asked.

"Yeah," Kyle said. "For what?"

Travers gave his son his best parental this-is-none-of-your-
business look, one that was always guaranteed to work. Of
course, now Travers wondered if the look worked because he

had the glare down pat or if he broadcast his thoughts when he had that expression on his face.

"Both, Dad," Kyle muttered.

Zoe looked back and forth between them. She seemed to know what was going on.

"Well, then," Travers said, "catch the hint."

Kyle sighed and carried Bartholomew Fang into the suite's kitchen. The dog's tail started pinwheeling when he realized where they were going.

"Apologize for what?" Zoe asked softly.

"How harsh I was in your office," Travers said. "I shouldn't have threatened to abandon the Fates. It's pretty clear that they can't survive on their own."

Zoe shrugged one shoulder. "I'm sure they can survive just fine."

"They don't even understand money," Travers said. "They thought three dollars would buy them a bus ticket."

"And they would learn fairly quickly that it can't." Zoe sighed. "They're older and smarter than both of us. They'd learn how to survive."

"I'm just sorry," he said. "I wasn't fair to you."

She looked at him then—really focussed those brown-and-gold eyes on him, and he had to concentrate not to get lost in them. "It seems to me that no one was fair to *you*," she said. "No one's bothered to explain anything to you. About them, about Kyle. About yourself."

He felt his cheeks warm more. "I'm sure they've tried."

"A lot of us refuse to believe when we learn about magic," Zoe said. "That doesn't mean your mentor should have given up."

"I don't even know who this mysterious mentor was," Travers said, "so it really doesn't matter."

She put her hand on his arm. "All I'm saying is that you

don't have to apologize to me. It's been an unusual day for you, and you've been under strain."

That was an understatement. He felt like he'd been through an emotional wringer—and he wasn't an emotional man.

"It just looks like you're under a strain, too," he said.

She gave him that look again. Each time she did, she tilted her head sideways, as if she could see him clearer through the corners of her eyes. Her black hair fell against her cheek like a caress.

"I'm fine," she said, obviously lying.

He decided to try again. "What's wrong with the place they want you to go?"

She sighed, and looked at one of the couches. "Mind if I sit?"

"Be my guest." Travers swept a hand around the room as if he had decorated it himself.

Not that he would have. There were three couches—which was one too many for the size—and only one easy chair. The end tables were scuffed, and the art was badly done photographs of Vegas at night. The vases, filled with fresh flowers, were plastic, and the see-through table in the kitchen was made of plastic instead of glass.

Zoe sat on the nearest couch, pulled off a high-heeled shoe, and rubbed her delicate foot. Travers thought of offering to help her, but had a hunch she'd balk.

"You want to know about Faerie," she said.

He nodded, and sat on the same couch, careful to keep a cushion between them.

From the kitchen, he heard the banging of plates and his son's giggle. So far as Travers could tell, Kyle wasn't paying attention to this conversation.

For some reason, Travers found that very important.

"When we're born," Zoe said, still looking at her aching foot, "we're all given a prophecy, all of us."

"Everyone?"

"Mages," Zoe said. "The Fates come up with the prophecies, and generally, you learn about it the first time you visit them, or from your mentor."

Which meant that Travers had a prophecy which he didn't know about.

"The prophecy supposedly comes from the air—the powers that are even greater than the Powers That Be, whoever that is—but I'm not so sure. Especially after today."

"Why?" Travers asked.

Zoe set down her foot and dug her toes into the carpet. Then she pulled the shoe off her other foot and started to rub it. "Because of my prophecy."

"Which is?" Travers felt like he had to drag each word out of her. Was she that used to keeping secrets? Or were all mages like this?

"My prophecy?" Zoe's fingers worked the ball of her foot. "It's about—"

She stopped herself and looked at Travers, as if she could see through him. He felt as if she were analyzing him, as if she were trying to figure out something about him.

Then she shook her head. "I'm such a fool," she said.

"You don't strike me as a fool," he said.

"It's all manipulation," she said. "I've known that for a long time. I've just never understood why until now. They've been setting me up."

"Setting you up for what?" Travers wasn't quite following this conversation.

"A trip into Faerie. They were promising me big rewards, a reward I've always wanted. And just to get me to risk my life for them. They must have known this was coming." She rested her hand on the side of her foot, but kept looking down.

Travers could sense how tired she was, and something else, something rather sad and defeated about her.

"You think they knew that Zeus—" Travers still felt ridiculous talking about a Greek god as if he really existed, but he soldiered through it—"would try to toss them out of their positions? You think they could see that far into the future?"

"Kyle can see into the future, can't he?" Zoe asked, not answering Travers. She eased her hand off her foot, stretched her long leg, and arched her toes.

Travers tried not to think about her smooth skin or the delicacy of her movements. "You're asking me? The ultimate clueless man?"

She leaned her head back as if she were waiting for Kyle to yell the answer from the kitchen. But, true to his word, he had left them alone.

"If the Fates could really foresee the future like that," Travers said, "why didn't they try to stop Zeus from undermining them? Why did they give up their powers? Why did they put themselves at a disadvantage?"

"Who knows? They're not the most logical of women." Zoe put her foot next to the other one, and rubbed her toes in the carpet.

Travers had never seen a woman do that after removing high heels, but then, he hadn't dated since his wife left, and she hadn't been the high-heel type.

"They're very literal and pretty strange," Travers said, "but they have been somewhat logical."

"You're defending them?" Zoe asked.

He felt as if he shouldn't be, as if defending them was betraying her. "No," he said, not really sure. "I just—what if they can only see partial futures? I mean, Kyle can only hear me when I 'broadcast' my thoughts, or so he says. Which means that he's a partial psychic, not a full one. Maybe that's how their prophecies work. Maybe they gave you that prophecy and didn't realize they were tied into it."

Zoe shook her head. "It's dangerous in Faerie."

"I'm assuming, since you call this place Faerie, they have magic, too," he said.

"Oh, yeah." She sighed. "There once was a number of different groups with magical abilities. Some of them went so deep underground that we no longer know about them. Some of them, from what I understand, were destroyed. And a few of us survived. The mages, we survived—and mostly were remembered through myths and legends. The Faeries were a particular group that actually managed to grow. They've been worrying the Powers That Be for at least five hundred years."

"Worrying why?" Travers asked.

"Because they seem to get more powerful, and that's not good."

Travers shook his head. "Not good—for you?"

"Yeah," she said. "For us. We don't work on accumulating power for the most part. We work on love."

"Huh?" Whatever he had expected her to say, it wasn't that. "What do you mean, 'love'?"

Her body went rigid for a brief moment, but she didn't move. It was as if he had caught her saying something wrong. She waited so long to respond that he got the sense she was trying to make up an answer instead of giving him the truth.

"We're—um—all about romantic love," she said. "Except for those of our number who go evil, the rest of us work for the betterment of anyone who can fall in love."

That wasn't all of it, he knew, but she obviously wasn't ready to tell him the rest. "And the Faeries?"

"They're all about power,' she said. "They don't even believe in love."

"Do you believe in power?"

She nodded, keeping her head down. "Maybe more than I believe in love," she said.

Those words hung between them for a moment. He thought about it: he wasn't sure he believed in romantic love either.

What he had felt for Cheryl had been teenage infatuation and lust. If he had felt love for her, a psychologist friend had once told him, then he would have hated her for leaving.

All Travers had felt was relief.

Still, he believed in love itself. He would do anything for his son. Anything at all. Even accept three strange women, drive them to Las Vegas, and give up a week of his life.

"I don't understand," Travers said. "If you're equally magical, what can they do to you, these faeries?"

Zoe raised her head, bit her lower lip, and released it. It was almost as if she weren't planning to tell him, and then changed her mind.

"It's against our rules to steal someone else's magic," she said.

"Steal it?" Travers asked. "How can you do that?"

She waved a hand, as if it weren't important. "You have to be really talented to do it. It's forbidden for us. You get one of the worst punishments ever. But it's not forbidden for faeries. It's part of how they live. There's only one hitch."

"And that is?"

"They can't steal magic in the outside world. They can only steal it inside of Faerie."

Travers blinked, then frowned.

"All those stories you hear about faeries," Zoe said, "the ones about changelings, and about people eating food that sucks them into a magic land, and about faerie circles—they come from this. People who just came into their magic, people who weren't sure what they had, people like Kyle who had a lot of power, but it wasn't developed or hadn't reached its maturity, they got trapped by the faeries and had their powers stolen. The faeries grew stronger, which is, I think, how they've managed to survive for so long."

Travers swallowed. He felt suddenly quite nervous. "And Faerie is near here?"

"Don't worry," Zoe said. "They won't mess with you or Kyle. Not while I'm here."

He hadn't even thought of himself. He had only been thinking of Kyle.

"How can you know that?" Travers asked.

Zoe smiled at him. "I know where all the entrances to Faerie are in Vegas, and you two won't get near them."

"Can't they just—spell—us there?" Travers asked, wondering if he used the right words.

"They haven't done anything like that in centuries," Zoe said. "They haven't had to. Small talents like yours don't interest them and they would rather wait until Kyle has come into his full power."

"But you're different," Travers said, beginning to understand.

"According to the prophecy," Zoe said, obviously choosing her words carefully, "I'll lose myself there. All I am is my magic. Without it, there's no Zoe Sinclair."

Travers doubted that, but he didn't know enough to reassure her. "Then you'll have to say no to the Fates."

She nodded. "I've come to that conclusion, too."

"Is there someone you can recommend to them?" he asked.

"I don't know exactly what they want me to do," she said.

"They mentioned stealing something." He had felt very uncomfortable about that.

"I don't steal," she said. "I find. That's different."

"And yet," Travers said, "we have a dog here."

"He's not stolen." Her lips thinned. "He wanted to come. He makes his own choices."

"Maybe what they want you to find does, too."

She sighed. "If it's in Faerie, I'm not going."

Travers nodded. He hadn't even wanted to come to Las Vegas, and there was no real life-or-death risk for him here. He could certainly understand her position.

He stood, because if he didn't, he would touch her, and he wasn't ready for that. Not even a light, casual touch on the shoulder. He was still confused—about the Fates, about himself, about *everything*, and he needed time to think.

He also needed food.

"Let's order in," he said. "Make a quiet evening of it, and talk to the Fates in the morning."

The idea of ordering in was daring enough for him. He would not have suggested it if she hadn't looked so comfortable on his couch.

She stretched, then ran a hand through her hair. It fell back into place perfectly—just like his sister Vivian accused his hair of doing. He smiled. Something else he and Zoe had in common.

"If I don't confront the Fates tonight, I won't sleep," Zoe said. "Let's just get this over with."

Travers hid his disappointment behind a genial smile. "All right, then. Dinner out. Somewhere big and loud and filled with obnoxious tourists so that the Fates won't embarrass us."

Zoe pushed herself off the couch. "That's just about anywhere in this part of Vegas, although we'll need a little quiet so the Fates can hear me when I say no."

Travers nodded. He slipped his hands in his pockets so he wouldn't extend one to her. He wasn't ready to reveal his attraction—not yet.

"You know this town better than we ever could," he said. "You choose."

"Great," Zoe muttered, reaching for the purse she had dropped beside the couch. "My choice of tourist traps. This day just keeps getting better and better."

Thirteen

Zoe followed Travers and Kyle into the hallway, wishing she had not decided to wear heels that morning. Her feet ached, her calves ached, and this endless day promised to go on forever.

Even planning dinner was proving difficult.

First, Kyle wouldn't leave the hotel room without Bartholomew. No amount of argument from Travers seemed to help. Kyle was worried that Bartholomew wouldn't be able to handle even an evening alone in the hotel suite, and Zoe had the sense that Kyle was right. Good old Morton the Magnificent might try to take Bartholomew back (since who knew how the Interim Fates had left him in the familiar department) or Bartholomew, who was pretty high strung even for a dachshund, simply might use his meager powers to escape, perhaps claiming he was searching for food or his companions.

After a bit of an argument, Travers let the dog come along.

That limited their choice of eating establishments. Now Zoe would have to contend with tourist restaurants that allowed dogs inside. She doubted there would be any convincing anyone that Bartholomew was a seeing-eye dog. Worst case, she would have to use her magic to make him invisible, something she really didn't want to do around the Fates.

The hallway between the suites was long and wide, and it looked like every other hotel hallway in every other large Vegas hotel. Zoe couldn't imagine coming to places like this to spend her vacation. She actually missed the old hotels and all their history—the Sands, with the blue-gray cigarette smoke hanging in the air, and the ghost of Sinatra in every room. She'd seen the infamous Rat Pack performances in Vegas—and she still felt privileged.

Zoe glanced at Travers, who was walking with his hand on Kyle's shoulder. Bartholomew didn't mind being on his leash. He led the group, sniffing every corner, every doorway, as they made their way to the end of the hall.

Travers was looking straight ahead, his expression unreadable. He got a distant look at times, and she wasn't sure what caused it. She would feel close to him for a moment, and then that closeness would fade as if it never were, almost as if his entire personality had withdrawn from the room without his body going with it.

She had no idea how he did that.

But it made her nervous, and a little more comfortable with her decision not to tell him the entire truth about her prophecy. She didn't want him to know that she was supposed to discover her true love near Faerie.

They stopped in front of the door to 1435, the Fates' suite. The hallway smelled faintly of garlic, a scent Zoe hadn't really noticed until they stopped in front of the door. Travers knocked, and all four of them stood in front of the spyhole as if they were the perfect Norman Rockwell family, coming to the aunts' house for a visit.

Zoe let a single shudder run through her. How deceiving

appearances could be. A man, a woman, a boy who looked like the man, and an obese dog. What else could they be in this hotel in this part of Vegas except a family? A family of tourists.

She would have thought so, looking at a surveillance tape. She was sure the security guard who was supposed to monitor the corridors through the cameras mounted on the wall thought the same thing.

Finally the door swung open and Atropos appeared. Only she didn't look like Atropos—or, at least, not the Atropos of Greek myth, the one who carried the abhorréd shears and cut the thread of life to create death.

This Atropos grinned at them. She had a streak of flour on one cheek, and more in her hair. Around her waist, an apron had absorbed even more flour, and there were flour tracks on the living room carpet.

"Welcome! Welcome," she said. "We've been expecting you."

The garlic scent was even stronger now, accented by the smells of oregano and basil, along with the smell of bread dough. Travers looked at Zoe in surprise, as if she could explain the turn of events. She shrugged.

Bartholomew yipped, and Kyle shushed him.

"Come on in," Clotho said from somewhere inside the suite.

"We just came to get you for dinner," Travers said slowly.

"We're having dinner here." Lachesis's voice sounded a little closer than Clotho's, but not much.

"We cooked," Atropos said, pulling the door open as wide as it went.

"Without magic?" Zoe asked, feeling apprehensive. After all, why would the Fates know how to cook? They had lived for centuries with everything provided for them, and few restrictions on their magic.

"Of course without magic." Clotho stood in the door to

the kitchen, holding a wooden spoon as if it were a club. The spoon was dripping tomato paste onto the blue-and-white kitchen tile.

"Come in!" Lachesis said again. She was setting the table in the dining area. The curtains were open, revealing a view of Las Vegas that Zoe only saw in brochures—the city spread before her like a sea of multi-colored Christmas lights.

Bartholomew tugged Kyle inside, and Travers followed, moving hesitantly. He looked over his shoulder at Zoe, and she read his expression as if she had known him all her life.

Is this what you want? he was asking her. He was going to give her a chance to escape if she needed it.

But this was probably the best. If the Fates were angry at her for not taking their case, and they decided that she had failed the test; if they had lied about no longer having magic; if they had some kind of retribution planned, better to be inside a private room than in the Hard Rock Café, trying to shout over the music.

Zoe nodded just a little at Travers, enough so that he noticed, not enough for anyone else to, and then she stepped inside. The smells were overpowering here, and she could no longer separate out individual odors.

"What're we having?" Kyle asked.

"Everyone's favorite," Atropos said. "Pizza!"

"You ordered pizza?" Travers asked, and there was relief in his voice.

"Of course not." Clotho sounded offended. She let the spoon drop, and more sauce dripped off.

"We learned how to cook in the last few months," Lachesis said.

"It was quite intimidating at first," Atropos said.

"Henri Barou made us learn," Clotho said.

"He let us use his cave fortress," Lachesis said, "but he wouldn't supply fresh meals every day."

"Cave fortress?" Travers asked.

But as he did, Kyle stepped forward, his eyes bright. "Henri Barou? That's my Uncle Dex, right?"

"Of course, child," Atropos said.

"He has a fortress of solitude? Just like in the comics?" Kyle sounded thrilled.

Zoe's breath caught. The Fates hated all mention of the comic books. Henri had told her that years ago.

"It is quite the place," Clotho said. "We had to stay there until we were safe."

"Safe from what?" Travers asked.

"Eris was trying to destroy us," Lachesis said.

"We suspect that will be a common problem as people discover we've given up our magic," Atropos said with a grin. It didn't seem to bother her. She wiped her hands on her flour-covered apron, getting more flour on herself and on the floor.

"We learned many things while we were there," Clotho said. "How to cook—"

"How to make a fire with our bare hands," Lachesis said.

"And how to bake." Atropos smiled. "Which is my favorite."

"Sit! Sit," Clotho said. "Let us do all the work."

Kyle wandered into the kitchen, to be near the food and probably to discuss Henri Barou's cave. Bartholomew followed Clotho around, licking tomato sauce off the tiled floor, his tail wagging furiously.

Lachesis set wine goblets on the table, even in Kyle's place, then went back to the kitchen for more utensils. Atropos also went into the kitchen, probably to check on whatever creation she was making.

Zoe slipped away from the group and walked to the wall of windows. Her reflection—and that of the room—was superimposed over the lights of the city. She crossed her arms, and leaned her forehead against the cool glass.

At night, Las Vegas was beautiful. During the day, when the smog and haze hid the mountains, and the snakes of traffic lined the city's arteries, Vegas seemed like too much sprawl. But at night, the city lived.

"Penny for them," Travers said behind her. Then, before she could turn, he added, "Damn!"

His reflection towered over hers, but his head was down, looking at something between his fingers.

"Don't tell me," she said without turning. "A penny."

"Right between my thumb and index finger like I'm some sort of cheesy kid's magician." He sounded annoyed.

Zoe turned, and found herself inches from him. She had had no idea he was standing so close—the reflection in the window hadn't given her a sense of distance.

Travers's hair had fallen across his forehead, making him look as young as Kyle. Zoe resisted the urge to push the hair back. Instead, she looked at the penny.

"May I?" she asked, holding out her hand.

He handed it to her, his fingers shaking. They brushed her palm, and a heat ran through her. She struggled to keep her breathing even.

The penny was shiny and new. She rubbed her fingers over it, feeling the pressed metal, the perfection of the coin. It didn't have that slight sense of fragility that faerie money had—the sense that if you squeezed too hard, the money might vanish.

"It seems real," she said.

"You mean it might not be?" he asked.

She smiled. "Magic is mysterious and it follows its own circular rules."

"I thought it followed the Fates' rules."

"What they do is more like build dams in streams. They try to control the magic and don't always succeed."

Travers was very close to her but she didn't want him to move away.

"You've been quiet since we left the hotel room," he said.

"There's a lot I don't want to tell you," she said, and then her breath caught. She hadn't meant to say that out loud.

"Really?" he said.

Zoe shrugged, planning to brush the comment off. Instead, she said, "Really."

He stared at her. She stared at him, noting the fine blond lashes over his sky blue eyes. He was the most handsome man she had ever seen, something she was about to tell him when—

"Crap!" she said and thrust the penny back at him. "You keep this. Get it away from me."

"What?" he said.

"Take it!" she said. "Take it quickly."

"Why? What does it do?"

"Think," she said, struggling not to say more. "What did you say to me before you conjured up the penny?"

"I said 'A penny for your thoughts.'"

"Precisely." She stuck the penny in the pocket of his polo shirt. "Keep it. I don't want it. And you can't have my thoughts."

"Not even the ones you're hiding from me?" he asked with a smile.

This time, she didn't even feel the urge to answer him. The moment had passed. Returning the penny negated the magic.

"You don't understand, Travers," Zoe said. "You really wanted to know what I was thinking."

A slight frown marred his forehead. "Yes, I did. I thought that was clear."

"I mean, you weren't just making conversation."

"I know," he said.

"So," she said, "when you created the penny, you created a spell that got you what you wanted. And I bought into it."

"Interesting choice of words," he said.

"Maybe a little too accurate," she said.

"Actually, no," he said. "I'm the one who supposedly purchased *your* thoughts."

"And apparently you got your penny's worth," Lachesis said as she brought the silverware into the dining room. "Giving the penny back probably wouldn't make the spell continue. Apparently, a penny's worth of thought is only a sentence or two."

Thank heavens, Zoe thought, but didn't say.

Travers gave her a sideways smile. "Why're you so relieved?"

Zoe shrugged one shoulder. "I've always been a private person."

"Doesn't my son make you nervous, then?" Travers asked.

"I know how to prevent a broadcast thought," Zoe said.

"Most of the time," Kyle said from the kitchen.

Zoe's heart jumped, and then she realized that Kyle was, after all, eleven. He might have been simply saying that to make her uncomfortable.

Or he might have been telling the truth.

Lachesis finished setting the table as if they were going to have a five-course formal dinner.

"Wine for everyone?" Atropos asked as she came in from the kitchen, carrying an open bottle of Chianti.

"Not for Kyle." Travers stepped away from Zoe as he spoke, and she felt his loss, as if he'd been actually touching her. She hadn't realized that the air conditioning was on so high in this part of the room. Travers had been blocking the breeze.

"The boy would like some." As Clotho spoke, something banged in the kitchen.

"The boy," Travers said, "will not get any."

Lachesis took the bottle from Atropos and poured each glass a little too full, as far as Zoe was concerned. Atropos went back into the kitchen. Travers watched the pouring as if it were the most important event in his life—and then his shoulders visibly relaxed when Lachesis skipped one of the wineglasses.

"That looks good!" Kyle said from the kitchen.

Atropos emerged, carrying a large salad.

"When did you have time to shop?" Zoe asked. She hadn't been gone that long, negotiating with the hotel manager. Nor had she spoken to Travers longer than a half an hour. The Fates still had to have time to make the meal and cook it.

"You have such lovely conveniences," Lachesis said.

"Almost as good as magic," Atropos said.

"We called a local grocery store and had the food delivered." Clotho carried a large pan in each hand.

"And you paid for it how?" Travers asked.

"Paid?" Lachesis asked. "They didn't ask for money."

"What did they say?" Travers's voice had an edge to it.

"That the hotel would take the charge," Atropos said.

"That's not what they really said, is it?" Travers's eyes had narrowed.

Clotho paused before she set the food down. "They said the charge would go to the room."

"Voilà! The hotel pays for it." Lachesis grinned. "I'm amazed that you don't even know your own customs."

Travers's gaze met Zoe's. "See what I've had to contend with?"

"I'm beginning to understand why you don't want them left alone," she said, trying not to laugh.

"What did we do?" Atropos asked as she took the platters from Clotho.

"Charging to the room means that it gets billed to the person who is paying for the room," Kyle said, as he came in from the kitchen, Bartholomew at his heels. "Jeez, even I know that."

"Oh," Clotho said. "And here we thought they were all being so courteous."

"We had feared that someone had recognized us, and was paying us tribute," Lachesis said.

"We truly couldn't believe our good fortune," Atropos said.

"That should be a sign for you," Travers said.

"A sign of what?" Clotho asked.

"Whenever something seems too good to be true, it probably is," Travers said.

Somehow the cliché didn't sound as—well—clichéd when he said it. Zoe frowned at him. She had had two major relationships in her past, relationships in which she thought she had been in love, and she had never felt this kind of attraction on the first day.

It had taken her years of friendship before sliding into the relationship with Ramon, back when she had just come into her magic. Three turbulent years later, years in which he had left her four times and had two affairs, she realized that however she felt about him, he didn't feel the same way about her.

And now, more than a hundred years later, she couldn't even remember what he looked like. But she could remember how she felt around him. Comfortable, easy—at least in the beginning. And constantly annoyed the rest of the time.

She hadn't yet felt comfortable or easy with Travers. She felt a rapport, and she felt an attraction so fine that it felt as if they were joined by an invisible string. Part of her—the sensitive, magical part—believed that this man was an opportunity, an opportunity that she didn't dare miss.

Perhaps she had been reading too many Nora Roberts novels.

Atropos set the platters down, revealing the pizzas. Kyle had been right; they looked fantastic. Pepperoni, sausage, and a variety of vegetables thickly covered the delicately golden mozzarella cheese. The tomato sauce bubbled through, still steaming, and the crust looked perfect—thick and golden brown and baked to perfection.

Zoe's stomach growled. She couldn't believe how hungry she was.

"Well," Lachesis said. "I think your saying is foolish."

Zoe frowned. What saying? And then she remembered that Travers had spouted a cliché at the Fates. Perhaps she should warn him about talking to the Fates at all, particularly since he didn't really seem to understand his magic.

"You're in our world now." Travers shook his head. "I can't believe I just said that."

"But you did, Dad." Kyle came out of the kitchen, carrying one more platter. Three large pizzas for all of them, plus a salad. It seemed like too much food. "Maybe you're changing."

"Yeah." Travers didn't sound happy about it.

"Actually," Atropos said, pulling back her chair, "you are coming into yourself."

The Fates sat. Then Clotho looked pointedly at Zoe, Travers, and Kyle. "You are joining us, aren't you?"

Kyle climbed into the chair closest to the empty wineglass. Travers sat beside him. Zoe sat on the other side of the table.

Lachesis cut all of the pizzas with a carving knife. Apparently the Fates hadn't learned everything there was to know about cooking, or maybe serving utensils didn't exactly count.

Still, the pieces she cut were evenly proportioned, as if she had always had such skill with a knife. Zoe didn't even want to think about that.

Atropos passed the salad to Travers, who helped himself. Kyle took the first piece of pizza.

Zoe sipped her wine and wished that she were at home. Her stomach, which had growled a few moments before, was now churning.

She really didn't want to tell the Fates that she wouldn't work with them. But they had left her no choice.

"You look serious, child," Lachesis said to her, opening the door.

Travers's gaze met Zoe's. She got the sense that he didn't want her to say anything, that he was hoping she had changed her mind.

Or maybe she was simply reading him wrong. She didn't have the psychic talents that Kyle did, and for all of her imagined connection to Travers, it hadn't been tested yet.

"I am," Zoe said, taking one of the platters of pizza as it came by. She took three slices, even though her stomach kept flip-flopping.

"We're having a feast," Atropos said. "No need for seriousness."

"Oh, but there is," Zoe said, handing the platter to Clotho. "I'm afraid I can't take your job."

"Even after meeting those children?" Clotho asked, nearly dropping the platter.

"I am not sure how they relate to your task," Zoe said, "but—"

"Because you never allowed us to finish our explanation," Lachesis said as she helped herself to salad.

Zoe didn't point out that the Fates had made finishing any topic nearly impossible. She took the salad bowl from Lachesis, and placed a pile of greens on her plate near the pizza slices. Even though the food looked good, at the moment the wine looked even better.

Zoe didn't touch it.

"Your explanation doesn't really matter," Zoe said. "The key is Faerie. You say I have to go in there, and I'm not ready."

All three Fates turned toward Travers. Their movement was so obvious that he blushed.

"What?" he asked.

The Fates smiled at each other and then Atropos said to Zoe, "You're ready now."

"Oh," Zoe said, finally understanding them. They believed Travers was her soulmate. Or they were manipulating her into believing it so that she would work with them. "You are all so—"

"So what?" Travers asked.

"So . . . so . . ." Zoe wished he weren't in the room. She didn't want to say anything about true love or soulmates or manipulation. "I'm just not going to endanger my own life, that's all."

"Child," Clotho said, "what's the point of living if you don't have some danger now and then?"

"Said a woman who spent that past four thousand years in the same place, protected by the Powers That Be," Zoe snapped.

The Fates froze in position. Kyle looked from one to the other as if he expected a fight. Travers frowned.

Zoe couldn't believe she had said that. If the Fates ever did regain their powers, she might pay for that sentence more than for refusing them.

"Point taken," Lachesis said. "We have endangered ourselves now."

"So much so," Atropos said, "that we have had to go into hiding for much of our sojourn here."

"Yeah," Kyle said. "The fortress. Was it cool?"

"Kyle!" Travers whispered, obviously trying to keep his son quiet.

"It doesn't matter," Zoe said to the Fates. "I'm not going to help you with whatever this is. I don't steal, and I don't go into Faerie. So no matter how hard you push, I'm not going to change my mind."

The Fates looked at each other.

"Then we are—what is that word?" Clotho asked.

"Screwed," Lachesis said with the perfect dry tone.

"Not to mention the rest of the world," Atropos said.

Clotho leaned toward Zoe. "You do realize that you could be murdering true love."

"I doubt it," Zoe said. "It has to exist before it gets murdered."

All three Fates hissed in a breath. They looked as shocked as Zoe expected them to.

She pretended she didn't notice, and bit into one of the slices of pizza. The crust was crunchy on the bottom, thick and rich in the middle, and the tomato sauce had a bit of a bite to it. The pepperoni was the best she had tasted outside of New York City.

"Zanthia," Lachesis said in the most dire tone Zoe had heard from the Fates since they arrived in Las Vegas. "You do realize that what you're saying is heresy."

Zoe held the pizza slice in front of her mouth, poised to take another bite. "I don't think there is such a thing any longer, not so long as Zeus' daughters hold power."

She took another bite, savoring the mix of flavors.

"You'd side with them?" Atropos asked.

"I'd just like to live my life," Zoe said after she swallowed.

"Without love?"

That last question came from Travers. He had receded into himself again, and Zoe got no real sense of him.

Kyle's face was pale, though, and he picked at his salad.

"I'll live without it no matter who's in power," Zoe said. "I've already resigned myself to that."

Fourteen

Travers set down his piece of pizza so that no one would see his hand tremble. Zoe's words upset him more than he wanted to admit.

He had been enjoying the attraction between them and part of him had been nursing a hope that the attraction would become something more, something finer, something longer lasting.

Something like love.

But how could that happen if she didn't believe in love?

Kyle pushed a slice of cucumber off his plate and hid it in his napkin. Travers pretended not to notice.

Bartholomew Fang sat on his hind legs between Kyle and Travers, occasionally whining and pushing at them with his front paws. Travers reached down and absently petted the dog's head.

He would wager if someone asked Bartholomew Fang whether or not love existed, the dog would say that it did. Of course, his definition might vary—he might say that love was little more than a warm bed and a good meal—but with the right person, that would be enough.

After Zoe had made her pronouncement, her gaze connected with Travers's and then slid away. Now she was looking from Fate to Fate to Fate, probably resigning herself to some other kind of fate.

The Fates seemed shocked to their core. Travers had never thought of them as fundamentally serious women—perhaps because he had not taken them seriously at first—but now they looked like their world had come to an end.

Then the table rattled.

The glasses slid toward the windows, and so did the plates, the silverware, and the serving platters. Travers grabbed his dishes, then realized that he was rattling, too. He bit the tip of his tongue and winced with pain. Blood mixed with the taste of tomato sauce in the back of his throat.

"It's an earthquake!" Kyle said and dove under the table.

He was right. Travers had lived through enough of the things to recognize that moment of indecision, that inability to accept that terra firma wasn't so firma after all.

He slid under the table as well.

"What're you doing?" Clotho asked.

"Get down here!" Kyle said. "You could die."

Clotho, Lachesis, and Atropos slipped under the table. Atropos was still holding a piece of pizza and Bartholomew Fang lunged for it.

Travers caught him just in time.

"There aren't earthquakes in Las Vegas," Zoe said.

"There are earthquakes everywhere," Travers said. "Get down here. We're in a hotel. If the ceiling falls in—"

"I'll hold it up," Zoe said.

The statement would have sounded ridiculous coming from anyone else, but Travers didn't doubt that she would. Her shapely legs moved away from the table, her narrow high heels making a clicking sound on the floor that was almost inaudible under the rattling dishes.

"I'm not worried about the ceiling," Kyle whispered. "I'm worried about the floor."

"What *is* this?" Lachesis asked.

"It's like that abysmal movie," Atropos said. "Remember? Clotho didn't want to watch it because it had an exclamation point in the title."

"And I was right, wasn't I?" Clotho said, wrapping her arms around her legs. "Exclamation points in movie titles are always bad."

Travers couldn't believe they were discussing movies at a time like this. He put his arm around Kyle and pulled the boy close. Kyle grabbed Bartholomew Fang, who whimpered in protest.

"Now isn't that strange?" Zoe asked.

Her feet were near the window which, if she hadn't had magic, Travers would have warned her against.

"What's strange?" Kyle asked, his voice vibrating.

"No one has stopped driving. No one has run onto the street. Everything looks normal outside," Zoe said.

"Oh, dear," Lachesis said.

"Better trace the magic," Atropos said.

"Magic?" Travers asked.

And then blue smoke filled the room—powder-blue smoke that smelled faintly of Limburger cheese. A cackling laugh that Travers didn't recognize followed, and then a wizened face peered under the tablecloth.

"Hiding, ladies?" The laugh apparently belonged to the face, which seemed to belong to a man who bore a strong resemblance to the apple witches Travers's sisters used to make when he was a kid. "And you brought friends."

Clotho sighed. "What do you want, Nero?"

"Nero?" Travers asked, feeling his heart rate increase. *"The* Nero?"

"Of course, *the* Nero," said the apple witch, sliding under the table to join them. He was wearing a purple satin shirt with poet sleeves and white bell-bottom pants, also made of satin. His hair was silvery black, and his eyes were the same odd color.

He reached for Travers. Nero's hand was as shriveled as his face. "This one has raw magic, ladies."

Nero grinned, which made his eyes virtually disappear among the wrinkles.

"Raw magic is so easy to steal. How did you let him by you? I thought you were supposed to protect all the baby magicians so that they couldn't lose their powers."

Travers ducked so Nero couldn't touch him.

"Leave him alone!" Kyle said, as Bartholomew Fang growled.

Nero's eyes lit up. "Another one. And so young. The power's not ready in him. But I can use it. I can definitely use it . . ."

He reached out again, and this time, Atropos slapped his hand. He clutched it to his chest and looked like he was about to cry.

"He's not *the* Nero," Lachesis said, with contempt. "If by Nero, you mean that horrible little Roman man with delusions of grandeur."

"This one is, though, the first Nero," said Atropos.

"And he's been trouble since the day he first wandered into the halls of Justice," Clotho said.

"Only then, he didn't have much magic." Lachesis narrowed her eyes. "You've been stealing."

Nero laughed. "Go ahead, punish me. I hear you ladies are out of power and magickless."

Kyle bit his lower lip, which he always did when the lip

threatened to tremble and reveal how frightened he was. Bartholomew Fang continued to growl, baring his teeth as he did so. Maybe he did deserve the name "Fang" after all. Those teeth were mighty impressive.

"We're merely—" Clotho started to speak but didn't get to finish. Instead, she and the other two Fates vanished.

Nero looked at Travers in surprise. Travers was equally surprised. He had no idea they could do that, either.

Then Nero smiled. "Well, now that they're gone—"

Duct tape appeared on Nero's mouth. He lifted his hands toward it, and suddenly they were bound with duct tape as well. He made little "mmph-mmph" sounds, and pushed himself away from Travers with his feet.

Then more duct tape appeared, wrapping itself around Nero's ankles. Little puffs of smoke—that silly blue, smelling of Limburger—appeared around his face and his hands, as if he were trying to free himself and couldn't.

"Nero!" Three female voices spoke in a rough unison. *"You shall not disturb us or our friends again. Warn everyone you see that the rumors about the Fates are untrue. You shall escape serious punishment this time, but in the next, you will receive exactly what's coming to you."*

Nero's oddly colored eyes grew wide and filled with tears. He struggled, but he couldn't free himself.

Travers wanted to get out from under the table, but he couldn't. Kyle was rooted to his spot. And Bartholomew Fang was drooling as he growled, making him look as fearsome as a dachshund could.

"Begone!" the voices said, and then Nero vanished, this time without the blue smoke. The smell lingered, oddly strong, which made Travers wonder if the cheese odor wasn't Nero's own unfortunate personal scent.

The tablecloth went up and Zoe peered beneath it. "You gonna stay under there all day?"

Kyle looked at her as if she were his savior. "Is the earth-quake over?"

"It never was," she said, extending him her hand. "It's a sign of badly used magic when someone about to transport in from somewhere else gets the vibrations wrong."

Kyle crawled out from under the table. Bartholomew Fang still growled. Travers put his hand on the dog's back, and Fang whirled, snapping and snarling.

Travers held his hands up like an outlaw about to be arrested. "It's just me."

The dog breathed heavily through his long snout, then sat on his haunches. He looked tinier than he had a moment ago.

"You're one tough pooch," Travers said.

"And you're one strange man." Zoe was peering under the table again. "You want to come out now?"

He did. He scooted out to find Kyle on a nearby couch, a pillow clasped against his stomach.

"That man," Kyle whispered. "He was going to hurt us."

"He wasn't going to hurt anyone," Zoe said. "He was just after the Fates. Which reminds me."

She snapped her fingers.

The Fates reappeared in the center of the living room floor, only they sat in the same positions they had held when they were under the table.

"—experimenting," Clotho finished. Then she looked around, surprised.

"What is the meaning of this?" Lachesis asked. But her voice, which should have sounded booming, actually sounded tiny and a bit scared.

"Someone tampered with us," Atropos said.

"I made you disappear." Zoe remained near the table. She took a piece of pizza off her plate. "That idiot Nero had no idea I was in the room."

"So?" Clotho asked, her voice shaking.

"So," Travers said, understanding what happened, "Zoe made it seem like you still have magic."

"I bought you a few days of protection," Zoe said. "But not much. A lot of people aren't happy with you all. You never did make many friends."

"Our job wasn't to make friends," Lachesis said.

"We're judges," Atropos said. "We're supposed to be impartial."

"Unfortunately," Clotho said, "impartiality often leads to difficult rulings."

"Which leads to difficult sentences," Lachesis said.

"Which leads to difficult interpersonal relations," Atropos said.

"It's just easier to say that most people hate you," Zoe said, and then took a bite of pizza.

That seemed harsh to Travers. Just because the Fates had done their job well didn't mean they were despised. But he didn't know a lot about this magic system he was supposed to be part of. And, if he admitted it, that Nero guy had frightened him.

"What'd he mean about the raw magic?" Kyle asked, still clutching the pillow.

"Magic can be stolen," Clotho said.

"Especially," Lachesis said, "from people who don't have theirs under control."

Travers wasn't sure that was a bad thing. "So?" he said. "Who'd miss what they didn't know they had?"

"You are at the most risk, Travers," Atropos said.

"You have had your magic so long that it has integrated into your personality," Clotho said.

"If you lose the magic," Lachesis said, "you will lose yourself."

"Hmm," Zoe muttered. "I thought that was *my* problem."

The Fates ignored her, but Kyle gave her a frightened look.

His boy was traumatized. Travers pushed himself off the floor and walked over to his son, putting his arm around him.

"What about Kyle?" Travers asked.

"He will be in even more danger when he turns twenty-one," Atropos said. "He will have a great magic. Yours is tiny. But his is already incorporating into himself."

Kyle was trembling so hard it felt like he was having his own private earthquake. Travers pulled him even closer.

"So what do we do?" Travers asked.

"Learn," Clotho said.

"And learn quickly," Lachesis said.

"You'll both need mentors," Atropos said.

"Both of us?" Travers asked. "Not just me?"

The Fates nodded in unison.

Zoe continued to chomp on that piece of pizza, as if she hadn't eaten for days. She watched the proceedings with wide eyes. Travers couldn't tell if she approved or not, and for the first time since meeting her, he didn't care.

"We believe," Clotho said slowly, "that we can mentor young Kyle for a short time until the appropriate person is found."

"You can?" Travers blurted. He didn't want these women training his son to do anything.

"Mentoring is a complex process," Lachesis said.

"Requiring active magic." Zoe's mouth was full, but her meaning was clear. The Fates couldn't help Kyle if they had no magic.

"Not in the early stages," Atropos said. "When the student has no magic, no magic is needed to block the errors. Early training is simply theory."

"But Kyle has magic," Travers said. "He can read minds."

"It is not exactly magic," Clotho said. "More of a manifestation of a later problem."

"Manifestation?" Kyle asked.

"Don't worry about it," Zoe said. "It's not that important."

"Are they right?" Travers asked her.

"You're checking with someone else about magic issues?" Lachesis's back stiffened. In fact, all of the Fates sat up straighter. Travers wondered what that trick looked like when the women actually had magic to help them look taller.

"Well," he said, "I mean, I've never known you with magic, and—"

Atropos made a sound between a growl and a sigh. "This has got to end soon."

"We were too easily persuaded to go along with this charade," Clotho said.

"You were the ones who wanted to cook dinner," Kyle said, sounding perilously close to tears.

"Not that charade," Lachesis said. "The one Zeus perpetrated. The one that has led to those . . . children. The one that will allow licentiousness and loveless futures for the next thousand years."

"Being a bit dramatic, aren't we?" Zoe asked.

"You saw them," Atropos said. "You know what we're talking about."

"Actually," Zoe said, "I heard that you weren't exactly competent when you took over the job."

This time Clotho made the growly, sighing sound. And it made Travers nervous. He pulled Kyle even closer.

"We were never that bad," Clotho said. "We at least knew our mages, knew our job, and knew our powers. These children don't know anything. They're puppets of their father's. If they get the post permanently, everything will be ruined."

"Well," Zoe said, setting her pizza crust down. "Not everything."

"How can you say that?" Lachesis's voice was growing shrill. "After you've—"

"Seen them?" Zoe said. "Because I know incompetence,

and even their father will get tired of this at some point. But that doesn't mean these girls can't seriously screw up in the meantime."

Atropos sighed. The Fates eased back down to their normal size.

"What I don't understand," Zoe said, "is what you can do without magic."

"That's easy," Clotho said.

"Not easy, exactly," Lachesis corrected.

"But understandable," Atropos said.

"All we have to do is find the wheel," Clotho said.

"What wheel?" Zoe asked.

Travers was watching all of them speak, moving his head to track woman to woman to woman. He was getting tennis neck.

"Our spinning wheel," Lachesis said, as if that explained everything.

"Spinning wheel?" Zoe asked.

"I thought you knew all about our history," Atropos said rather bitterly.

"Apparently I don't." Zoe sighed and sat down. She crossed her legs and tugged her skirt closer to her knee. She looked lovely, even though she was clearly tired.

"Um." Travers raised his free hand slightly, feeling like a recalcitrant school child. "Before we get too far off topic, can I ask one question?"

"You mean two questions," Clotho said.

"No," Travers said. "I mean one."

"But you already asked one," Lachesis said. "So you need permission for two."

He was getting a headache. He wanted to blame the lingering smell of stinky cheese, but he suspected it was caused by the heat and an entire day of conversation with the Fates.

"Okay," he said, as if he were humoring a three-year-old, "two questions."

"You may ask one question," Atropos said.

"Then he can't ask anything," Kyle said. "Be fair!"

"We *are* being fair," Clotho said. "He wasted one question. Only one is left."

Okay. There was a circular logic to that, but not one Travers wanted to explore.

Zoe gave him a sympathetic glance, and he wondered if she realized that he had just saved her from finding out what the case was. He wondered if she appreciated his efforts, or if she had changed her mind again.

"I was wondering," he said slowly, "how long you would mentor Kyle?"

"Until Zoe's done with you, of course," Lachesis said.

"Like hell," Zoe said. "I told you. I'm not taking on a baby magician."

Travers felt his cheeks heat. What was it about this woman that made him feel at turns like a desirable man and a teenage boy?

"Train him, Zanthia," Atropos said. "You won't regret it."

"Just like I won't regret going into Faerie?" Zoe asked.

"We're not sure you have to go into Faerie, dear," Clotho said. "That's just where you start."

"Huh?" Zoe asked.

"Looking for the wheel," Lachesis said.

"Perhaps you two could do it together," Atropos said with a smile.

"So that's it," Zoe said, as if she had made a realization. She threw the pizza crust down like it was a weapon she no longer wanted. "He's not my true love. You can't manipulate something like that. When are you going to learn?"

"What?" That word came out of Travers's mouth, and he

didn't recall thinking it, let alone sending the signal from his brain to his lips. No one had mentioned love before, let alone true love.

Except Zoe. In the context of never having any.

Travers's cheeks heated. "This is some kind of joke, isn't it?"

All of the women looked at him. Kyle pressed closer.

"The magic, the tricks—you got me to believe those. But you—" Travers pointed at the Fates—"you lied. You and my sister did collude, didn't you? On getting me 'trained' and getting me married at the same time. She's happy so she wants me to be happy."

"That's not a bad thing," Kyle whispered.

"I *am* happy!" Travers shouted, which, even to him, didn't sound happy at all. He lowered his voice. "I mean, I *was* happy. I have a great kid and a great life, and I don't really want to change that. I've been dragged to this city against my will. I've stayed, I've done my part, but I'm not falling in love on command."

He had to force himself not to look at Zoe. He hadn't fallen in love with her. He *hadn't*. He knew he hadn't. It wasn't possible. Love at first sight or, at least, love during the first day—only happened in fairy tales.

Kyle elbowed him.

Travers frowned. Kyle overheard that thought and had a point. Or might have a point, if Travers was exactly sure what Kyle was thinking. (It wasn't fair that his own kid had an advantage in this area.) They were in a place with faeries—real faeries, with magic, and everything. And three women who used to have magic powers, and one woman who still did.

Maybe this was a faerie tale.

"Bingo, Dad," Kyle whispered.

"I don't care," Travers whispered back.

"What?" Clotho asked.

Travers sat up straighter. Zoe was staring at him, her beautiful eyes wide. She apparently hadn't expected him to object to being in love with her. And he wasn't, really. He was objecting to losing control over his life, to being manipulated and forced out of his rut and being commanded to change.

He didn't want to change. He liked himself. He liked Kyle. He even liked L.A.

"Dad," Kyle whispered, nodding toward the Fates.

They were still staring at him, as if they expected him to say something.

"I don't care what you all want," Travers said. "I'm my own man. I make my own choices. And if you're trying to manipulate me into spending time with Zoe, then that's the worst way of getting me to do it."

"Me, too," Zoe said, crossing her arms.

"Stubborn," Lachesis said.

"Usually that would be the basis of a relationship," Atropos said. "Look how much they have in common."

It was clear that the Fates were no longer talking to Travers or Zoe. The Fates were talking to each other.

"Strong personalities," Clotho said.

"Similar belief systems," Lachesis said.

"All lost," Atropos said with a sigh.

"Lost?" Kyle sat up, pushing away from his dad. "What do you mean, *lost*?"

"It's clear," Clotho said, "that the laws of romance are already breaking down."

"Zeus wants love out of the equation, and somehow those children of his, through their incompetence, are making that possible," Lachesis said.

"Otherwise, the two of you would fall into each other's arms," Atropos said.

"Or maybe," Zoe said, raising her chin slightly, "we're not meant to have a relationship."

Travers felt his stomach twist. He didn't want to be forced into a relationship with anyone; then again, Zoe was the first person who had interested him in a long time.

That feeling couldn't be wrong, could it? It couldn't be magically applied, like paint to a wall, could it? Feelings had to come from the inside, didn't they?

"Perhaps you're right," Clotho said to Zoe.

"Perhaps we made a mistake," Lachesis said.

"It could be us after all," Atropos said.

"We've been without magic for so long now that we might be making errors that we're unaware of," Clotho said.

Then all three Fates sighed.

"Maybe we're the only ones who want the world the way it was," Lachesis said.

"Now wait a minute," Zoe said. "I met those Interim Fates. They're a disaster."

"Then at least help us locate the wheel," Atropos said.

"And then you'll take this problem to someone else?" Zoe asked.

"We'll take ourselves along with it," Clotho said. "Isn't that what you want?"

Zoe glanced at Travers, and quickly looked away. Not before he saw something vulnerable in her eyes, something almost fearful.

"Our lives would be our own again," Travers said to her.

"And you can make your own decisions," Lachesis said.

"About life," Atropos said.

"About love," Clotho said.

"About everything," Lachesis said.

Zoe let out a long breath. "All right," she said. "That I'll do."

"What about Dad?" Kyle asked, echoing Travers's thought, one he had decided not to vocalize. He could've muzzled his kid, but instead, he just shook his head slightly.

"He has many options," Atropos said.

"But we must warn you," Clotho said.

"Others will try to steal your magic, now that you've tapped it," Lachesis said.

"The drive across the West is particularly treacherous," Atropos said.

"There are many lost and lonely and starving mages," Clotho said, "looking for any advantage they can get."

Travers bit his lower lip. The Fates looked at each other, as if they weren't talking to him at all.

"I worry most about the child," Lachesis said.

Travers's arm tightened around Kyle. Kyle eased in closer.

"This still feels like manipulation," Travers said. "I've taken care of myself for years. I'm sure I'll be fine on a trip back to Oregon, a trip I've taken dozens of times."

Zoe made a clicking sound behind her teeth, almost a tsk-tsk. Travers glanced at her. She gave him a sheepish shrug.

"I'm afraid in this case the Fates are right," she said.

"In this case?" Atropos asked, sounding indignant.

"There are mages who would steal your magic," Zoe said, as if Atropos hadn't spoken.

"But only now, only after I've met all of you." Travers couldn't keep the sarcasm from his tone. Kyle leaned in even closer. Travers wasn't sure his son could hug him any tighter.

"You've deliberately tapped your magic," Zoe said. "It's like taking a cover off a pool. Now it reflects the light, and everyone can sense it. Before, it wasn't as obvious."

"So I'll put the cover back on," Travers said.

"It's not that simple," Zoe said. "The analogy breaks down. It's as if in taking the cover off, the cover has vanished and the pool will keep growing. You're a magic attractor, so long as your powers remain untamed."

"I'm sure you've had trouble before," Clotho said.

"But you probably explained it away as some other circumstance," Lachesis said.

"Like those smoke rings," Kyle whispered.

Travers looked at his son in horror. They had to vacate a hotel near Redding on the way to Vivian's wedding because the room they were staying in—and only that room—was filled with smoke rings. When Travers tried to explain it to the desk clerk, he had said it was as if an invisible person sat in the room, smoking a pipe and exhaling in little rings. The clerk had muttered something about the Caterpillar in *Alice in Wonderland,* added a rather snide comment about everyone imagining hookah pipes—and pointed to the smoke rings that had followed Travers into the lobby.

That was when he decided to leave. He had driven nearly fifty miles before he found another hotel to take them. By then the smoke rings were gone.

The next morning he scanned the local news channels, expecting to hear about a hotel that had burned down near Redding, but nothing got reported. It didn't make any California papers the following day, either, and Travers *had* chalked the whole thing up to an oddity, even though Kyle had told him that the smoke seemed evil.

Travers shook his head. "This has been the most incredible day of my life," he said.

Zoe gave him a sympathetic smile. "Sadly, it won't stay that way."

His gaze met hers and held it. This time she didn't look away. The attraction still floated between them, but now he questioned what caused it—a real attraction or even more magic.

And the questioning made him feel sad. He wanted the attraction to be real.

She closed her eyes, her long, dark lashes brushing against the skin of her cheek. Then she sighed, as if she had made some kind of resolution. When she opened her eyes, they seemed slightly different—a little more determined maybe, or a little more resigned.

"I can teach you a few survival skills," she said. "I can get you started enough to make the trip to Oregon to be mentored."

Travers should have felt relieved, but he didn't. He didn't want survival skills. He had been speaking the truth when he said he wanted his life back.

"How long will I have to stay in Oregon?" he asked the Fates.

"Mentoring takes anywhere from two to five years," Atropos said.

"Depending on the student," Clotho added.

"And the level of ability," Lachesis said.

"In your case," Atropos said, "two years should do."

"Two *years*?" Travers asked. "But I have a job, a business, a life in L.A."

"Then perhaps those children can find you a new mentor there," Clotho said, sniffing as if the Interim Fates were in the room and hadn't bathed in weeks.

"Either way," Zoe said, "I'll get you enough control to go wherever you need to."

She spoke softly, making it clear that she was only talking to him.

"How long will that take?" Travers asked, knowing he sounded ungrateful.

"A few weeks," Zoe said. "Depending on my caseload, and how long it takes me to find this wheel."

"You're taking our job?" Lachesis asked.

"Against my better judgement," Zoe said.

"And she's mentoring young Travers," Atropos said in a stage whisper. "How much better could it get?"

"I don't know," Travers said. "it would be kinda nice not to be mentored at all."

Kyle buried his face in Travers's chest, as if he didn't want to see the fallout from that comment. But Travers didn't care. In the last week, his life had veered out of control, and it would never be the same again. He was smart enough to realize that.

He also knew that some of his disappointment came from the interaction with Zoe. He did want to spend time with her, but not as a student with a teacher. He wanted to get to know the woman, to understand how she felt about life, not learn how she made the Fates disappear or how she convinced a guy who looked like an apple witch that the Fates hadn't lost their magic.

"I think we all wished we had the luxury of forgoing a mentor," Zoe said, "but none of us do. I promise not to be hard on you."

Travers leaned back in surprise. "Hard on me?"

"In the training," Zoe said.

"Like her mentor was with her," Clotho said.

"It's okay, Dad," Kyle whispered from somewhere near Travers's chest. "I believe in you."

Travers was glad someone did. Although he doubted Kyle would like this situation much when he really realized how much their life would change. Right now, Kyle probably saw this as a way out of summer school.

But it was more than that. It was a whole new way of living, a way Travers wasn't sure he would ever learn to like.

Fifteen

Zoe leaned her head against the ripped leather seat in the back of the cab. She was exhausted, but she knew better than to close her eyes. The ride from the Strip to her house would only take about ten minutes at this time of night. Normally, she would have walked, but her feet had ached for hours now, and even if she spelled her high heels into tennis shoes, the walk wouldn't be any more pleasant.

The cab headed east on Tropicana, past the UNLV campus. There, as Zoe gazed out the window, she saw people walking—summer school students heading to the library, going to their dorms. The University of Nevada-Las Vegas was a little oasis of normality in a town that didn't believe in it. Students came here, and although they indulged in the Vegas nightlife, they didn't really become part of it.

They never saw beneath the city's surface.

Perhaps that was Zoe's problem. She always saw beneath the surface.

Zoe sighed. She still wasn't sure how or when she had decided to take the Fates' case. They said she would have to locate the wheel, and that was when she got the idea: she might be able to find it—maybe even take it—without venturing into Faerie herself.

The cab turned north on Pecos Road, heading into the quiet neighborhood that Zoe had lived in since the mid-1970s. Her house was in a cul-de-sac off two other side roads. She had nearly an acre with tall trees and a lot of landscaping which had cost her a small fortune to put in. It also cost her a small fortune to maintain—Vegas was high desert, and keeping any kind of plant alive in this climate required a drip irrigation system, more water than the city wanted her to use, and the services of a gardener.

She could afford it. She had lived pretty frugally most of her life, making sure she always had enough money to last her several years without work. The gardener felt like a major indulgence, one she couldn't live without.

The house was a two-story, modified adobe style split-level, about as trendy as she could have gotten back when she was buying. She had grown tired of her 1950s ranch with its 850 square feet, and thought she needed 4,000 square feet of privacy.

Most of the rooms were closed off now, but she wasn't willing to sell the house. She didn't want to lose the yard, the landscaping, and the pool.

The pool was her secret pride and joy. She had learned when she lived in Los Angeles in the 1930s that living in a desert climate without a pool was like living in Aspen without a pair of skis.

She had expanded the pool thirty years ago, making it twenty-five meters long, with a small concrete island in the center. There were bridges to that island, and a pavilion built in the middle, providing shade even in the middle of the day. She swam every morning, and often in the evenings, and on days when she had no work, she sat in the chaise longue and read, enjoying the warmth and the shade and the bits of privacy she had bought.

It was not the life of an average detective. It certainly wasn't the life she had imagined for herself when she had come to Vegas. And it was light years from the Hammett/Chandler ideal of a grungy apartment with a disillusioned detective who only spent as much time in the room as she needed to sleep off the previous night's drunk.

She had lived that way for a few years, and while it played well in fiction, in practice it left her muzzy-headed, lonely, and dissatisfied. Somewhere along the way, she realized that her office could be sparse and noir, but her home had to be comfortable, maybe even spectacular, or her life wasn't worth living.

The cab pulled up in front of the arch-shaped garage door. A hedgerow going off in either direction hid the rest of the house from view except for the solar lamps she had installed last year, illuminating the base of the adobe through the cactus garden.

"You gonna be okay, miss?" the driver asked through the window, before he requested his fee.

Zoe blinked and sat up, wondering for a moment if she had fallen asleep. But she hadn't. She had paid attention to the entire drive.

Then she realized that he thought she was a tourist, coming to visit a local, and something about her home made it seem like her visit would be an uncomfortable one.

She smiled at the man, grateful for his concern—that was the thing about Vegas that no one mentioned: the locals still acted as if it were a small town—and unzipped the top of her purse, looking for her wallet.

"I'll be fine," she said. "I live here."

He raised his eyebrows as if he didn't believe her, but he didn't say anything more. She gave him his fee plus a healthy tip, and let herself out into the warm desert night.

The temperature had dropped twenty degrees, making it in the low nineties, which wasn't so bad, considering. The temperature might actually dip into the eighties before dawn.

She could remember when Vegas summer nights got truly cool—no asphalt and car exhaust and haze to hold in the day's heat. But that seemed like a long time ago.

Everything seemed like a long time ago.

She was feeling old tonight, perhaps because she was attracted to a much younger man.

Zoe smiled at herself, and threaded her way through the hedgerow to the front door. The plants were damp—her gardener clearly had misted them against city regulations. She didn't have the heart to reprimand him.

She unlocked her front door, shut off the security system, and took a deep lungful of air-conditioned cold. She left the house at a consistent 75 degrees in the summer, which felt positively frigid on days like today, and didn't waste nearly as much electricity as the old days, when summer air conditioning temperatures were a standard 60 or below.

She kicked off her painful shoes and walked barefoot across the shag carpet. The entry was the most spectacular part of her house.

Designed for faculty parties, the house had a number of features that made it the perfect home for the UNLV basketball coach or provost. Not too far from the university, but fancy enough to impress all those alums.

But the builder had forgotten that university salaries, even in the cash-rich UNLV basketball program, weren't the same as, say, mobsters' salaries, and the house had remained empty until Zoe bought it, three years later.

Still, she loved the weird opulence. In this, the entry and great room, the ceiling was high enough for Rick Fox to stand on Shaquille O'Neal's shoulders and barely brush the painted wood. A minibar stood to the left of the door, but there was nothing mini about it. Made of rich, dark wood, the bar looked more like it had been stolen from the front of a church than a place for people to enjoy drinks.

And then there was the fireplace. It stood directly across from the door, and was lined in marble. The fireplace was large enough for three witches and a cauldron to stand inside it—or three Fates and a cooking pot, at least.

Zoe shook her head. She wasn't going to get the Fates out of her mind as quickly as she had hoped. She glanced at the grand piano, which was the final finishing touch in this front room, and knew that playing wouldn't relax her tonight.

Nothing would, not even that hot bath and book she had promised herself earlier.

She reset the alarm and walked through the great room to the kitchen. She had remodeled the kitchen ten years ago, but it was still small compared to the rest of the house. She didn't mind. She liked cozy, and she didn't cook enough to make an elaborate kitchen worthwhile.

She pulled open the fridge, got out a fat-free strawberry yogurt drink, and sipped on it while she turned on the radio. Soft jazz with a '40s edge, making her think of the days just after the war, when L.A. was still a small town, and she was thinking of moving away from it, thinking that she'd find less corruption somewhere else.

And, she had to admit, she was getting away from yet another failed relationship, this one with a bookie she'd met while on the job. Odd that after she had broken up with a bookie, she had moved to a town that made its living off gambling.

She had thought she had a lot in common with the bookie—a taste for lowlife, but no urge to live it; an understanding of the way the world worked, or didn't; and a willingness to put up with the seamier sides of a town that seemed composed of seamy sides.

In the end, though, she realized that what she had thought were compatible traits were simply excuses. He liked her because she gave him legitimacy and she, in turn, had used him for leads.

And then there had been the issue of the magic.

He had none. And he had accidentally found out about hers, creating a scene she'd never forget. He wanted her to use it, to abuse it, to make them both rich, to make them famous, to make them the couple of the century.

And he begged her for immortality, as if that were in her power to give.

She was breaking up with him when she had been summoned to the Fates, who reminded her about the no-talking-to-mortals rule. Zoe had outlined what happened, trying to make it clear that his discovery was an accident.

She wasn't ever sure if the Fates believed her, but they didn't punish her. They made it clear, though, that future violations wouldn't be tolerated.

They had scared her that day, and she had believed them. She'd heard of their punishments—Sisyphus and the rock was their idea, although no one remembered what the crime had been—and she wanted nothing of it.

So she vanished from L.A. Vanished and went to Vegas, but stubbornly did not change her name.

Maybe she thought the bookie would come looking for her, riding into the neon-coated streets in his white convertible, a hero on a white horse.

But she never heard from him again. And even though she dated, she never got involved again, either. Better to keep her emotions in check than go through another wrenching experience of a serious breakup for the umpteenth time in a hundred years.

And now she had promised to help Travers Kineally. He wasn't mortal, but he was the next best thing—a man newly arrived in his magic. A man with eight years of misunderstandings and mistakes behind him.

A man with an eleven-year-old son, which made him a man with a history, although not a history as bad as hers.

Zoe carried the yogurt drink into the nearby half-bath and looked at herself in the mirror. She still looked mid-thirties. No new wrinkles had appeared on her face since Lincoln was president. She didn't have any gray hairs, and she worked hard to keep her figure without resorting to magical treatments.

But even if she were to take how old she looked, as opposed to how old she was, she was too old for Travers. She had been over one hundred years old when Travers Kineally was born. When that sank in, what would he think?

Modern American men had enough trouble being younger than the women they dated. Imagine being this much younger.

Then Zoe smiled, and the crow's feet she'd had since she got her magic reappeared like valued old friends. She wasn't going to date Travers Kineally. She was going to teach him. The way old crones were supposed to handle young and studly men.

Zoe sighed, took another sip of the artificially sweetened yogurt drink, and stepped out of the bathroom. She wandered into the TV room, turned the jazz on in here, and sank into her 1970s couch. Big as a single bed with cushions that had only gotten softer with age, this couch was where she went when she needed to think.

And she really needed to contemplate all that she had learned this day—beyond Travers Kineally, who was a problem in and of himself.

"Aaaack! Where you been? Where you been?" The voice sounded almost machine-like, but it belonged to her temporary familiar, Black Bart. He sat on his perch near the couch and peered down at her, his parrot's eyes glittering as he took her in.

"Working, Bart," she said with a sigh. She was glad that

Black Bart was her temporary familiar—an Interim Familiar, just like the Interim Fates, and just about as competent. Fortunately, in the short term, she didn't need a competent familiar. She just needed one that would keep her magic pure, and the familiar's very presence did that.

Otherwise, she wouldn't have been able to use Black Bart as a substitute at all.

"Bartie like the Babe," the bird said, and hopped down to the side of the couch, wanting his feathers stroked. He'd been saying that about babes ever since he met Zoe.

The proprietor of the magic store, who catered to both faeries and mages, said Bart found Zoe attractive. She certainly hoped that analysis was wrong—the last thing she needed was a jealous parrot—but Bart certainly seemed proprietary in his own little avian way.

What she needed was her own familiar, not a borrowed one, and one of her many realizations today was that she wouldn't get her own familiar, not as long as the Interim Fates were in office. They didn't even know enough to clean up after a rather panicked dachshund; they certainly wouldn't know how to create the perfect match between the right mage and the right familiar.

"Babe need lunch?" Bart asked, which was his way of asking if she would make any food soon. He usually got a treat when she did, mostly to keep him quiet.

She did a lot to keep him quiet.

"Not at the moment, Bart," she said, feeling lucky that he hadn't heard her open the refrigerator door. "Maybe later."

"Later, later, later," he said, like a rejected child. She half expected him to add, *It's always later with you.* But of course he didn't. He might be a familiar, blessed with his own peculiar magic, but he couldn't really speak any more than any other familiar could. She would have to spell him to give him a capacity beyond a normal parrot's.

Zoe leaned back in the couch, letting the cushions envelop her. She put her bare feet on the coffee table and closed her eyes. The Interim Fates had worried her, and Nero had scared her. Partly because he had appeared so abruptly, but mostly because of his own personal brand of incompetence.

He had only a little magic—as evidenced by his entrance—yet he was willing to use it to attack the Fates. Fortunately, he wasn't very bright, and Zoe had been able to fool him.

But she might not be so lucky next time.

And if something happened to the Fates, then the mages would be stuck with the Interim Fates for good.

So she had agreed to take the case, against her better judgement. She didn't want to be in the middle of magical politics, but she felt like she had no choice.

Travers certainly couldn't help the Fates, even if he had wanted to, and getting them to someone else—someone competent—might prove difficult. It wasn't until after Zoe had completed her disappearance spell that she realized what danger she had put the Fates in.

She had held them in the magic stream while she dealt with Nero. Someone else could have found them and swept them along, and Zoe might never have been able to find them.

It had taken nearly two more hours, between her and Travers, to get the entire story of the wheel out of the Fates. The women went through dozens of digressions, and one small magic tutorial session for Kyle (who seemed oblivious—only Travers seemed interested).

Finally, something like a coherent story emerged: the wheel was a spinning wheel and, of course, it had magic. Thousands of years ago, the Fates used it to enhance their powers whenever they were called upon to administer justice. The wheel increased the Fates' ability a thousandfold, and they needed it in those long-ago days.

At least, Clotho believed they needed it. Lachesis didn't, calling it a crutch, and Atropos tried to calm the disagreement—one that had clearly been going on for centuries.

Zoe put the heels of her hands against her closed eyes. She couldn't even think about the Fates without going into a digression. They were rubbing off on her and she hated it.

"Babe need a backrub?" Bart asked, apparently sensing her distress.

"Babe needs a new life," Zoe said without opening her eyes.

"Backrub only," Bart said, with his uncanny ability to communicate.

"No thanks, kiddo," Zoe said, and sank deeper into the couch.

The wheel had disappeared three thousand years ago. At least, the Fates thought it was about three thousand years ago. Their sense of time was so fluid, though, that Zoe couldn't be sure if the wheel vanished a thousand years ago, three thousand years ago, or last week.

Well, she was fairly certain that it hadn't disappeared last week since the Fates were already looking for it then.

Still, she had never worked on a case this old or one this cold. The Fates had done nothing to find the wheel. They hadn't used magic and they hadn't done the old-fashioned asking-around either.

They believed they knew what happened.

At the time, the faeries and the mages were having a power struggle over dominion of the mortals. (The Fates had a long digression over this: Lachesis had called the conflict a war; Atropos had said it was merely a struggle; and Clotho had called it unimportant.)

The faeries were coming up in importance—they were gaining footholds in parts of Europe that the Fates couldn't seem to touch—and they wanted even more power. The Faerie

Kings snuck into the Hall of Justice and made off with the wheel.

At least, that was what Zoe thought happened. The Fates had erupted into a very bitter, very personal argument that had stopped as suddenly as it started. Travers had given Zoe a perplexed look and she had shrugged.

She had never heard of the Fates fighting before that night.

There was more to this Faerie King story than the Fates were willing to admit.

The upshot, though, was that the Fates had survived just fine without the wheel. It had augmented their powers in the early days, but it hadn't done much once they learned how to control their own enhanced magicks.

But the wheel had powers of its own, powers that amplified—and sometimes created—magic where there was none. And because the Fates had used the wheel in the past, they had a tie to it.

The wheel could restore their magic, not just at the level where it was before they gave it up, but strengthened a thousand times. The Fates would be strong enough to take on Zeus and any cohorts he had among the Powers That Be.

And that was more than enough to get Zoe to sign on—that, and the Interim Fates, and Nero.

"Bart want cracker," Black Bart said.

"No, you don't." Zoe let her hands drop. "You hate crackers."

"Okay. Lunch." The bird was hungry. She would have to check his food dish. It was probably empty. He always stuffed himself when she left him home alone.

"Lunch, then," Zoe said and stood up. She had a lot of work to do. Tracing the wheel would not be easy. She hoped that it had found its way out of Faerie and into some museum collection, but she doubted that had happened.

Still, she had to start somewhere. The Internet would be her initial guide—there had to be art or artifacts that pictured the wheel. They might not be accurate (some of the early drawings of the Fates pictured them as wizened old women, a guise they had never worn), but the pictures would at least give her a place to start.

She might also try to hack into some of the faerie sites, and see what was listed in their version of e-Bay. Faeries didn't care about money; they collected items with totemic and magical value. That was one of the many reasons faeries ran casinos; people came in with their lucky rabbits' feet or their good-luck hats and often left without them. Superstition imbued those items with a slight radiance, and faeries valued that radiance.

Zoe had no idea how much power the wheel gave off, but she suspected it was a lot. And maybe, just maybe, she'd be lucky enough to find traces of it on the Web.

Otherwise, an actual search might take her into Faerie, where she didn't want to go.

And she certainly didn't want to go alone, with no one to back her up. The Fates had no power, and Travers didn't know how to use his—he'd just be a victim in there.

Zoe had no one else to ask.

If she were even strong enough to get past her fears, which she most decidedly was not.

"Lunch," Bart said, and it was not a question. It was a demand.

"Sorry," Zoe said. She had gotten lost in thought. Just like she would get lost in Faerie.

This case was going to be dangerous. She would have to do everything to remain alert, cautious—and safe.

Even if it meant going back on her promise to the Fates.

Sixteen

The next morning, Travers had definitive proof that he had not been dreaming: he woke up in a king-sized bed in a hotel suite in Las Vegas.

He had hoped that the last week had been some elaborate nightmare, dreamed in installments, rather like a mini-series sent by Mr. Sandman.

Of course, Travers couldn't get that lucky.

He ordered breakfast from room service, and managed to be showered and dressed long before it arrived. He set the complimentary *USA Today* next to his chair, since a newspaper was always part of his morning routine, and he waited until the waiter had left and the food was spread on the table before waking Kyle.

Kyle was not—by any stretch—a morning person.

Travers was. Each new day was a new opportunity, and he liked looking at the day as if he were starting over with a clean slate. Only this morning, he felt like the slate was rather smudged, and he didn't know what to do about it.

He had called his office, sent the clients with emergencies

to another CPA whose work he respected, and told his secretary to let the rest of his clients know that Travers wouldn't be back for another week due to family problems.

Kyle staggered out of his own room, and shuffled to the table, looking more like an old man than an eleven-year-old boy. He had splashed water on his face, but forgot to dry it off. His skin was dotted with droplets, his hair slicked back against his scalp. The front of his pajama top was soaking, but Travers didn't say anything.

Kyle would notice eventually, when he became awake enough.

Right now, he wasn't even awake enough to notice that his father had ordered him waffles with strawberries and whipped cream, a meal that Travers usually called dessert and not breakfast. Travers had also ordered a plate of sausages which, he figured, if they didn't eat them, Bartholomew Fang would. Travers got pancakes for himself, and a fruit bowl, which he would save for later.

The thing that smelled the best, though, was the coffee. Travers didn't realize how very exhausted he was—the stresses of the last week, and the revelation about himself, had put a strain on him that he wasn't used to.

Kyle was halfway through his waffle and strawberries before he paused to rub his eyes. Then he stretched, sighed, and returned to his breakfast.

Travers smiled. At least this part of the morning was normal. Kyle would finish eating and soon the conversation would start, as his son slowly realized the day had begun.

Only this time, Travers wasn't quite as willing as usual to have a conversation. He still had a lot of thinking to do. He no longer doubted that he had magical ability. In fact, his point of view on that had changed so much in the last twenty-four hours that he now wondered how he could have doubted it.

His own capacity for self-delusion startled him. Last night, he had made the mistake of trying to fall asleep by counting the magical incidents that he could remember—anything odd, anything out of the ordinary. He paused with each one, recalling the events, and started to wonder how anyone could have missed the cause.

He was sure the Fates had a theory as to how he could have missed it, and he knew that Zoe would have an opinion.

She seemed to have an opinion about everything else.

He liked that about her. Her self-assurance, her strength, her obvious intelligence. During his long bout of self-analysis the night before, he realized he would have been attracted to her, magic or not.

And that presented a problem.

It presented several problems, actually. The first was how to deal with his attraction to a woman who was going to act as his teacher. The second problem was how to convince her that he was interested—truly interested, not just magically obligated. And the third concerned Kyle.

Travers had vowed not to get involved with anyone while his son was at home. Travers had seen too many of his friends bounce from "serious" relationship to "serious" relationship, leaving their children confused, scared, and hurt.

Cheryl had already done a lot of damage to Kyle, by leaving and not returning, not writing, not caring about anyone but herself. Travers was determined to cause as few injuries to his son as possible, and one way to guarantee that was to make sure Kyle didn't bond with anyone who wouldn't be in his life for the rest of his life.

You couldn't guarantee that with girlfriends, and you couldn't explain casual relationships to a child—maybe not even to an eleven-year-old boy. And explaining attraction was even more out of the question: Travers couldn't ask his son for permission to explore an interest in a woman who might simply turn out to be a passing fad.

Kyle pushed his plate away as Bartholomew Fang padded out of the bedroom. The dog, apparently, was even less of a morning person than Kyle was.

"Does the dog have to go out?" Travers asked.

"I took him out a few hours ago," Kyle said.

Travers felt the pancakes he had eaten turn to lead in his stomach. "Without waking me?"

"Don't sweat it, Dad," Kyle said. "We went onto the patio. There's some plants tucked against the rail."

Travers wasn't sure if he was more appalled at Kyle's willingness to let the dog use a patio plant as a bathroom or the fact that Kyle thought it was appropriate.

Then Kyle giggled. "You're too tense, Dad. We went just outside the front door. Of the hotel."

The pancakes felt even heavier. Kyle had no idea how dangerous other cities were. He and Travers lived a pretty secluded life in their little portion of Los Angeles, and Kyle knew the risks there. He just couldn't assume every place was as safe as the ones he knew at home.

"Kyle, you have to let me know when you're leaving the room," Travers said.

"You'd've figured it out," Kyle said.

"Next time you tell me." Travers heard his own father in his voice, and he didn't care. "It's dangerous out there."

"The bellman was watching the entire time," Kyle said.

"I don't care," Travers said. "You don't know this place."

"Neither do you." Kyle grabbed a sausage and broke it into little pieces with his fingers. He set the pieces on the floor, and Bartholomew Fang vacuumed them up so quickly that Travers wondered if the dog got some of the rug as well.

"Just promise me," Travers said. "Promise me you'll let me know where you are at all times."

Kyle sighed. "I didn't think you'd be so mad."

"I'm not mad," Travers said. "I'm just . . ."

How to explain to his son how unnerved he was? How off balance? He hoped he was broadcasting, as they called it, because he didn't want Kyle to sense the anxiety as well. Travers had worked really hard to be solid for Kyle, and now Travers wasn't even sure who he was, let alone what would happen next.

"Scared?" Kyle whispered. He didn't look up.

Travers wondered if Kyle could sense anything, and he toyed with lying.

"Am I scared?" Travers repeated while he thought about how to field that question.

Kyle nodded, still watching Fang snuffle at the carpet, searching for more sausage.

"I guess maybe I am," Travers said, deciding on truth as the best strategy. "I don't know what's ahead."

"Lots of lights," Kyle said.

"Hmm?" Travers didn't understand. It sounded like a non sequitur, but sometimes Kyle made predictions that came true.

"You didn't know what was ahead," Kyle said. "But I can see it. Lots of lights. Neon lights."

Travers gave him an indulgent smile. "We are in Las Vegas."

Kyle shook his head. "No, Dad. The lights are swirling, and they come in very close, and I'm not sure you escape them."

"Escape them?" Travers asked, feeling as if his son had had too many conversations with the Fates.

"And Miss Sinclair, she's there, too, along with these guys who seem really mad." Kyle pushed his plate away, something astonishing, considering he still had some strawberries and whipped cream on it. Even Bartholomew Fang gave him a sideways look, although that might have been a request for more sausage.

Travers tried to comprehend what Kyle was telling him.

In the past, Travers would have dismissed it as dream fragments, left over from Kyle's sound sleep, and it was hard to fight those tendencies now.

Kyle must have seen the struggle on Travers's face. Kyle put his hand on Travers's arm and leaned toward him, looking both scared and sincere.

"Dad," Kyle said, "if I promise to be good and do icky basketball without complaining and stuff, can we just go home? I won't write any more comics or talk about magic any more or anything."

Travers stared at his son. Kyle had just offered to give up two things he loved for something Travers had to force him into every year. Had the vision frightened Kyle? Or was something else going on?

"This vision thing," Travers said—he couldn't call it a prophecy without giving it too much weight, and he didn't want to call it a dream without detracting from his son's fear—"it scared you, didn't it?"

Kyle bit his lower lip. Bartholomew Fang whined and pressed his nose against Kyle's knee. Kyle petted him absently, but didn't look at him.

"You like things normal, Dad." Kyle's soft words echoed Travers's earlier thoughts. Travers felt uneasy about that, too. "Because of me, everything's all screwed up."

Travers grabbed his coffee cup as if it were a lifeline, even though he knew that the confusion he felt didn't come from sleepiness, so caffeine wouldn't help. "Everything?"

"We're here because of me," Kyle said. "I begged you to drive the Fates here. And I helped Aunt Vivian convince you to take them to L.A. in the first place."

Bartholomew Fang whined again and shoved his nose against Kyle's hand. Kyle ignored him.

Travers snapped his fingers, and Bartholomew Fang ran

to him. Travers took a piece of sausage and gave it to the dog, who—to his surprise—ignored it.

So the dog did have some powers of his own. He sensed, in canine fashion, the tension in the room and was trying to ameliorate it.

"What are you most afraid of, Kyle?" Travers asked.

To his surprise, Kyle's lower lip trembled, even though his teeth were trying to hold it in place. A tear ran down his cheek, and Kyle wiped at it with the back of his hand.

"Ky?" Travers kept his voice soft.

"Did . . ." Kyle swallowed visibly and had to start again. "Did Mom run away because of the magic?"

Kid psychology, and reinventing the past. Kyle must have thought that Travers was denying his magic for a reason, not because he truly hadn't figured it out.

"Did she leave me because I'm magic?" Travers often started by repeating the question with slightly different wording just to make sure he understood. "I—"

"No," Kyle whispered. "Did she leave because of me?"

Travers felt his breath leave his body as forcefully as if he had fallen from a great height. Kyle had never asked a question like that before, he had never once asked if it was his fault that Cheryl left, even though Kyle's sister Megan, the child psychologist, often asked if Kyle worried about that.

Kyle must have worried about it and not said a single thing. How much else had that kid bottled up inside?

"Your mom and I," Travers said slowly, uncertain if he'd ever talked to Kyle about his mother in quite this way, "we got married when we were seven years older than you."

Another tear hung on Kyle's lower eyelashes but didn't fall. Travers found himself staring at it.

"I know that seems old to you, but it's not. Not really." Travers sighed. He didn't entirely understand what happened, either. He knew what broke up the marriage. He just didn't know why Cheryl had abandoned her son. It was inconceivable to Travers that anyone would ignore this child, let alone never see him again.

Kyle was staring at him as if trying to memorize every single word.

"When you get married," Travers said, "you declare that you're grown up. My parents made it pretty clear that I'd be on my own if I married your mother, and she didn't have any parents, just a grandmother whom she really didn't like. So we were on our own. And it was hard. All we had was a high school education. We couldn't get good jobs and we couldn't rent a nice place, like they have in the commercials."

That last was bitter, and Travers heard it. He had worked all of Kyle's life to keep the bitterness out of his conversations about Cheryl. He wasn't about to let the bitterness creep in now.

"She was happy when she got pregnant," Travers said. "It was just like in the fairy tales, you know? Babies are part of happily ever after."

Kyle blinked and the tear fell. This time, Travers caught it with his forefinger, and then he caressed his son's cheek.

"I was the one who was worried," Travers said. "I worried about money and finding a safe neighborhood for you to grow up in and being the best dad in the world, and maybe in all that worrying, I scared your mom. I don't know."

Kyle's lips had thinned. He looked like he was stretched so tight he would shatter.

Still, Travers knew he had to continue. This was important, maybe the most important conversation they'd had.

"All I know," Travers said, "is that the day you were born, it was like your mom and I switched attitudes. I was thrilled. I'd never seen anyone like you before and I thought you were just the best thing that had ever happened to me."

"And Mom thought I was the worst?" Kyle's voice shook.

Travers's breath caught in his throat. He hadn't meant that, but he understood how his son could hear it that way. That's what made this conversation so very difficult.

"No," Travers said. "Your mom realized that fairy tales weren't true. Babies, particularly newborn babies, are a lot of work. They can't do anything for themselves. They can't talk, they can't tell you what bothers them, all they can do is cry, and eat, and poop. Some newborns can't even really smile, but you could. You had the best smile I'd ever seen."

Travers had told him that before and it always made Kyle grin. Except this time. This time, Kyle couldn't be easily calmed. "So she left because she didn't like taking care of me."

Travers was being very careful to control his thoughts—he wasn't even going to think the adult answer if he could avoid it.

"I don't know why she left," he said, "but here's my guess."

Kyle sat very attentively. Even Bartholomew Fang watched Travers as if the world hung on his answer.

"I think being a grown-up was too much for her," Travers said. "Me, the lack of money, the fact it was so different from the way it looks in the movies—I think she couldn't take it anymore."

"But she left after I was born," Kyle whispered. "It had to be my fault."

Travers shook his head. "It was probably mine. I expected her to be someone she wasn't. I expected her to be the fairy tale wife and mom, and she was just a young girl pretending to be a woman."

He could tell from the slight frown on Kyle's face that the explanation was too adult for his son.

"Some people," Travers said, trying again, "are really good at taking care of other people, whether they're married to them or friends with them or related to them."

"Like you and Aunt Viv," Kyle said.

"Yes," Travers said. "But some people need to be taken care of themselves, even though they're grown-ups."

"Like the Fates," Kyle said.

"Kinda," Travers said. "Only worse. The Fates are trying to take care of themselves. They're just not doing a good job of it at the moment. They've done a good job in the past."

"But they don't understand this world," Kyle said.

"And your mom didn't understand the grown-up world of marriage and children. She ran away from responsibility, Kyle, not from you."

"But I *was* her responsibility," Kyle said.

Travers nodded. He had hoped his son would miss that part, but Kyle proved too intelligent once again.

"You were," Travers said. "But she didn't stay long enough to get to know you. She didn't even try, Kyle. It was just like if the Fates ran away the first time they realized their magic didn't work here. They would never have gotten to see this world; they just would have run away from the first thing that scared them."

Kyle bit his lower lip again. He was still disturbed. It was obvious from his downcast expression and his unwillingness to ask the question that was on his mind.

"Kyle," Travers said, taking his son's hand and holding it tightly. "It wouldn't have mattered if you were a baby or a puppy. She wasn't running away from you. She was running away from me and the failure of our dreams. That's why she hasn't been back."

"Huh?" Kyle asked. He didn't seem to understand this part.

"If she saw you as a real person, if she knew what she had actually left behind, then she might feel some regret. She might have to change her behavior." Travers gave his son a rueful smile. "I don't think she's willing to do that, even now."

"She doesn't sound very nice," Kyle said, and there was anger in his voice. "How come you married somebody who wasn't very nice?"

Travers resisted the urge to contradict Kyle, and reassure him that she was nice.

"I was eighteen when I fell in love with her," Travers said. "I didn't see her any more clearly than she saw me. I don't think we fell in love with people. I think we fell in love with what we made up. And when that turned out to be wrong, she ran away, and I—"

He took a deep breath, and studied his son. This part, Travers had never admitted to Kyle.

"—I let her."

"You could've gone to find her?" Kyle asked, and there was hope in his voice. He probably wanted Travers to do that even now.

"I could have," Travers said. "I don't know what good it would have done. Maybe not any. But I didn't."

"How come?" Kyle asked.

"Because," Travers said softly, "if she couldn't stay when she had something as perfect as you in her life, nothing I had to say would make any difference. She would never see the good things. She would spend her life thinking other people had them, and never realize how wonderful the stuff in her life really was."

There it was, part of the adult theory. But Kyle seemed to understand it.

"You think there was something wrong with her?" Kyle asked.

"Yeah," Travers said, wishing he had thought of putting it that simply. "Yeah, I do."

"Oh," Kyle said, and leaned back in his chair. He stared at his half-finished breakfast. "So you thinking you didn't have magic, that had nothing to do with Mom?"

It took Travers a moment to understand the logic of the question. Kyle had brought all of this up because he believed that Travers had been pretending not to have magic with the thought that magic had driven Cheryl away. So in accepting magic, Travers would have been guaranteeing that Cheryl never came back.

"It had nothing to do with your mom," Travers said. "Just my own blind stupidity."

"You're not stupid, Dad," Kyle said.

"Thanks," Travers said.

Kyle nodded. He slid his plate back, grabbed his fork, and scooped up a large bite of whipped cream and strawberries.

But before he stuffed it in his mouth, he looked at Travers. "Dad, I'm really glad you stayed."

Travers ruffled his son's hair. "Best decision I ever made, Kyle."

Kyle grinned, then set about finishing his breakfast. Travers watched him, feeling even more disconcerted than he had all night. Kyle was feeling the changes, too, just not in the same way. And the stresses on Travers would influence his son as well.

Travers just didn't know how to prevent it.

Seventeen

Zoe felt like she was a general in charge of too many troops. At ten A.M., she went to the hotel to find the Fates still lounging over breakfast and no sign whatsoever of Travers and Kyle. Zoe wasn't sure who to be more irritated at: the Fates, who seemed to think that there was no such thing as time and a schedule; or Travers, who knew there was, but apparently ignored it.

She packed the Fates off to their separate rooms for showers, and was about to pick up the phone to summon Travers and Kyle, when a knock came at the door.

Since the Fates were singing the same song in three different showers (which would have been creepy even if the song hadn't been "Boogie-Woogie Bugle Boy of Company B" [which the Fates mispronounced, in three-part harmony worthy of the Andrews Sisters, as "Boegie-Woegie Bugle Boy"]), Zoe decided it was the better part of valor to answer the door herself, rather than interrupt one of the three chanteuses.

Zoe pulled the door open to find Kyle and Travers standing before her. Kyle looked subdued; his glasses had slid to the end of his nose and were smudged, his hair was badly combed, and he sniffled. Zoe wanted to smooth his hair and ask him what was wrong, but she felt that would be inappropriate, at least in front of his father.

Travers looked even better than he had the day before. His light blue polo shirt and dark jeans emphasized his lean, elegant body, and made his blond hair seem even lighter. The clothes also accented the blue of his eyes. He smiled at her as if nothing was wrong.

"You don't look like a Fate," he said.

"That's because I'm not one, thank heavens," Zoe said, and stood aside.

The first one across the threshold wasn't Kyle or Travers, but Bartholomew, whom she hadn't even noticed. The little round dog waddled past her as if he were king and she was his servant.

"He seems to be doing pretty well," Zoe said.

"Considering how much he's eaten, it's amazing he can walk," Travers said. "What are familiars supposed to do? Eat all the calories in the room so the mage doesn't have to?"

"Only some familiars," Zoe said. "And only if they're named Bartholomew."

"He's still hoping for 'Fang.'" Kyle's voice was a bit watery, too, as if he had been holding back tears.

Zoe closed the door. The singing continued as if it were in surround sound, and Travers looked from one closed door to the next.

"They're not in the same shower, are they?" he asked.

Zoe shook her head.

"They decided on the song and the misinterpretation of the lyrics before they went in, right?"

Zoe shook her head again.

Travers sighed. "Some things I'm never going to get used to."

He stepped farther into the main room, and stopped. He was clearly as appalled as Zoe had been when she first walked in.

The living room was a disaster. Zoe hadn't even tried to clean it up. It looked like the Fates had hosted a group of visiting thirteen-year-old girls. Pillows rested on the floor, along with a pile of blankets. Empty A&W Root Beer cans leaned against Hires Root Beer cans which leaned against one or two regular beer cans, all apparently empty. A box of chocolates, with all but the center two pieces picked out, lay open on the coffee table, and pizza crusts littered the floor near the couch. The television had been turned so that whoever leaned against the pillows could see it, and a bunch of DVDs were stacked next to the DVD player.

Travers walked over to the DVDs and picked one up. "The first season of *CSI*?" he said with a frown. "Who are they kidding?"

Kyle joined him.

"Look," Kyle said, crouching next to the stack and pulling some videotapes from behind it. "A whole set of *City Confidential,* and *American Justice.*"

"What are they looking for?" Travers asked.

"I'm not sure we need to know," Zoe said.

He looked at her as if he were seeing her for the first time. His eyes were electric, and they sent a charge through her every time they met hers. She felt her heart rate increase, and hoped the changes in her breathing weren't obvious to anyone but herself.

Is everything okay? she mouthed toward him, and nodded at Kyle.

Travers shrugged. *Tell you later,* he mouthed back.

A crunching sound came from behind her. Zoe turned in time to see Bartholomew inhale the last pizza crust.

"Oh, man," Travers said. "He's going to be sick later."

"I don't know," Zoe said. "He's an eating machine."

"Wonderful," Travers said. "So nice of you to share him."

Even though his tone was dry, he smiled, and she felt weak in the knees. She also felt a surge of anger at her own susceptibility to him. She had resolved to keep her distance the night before, but apparently her body hadn't gotten the message.

"Listen," Travers said, "I've been thinking about the training and the case and I realized no one talked with you about money."

Zoe shrugged. She hadn't expected to be paid, once she figured out that she really was working for the Fates.

They had switched, somewhere in the last few minutes, to "Don't Sit Under the Apple Tree (with Anyone Else but Me)" which was marginally less annoying, only because they were mispronouncing fewer words.

"We're all going to be taking a lot of your time, and I think you'll need to be compensated—"

"It's all right," Zoe said.

"No, it's not." Travers was cute when he was concerned. "The Fates can't pay you, but I can and—"

"It's all right," Zoe repeated.

"No, seriously—"

"Seriously," Zoe said, feeling more annoyed than she should have. He wanted to be fair to her, after all, and she wasn't allowing it. "I can't accept money for training. No mentor does."

"But—"

"And as for the case, for all I know, this still might be a test on the part of the Fates."

"You think the Interim Fates were fake?" Kyle asked from

the floor. He was still going through the piles of videos and DVDs.

"I don't know what to think," Zoe said. "So it's better if I just play this straight."

"Which would seem to me that you'd need compensation," Travers said. "It's unusual for you not to take payment for your detective work, right?"

Zoe held up a hand. "It's my decision. I'm not hurting for money."

"And as for being my mentor," Travers began.

"Yes?" Zoe's hands clenched, and she had to will them apart. She didn't want him to change anything, and yet she wanted everything changed. She wasn't being as rational as she liked this morning, and it was irritating her.

"I thought we'd agreed that I just needed some tricks so that I could get to Oregon."

"You don't want me as a mentor?" she asked, and then wished she could take the words back. They sounded bitchier than she intended. Mostly, she was trying to clarify.

At least, she thought she was.

But with her emotions all over the place, she wasn't sure what she was doing.

Except that she had been fine before he had arrived. Calm, planning ahead, barely annoyed at all by the Fates' mess and their lack of timing.

"I didn't say that," Travers said. "I thought we decided yesterday that it was better for me not to take too much of your time."

"I thought we decided that we'd decide later," Zoe said. "Once you figured out what you needed to do for yourself and for Kyle."

"No one ever exactly said that." Kyle paused in his sorting of the videos. "You both thought it, but no one actually said it."

He would be useful to have around. Useful and unnerving.

Still, Zoe smiled at him. "Thanks, Kyle. Why don't we leave things that way? We need to get started today anyway."

"I thought the Fates' case took priority," Travers said.

"It does." Zoe bent over and grabbed one of the blankets. As she started folding it, Cheetos fell out. Those women were going to have to start watching their figures now that they didn't have the magic to maintain them. But she wasn't going to be the one to tell them.

"Then I don't understand," Travers said. "How will you do both?"

"There's no formal program." Zoe folded the blanket and set it on the couch. Then she grabbed the next blanket, this time shaking it to rid it of its Cheetos.

Oh, the maid was going to love this room.

"So?" Travers asked.

"So you'll learn as the day progresses. Whatever happens to us will give me a chance to train you."

Travers glanced at Kyle. He was reading the back of a video, and didn't seem to be listening. Although Zoe had a hunch that boy heard more than he let on.

"Um, if I go anywhere with you, Kyle will have to as well."

Zoe shook her head. "I did some Internet research on that wheel this morning. The places we're going to go, you can't take an eleven-year-old."

"I'll stay in the car," Kyle said.

"Even then." Zoe folded the blanket and set it next to the first one.

"We're going to have to find another way," Travers said. "I can't leave him alone."

"You could leave him with the Fates," Zoe said.

Travers raised his eyebrows as if she had suggested leaving his son with a group of well-known cannibals. "And who would take care of all of them?"

"The Fates are older than all of us combined, and they have run an entire justice system. They know a lot about crime and punishment and—"

"And magic," Travers said. "And they have evil mages after them, they've lost a spinning wheel, and they don't know what a dollar bill is. They're not appropriate guardians for my son."

Zoe took a deep breath, trying to keep herself calm. If Kyle were her son, she'd be just as worried about him. But there were other considerations, ones that Travers didn't know about.

"Let me take your concerns in reverse order," Zoe said. "First, Kyle knows what a dollar bill is, so he'll be able to help the Fates with the practical modern stuff. You and I are going to search for the wheel, and the faster we find it, the faster all of us can leave each other's company."

She hadn't meant for that sentence to have as much bite as she put into it. It made her sound like she didn't want to be with him, either, which wasn't true.

"And finally," she said, "I've taken care of the mages, at least for a couple of days."

"What if you're wrong?" Travers said. "It's my son's life you're risking, and the Fates can't do any of that stuff you did yesterday to save him. What're they going to do, get hotel security because some evil magician tries to kidnap them?"

"They're not as helpless as you think," Zoe said. "They do know how magic works, even if they can't practice it themselves right now. They survived with you and Kyle before either of you knew about their powers. I think they'll be just fine with Kyle, and he won't be in any danger."

"But you don't know that," Travers said. "You're asking me to risk Kyle's life on a guess."

Zoe felt her cheeks heat. What was it about this man that had revived her talent for blushing?

"So we're at a stalemate. Either Kyle comes with us, or you go off on the case alone," Travers said, "and train me at some other point."

The music stopped. The air rang with the echoing last chord. The Fates weren't bad musicians; they just weren't very good with lyrics.

Kyle had set the last video down. He stood beside the television, looking as uncertain as he had at the door. Something had bothered him this morning, and Zoe couldn't tell what it was.

"Kyle," she said, "has anyone trained you to project?"

"Huh?" he asked.

"To send your thoughts, like a shout, into someone else's mind?"

Kyle shook his head slowly, as if the idea of anyone training him at all—maybe even noticing him—was foreign to him.

"Can I teach you?" Zoe asked.

"To what purpose?" Travers asked.

"To great purpose," Zoe said. "He should have learned this one long ago."

Travers crossed his arms, and Zoe got the sense that he interpreted her words as a criticism of his parenting.

"Unlike mortal children," Zoe said, "Kyle doesn't need to carry a phone to stay in touch. If he's in trouble, he can project his need for help to you—like a shout over a very long distance. Once you learn how to use your own magic, you can transport from wherever you are to wherever he is, taking care of the problem right away."

Travers's shoulders relaxed, and he glanced at Kyle. "Really? He can do that?"

"Anyone with his powers can do that," Zoe said. "He just has to know how to use them."

Bartholomew had stopped eating pizza crusts and had waddled to the center of the conversation, sitting near Travers as if Bartholomew were protecting Travers from Zoe. Zoe would have thought it cute if Bartholomew hadn't had an orange Cheetos mustache. That dog had apparently been snacking while he had been finishing off the pizza.

"How long will it take to train him?" Travers asked.

"Not long," Zoe said. "Half an hour at the most. Less time than it'll take for the Fates to get dressed."

Travers sighed, bent, and absently petted Bartholomew. For a man who claimed he didn't like animals, he was very affectionate with this one.

"I still don't like the plan," Travers said. "The Fates aren't going to know how to take care of him. They'll let him do all sorts of things that I wouldn't let him do."

"So does Aunt Viv," Kyle said, "and you let me stay with her."

Travers gave Kyle an exasperated frown. Then Travers let his arms drop. "Tell you what," he said to Zoe. "You train Kyle how to—what is it? Project?"

She nodded.

"And I'll call my sister, Megan. Maybe she can get a few days off, until you have me as trained as we can get me for that trip to Oregon."

Zoe had to ask: "Will your sister be able to handle the Fates?"

"Megan?" Travers looked at Kyle, who smiled for the first time since he came into the hotel room.

"My Aunt Megan makes my dad look like he's flexible." From the way Kyle said that, Zoe could tell Kyle had used that example before.

"I *am* flexible," Travers said with only a little irritation.

"Not compared to Aunt Viv," Kyle said.

"Perhaps you should call that aunt," Zoe said.

"Can't," Kyle said. "She's on her honeymoon. She'd want to hear from me and Dad about as much as Dad wants to have his day disrupted."

Zoe looked at Travers. "Your sister Megan doesn't sound appropriate. Is there someone else you can call?"

Travers shook his head. "I'll call Meg. When she gets here, we'll make sure she and Kyle stay away from the Fates. That's all it'll take."

The man was truly an optimist, but Zoe didn't say that. He had only had a few days to get used to the ways of magic and of the Fates. She had had an entire lifetime, and she knew that getting rid of them wasn't all that easy.

"The best thing to do," she said, "is find that wheel. Once the Fates have it, we can continue with our lives."

"Whatever that means," Travers said.

Zoe smiled. "Let's hope you get a chance to find out."

Eighteen

Against his better judgement, Travers left Kyle with the Fates. Travers also left Bartholomew Fang there for good measure. While waiting for the Fates, Travers had checked with the hotel about a baby-sitting service, then decided that wouldn't work, either.

Kyle was too old for conventional baby-sitting, and the Fates probably would be in and out. They were trouble enough when they were behaving. Travers couldn't imagine what the hotel would do when the Fates got out of hand.

Instead, he called Megan and left a message on her voice mail and another with her secretary. Megan would return his call as soon as she was back in the office. By then, he'd be out with Zoe, but at least he had made contact. Maybe in a few days (or less!), Megan would be able to join him in Vegas; maybe she could even take Kyle home. It wasn't too late for him to start those classes.

In the short term, however, Travers had to count on Kyle's ability to "project," and the Fates' good sense, neither of which seemed exceedingly reliable. While the Fates got dressed and while Travers was on the phone, Zoe taught Kyle how to send his thoughts outward.

Kyle practiced on his father. The scream was so loud, it felt like someone had blatted a trumpet right next to his ear. Yet somehow Travers had known that the sound was internal. Or maybe the resulting headache, which only needed circles, stars, and little cheeping birdies going around his head to complete it, convinced him.

Zoe saw Travers's distress (or maybe she saw the circles and stars and little cheeping birdies), and touched his forehead. The headache had disappeared as magically as it had arrived.

Then Zoe pronounced Kyle fit for projecting. He would have to learn control, she said, and Travers could second, third, and fourth that, but once Kyle had the control, he would have a very subtle ability to project his thoughts.

Which was just exactly what Travers needed from a son about to head into puberty.

Travers didn't object, though. He left his son with three women who had taken forty-five minutes to put on blue jeans, matching white blouses, and sandals. All three Fates wore their hair down, and none of them was wearing any makeup.

For the life of him, Travers had no idea what had taken them so long to prepare for the day and he knew he never, ever wanted to find out.

He and Zoe didn't even discuss it as they left the hotel. Zoe had questioned Travers's judgement just once, when he gave Kyle enough money to get him and the Fates lunch, dinner, and tickets to the *Star Trek Experience*. The Fates, it turned out, were big Star Trek fans; while they were staying in Dexter's coastal hideaway, they saw every single episode of every single show.

Travers also gave Kyle his cell phone, along with Zoe's number. With every base covered, Travers hoped that nothing would go wrong.

Of course, with the Fates involved, that was a pretty big hope.

This morning, Zoe was driving. Her car was a racy red Jaguar convertible, which she used with the top down. The car didn't surprise Travers—somehow the Jag suited Zoe—but the top-down part did. Even though it was only eleven A.M., the temperature hovered around 110 degrees. Air conditioning wasn't advised at this temperature—it was a requirement.

And Zoe didn't seem to notice.

Travers would. His blond hair would be blonder, which was actually a look most women liked. Unless it was coupled with the beet-red sunburn on his scalp, along with the tiny sweat blisters that he always got when he was in the heat too much.

By the end of the day, he would look like Lobster Man in a blond wig.

He hadn't complained yet. He had used the drive from the Strip to downtown to examine the car's dash, looking for signs of working air conditioning.

He found two: a dial and a lever, both of which were in the "off" position. The Jag was old enough, and had been refurbished enough, to make the assumption that the air conditioning worked an iffy proposition.

He would wait until they stopped before mentioning his delicate white skin. Zoe was going to her office to look up a few last-minute details and then they were, in her words, going door-to-door at the faerie casinos.

Travers didn't know if "faerie casinos" was the name of a chain, or if it was actually a series of casinos owned by faeries, or both. He was going to ask about that, too, when they stopped. Traveling in a convertible, even in the stop-and-go Vegas midday traffic, made conversation nearly impossible.

This morning, Vegas looked as dingy and grimy as its

history. Even though a lot of the buildings weren't very old, they had a worn look that he recognized, one that buildings got after only a few years in the desert.

The city also had an unusual kind of sprawl. Los Angeles was divided into clear neighborhoods with different types of architecture throughout. Yes, it was strip mall heaven, and parts of L.A. looked no different from other parts. But Vegas, off the freeways and on the side roads, was a series of housing tracts. However, neighborhood to neighborhood changed only by landscaping or by the year of the housing development. Most were upscale, but the closer he got to downtown, the older the housing developments got, and the more dilapidated.

Gang tags started to appear on the side of abandoned warehouses and on fences near gated neighborhoods. Broken-down cars littered a few blocks, and most had glass covering the streets.

Zoe didn't seem to notice, or if she did, she didn't seem to care. She zoomed by with a confidence that Travers would never feel in such a neighborhood.

The streets made him nervous, so he studied her instead. The wind blew her hair back, revealing her strong jaw and high cheekbones. Her neck was elegant and flawless, and her lips were perfectly formed.

For the first time in his life, Travers wished he had the freedom other men his age had. He wished he could just pick up and go, just change his life, stay in Vegas a while and get to know this woman without any cares in the world.

But the moment he had that thought, he got a shivery sense of worry about one of those cares. Travers leaned his head back against the car seat and hoped that shivery sense wasn't Kyle attempting to send a message, just a father's worry about leaving his son with three slightly insane women.

"He'll be fine," Zoe shouted over the roar of the car as if she were the one who could read minds, not Kyle.

She hadn't even looked at him. Her gaze was still on the road, her left arm braced above the wheel, her right hand resting on the stick shift.

Travers felt his unease grow. "How'd you know that's what I was thinking?"

Zoe gave him a quick glance and a matching grin. "I would've been surprised if you weren't."

He smiled in return, then leaned back in his seat. The wind from the passing cars smelled of exhaust, and felt like hot air, instead of cooler the way that driving in a convertible should be.

The neighborhood was growing steadily worse—dilapidated buildings, more broken-down cars, boys huddled in doorways making the kinds of deals that Travers didn't want to think about.

He didn't understand Zoe. She drove a Jaguar—a classic—and yet, she kept her office in a neighborhood this bad. Was the neighborhood because of the class of clients a private investigator got? Or was it camouflage, away from the "mortals," as she and the Fates called normal people?

Or was it something else, a chance to emulate the private detectives from the books and movies, the ones who talked tough, and played even tougher, and fell in love with tough dames, if only for a chapter or two?

Zoe rounded a corner, and Travers recognized the sunwashed frame of her office. She bounced over a rut in the driveway, heading into the back, and under a carport that looked like it had been added onto the building decades after the building's initial construction.

Zoe shut off the engine, got out, and ran her hands through her hair. It fell, shiny, smooth, and neatly combed, against her face. Then she raised her eyebrows at Travers.

"Aren't you getting out?"

"Shouldn't you put up the roof?" he asked.

"Why?" she asked. "It's protected here."

"From sunlight," he said. "But not from the neighborhood itself. I've led a pretty quiet life and I know how to hot-wire a car this old."

"You do?" Her grin grew. "You have hidden talents, Mr. Kineally."

She had meant that as a joke, but it hit home. He did have hidden talents, hidden even from himself.

He sighed and got out of the car. Although he was in the shade, his skin felt hot and he knew that he had burned.

"It's your car," he said.

"And my office." She raised a hand. "Watch and learn."

She held the hand over the center of the car, then clenched her hand into a fist. After a moment, she released the fist, spreading her fingers wide.

The car wavered like a heat mirage. It got an almost silvery glow, and then it winked out—just like the Fates had the night before.

"You made it disappear?" Travers reached down, and touched hot metal. He brought his fingers back. They'd been burned.

"I didn't make it disappear," Zoe said. "I just made it invisible."

"Oh," he said, because he didn't know how to respond. "I thought you weren't supposed to use magic for personal gain."

"I'm not," she said. "I'm using it to prevent personal loss."

She crossed her arms, and tilted her head slightly. She still stood near the driver's side of the car, although that wasn't immediately obvious, since the car was impossible to see.

"Aren't we going to go in?" Travers asked, a little worried about walking to her side of the car. He couldn't remember how long the vehicle was, not exactly, anyway, and he didn't want to bash into the side of the car, making himself look like a complete dork.

"Aren't you going to ask me how to make things invisible?" Zoe said.

It hadn't crossed his mind. He blinked, looked at the non-existent car (well, that wasn't true. It did exist. It just didn't seem to exist. Even though he could feel the heat radiating from its body, and hear the engine ticking in the shade), and frowned.

"I thought you said I have a small magic," he said, knowing it sounded lame. But he really hadn't associated himself with that trick she had just done.

"This *is* small magic," Zoe said. "It's barely above a parlor trick."

Travers touched the car's warm metal. As he did, he looked down. The tip of his finger had disappeared.

Somehow that felt like more than a parlor trick.

"I don't want you to practice on my car." Zoe looked around the small parking area behind the office. Except for the carport, and the invisible car inside of it, there wasn't a lot surrounding them. A ratty fence, a few garbage cans, some dying plants. Not much else.

Travers let out a small breath. Maybe she wouldn't have him do anything, after all. At least, not out here.

"Let's try that." Zoe pointed at the nearest garbage can.

"And what exactly are we trying to do?" Travers asked.

"You'll make it invisible," Zoe said. "Right down to its shadow."

Travers frowned. The shadow was short, since the sun was getting close to its zenith, but still visible. He was beginning to understand the level of detail magic took—he would never have thought of the shadow if Zoe hadn't mentioned it—but a shadow with nothing to cast it was suspicious.

"Am I just supposed to try thinking 'invisible!' or—"

"Don't!" Zoe held up her hand, then lowered it slowly. "Crap."

"What?" Travers asked.

Zoe shook her head. "You're too quick."

"No one's ever accused me of that before." Then he flushed, wishing he could take the sentence back. That was what passed for banter in high school, not among adults. Of course, high school was the last time he had wooed a woman, and look how well that turned out.

Zoe put her hands on her hips. "Just look at yourself."

Travers looked down—and his heart nearly stopped when he saw nothing but pavement. Not even a shadow.

Not even a shoe print.

He wasn't sure whether he should be impressed with his own first-timer's skill or if he should be frightened that he had done something wrong.

So he felt both emotions at once, letting them mix and blend, one emotion dominating the other for half a second, then the other taking over.

"Now what do I do?" he asked. Then he frowned. "You can hear me, right?"

"I can hear you." Zoe sighed. "This is going to be harder than I thought."

"Turning me back?' he asked, not trying to keep the panic out of his voice.

"Teaching you. There are subtleties involved that I've never bothered to think about." Zoe sighed again, as if the burden she had undertaken was much too great.

Travers could feel his face flush—and it wasn't just from the sunburn. "Can I turn back or not?"

"You'll have to do it," Zoe said. "It's the only way you'll learn."

"Learn what?" Travers asked.

"Two things," Zoe said. "How to reverse a miscued spell and how to avoid undisciplined thinking."

Travers's spine stiffened. He'd never been an undisciplined thinker in his life.

Yet, he stood here, beside an invisible Jaguar, in a town he had never wanted to visit, as clear to the world as a sheet of newly cleaned glass.

He wisely refrained from saying anything.

"Okay," Zoe said. "Here's what you do. You say, 'Reverse!' and as you do, you think exactly what you were thinking when you changed."

He didn't know what he had been thinking. He didn't even feel that little *poof* he had felt the day before as the magic had worked.

"Um," he said, "what if I don't know what I was thinking?"

Maybe he was an undisciplined thinker. Maybe he just hadn't realized it until now.

"Oh, for heaven's sake." Zoe walked toward him, stopped, and put out a hand. She was feeling for the back of the car, just like he would have had to do. Suddenly he didn't feel quite as stupid as he had a moment earlier. "You'll remember. Just think about what we were talking about."

"We were talking about invisibility," Travers said.

"We were talking about how to spell the garbage can, and you felt the need to make some witty comment."

"I didn't feel the need," Travers said. "I was just asking a question. It was a logical question, actually, given the circumstances. I mean, I've never done stuff like this before, so how would I know what I'm doing? I've never even seen stuff like this before yesterday, so I'm really out of my depth."

"We can argue that last point later," Zoe said. "The one about yesterday, not the one about being out of your depth. It's pretty clear that you're out of your depth."

"Thanks," Travers said.

"So," Zoe said, her hands down slightly. She hadn't moved

any farther, and apparently, she hadn't touched the car. "Are you going to try to reverse the spell?"

"Oh, yeah." Travers bit his lower lip. Say "reverse" and think of England. He felt a *poof* and he was standing on a bridge, overlooking a slow-moving and sludgy river. It was dark, and the lights below him came from ships. A city spread before him—obviously not Las Vegas.

Even the air smelled different. Raw, damp, and filled with humidity.

England.

Travers swore, said, "Reverse!" and thought of England. Seriously thought of England, instead of a silly pun, like he had done before.

Another little *poof* went through him, and then he blinked in the sunlight.

He was standing behind Zoe now, near the garbage cans. She was still facing the carport, and she was talking.

"Travers," she said. "We don't have all day. This was just supposed to be the first lesson."

And he'd performed it. Really well, only he didn't tell her that. He didn't even want to tell her that.

The trip to England (was that really London Bridge?) was his own little secret.

He snuck toward the carport, his feet crunching slightly on the gravel.

Zoe turned, her expression sharp. "Who's there?"

Travers held his breath as he walked. He tried to make as few sounds as possible, but each echoed as if it were the only sound in the world.

"What's going on?" Zoe asked, still looking around. She wasn't looking at him, though, so she didn't know where he was. Maybe she couldn't hear the drumbeat of his heart as he moved. "Travers?"

He had to touch the car to go around it. His fingers found

the metal, cooling in the shade of the carport, and traced their way to the front. He had to squeeze through the small space between a beam and the car, then move to the other side, as if nothing happened.

"Travers?" Zoe asked again, her voice rising.

"Just say 'reverse'?" he asked, as if he had been in the same spot the whole time.

She whirled, looking visibly startled. She glanced over her shoulder once, as if she thought someone might be behind her, and then said, "And think about what you had thought before. That's the important part. Undisciplined thought—"

"Is dangerous," Travers said. "I'm beginning to figure that out."

Zoe kept looking around as if she sensed someone else's presence. But Travers couldn't think about her or England. He had to think about invisibility and wondering how to achieve it.

He kept that thought at the forefront of his brain as he said, "Reverse!"

For a moment, he thought everything stayed the same. Zoe was staring just past him, and he felt no different.

Then he looked down, saw his narrow feet in their sandals, saw his pants, his hands—which looked fine—his arms, which were sunburned, and the rest of him.

He wanted to pat himself to see if he was all there, but he had always been all there, just not visible to anyone else, not even himself.

Zoe frowned. Her hands hadn't left her hips. "What happened to you?"

He blinked, looked down, didn't know what she was referring to. He didn't even want to speculate about it—didn't want to think about the possible things that could have gone wrong, in case he would now make them go wrong.

He wondered if he was covered with some kind of obviously English patina—a bit of rain, a touch of dew, maybe a little bit of malt vinegar from a passing fish-and-chips truck.

"I—um." He looked down at himself again, unwilling to admit that he had made not one, but two mistakes. "I—what are you talking about?"

"You're all red." She sounded annoyed.

Travers looked at his arms and grinned. "I'm sunburned."

"From being invisible?"

"From riding in your car."

"Nonsense," she said. "No one can get sunburned that fast."

"I can get sunburned in ten minutes on a cloudy day," Travers said. "Just ask Kyle."

"I'm not going back to the Strip to confer with your son," Zoe said. "You thought something and it turned you red."

"I thought I could handle the top down in your car for the few short miles it took to get here," Travers said. "I thought wrong."

"You should have said something," Zoe said.

"I planned to," Travers said, "and then we got here and everything got—"

He made himself pause. Maybe the use of metaphor was the problem. After all, he had disappeared when he metaphorically thought of another country, a pun on the way that Victorian women were told to suffer through sex. (Close your eyes, dear, and think of England.)

Maybe he would have to change the entire way he thought, the way he looked at the world, everything about his life—

"You look particularly glum," Zoe said. "What's the matter?"

"Besides the fact that I just did a spell by accident and I might be dying of heatstroke?" Travers asked. "Why, nothing's the matter."

Zoe raised her eyebrows at him. It was an attractive look,

and one she used often. He longed to touch the side of them, feel how soft her skin was, and maybe kiss the corner of her eye.

"You want to try this garbage can spell or not?" she asked.

He didn't. Not really. "Can we just go inside? I'd like some water and some sunscreen, and a relief from these temperatures."

And not the relief he had gotten a few minutes ago.

Zoe shook her head, let her arms drop, and shoved her keys into her pocket. "Avoiding the lessons won't teach you anything."

"I learned about 'reverse,'" Travers said. "That's something."

"And it doesn't always work," Zoe said. "Especially if you can't remember the sequence or you stick a new sequence in the middle of it."

Yeah, he got that one, too, but he didn't want to talk about it. "How about I disappear your garbage can inside, where there's air conditioning?"

Zoe sighed. "All right, you can make tiny things invisible while I double-check my research. And then we have to get on the trail of that wheel."

"How long do you think it'll take to find it?" Travers asked, hoping that it would only take a few days. He wanted the Fates out of his hair as soon as possible. He'd really like it if it happened before his sister Megan arrived.

"I have no idea," Zoe said. "With the way things are going this morning, it might take us centuries."

"Centuries?" Travers's voice shook. "I hope you're exaggerating."

Zoe headed toward the building's back door. "I hope I am, too."

Nineteen

Zoe stepped into the coolness of her office. At least, it was cool compared with the great outdoors, where the temperatures had to be heading toward 110. Sometimes she loved the summer heat, and sometimes she wondered why she suffered through it when she could easily go someplace cool, like the Pacific Northwest or the North of England.

Travers was only a few steps behind her. She could hear his soft footfall in the hallway. It sounded familiar—almost like the footsteps she had heard outside.

A shiver ran down her back. When he had gone invisible, and the car had been invisible, Zoe had been uneasy. Then, when she realized that someone was behind her, her unease grew. She hadn't gotten a sense of evil, like she had when that mage showed up to take the Fates, but she had been surprised that someone else had gotten so close.

Perhaps he was just walking around, exploring his invisibility.

Or perhaps the newness of his magic, and his inexperience,

had brought the wrong kind of mage to watch their lessons, someone who might target Travers in the future.

Zoe would have to warn him again, but she didn't know how. She wasn't even sure if she believed him about the sunburn. She had been telling the truth when she had said that she had never seen anyone get sunburned that fast.

She flicked on her overhead office light. Chairs were scattered everywhere, and a few five-dollar bills still littered the floor. Right in front of her desk, a scrape of pink material caught on the edge of a chair.

The office smelled strongly of wet dog. She hadn't gone into the bathroom to see the damage that Kyle had done, but she probably should have. She hadn't thought it through—an eleven-year-old, a stubborn dog, a bath. It probably didn't take prescience to know that the bathroom was a disaster.

Zoe sighed. She would never get to the case. And because of that, she'd never be free of the Fates. She was going to have them around until the end of time, rescuing them from angry mages, and trying to sort her way through their conversations.

She shivered again. That was not her idea of a good time.

"The air conditioning isn't on high enough to make a person shiver," Travers said from behind her. "Is it?"

She turned, and found herself against him. His skin radiated heat. The burn looked painful, but he was smiling at her.

She liked that smile. It had a softness to it, a softness mixed with just enough humor to take the edge off his good looks. This morning, she was finally getting to see him as a person, not just as the best-looking man she had ever laid eyes on.

"The air conditioning is on as high as it goes," she said, not moving away from his chest. "The problem is that the entire system needs to be replaced, and the landlord won't do it."

"In Vegas," Travers said, "that would seem to me to be a violation of landlord-tenant law."

"Which varies from state to state and city to city," Zoe said.

"Except for one provision," Travers said. "The landlord has to make certain that living conditions don't threaten the lives of the renters."

Zoe felt the heat from his body run along her neck and up her cheeks. Or maybe she was blushing again. This time, it wasn't from lewd thoughts; it was from the fact that she might be guilty of something that she hadn't even been aware of.

"You okay?" Travers asked.

"Let's go inside," she said, and stepped across the threshold.

The wet-dog smell was even stronger in here. Part of the carpet squished under her feet, and for a moment, Zoe thought that Bartholomew's bladder problems had extended to this dimension.

Then she realized that she hadn't had a towel in that bathroom—at least not one big enough for a squirming, obese dachshund. The creature had waddled into her main office, sat down, and proceeded to drip water on her terribly thin, poorly maintained carpet.

"Whew!" Travers said. "Stinks in here."

"No kidding," Zoe said.

"I'd advise you to open a window, but then it might take all day for the air conditioning to get the temperature back to this."

"Try all week," Zoe said.

She snapped her fingers, and the rug dried instantly. Then she went into the bathroom. For a moment, she just stared at the mess—hair everywhere, all of it short and brown and probably canine. The sink was filled with hair and the remnants of soapy water. Kyle hadn't even pulled the plug to drain it.

Travers peered over Zoe's shoulder, startling her.

"I forgot to check on him," Travers said. "My fault. Cleanup still isn't his strong suit."

"It's okay," Zoe said, and snapped her fingers again. The bathroom sparkled, all the hair gone, and the smell with it.

"I'm still confused," Travers said. "I thought you weren't supposed to use your magic except in emergencies."

"I can use it whenever I want," Zoe said, "except when I would compromise some mortals."

"Compromise?"

"Make them understand that magic exists," Zoe said. "And I shouldn't use it for personal gain, whatever that means. And most of all, I should try to live my life as anonymously as possible, since the Fates—our Fates—were trying to crack down on new myths and legends, or as they called them, leaks from the magical realm."

"Leaks." Travers grinned. "Sounds like something Fang would do."

"You're calling him Fang now?" Zoe felt surprised. The dog wasn't even close to a Fang.

"Bartholomew Fang," Travers said. "It suits him."

Zoe shook her head, but didn't argue. The dog really was bamboozling him, and it was kind of sweet.

Travers leaned against the doorjamb, then stood as if the pressure against his skin hurt him.

"So," he said, perhaps to cover that awkward moment, "you can use your magic at any time without penalty."

"I didn't say that." Zoe ran a finger in the sink. She had gotten it clean, but the wet-dog smell lingered. Maybe the odor had just gotten caught in her nose. "There is a penalty. The more power I use, the more I age."

"Power," Travers said. "Not magic."

She shrugged. "Sometimes they're related."

She turned to head out of the bathroom. Travers put a hand on her shoulder, stopping her. His touch seared through her shirt, running through her entire body as if he were current and she were the conductor.

"You must not have used very much power," he said. "You don't look old to me."

She felt torn: part of her flattered at his compliment, and the other part worried about their age difference. He ran his other hand along her cheek.

"In fact," he said, "you're probably the most beautiful woman I've ever seen."

And you're the best-looking man, she thought, but didn't say, grateful that Kyle wasn't here. She was certain she was broadcasting.

Travers leaned toward her. He was going to kiss her, and she should use the better part of valor to move away. Not that it would be easy to move in this small bathroom. And not that she wanted to move. But it would be better for both of them and the Fates, and Kyle, and even that stupid dog, if she just stepped aside.

But she dithered too long. Travers's lips touched hers, and hers parted. Somehow her arms found their way around his neck, and his found their way around her waist, and she was pressed against him, her body fitting his as if they had been made for each other.

She willed her brain into silence, not that it took much work, and surrendered to the kiss. It was slow and leisurely, as if their mouths were getting to know each other as a prelude to them getting to know each other.

In the middle of it, Zoe forgot to breathe. She realized she was getting short of air at the moment Travers's lips left hers.

"Wow," he said, his mouth only an inch or so from hers. "I haven't kissed anyone in a long time, but I don't remember it ever being that good."

Neither did she. And she'd probably kissed a lot more people over a lot longer time.

She leaned her forehead against his, felt the heat of his skin, and realized she was probably hurting him.

She stepped back, out of his arms, and held out her hand. A bottle of lotion appeared in it.

"Let me take care of that burn," she said, and winced inwardly. She had meant to say that she would give him the cream and *he* would take care of the burn—maybe even learn a simple healing spell—but that wasn't what she said.

He looked at the lotion, then at her, as if he were trying to understand the transition. Finally, he nodded.

"What do we do?" he asked.

It was another opening. *We* as opposed to *me* or *you*. But she didn't take it. And now she couldn't believe that her subconscious was guiding her. Her conscious brain knew what her subconscious was doing, and heartily approved.

Maybe only one other part of her disapproved and that part came out of fear.

"Sit here," she said, moving ever so slightly so that Travers could sit on the closed toilet seat. "And take off your shirt."

As well as everything else. But that sentence stayed inside. She was managing some control—just not enough.

Travers pulled his shirt over his head, moving slightly so the fabric didn't brush his skin. He was as well-built as she had guessed—broad shoulders, a firm, muscular chest, and a flat stomach. The muscles didn't ripple on him—for which she was grateful; she never liked ripply men—but they were visible with his movements, giving him a strength he didn't have when he was clothed.

He was lightly furred, the hair as blond as the hair on his head, and it tapered down his chest, into a line that pointed even lower—

Zoe made herself look at his sunburn, as she struggled to control her breathing.

Underneath his shirt, his skin was very white. A firm line had been etched in his biceps, where the skin went from white to bright red.

It was a sunburn—no doubt about that—and part of it was already beginning to blister.

"You should have said something," Zoe said as she squeezed lotion onto her hand.

"You probably would have moved away if I had," Travers said.

Zoe felt her face heat. She was blushing. Dammit! She continued to blush around this man. She had been so certain she had outgrown that habit.

"No," she said. "I mean, I meant that you should have said something about the sunburn."

"Oh." His head was down. She couldn't quite tell what he was thinking, and that made her feel odd. "I figured it would be okay to say something when we got here."

"Well," she said, "it clearly wasn't okay. You're wind-burned and sunburned, and beginning to blister."

She rubbed the lotion on her hands, and then applied it to the back of his neck. The skin there was almost too hot to touch. She silently recited a small spell that would take the pain from the burn and heal the skin.

"I get burned a lot," he said. "I just live with it—hey, what're you doing?"

She pulled her hands away, afraid she was doing something wrong. "I'm sorry. Did I hurt you?"

"No." He sounded surprised. "In fact, the places you touched feel even better than they felt before the burn."

Maybe a bit too much healing, then. Or she was taking tension out, too. She poured lotion on his burned right arm, and rubbed, relishing the feel of his skin beneath hers.

"Are you doing magic?" he asked. "I mean, besides making the bottle just appear?"

"Yes," she said. "It's a simple healing spell."

And the next sentence out of her mouth should have been about teaching him the spell, but she didn't say a word. Instead, she ran both hands along his arm, feeling the muscles, the firm skin, the warmth. Then she took his hand in her own, caressing it, massaging the fingers.

He sat very still, almost too still, as if he were trying to hold himself in reserve. But that sense she had had the day before, that sense of him vanishing, wasn't there. It was almost as if he had tried to vanish, and couldn't, as if he had forgotten how.

She moved to the other arm, and massaged it, taking the pain away with the burn, the lotion making her movements quick and gentle.

Travers's breathing was ragged, and he closed his eyes. But somehow he maintained the stillness.

She wanted to interrupt that stillness, to break through it, to take away his control. She moved in front of him, planning to sit on his lap while she put the lotion on his face when he grabbed the lotion bottle from her.

"Okay," he said, and his voice was a little raspy, "now explain to me how this is done."

His gaze met hers. His eyes were a slightly different color than they had been before—a deeper blue, as if she had gotten closer to his core self.

He was clearly as aroused as she was.

"Later," she said, and reached for the lotion.

He pulled it back toward the wall, out of her reach, like a little boy playing keep-away on a schoolyard.

"Teach me now," he said. His voice had a little more control.

He was the one who had started this with his kiss. He was the one who let her touch him like that, who clearly enjoyed it. Why was he stopping now?

"What's wrong?" she asked.

"Wrong?" He stood slowly, so as not to bang into her. She still had to step out of the bathroom to get out of his way. "It's not you, Zoe."

She frowned. If he wanted her to be off-balance, he was succeeding. She couldn't remember the last time a man made her feel so many emotions at the same time.

Including frustration. That little dance in the cramped bathroom had let her feel just how attracted she was to this man, and she was willing to explore that attraction, even if there was no future in it.

"I don't understand," she said.

He set the lotion on the sink and looked at his arms in the mirror. They were considerably less red than his face. The heat and pain had clearly left them.

He looked at his skin for a moment, as if he were trying to think of what to say, and then he spoke. "I can't have a casual relationship, Zoe. Not as long as Kyle's living with me."

"Not at all?" she asked, not sure if "casual" was what she wanted, either.

Travers shook his head. "My ex-wife walked out on my son, and the only women I want in his life are the ones who are going to stay."

"Like the Fates?" Zoe asked, confused.

"No." Travers turned and leaned against the sink. His face almost glowed. She longed to touch it, to remove the ache, but she kept her lotion-covered hands clasped at her sides. "He understands friendship and casual acquaintances. But I'm not going to lie to him about my relationship with someone, and I'm not going to subject him to loss like the one he experienced before."

"Him?" Zoe asked. "Or you?"

Travers gave her that sideways, rueful smile that she liked. "Believe me, I thought of that. And it's not me I'm protecting. It's sad to say I don't think I ever loved Cheryl. I was a teenage boy, lost in hormones, and I thought marriage was the right thing."

"That still had to hurt," Zoe said.

Travers nodded. "It hurt, but it was eleven years ago. I'm long past it."

"Except that you haven't had another relationship."

"Because of Kyle," Travers said. His certainty made her doubt him even more. Travers hadn't looked at this at all. "If I bring someone else into his life before he graduates from high school, she'd better be the woman I'm spending the rest of my life with."

"Or?" Zoe asked.

"Or there's no relationship."

"It sounds impossible," she said. "How are you going to know the woman you want to spend the rest of your life with— and it's going to be a very long life, you know—without giving a few other women a test run?"

"I'll know," Travers said.

She didn't believe him. She sighed. Now was the time. Now that they were putting everything between them, making their sides clear.

"I've been around for more than a hundred years, Travers," Zoe said. "I've fallen in love a few times. But none of those men were the One the Fates talk about—the soulmate, the man I'll spend the rest of my life with."

"But you knew that going in," Travers said, once again not noticing the age thing.

"I knew that once I was already in," Zoe said. "There's no

such thing as a bolt out of the blue that makes you believe you've found your one and only."

Something changed in his eyes, something cooled, and he finally achieved that distance she had noted the day before. It felt as if he had left the room, even though he was still only a few feet from her.

"So is that why you kissed me?" he asked. "For fun? For experimentation?"

"You kissed me," she said, with more heat than she wanted to. "And I liked it, so I kissed you back. I thought we had something going here."

"If Kyle weren't in my life," Travers said, "maybe. But he is."

"This kiss, then," Zoe said. "It was—what? Impulse? A tease? An experimentation to see how I'd react?"

He dropped his gaze, his eyelashes brushing against that inflamed skin. "I just—wanted—I couldn't—you're so beautiful, Zoe. I just wanted to—just once . . ."

His voice trailed off. He didn't look up. She felt her own skin coloring. It had been impulse, and it embarrassed him. Or she had embarrassed him by taking things one step farther.

"Give me the lotion," she said, suppressing a sigh. "Let me teach you a very simple spell for healing."

Twenty

The spell was simple. Travers performed it slowly, carefully, with a single finger tracing a visible path on his sunburned skin. He stood in front of the mirror, and examined his face with a care he hadn't used since he was a teenage boy about to go to his first prom.

At first, his fingers had shaken. Zoe had given him a cool smile, told him that was normal, and decamped for the main part of the office. He supposed he could call her if something went wrong.

But nothing did. His skin stopped looking so red, and the pain—which felt like someone had placed a hot mask over his face—eased to nearly nothing.

Now, as he examined his arms, he realized the sunburn had faded into a tan, something that hadn't happened to him in his entire life.

Just like that kiss. He had never experienced a kiss like that in his entire life, either. And then, with her hands on his, taking his own hand between them, rubbing—

He had to end it. Just to maintain his own control.

He had thought he was past that, that loss of control which would lead him into making a mistake he would later regret. Not that he regretted Kyle. But Travers regretted the circumstances of his marriage, which no one knew except himself and Cheryl, and he regretted being the cause of it all.

Hormones.

Maybe he had misunderstood the magical explanations. He thought the Fates (or was it Zoe?) had said people came into their magic when their hormones no longer controlled them.

He snorted, and shook his head. Until today, his hormones hadn't controlled him for a long time.

But he couldn't pass up that kiss. Zoe had been so close and the floral scent of her hair, mixed with a scent that he had already come to recognize as uniquely Zoe, enticed him to act on impulse.

Now he wished he hadn't. She was angry at him, and he was angry at himself, making a physical promise that he couldn't keep.

He knew the arguments: he could have let that moment continue, taken it all the way; they were both adults. But he didn't dare. Not with his heart already intrigued. And not with Kyle able to read—what did he call it?—*broadcast* thoughts.

The last thing Travers needed was explaining risky, unprotected (and impulsively enjoyable) sex to his son.

Travers finished the spell and washed the lotion off his hands. Then he squared his shoulders and carried the bottle into the main part of the office.

Zoe sat at her desk chair with her back to the room. She was hunched over her computer, her fingers dancing across the keys. Rays of light peeked through the blinds, making her skin look striped.

"What do you want me to do with the lotion?" he asked.

"Keep it." Her words were clipped. "It's a gift."

He sighed, ever so silently, knowing he deserved her withdrawal, and not sure how to apologize for giving in to his impulse without sounding like he was apologizing for the kiss. He hadn't felt sorry for that.

Sometimes his own rules seemed harsh, even to him.

"Finding anything?" he asked.

She rotated her chair with the tips of her toes. "You ready to talk business?"

As if he hadn't been. As if the discussion of invisibility and the lessons in healing had been his idea.

But he didn't let those thoughts out. It was better for him to keep as much control around Zoe as he could, so he wouldn't make another mistake.

"Yes," he said. The word sounded meek. He wasn't feeling meek. The irritation he felt was fueled by a sexual tension he had buried long ago. He wished he could bury it again.

"All right." She nodded toward a chair. "Sit."

He walked into the office, set the lotion on the desk, and sat in the chair closest to the desk. While he had been healing his face, Zoe had cleaned up the front. The smell of wet fur was gone, along with the remaining five-dollar bill, and that embarrassing scrap of pink cloth.

"This is going to be difficult for you," she said. "You'll be learning about two magic systems at once. You'll have to keep firmly in mind which refers to our system and which refers to the faerie system."

"How do you know that I'm not part of the faerie system?" he asked.

To his surprise, she grinned. "You don't have pointed ears and a rude manner."

"Excuse me?"

"The faerie's magic is hereditary. Occasionally, the faeries bring in a civilian, but the faerie traits dominate. You'd have a particular look if you were faerie."

Travers was intrigued. "So how do we get our magic?"

"No one knows. We're all orphans. We just appear on someone's doorstep one day." Then Zoe peered at him. "Except you. You have a family. Kyle has magic. He's your son, right?"

"Oh, yeah," Travers said. "Can't you tell?"

She smiled. "You look alike, but sometimes that doesn't mean anything. Especially when you're dealing with magic. What about the rest of your family?"

"My sisters and I were adopted," Travers said. "Kyle says that Vivian has magic—or will. She's psychic, too, although I never believed it before this month."

"And your other sister?" Zoe asked.

"Megan?" Travers shrugged. "She's as normal as they come."

"Like you."

He felt the words as if they had a steel edge. The ease he had thought was returning between him and Zoe disappeared.

"Good point," he said.

"Still, two or three in one family is very unusual for us. Did the Fates say anything to you about this?" Zoe asked.

Travers shook his head.

"So they knew about it." She steepled her fingers and leaned back in her chair. It squeaked. "Fascinating."

He didn't want to think about his family. Not about his sisters or his parents or Kyle. Especially not Kyle, who, if Travers was lucky, was at this moment talking Klingon to some poor, unsuspecting *Star Trek: The Experience* employee.

"Your parents have no magic?" Zoe asked.

"My parents found Viv appalling," Travers said. "Not because she had psychic experiences, but because they often made her black out. My folks took her to all kinds of doctors, but it wasn't until our Aunt Eugenia—"

He stopped and frowned.

"Your aunt," Zoe said.

He shook his head. "She wasn't really an aunt. But she did help Viv. She even left her fortune to Viv. And Aunt Eugenia was weird. She had a way of making things happen."

"So your sister had a mentor," Zoe said. "I wonder what exactly happened to yours."

Travers shrugged. "It doesn't matter. You were going to explain the different systems to me."

"No," Zoe said. "I was going to tell you about my progress."

She tapped her steepled fingers against her chin, as if she were thinking about how to discuss this. He couldn't believe this was the same woman he'd kissed not half an hour before. She was cool and distant, not laughing and warm like she had been when they'd arrived.

"The faeries," she said after a moment, "believe in collecting power."

"I think someone mentioned that yesterday," Travers said.

"They take it from even the tiniest sources," Zoe said, undeterred. "Sometimes they use it, and sometimes they keep it. They hoard magical power for the future, so that if something happens and they need extra power, they can tap it, like a reservoir."

"Our people don't do that?" Travers asked.

"We consider it theft," Zoe said.

"Like what nearly happened last night," Travers said.

Zoe unsteepled her fingers, opened her hands in an I-don't-know gesture, and, for good measure, shrugged. "That's extreme, at least for faerie. Pretty common for us. Faerie goes after items—totems. You know, if you had a lucky quarter and whether or not it was lucky, you believed that it was, the faeries would want it."

"Because I have magic," Travers said.

"Even if you don't. The faeries think belief transfers a magical essence and, from what I've seen in this town, they may not be wrong."

"So by stealing this spinning wheel—"

"They stole great power from the Fates," Zoe said.

"Why didn't the Fates go after them?" Travers asked.

"That is the question, isn't it?" Zoe stood up. She paced behind her desk like a detective in the last scene of a locked-room mystery. "I've been asking myself that since yesterday. Part of it is pretty simple: the Fates didn't want a war with Faerie."

"Isn't that what they said?" Travers asked. A lot of the day before was a blur. His mind had to reorganize itself, and it still wasn't done. He thought he was doing pretty well for a man who believed he wasn't anything special, only to discover that he had an ability that made him extremely unusual.

"That's part of what they said." Zoe leaned against the desk, revealing a great deal of thigh. Travers had no idea why she wore skirts when so many women didn't anymore, but he didn't object.

Not even now, when he was pretending he could get his hormones back under control.

"They also said they didn't need the wheel anymore," Zoe was saying.

It took Travers a bit to concentrate on that last. The thigh had distracted him even more than he thought it would.

"But they need it now," Travers said. "What if it doesn't have any magic left?"

"If the faeries have stolen the power?" Zoe let out a whistling breath. "Oh, dear. That might be war. Some magical items—not totems like we were talking about, but items with true magic—they can't be depleted, except through overuse or misuse."

"And ruining this spinning wheel, which has been gone for longer than the Western World has recorded history, would be a cause for war?"

"Don't ask me," Zoe said, tugging at the edge of her skirt. "For a mage, I'm pretty young."

She wasn't looking at him when she said that. This was the third time she had brought up age. Perhaps it bothered her. It only intrigued him, although it might not have, if he still believed he had a limited lifespan.

Perhaps that was the best factor, the most mitigating. He might have all this pesky magic, but in exchange, he got to live what, in his mind, seemed like forever.

"It just seems odd," Travers said, thinking that sentence was odd. Everything had been odd since Viv's wedding. Only some things had been odder than others. "We're not going to start a war, are we, by stealing the thing?"

"We're not going to steal it." Zoe hopped off the desk. There was something she wasn't telling him. Some plan.

"And shouldn't we even see if the wheel still has some power?"

Zoe looked at him over her shoulder. Her hair had caught on the edge of her lip, and she brushed the strand away.

"You don't get this, do you?" Her voice was low, almost dangerous. "What the Fates want us to do—want *me* to do—is go to one of the most unstable places on the planet and re-connoiter for them. I'll be lucky to get out alive, Travers."

"I thought you said you wouldn't have to go into Faerie." He matched his tone to hers. He wasn't going to let her intimidate him, no matter what.

"I'm hoping I won't," she said. "I have a few tricks that might work."

Travers sighed. He felt awkward sitting while she stood over him, looking like one of those mythic amazon women. Or maybe they weren't mythic, if Zeus ruled the world (or part of it) and faeries really did exist. Travers blinked, not willing to contemplate all the implications of that particular thought—wishing he had time to sit in a dark room for maybe—oh, who knew? A year or more—and assimilate all that he had learned so far.

But he didn't have that kind of time. And he was supposed to apprentice magic with a woman who might have to walk into danger at any moment, a woman he still wanted to kiss even though he vowed not to, a woman he would make love to if she only touched his skin again like she had a few minutes earlier.

He cleared his throat, hoping she hadn't noticed all the various emotions he had just run through—particularly the last one. "You were going to tell me what you found."

She nodded, and leaned against the desk again. Only this time she was facing him. If he were cruder, or younger, or bolder, he would adjust his chair ever so slightly. It wouldn't take much to peer along those thighs, underneath that skirt—

Travers clenched his fists so hard that the nails bit into his skin. He had to control his thoughts, if not for his hormones' sake, then for the sake of his magic. He didn't want to make another English mistake—only this time, with Zoe.

"You ready for a history lesson?" Zoe asked.

This time, Travers sighed loudly. All he'd been getting the last few days were history lessons. And he'd been a math major. History and fiction had never interested him.

"Do I have a choice?" he asked.

"Not if you want to know what's going on," Zoe said.

"I figured as much," Travers said, and braced himself. He would need some trick for paying attention, besides avoiding looking at Zoe's knees.

To his relief, she went around the desk and plopped in her chair.

"Let me tell you a true faerie tale," she said, and started to talk.

Twenty-one

Kyle sat under one of the big umbrellas at the water park, feeling nearly naked in his swim trunks. He was sipping a vanilla milkshake, his feet propped on the chair beside him, while the Fates were splashing around in one of the nearby pools.

Through the gate, he could see the Strip—more cars and people than he wanted to think about—and all the grand Vegas stuff folks were always talking about: the big towers, the glass-sided hotels, and casinos, casinos, casinos.

If he saw another person carrying one of those plastic jugs of nickels and thinking, *One more chance—all I need is one more chance,* he'd knock the jug from their hands, scream *One more chance isn't going to make you any richer than you already are!* and run away.

He had never realized how badly adults could delude themselves until he came here.

He had been banned from the water into the shade of this poolside umbrella because his skin was turning that lovely shade of red his dad called "lobster." Kyle had even bought sunscreen—planning ahead because he knew swimming was an option. But he couldn't get anything above an SPF of 30 and he needed at least 50 to spend a lot of time in the sun.

So the Fates had banished him to the shade, where he got to watch their matching purses, their towels, their clothes, and their milkshakes.

Kyle really wanted to get back to the air conditioned hotel room, see how Fang was doing, and take a nap. But he didn't want to admit the nap thing to anyone. It was just, after some hours of sightseeing and goofing in the sun, he was tired.

He was also tired of being vigilant. The Fates were naïve— it felt like he was baby-sitting them instead of the other way around. They didn't even notice how all the grown-up men in *Star Trek: The Experience* were hitting on them.

Clotho got asked out the most (Kyle was keeping track) but that was probably because she was blond and looked a lot like Heidi Klum. (So, Kyle assumed, people were probably mistaking her for the supermodel.) Lachesis and Atropos tied with the same number of men asking them out—sometimes the same men, who would go from one beautiful woman to the other without taking a breath.

Kyle was actually glad to get to the darkness of the shuttle simulator, and when the ride was over, he turned down the Fates' offer to take him to Quark's Bar and Restaurant just so he could get them out of the building.

He hadn't expected them to immediately head for the water park. But they'd brought their giant purses, and one of the Fates had been smart enough to shove his swimming suit into the bag with theirs. He argued the whole walk over from the Hilton, where the *Experience* was, to the water park, but the Fates wouldn't budge.

They had it in their heads that they would give him a good time, whether he wanted it or not.

What he really wanted was for those weird men to stop following him.

Actually, Kyle wasn't sure the weird men were following him or the Fates. At first, Kyle thought the men were extras at *Star Trek: The Experience.* They looked like short, thin Vulcans wearing the wrong kind of makeup. Their skin was darker than Spock's but not as dark as Tuvok's or T'Pol's. Their eyebrows didn't slash darkly like a Vulcan's, but soared over the eyes like wings.

But the thing that made these guys the most like Vulcan were their pointed ears. These things were masterful, even better than the ones on the current show. They looked real.

In the Hilton, Kyle had gone from escalator to elevator, trying to see if the guys were really following (just like detectives did in television chase scenes) and sure enough, the guys kept turning up— as his dad would say— like a bad penny.

So Kyle had mentioned this to the Fates on the way out of the Hilton, suggesting maybe a stop at their hotel (and thinking hopefully of a nap), when the Fates actually stopped in the middle of the sidewalk and turned around.

Kyle had to stop next to them, and hang there while the Fates looked for the guys—not that they were hard to miss. These guys kept walking toward the Fates, all determined, their expressions really serious.

The guys wore black, too, which had to be really hot on the sidewalk, without any shade at all. Kyle wasn't wearing black—his t-shirt and shorts were appropriate to the weather — and the heat, which he was kinda used to from L.A., was killing him.

These guys didn't even notice.

It took a moment for the Fates to see the guys, but when they did, all three women giggled.

Giggled!

Like Caitlin always did in math class when Jason Budregas made faces at her. She would just giggle and giggle and giggle like she couldn't stop and finally the teacher had to separate them.

The Fates giggled, and blushed, too, and for a minute, Kyle thought they wouldn't be able to stop, but they did, told him not to worry (in three different, yet confusing, ways) and urged him on to the water park.

He checked as they paid on the way in. The guys didn't follow. Instead, they kept walking like they weren't even interested in the water or the Fates or anything.

The Fates kinda deflated then, and Kyle asked them if they knew those guys. And the Fates said no, but he couldn't tell if they were lying.

And he never did get close enough to the guys to see what they were thinking. But Kyle knew if he ever saw them again, he would try to find out.

He finished his milkshake, sucking the last bit of vanilla creaminess out of the bottom with his straw, enjoying the slurpy sound. No one here to tell him to knock it off. No one to annoy.

And no one to mentally eavesdrop on, either. All people were thinking about was what a great day they were having, how nice the sun was, how nice the water was, and how much they hoped their (kid, mother, grandfather, best friend) was enjoying the trip.

Kyle burped and reached for Lachesis's strawberry shake, then changed his mind. He was stuffed, even if he hadn't had lunch yet.

He glanced at the water slide, watched Atropos go down with her hands up and her head back as she laughed and screamed at the same time. He wanted to go, but he didn't. He remembered the last time he'd gotten badly sunburned.

Dad had actually had to take him to the emergency room where they reamed out Dad, not Kyle, and it hadn't even been Dad's fault.

Kyle stretched. Maybe the nearby vendors would have sunscreen with the right SPF. He stood, wrapped a towel over his shoulders like a cape, and padded barefoot across the hot concrete to the nearest shop.

He had some money stuffed in the pocket of his suit. Too late, he realized he'd left the Fates' purses behind. He turned around and headed back to the umbrella, only to see those three guys walking toward it from the opposite direction.

Kyle felt like he was in one of those old Western movies, where the good guys and the bad guys face off in the noonday sun. Only he'd forgotten to bring his share of the good guys. There was just him, and these three guys with pointed ears.

The guys had changed out of their black leather. They were wearing Speedos, and the suits looked okay on them, too. Only these guys had tattoos across their tummies and backs and down their arms, tattoos of things like women with wings and dragons and other stuff that Kyle had only seen on fantasy novels.

They also had pierced nipples, which made Kyle hurt. He clutched the towel even tighter and kept walking. Given luck, he'd get to the umbrella table at the same time as the guys.

He opened his mind as he hurried, hoping to catch their thoughts. But he got the same old *great sun, great day, great vacation, wish you were here, hope Mom's enjoying herself, dang! I stubbed my toe, oh, I ate too much* and all of that.

Nothing that three guys with pointed ears and tattoos would be thinking.

Kyle ran back to his chair and slipped into it before the guys arrived. Then he thought sitting was a really stupid idea because he was at a disadvantage—he couldn't move quick and he couldn't get away. And, not to mention, his back was to the guys.

He turned around, but the guys were gone.

Kyle looked for the Fates, and didn't see them, either.

Then all three came down the big water slide, their legs wrapped around each other, screaming joyfully in three-part harmony.

Kyle sighed and stood. He was going to have to be the grown-up on this one, and he hated being the grown-up. If he'd learned anything this morning, that was it. He wanted someone else to make the decisions.

The Fates surfaced in the pool, their blond, red, and black hair looking weirdly bright in the Vegas sun. They waved at Kyle and he beckoned them forward.

He still couldn't see the guys anywhere.

The Fates swam over to him.

"I think we have to go," Kyle said. "Those guys are here."

"Really?" Clotho asked, turning. "Where?"

Lachesis and Atropos turned, too, as if they couldn't contain themselves.

"I'm serious. Those guys are scaring me," Kyle said. "They're stalking us."

"We'll be fine," Lachesis said, and dunked under the water. Atropos followed. Clotho gave him a wicked grin and sank beneath the surface, too.

Kyle clenched his fists, feeling as helpless as he ever had in his life. He wondered if he should send one of those screaming messages that Zoe taught him about this morning.

He didn't know if this was the right kind of emergency. He sure didn't want to cry wolf or anything.

Kyle scanned the entire crowd, turning round and round and round, looking at faces and ears and Speedos, wondering if the guys had just vanished.

After a full 360 search, Kyle didn't see them. Maybe he was imagining the whole thing. Maybe those guys weren't anybody.

Or maybe he was getting a weird kind of future vision—something that hadn't happened yet, but might.

Kyle went back to the shade and grabbed Atropos's chocolate shake, which was pretty melted. He started to drink it as he stared into the pool.

What he would do was simple: if he saw the guys again, he'd let out one of those mental screams. And then he'd get the Fates out of here as fast as possible.

He was ready, even if they weren't.

Twenty-two

The history of Faerie, as told by Zoe Sinclair, was short, dark, and surprisingly brutal. Travers found himself slumped in his chair, his hands clasped behind his head, trying hard not to let the images she gave him form pictures in his head.

The *Reader's Digest Condensed* version was, as best as he understood it, that the faeries abandoned their woodsy, nature-vibe lifestyle sometime after Christianity made it into the British Isles, but sometime before industrialization. Most of the faeries moved to America, where they thought they could live in peace and harmony, mingling with the natives. Then they realized that the natives had their own form of magic (one that Zoe refused to discuss—saying a third magical reality was more than Travers could bear. He figured he had the right to decide what he could bear and what he couldn't, but he'd already irritated her once today, so he decided not to irritate her again).

A lot of the faerie myths were true, just like a lot of the mage myths were true, but the truth was hidden in the storytelling.

"What does that mean for us?" Travers asked.

"It means we can't trust them," Zoe said. She was still leaning against the desk, still looking beautiful, and still enticing him, whether she was trying or not.

Travers kept his eyes on hers, so he wouldn't look at those knees, which led to the thighs, which led to —

"I figured that much out on my own," Travers said. "About not trusting them, that is. What I haven't figured is how all this matters to our case."

The "our" came out before he could stop it, but Zoe didn't seem to notice. Or if she did notice, she didn't mind.

"You know the story of Rip Van Winkle?" Zoe asked.

"Yeah," Travers said.

"The story's true," Zoe said. "A lot of the stories you heard about that part of New England were true. The faeries were trying to get rid of the Europeans who might recognize them. What do you think happened to Roanoke?"

"Huh?"

"The first colony, the one where all the colonists mysteriously vanished?"

"I've never heard of it," Travers said.

Zoe crossed her arms. She shook her head. "What do they do for education these days?"

"I studied math."

"I studied everything." She sighed. "Of course, there was a lot less of everything when I was young."

She made herself sound ancient. It was her fourth mention of age. Clearly it bothered her, and he was going to see if he could change it.

"Anyway," she said. "Rip van Winkle, the Headless Horseman, all faerie tricks to get rid of the colonists."

"That worked," Travers said.

Zoe smiled. "The faeries have always underestimated mortals."

"And mages haven't?" Travers asked.

Zoe shrugged and stood. Her skirt fell across her knees, and Travers felt a stab of disappointment. Another opportunity lost. Not that he was going to take advantage of it.

"That's the nice thing about focussing on love," Zoe said. "You don't worry about advantage or disadvantage. Your concern is with finding the perfect mate and living happily ever after."

"Then how come all of the mages I've met are single?" Travers asked.

Her expression fell for a brief moment. It was as if she couldn't control the muscles on her face. And then she shrugged again, a slightly empty smile crossing her lips.

"You haven't met very many of us," she said and turned away.

She grabbed some papers off her desk, shuffled them, then stacked them. She sighed once, and said, "Faeries are tricksters. That's what they did to old Rip Van Winkle. They tricked him out of a very important decade of his life. What the story doesn't tell you is that they raided his land and his business, taking items of magical power. He was a strong believer in many things, and the faeries wanted those things. But he recognized them for what they were. And as punishment, they kept him in magic time for longer than they needed to. He lost everything. Wife, children, friends. Even his country."

Her voice was soft.

"That's what you're afraid of?" Travers asked. "Afraid they'll trick you out of everything?"

She shook her head. "They've become a lot more sophisticated now. They can take magic from you or even from me in the right circumstances—and if they have enough power."

"You mentioned that yesterday."

"What I didn't mention yesterday is that the faeries have stockpiled magical items all over the United States. There are places in this country where they keep the most important items." Zoe ran a hand through her hair. The hair tangled, then fell against her cheeks.

Travers wanted to smooth it out, but he didn't touch her. Not after that earlier encounter.

"The faeries use those items to maintain their powers and also to maintain what they call Faerie—their mystical home."

"Like your Mount Olympus."

She gave him a sideways glance. "Look at your map, sweetie. Mount Olympus exists."

"But no one ever saw Greek gods living there," Travers said.

Zoe raised her eyebrows at him, then shook her head slightly. "Mount Olympus is the highest mountain in Greece. The top is always hidden behind a layer of clouds. And there's a reason for that."

"Yeah," Travers said. "At a certain level in the atmosphere—"

"No," Zoe said. "It's magic. There is a palace on top of that mountain and the Powers That Be live there. The Muses live on the mountainside and manage to keep their homes invisible most of the time, and the judicial courts, it is said, float among the clouds."

"You don't know where they are?" Travers couldn't quite keep the sarcasm from his voice.

"No one does." Zoe set the papers down. "You've seen how people are reacting to the Fates lacking their powers. Imagine if people knew where the Fates lived and worked. America didn't invent going postal, you know. You just named it."

"So the faeries didn't have a mountain," Travers said.

"They could have, I suppose." Zoe tapped her computer keyboard, bent over it, and the printer snapped to life. "I mean, they were in Europe, after all. But early on, faeries lived in tribes, and they were pretty hostile to each other."

The printer beeped twice and then began spitting out paper.

"But the faeries chose to create their hideaway out of thin air, and they've continued that practice in the States. They have several, and they're all interconnected. Magical totems keep the things going. If you can imagine that Faerie itself is like an oven, and the totems provide the electricity to keep the thing running, then you have an idea of what we're talking about."

She took the papers out of the printer, and rolled them in one hand. Then she shut the printer off.

"Okay," Travers said. "So there are thousands of magical items."

"Millions," Zoe said. "Maybe billions. So many that only a few can keep track of them. But, thanks to the Internet, and all those internal faerie conflicts, we actually have a chance of figuring out where some items are stored."

"Internal conflicts?"

She waved her hand, dismissing that. "As I said, they're tribal. These conflicts have existed since the first ear got pointed. Don't even try to follow it all."

"I don't see how it relates to the Internet."

"Faerie e-Bay," she said with a grin.

"Faerie what?"

"E-Bay," she said. "Except that it's not really e-Bay, since that's a trademarked name and a real business. But faeries do steal and then trade magical items, always looking for the better totem. Some of those items actually are on e-Bay— original rabbits' feet from the 1930s, wishing-well pennies, things like that, only with descriptions that make them appealing only to faeries in the know."

Travers shook his head. The secret worlds had secret worlds, which probably had more secret worlds. And they all seemed to have secret passwords and understandings and ways of doing business.

No wonder Zoe didn't want to tell him about any other magical systems.

"So we go on e-Bay and look for a spinning wheel?" Travers asked.

"Tried that late last night," Zoe said. "I found a lot of spinning wheels, but none old enough and none with the right description. So I had to follow a few digital trails. I managed to locate Faerie e-Bay. Its domain changes from week to week, and finding it is always a trick."

"Of course," Travers muttered.

"But I found it and a few other sites, and managed to discern that the wheel hasn't been on the market."

"Recently?"

"Ever," Zoe said. "So whoever originally stole it still has it."

"Okay." Travers's headache from the day before was returning. Was there a maximum amount of information the brain could handle? He didn't know, but if he had to guess, he was beginning to think he had reached it. "There was no Internet several thousand years ago, so that means the trail's a dead end."

"Ah, Travers," Zoe said, slapping the rolled papers against her hand. "You've forgotten the whole point of this discussion."

"There was a point?" he asked, then realized he had said that out loud.

But Zoe didn't seem to notice. "There was. Myths, legends, slipping into the mortal consciousness. I looked up fairy tales and local legends, starting in Greece and working my way outward."

"Legends about spinning wheels?"

Zoe nodded. "There are more than you would think."

"I'm surprised there's even one," Travers said.

Zoe sighed. "You have to start paying attention. The Fates told you the first one. It was about them."

"Oh, yeah," he said, although he wasn't sure he remembered a fairy tale. He remembered them saying they had a spinning wheel, and that was all.

"Anyway, I traced the wheel to the dominant tribe of faeries, the ones that lived in the British Isles for so long. That's good luck for us."

"It is?" Travers asked.

Zoe nodded. "It means that the wheel is somewhere in North America. When the tribe came over, it wasn't going to leave its most powerful possessions behind."

"'Somewhere in North America' is a big space," Travers said.

"But here's the great thing about Faerie," Zoe said. "The rules of time and space don't exactly apply."

Travers rubbed the bridge of his nose. That headache was growing worse. "Meaning?"

"Meaning that like Rip Van Winkle, if you go into Faerie and aren't careful, you'll lose years in the space of minutes."

"Oh, good," Travers said.

"And if you enter Faerie in Las Vegas, you can go anywhere on the North American continent—provided there's a Faerie portal leading out."

"I can go anywhere on the continent now," Travers said.

"In a matter of seconds," Zoe said.

"Oh." Travers frowned. "But I'd lose years."

"No," she said. "Distances aren't as—distant—in Faerie. They're only as long as you want them to be."

He leaned forward in his chair, suddenly very uncomfortable. "It sounds like you want to go into Faerie now. What happened to 'it could be the death of us,' and all that danger stuff?"

She bit her lower lip, then seemed to catch herself. "I'm hoping we won't have to go in. I'm hoping we can get someone to go for us. And it won't take long, and we'll be done with helping the Fates. They'll become someone else's problem."

"I suppose you have someone in mind," Travers said.

"Yes," Zoe said, and her smile was radiant. "I certainly do."

Twenty-three

Zoe knew her plan verged on crazy. But she also knew that if a person couldn't trust her friends, she couldn't trust anyone.

She was going to have to go to Herschel and Gaylord. But first, she wanted to double-check her information.

She wasn't going to explain this part of the plan to Travers. He didn't need to know that she had a bit more research to finish before sending anyone into Faerie. Zoe managed to get him out of her office by promising lunch. She didn't tell him until they pulled up outside Rigo's Tacos that lunch would be a fried pork burrito on the run.

To his credit, Travers didn't complain. He just took a lot of extra napkins, and ate in silence.

Zoe sipped the take-out iced tea she'd gotten at Rigo's and drove one-handed through the North Las Vegas traffic.

North Las Vegas was a different city from Vegas. North Las Vegas sprang up around the air force base, and never really took off the way Vegas proper did. But North Vegas had its own charm, and it felt like a real city, with truly ethnic neighborhoods and old buildings ripe for redevelopment, and urban renewal taking place in the Golden Triangle section.

Zoe wasn't heading to the Triangle. She was driving to one of the old neighborhoods, filled with buildings that had become ramshackle in the desert sun. Bars on the windows, walls with gang tags, and broken-down cars huddling next to the curb made the area seem more dangerous than it was.

She could feel Travers tense beside her, and she didn't care. She felt more at home in places like this than she did in the bright and shiny Strip. The Strip was for tourists. North Vegas was for locals.

She parked in an alley behind a row of single-story buildings made of a bad combination of wood and adobe. The original building, in the center, was made of real adobe, and had once been the only business on this road. Over the years, the other buildings sprang up around it, and Zoe could remember, in the late 1950s, when this block looked nice and clean, and the new buildings made the old building seem like it had been freshly built, too.

Now all of them tottered against each other like elderly friends heading into a buffet. Two buildings housed pawnshops, two others hosted liquor stores, and two more were closed.

The building in the center, the original, was shrouded, the windows impossible to see. Zoe didn't care about that—the building housed one of those shops only a handful of people knew about, because only a handful of people needed to know.

Occasionally mortals—local and tourist—wandered into the shop and thought they'd come upon a curio store. Usually they ended up regretting their stop; they picked up something cursed or too magical for them to understand, and no matter how many warnings the clerks gave them, the mortals bought the item anyway.

Zoe had no patience with those people, but she did try to protect them. That's why she had never, in all her years in Vegas, brought anyone here before.

Today, she felt she had no choice.

No one else was parked in the alley, and the nearby roads were deserted. The afternoon sun bleached the area white, making the asphalt, the iron bars, even the once-pink walls of the buildings seem to glow with reflected light.

Travers's skin wasn't glowing this time, though. The potion she'd cobbled together worked as both healing lotion and sunscreen. He didn't know that yet, either, but he would by the time they got back to the hotel.

He climbed out of the car. She walked to his side of the car and protected it—not with an invisibility spell (in this neighborhood that would be a neon "Steal Me" sign) but with the Club, which she carried in her trunk for just such an emergency.

Travers didn't even ask her about that—why she would use a regular, manmade protection device in one neighborhood and a magical one in another.

That bothered her as well—shouldn't he be more curious about this stuff?—and then she realized that he felt nervous in this alley, looking over his shoulder at the black spray paint shouting its affiliations on the side of a nearby Dumpster.

He was uneasy, and he was trying to pretend that he wasn't. Zoe smiled. It had been clear from the moment she met him that he had led a sheltered life, even though it had been in Los Angeles.

The longer he stayed around her, the less sheltered it would become.

"Come on," she said, and walked down the two concrete steps that led into the back door of the shop. She pulled the door open by the decorative iron bars that covered it, listening to the hinges squeal as she stepped into the darkness.

The transition from early afternoon sunlight to badly lit

shop was always a difficult one. When she entered this place, she always felt as if she had to step through a dark cavern to get into the real store. It was almost the way a fade-out in a movie would feel.

For one entire minute, the world went black: no sight, no sound, no texture.

But a lot of smells. Incense and pot and something fetid, mixing with that ancient sweet-plastic smell that drugstores used to have. Then the fetid smell faded, the pot smell became expensive pipe tobacco, and the incense became expensive soap, making the place seem even more enticing.

The first few smells—and the darkness—often discouraged the casual customer. (And if they couldn't be discouraged, well, that was their problem.) The other smells were real—or as real as anything was in this particular store.

Travers stayed close to Zoe, not complaining, but she could still sense his unease. She hadn't warned him about this place, deciding that he had to get used to surprises; they would be part of his life from now on.

Gradually, the darkness faded or her eyes adjusted or the entrance spell wore off—she was never sure which it was—and the room revealed itself, one small area at a time. The store never looked the same: sometimes it resembled a down-on-its luck antiques store; sometimes it reminded her of a 1960s head shop; and sometimes it seemed like a casino gift shop gone bad.

This time, the décor was a mixture of 1960s kitsch and a designer dinnerware outlet store. Mixed in among the orange bubble lamps and the once state-of-the-art hi-fis was very expensive crystal glassware. Near the purple-and-blue plastic cups were stoneware dishes that would cost most people a small fortune to buy new, and beside the square color TV with its very own rabbit ears were Erte sculptures that Zoe suspected were original.

The smells had settled down now, too—the pipe smell faded, replaced by the dusty odor of an desert antiques store; the sweet-plastic drugstore odor remained, but instead of the expensive soap smell, the dominant scent in the room became the sharp, bubbly, gummy smell of Dippity Do.

"What is this place?" Travers whispered.

Zoe shushed him, but it was too late.

Elmer the Shaman appeared in a cascade of tiny, multi-colored lights. His rumpled face looked even older than it had the last time Zoe saw him, not three weeks ago. His eyes were sunken into his skull, and his skin, pockmarked from a smallpox epidemic at least three centuries before, seemed even darker than usual.

He wore a bright orange-and-green polyester shirt, its collar open 1970s disco style, and a pair of matching green polyester bell-bottom slacks. White platform boots peeked out from the bell-bottoms. He wore too much jewelry—several gold chains around his neck, an oversized ruby ring, and a watch three times larger than his wrist. The only thing that really didn't go with his 1970s outfit, however, was the battered bowler hat that he had stuck on his head.

He chewed on a toothpick, obviously trying to break his smoking habit once again, and peered at Zoe.

"You don't change, do you, girl?" His voice was deep, laconic, and tired.

"Once every fifty years I redo my style whether I need to or not," Zoe said, even though not a word was true. She did update her wardrobe all the time. She just didn't go from clothing period to clothing period in the space of a week like Elmer did.

Zoe put her hand on Travers's arm and pulled him forward. She could see his reflection in one of the glass-fronted curio cabinets. He looked like a man who had swallowed something awful.

"Elmer," Zoe said, "this is my friend Travers. He's new."

Elmer tucked his hat back slightly, and leaned forward on his platform boots. He looked like he was going to tip over.

"I'll say he's new." Elmer spoke with the toothpick in his mouth. It bobbed every time his lower lip moved. "New and worn at the same time, with a lot of out-of-control power."

Elmer pushed a finger in Travers's chest.

"This is the last town you should be in, boy," Elmer said.

Travers gave Zoe a help-me look.

She ignored it. "He's here for a reason."

"He should leave before that reason comes back to bite him," Elmer said. "He's bait, Zoe-babes. Let him go, and find someone more suitable."

"I'm not here to discuss my friends," Zoe said. It was unusual for Elmer to discuss them as well. Usually he ignored whoever she brought into the store.

"Friends?" Elmer stuck his hand through her arm. His fingers gripped her skin a bit too hard, just like they always did, as if he could draw strength from her just by touching her. "Now Zoe, you know you're more than friends."

She narrowed her gaze at him, first looking at his hand on her arm, and then at his face. "He's my friend, Elmer."

"Well, I certainly hope not because you're wasting a lot of spark," Elmer said. His grip on her arm grew even tighter. Zoe wondered if he had shut off the circulation.

"Spark?" Travers asked.

"Auras," Elmer said. "You two—you just spark off each other, like a fireworks show. Damn beautiful it is, but dangerous if you don't do something about it."

"Like what?" Travers asked.

"Like not believing everything you hear." Zoe slipped her arm out of Elmer's grasp. Her skin ached where his fingers had been. "I'm here because I need a few things, Elm, not because I need a reading."

Elmer shoved his hands in his pockets and shrugged. "Looks more like you need a reading."

"A reading?" Travers asked.

Poor Travers. He really was out of his depth. Zoe decided to throw him a tidbit.

"Elmer here is a shaman," Zoe said. "Or he thinks he's one, at any rate."

"Zoe," Elmer said. "Just because you've never taken advantage—"

"I don't need your prophecies," Zoe said. "We get enough from our Fates."

"Only one," Elmer said. "How can you guide your life with one prophecy? It's why you run scared, why you and this man are simply 'friends,' why you—"

"Elmer," Zoe snapped. "That's enough."

"Actually, I'm interested," Travers said.

"I'll bet you are," Zoe mumbled under her breath.

"I see things," Elmer said. "I explain them."

"You're psychic," Travers said as if he had figured out the answer to the hardest test ever written.

Elmer pushed the bowler back, away from his brow. "No."

His tone was so cold that Zoe shivered.

"Has the mage education system become that poor?" Elmer asked. "Who is his mentor? He shouldn't be asking questions like this."

"That's a long story," Zoe said.

Travers frowned. "I didn't mean to offend you. I just thought—"

"Thinking," Elmer said. "That's your first mistake."

Zoe stepped between Travers and Elmer. She kept her back to Travers, and stared down at Elmer. "I came here to shop, not to have a reading. If you don't want my business, then we can just leave."

"Didn't say that." Elmer squashed the bowler farther down

his skull. "Just thought Tall, Blond, and Confused here was interesting, that's all."

Travers stiffened beside her. She could feel his irritation growing.

"Is there a reason we're putting up with this?" he asked her in not-quite-a-whisper. His lack of subtlety made Elmer smile.

Zoe put a calming hand on Travers's arm. "Yes. Elmer, for all his flamboyance, has some talents that I lack."

Elmer grinned. "I have a lot of talents you lack, honey, and some we'd have to test."

Zoe felt the muscles in Travers's arm move as he clenched his fists. She patted his arm, then nodded at Elmer. "Let's go in the main part of the store, shall we?"

"I suppose," Elmer said, "but your boyfriend can't come. His magic is still too wild."

Zoe glanced at Travers. "Will you be all right out here?"

He shrugged. "This is all new to me. It's your decision."

His voice had a strained anger to it. He obviously didn't like being out of control.

"Just don't touch anything," Zoe said. "I'll be back as soon as I can."

"Fine." Travers nodded toward a small, red upholstered chair. "Can I at least sit while I wait?"

"I wouldn't," Elmer said, "unless you want to visit 1755. It's an antique, and it really doesn't like this century."

"Is there any place he can be comfortable?" Zoe asked.

"Not in here," Elmer said with a grin. He pulled back the curtain behind some of the curios. "Coming, doll?"

Zoe sighed. She knew that Elmer wouldn't help her with Travers present.

"Sorry," she said to Travers. "I'll hurry."

"Don't worry about me," he said. "I'll just stay out here and try not to speculate about what all this stuff does."

Zoe gave Travers an apologetic smile, then followed Elmer through the curtain. She went through another wave of darkness, and had a moment of doubt.

Maybe she didn't know what she was doing. Maybe she should simply tell the Fates they were on their own, pull up her stakes and leave Vegas, get as far from the nearest Faerie Circle as possible, and live out her life in quiet.

But she knew she couldn't do that, any more than she could leave that man standing in the front of Elmer's store. She felt for Travers.

She only hoped that, while he was waiting, he kept his thoughts and his fingers under control.

Twenty-four

By the time they'd finished lunch, Kyle's stomach felt as solid as a basketball. He had put a hamburger and fries on top of all three milkshakes, and he was already paying for it.

Except for *Star Trek: The Experience,* the day was pretty much a bust. Kyle was sunburned and nauseous, jittery and frightened, and worried about those three guys, who still appeared at the oddest times.

Since he got in the neighborhood of his hotel, though, he hadn't seen them. The Fates flanked him, talking happily about their rides, the water park, and the Rainforest Café where they'd coaxed him into that last bit of food.

He had known better than to eat when he was already stuffed. Now he felt like that guy in the Monty Python movie his dad had yelled at him for watching—the really fat guy who ate one last thing: a wafer-thin mint.

The very thought of a wafer-thin mint made Kyle's stomach turn over, and the act of it turning over made it turn over again. He put a hand on the small basketball he was growing there, and hurried along the block.

The Fates had to struggle to keep up.

Kyle glanced over his shoulder. No three guys. They had shown up in the Rainforest Café just as he and the Fates were leaving. They were sitting underneath a giant tree branch, studying the bright green fake frog on the table beside them.

As far as Kyle could tell, the men didn't see them leave.

Still, he glanced around before slipping into his hotel's lobby. No Vulcan men, no strangers. Only tourists on the street who looked like normal people.

Of course, he and his dad looked like normal people, and they were about as strange as it got.

"I do think we should change clothes and go to one of the casinos," Clotho said. She slipped her hand on Kyle's back, making his sunburn sting.

He pretended it didn't hurt.

"I would love to crap," Lachesis said.

"Play craps," Atropos said.

"Is that the proper way to say it?" Clotho asked Kyle.

"I don't even know what it is." He sounded as grumpy as he felt. Maybe just a little less. If he sounded as grumpy as he felt, he would be yelling at them.

"It's a game of cards," Lachesis said.

"Dice," Atropos said.

"It's gambling, though, right?" Kyle asked.

All three Fates nodded.

"I can't go with you if you do that, and my dad'll be really mad at me for letting you go alone." Especially if he gave them any of the money he carried in his wallet. The Fates didn't understand money, and they didn't understand games, and they certainly didn't understand gambling.

Kyle hurried them along the lobby, filled with mirrors and video poker machines, and onto the elevators. He wanted nothing more than a cool shower and a long nap.

The elevators were large and mirrored as well. Kyle saw

himself in the reflecting glass as he stepped on board. He had gone past lobster an hour ago. Now he was fire engine red. His dad would be so furious with him. Sunburn avoidance was like topic number one between the two of them in the summer—the fate of natural blonds in California, his dad liked to say.

Only they weren't in California. They were in Nevada, and even though Kyle was happy to miss school, he really wanted to go home.

"Who're those guys?" he blurted as the elevator doors closed, narrowly missing Atropos's foot.

"What guys?" Clotho asked, but she didn't sound innocent. She was clearly pretending not to know exactly what he was talking about.

"Those three Vulcans who were following us everywhere," Kyle said.

"Vulcan is here?" Lachesis asked.

"Aphrodite let him off the mountain?" Atropos glanced at the other two Fates in surprise.

"He doesn't like to leave his forge," Clotho said. "And no one has called him Vulcan in years."

"Well, they're not calling him Hephaestus, either," Lachesis snapped.

Atropos let out a long breath. "Real name," she breathed, and in it, Kyle heard a warning.

He wasn't entirely sure he understood it, but he guessed that Lachesis had just used someone's real name, and that was bad.

"No," Kyle said. "Not a single Vulcan. But people from the planet Vulcan, like in *Star Trek*."

"Like Spock," Clotho said with a smile. "I must admit, he's my favorite."

"I prefer Kirk," Lachesis said. "A man of action is always more interesting."

"Picard combines both logic and action," Atropos said. "And his head is delightfully bald—"

"Stop!" Kyle held up his hands. His queasy stomach put him in no mood for their conversations. "I just asked about the three guys who've been following us all day. You know, the ones with pointed ears?"

"Oh, them," Clotho said, crossing her arms and leaning against the brass railing that circled the elevator. "I didn't see them, did you?"

"No," Lachesis said, looking up at the floor numbers ticking away. "I didn't see them anywhere. Certainly not at the café or the water park."

"Or Quark's," Atropos said, studying her fingernails. "I didn't see them at Quark's, either."

Kyle couldn't read the Fates' minds (for which he said a grateful prayer every night), but he didn't have to in this instance. And he was just queasy enough to forget that they were adults and he wasn't. Confronting the Fates didn't bother him.

"You know these guys, don't you?" he asked.

"Of course not," all three Fates said in unison, but not one looked at him, not even through their reflections in the mirrors.

"What's all this about?" Kyle asked, but as he did, the elevator bobbed to a stop, and the doors slid open, revealing their floor.

"Nothing," Clotho said.

"Don't you worry about it," Lachesis added.

"Really, it's nothing," Atropos said, and then all three Fates giggled as they headed to their room.

Kyle was going to ask if he should come with them, and then he decided he didn't care. They didn't have any money, so they couldn't go out, and they knew where his room was, so if they wanted to leave, they could just come and get him.

Besides, he'd made his desire for a nap known, and they had said they wanted one, too.

If they were lying to him, and bringing in those three weird guys, well then, that was their problem, wasn't it?

The thought made Kyle shiver. His dad wouldn't like it.

"Hey!" he shouted. "Either you gotta come to my room or I gotta come to yours!"

"We'll shower, nap, and then come find you," Clotho said.

"We promise we'll be good," Lachesis said.

"The only strange men we'll see will be on television," Atropos said.

Kyle rolled his eyes. He still wasn't sure he believed the Fates, but at least he could say that he tried. He shuffled down the hall to his room, used the key to open the door, and was nearly assaulted by a very lonely dachshund who needed to go out.

Kyle looked down the hallway and sighed. His stomach still ached. His skin felt like crispy chicken. And the nap was coming whether he could hold it off or not.

But Fang had his back legs crossed, almost literally. So Kyle dropped his towel inside the door, and headed back to the elevator, this time leading a dachshund who was so glad to see him, Kyle nearly forgot how awful he felt.

He got in the elevator and closed his eyes, but not before checking to make sure the hallway outside the Fates' room was empty.

He had given those three guys the slip.

Now he hoped they wouldn't find him—or the Fates—again.

Twenty-five

Travers stood in the center of the strange little shop, feeling even more out of place than he had when he first came into Las Vegas. He had no idea how this store would help him or Zoe find the Fates' spinning wheel. He didn't know what the strange man had that Zoe could need. And he wasn't exactly sure what a shaman was, at least not in the context of Zoe's many magical worlds.

The shop was dark and cluttered. The lamps, lit on various tables around the room, were all from the 1960s, and looked like they'd been rejected by Hugh Hefner for his bachelor pad. They were bubble-shaped and garishly colored.

They also didn't give off much light.

Travers was almost afraid to move across the matted shag carpet to peer at the various items. He recognized a Big Chief notebook in pristine condition and a fat pencil beside it, the kind kids used to have when his dad was in school.

There were ashtrays everywhere—collections of ashtrays, from the Grand Canyon and all of the old Vegas strip hotels and various bars. He could have sworn, when he came into the shop, that the ashtrays were full, but now when he looked at them, he realized they weren't.

This place played a lot of tricks on the eyes, and he didn't like it. He didn't like any of it. He felt awkward just standing in the middle of the room like a forgotten child, unable to touch anything.

Still, he had to do something. Maybe there were books here that he could buy, books that would help him study his new magical life. Travers sighed. It felt so odd to think about a new magical life.

A movement caught Travers's eye. A mirror bubbled to life, filled with fog like a steaming pot. He frowned at it, but didn't step any closer.

The mirror was oval-shaped, just like the mirrors in the movies, and it had a gilt frame that looked both heavy and sturdy. The mirror was mounted on the wall, and beneath it was a calligraphed sign that said in large letters:

Don't Touch!!

He didn't plan to. He had heard the warnings, and he was learning that they existed for a good reason.

Still, the mirror continued to fog as if someone had a dry ice machine running behind it. At the thought, Travers turned and saw only more tables behind him, tables with tiny items that he couldn't identify.

Finally a large cloud of smoke left the mirror. The smoke surged forward, dispersing in the already dark room. The air smelled faintly of burning leaves, and then the scent faded as if it never was.

The mirror cleared, like a pond after ripples faded away, and he found himself staring at a woman's face.

She had wild, green hair that exploded around her head as

if she were a cartoon character who had stuck her fingers in a light socket. The green, however, accented her opalescent skin, and made her green eyes glow.

The mirror only showed her from her face to her shoulders. She wore nothing on that part of her body, not even earrings or a necklace. The look provided the illusion of nudity, even if she were fully dressed from the chest downward.

She was oddly beautiful. Travers took a step toward her before he had to consciously think of stopping.

He wasn't supposed to touch anything, no matter what.

"There you are," the woman said, her voice rich and warm, filled with vibrato. It almost sounded as if she were singing. "I've been sensing you all day, and you're in Elmer's store. Your magic makes you unhappy."

Travers looked over his shoulder, hoping that someone else was in the store with him. No one was, of course. He was on his own.

She raised her eyebrows. They were black, which somehow accented all that green. "I heard Elmer's instructions. He said not to touch, but he didn't say not to talk."

"Who are you?" Travers asked.

She smiled. "Someone who can make your life a whole lot easier."

Travers crossed his arms. "I don't talk to mysterious people who refuse to give their names."

"I've gotten a sense of you," she said as if he hadn't spoken, "just from the short time that I've been observing you. It's pretty clear to me that you don't like this magic business. I can take your powers off your hands in exchange for the wheel."

"Wheel?" he asked, his heart pounding.

"The spinning wheel," the woman said. "The one your friends the Fates are looking for. I can give it to you."

Scam operators were the same in magic worlds and non-magic worlds. Somehow Travers found that reassuring.

"Who did you say you were?" he asked.

"Why does it matter so much?" Her voice was like melted honey.

"Because I don't deal with people I don't know," he said.

"Hmm." Her smile widened. "Savvy to the way of the world, are we?"

"I don't know about we Travers said, "but me, I have always made it a policy to deal with people I know, whose reputation has been verified, and who will work honestly with me."

He almost leaned against a nearby table, then caught himself.

The woman in the mirror didn't seem to notice his movement. Her startling green eyes had narrowed. She obviously didn't like the direction this conversation was taking.

"So," Travers said, "tell me who you are, I'll check with people I know about your reputation, and then we'll see if we can come to terms we both like."

She raised her chin. Her eyes seemed to be an even brighter green. It was almost as if they were lit from within.

"This is a one-time offer," she said. "Decide now, or lose the wheel forever."

Travers gave her his most charming smile. "I'm afraid I've made my decision."

"You'll regret it," she said, and winked out of the mirror. For a moment, its surface rippled as if it were a pond that had been disturbed. Then the smoke sucked back into the glass in one large cloud, almost like reverse photography.

The smoke swirled and boiled for a long time before it faded into nothingness. The glass now reflected the interior of the store.

Travers sighed. He hoped he had done the right thing. He hoped he hadn't screwed up their chance to find the spinning wheel.

But even if he had, he didn't entirely regret what he had done. Fairy tales had taught him not to trust women who hid in mirrors. And besides, he'd wanted to bargain. She just hadn't worked with him.

In his world—his old world—that was the sure sign of a flimflam artist.

He hoped it was in this new world as well.

Those were his superficial reasons for turning her down, but deep inside, he had one more, and it really unsettled him.

He was beginning to like the idea of having magic. He had been the most normal person in his family, a man who lived a normal life with a not-so-normal child. He had a normal job, and he lived in a normal house.

He'd never really had the chance to be different.

And now he was.

Strange what a difference a few days could make. He'd learned that before, when Kyle was born, but he was learning it all over again.

Travers's world had changed, and now that he was used to the change, he was growing to like it—chaos and all.

Twenty-six

The curtain swished around Zoe as she followed Elmer into his back room.

The space beyond the curtains was dark. Obviously this was Elmer's way of controlling the people around him. He had them step through a doorway into darkness, then gradually revealed their surroundings.

This time, the smells that engulfed her were mundane: a faint odor of dusty cloth mixed with an even fainter odor of mothballs. For all she knew, that was how the curtain could have smelled.

Then the lights came up, slowly, as if someone were turning on a variety of switches that operated fixtures all over the room. Zoe's back muscles were tight with tension; she had been here once before when Elmer had given a tour to some of his favorite magic-users. That day, the main part of the store had been the size of a warehouse. It had held posters from Houdini and little curios from the real magic users who had died in the Spanish Inquisition.

This afternoon, however, the room was tiny, barely the

size of an average bedroom. A single table lined the back wall, and two chairs sat in front of it. Both chairs were made of wood with plain wooden seats. A boombox sat on an otherwise empty shelf, but no sound echoed in the room except Zoe's breathing.

Elmer stood near the chairs. He had changed clothing in the seconds he was waiting for her. Now he wore a pair of faded blue jeans and a matching denim shirt. His raven-black hair cascaded down his back, and a single thin braid, decorated with beads, ran down the middle of the cascade.

Elmer's magic combined several Native American traditions, although he had also been trained in mage magic and more faerie spells than any other non-faerie magician. His real name wasn't Elmer, of course. Zoe had no idea what it was.

But she had heard that he had been in this region for centuries. He knew what happened to the Anasazi and after the Spanish introduced horses to the New World, he had ridden all over the Southwest in search of new spells.

He collected magic like most people collected books. He did not acquire magic to add to his own power, but instead he understood the history of most magic systems she'd ever heard of, learned as many of their spells as he could, and sold that knowledge.

He also collected magical items and sold them as well. Zoe knew he didn't have the spinning wheel because he had been the first person she had checked with, and she trusted him enough to believe him when he told her that he had never seen it, although he had heard of it.

"What is it that your young friend can't hear?" Elmer asked, his hands threaded before him.

"Actually," Zoe said, "I'm less concerned about him than I am about all those things you have in the back room. Elmer, I saw at least five portals."

He shrugged. "They're becoming less and less useful in this day of airplane travel. No one wants devices anymore. They want to learn how to do the work themselves."

Zoe didn't know how to respond to that. She looked around, wondering why he had changed the shape of the room. Was he out of inventory?

He swept his hand toward the chairs. "Take a seat, my dear."

His manner was different here, less abrasive. He sat first, put his hands on his knees, and waited.

Zoe perched on the edge of the other chair.

"I have a love potion," Elmer said before she even started. "But I don't think it will do you any good."

"What?" Zoe slid back in the chair. His comment surprised her. It was so far from what she'd been thinking about that it took her a moment to understand him.

"A love potion," Elmer said. "In fact, I could make up several. But attraction isn't the problem here. Understanding is."

"Excuse me?" Zoe asked.

Elmer frowned, the look making his narrow eyes nearly disappear in his face. "You want to make the relationship with the young man work, don't you? He is the one you've been waiting for."

Zoe hated it when people made assumptions. "First of all, I haven't been waiting for anyone. Secondly, I'm not here about a love potion. And thirdly, if I needed anything like that—which I don't—I would have made it myself."

"My mistake." Elmer said that as if he believed he hadn't made a mistake at all. "What are you here for?"

Zoe made herself take a deep breath. "Three things. I need a protection charm that will withstand most people with small magicks."

Elmer's frown deepened.

"I need a location spell that's guaranteed to work."

Elmer sighed.

"And," Zoe said, trying not to sound dramatic and knowing she was failing, "I need a map of Faerie."

"Faerie?" Elmer sounded like he choked on the word.

"Yes," Zoe said.

"All of Faerie?"

"If possible," she said. "Otherwise, I'll take the areas in current use. They're mostly in the U.S., right?"

That was what she had told Travers, but she hadn't been certain. The problem with Faerie, aside from the fact that it was an artificial environment, was that it moved around all the time. What was true about it a month ago might not have been true about it yesterday.

"What are you about, Zoe?" Elmer asked.

"I'm working on a case," she said, not lying.

"I thought you had an aversion to Faerie."

"I do," she said. "I'm going to try to complete this case without going in."

"Child, even if I give you the perfect spells, you'll be undermagicked. Faerie is one of the most powerful places not on the planet."

"I know that," Zoe said.

"And the moment your magic touches it, the faeries will know that you're searching for something."

"I know that, too," Zoe said.

"They might not take too kindly to whatever it is you're going to do."

"I'm not going to do anything." She hoped.

"You're messing in things that are above both of us," he said. "The wheel belonged to the Fates who work for the Powers That Be. It was stolen by the Faerie Kings so they could wrest power from the Great Rulers. The Faerie Kings

believe their strength comes from that wheel. You cannot—
dare not—touch it."

"Who said I'm going after the wheel?" Zoe asked.

"Power vacuums. The world is whirling, young Zoe, and
the magic is changing. The word is that the Fates will never
return to their work and that Zeus already leads the Powers
That Be. Aphrodite has lost, and the powers that have kept
love in the mortal equation for centuries are gone."

"I hadn't heard that," Zoe said.

"You don't listen as closely as I do," Elmer said.

"It's not your tradition," Zoe said. "I would know."

Elmer shook his head. "You fail to realize, as all of you
youngsters fail to realize, that the traditions come from the
same source. It was political differences that gave us our war-
ring philosophies, and the magicks developed by one culture
are often in opposition to the magicks developed by another."

That made sense, even though Zoe hadn't heard it before.
Then a faint odor of burning leaves reached her, and she immediately thought of Travers.

Elmer looked at the curtain. It was moving as if in a small
wind.

"You would like to help him," Elmer said.

Zoe shook her head, even though the very denial was a
lie. "I'm here to talk with you. He's strong enough to take
care of himself."

"His magic is small and undeveloped. Forces older than
both of us might like him to augment their power."

"He'll be all right," Zoe said, wondering if this was a test,
and if so, what kind. To see how determined she was to pre-
serve the romantic love her people were known for? Or to
see if she could remain focused on her task, no matter what
the distraction?

"A map of Faerie," Elmer said, returning to her original

request, "will only show Faerie as it is this minute, and will be of no use to you."

"Don't play games with me, Elmer," Zoe said. "We both know that you can make an accurate map of Faerie that changes as Faerie changes."

Elmer's lips thinned. "It will be costly."

Zoe nodded. "I'm prepared for that."

"I have no protection charms that work in Faerie," he said.

"That charm is not for Faerie," Zoe said, not willing to explain more. She didn't want him to know—if he didn't already—that she was hiding the Fates.

"Any charm I will give you will only protect once," Elmer said.

"That's all I need," Zoe said.

He stood. "And the location spell? It is for Faerie, isn't it?"

"Yes," she said.

"The magic will be traced to me. You know that?" Elmer said.

"You already have an agreement with the faeries," Zoe said, "or you wouldn't have so many magic items here."

Elmer looked at her sideways. His face had grown heavier, angrier, as if he hadn't wanted her to know about his connection to Faerie.

But she had been in Las Vegas long enough to hear of items lost in a faerie casino that later appeared in Elmer's back room. His connection to Faerie, whatever it was, was important to both sides.

"How do you know my location spell can be trusted?" Elmer asked, voicing a thought that had hovered at the back of Zoe's brain since she got this plan.

"I don't," she said. "But I'm hoping it can be. After all, as you said, the world is changing. New alliances are being formed. You certainly wouldn't want to be left out of the change, would you?"

Elmer shrugged. "Modern politics doesn't concern me."

"Unless it affects your livelihood," Zoe said.

Elmer glared at her.

"I know people, too," Zoe said. "Play fair with me and I'll play fair with you."

Elmer's stare was unnerving, but she met it. Finally, he looked away. His fingers brushed the table.

On it, a Cubs baseball cap, a glowing tube, and a scrap of paper had appeared.

"Last chance to change your mind, Zoe," Elmer said.

"I won't change it," she said. "Tell me how much all of this is."

"Your detection services for a case of my choosing at a time of my choosing," he said.

"Any time within the next hundred years," Zoe added, not wanting to be indebted to him forever.

"A thousand," he said.

"Five hundred," she said.

"Done," he said, and she felt as if she had given in too easily. Still, she didn't complain.

Instead she looked at the items on the table. He handed her the baseball cap.

"Your protection charm," he said. "Be careful with it. Once the magic has fled, the cap itself is worth a great deal to baseball collectors. It's old and important."

Zoe resisted the urge to roll her eyes. Most of the items that the faeries collected in their totem search were sports-related. She never understood the power that people gave their special teams, nor did she understand the superstitious rituals that went with certain items.

Obviously, this cap had some of that superstition believed into it, which made sense, considering it belonged to one of the losingest and yet most popular teams in baseball.

She tucked the cap under her arm, knowing better than to put it on.

Then he handed her the scrap of paper. It was small, barely the size of her palm, and the edges of it were brown as if it had been rescued from a fire.

"Your spell," Elmer said. "Keep it flat. Do not read it aloud, and make sure you've closed your eyes when you've thought the final word."

"All right," Zoe said, taking the spell and letting it rest on her hand. The writing was old and spidery and looked to be in medieval Latin.

"Finally," Elmer said, picking up the tube, "your map. It will serve you for exactly one month. After that, its power will wane and it won't be worth the paper its superimposed upon. Don't look at it too much, or you'll lose time. Don't hold it too long, or you'll end up at a place of the map's choosing. Don't try to extract the magic from the map, or it might kill you."

Zoe nodded.

"Any questions?" he asked.

"No," she said.

"Good." He tucked the map under her other arm. "I hope I see you again, Zoe. If your quest doesn't work, then I'm the one out a fortune in magic."

"It'll work," Zoe said, wanting to add that he would be out a fortune, but she would be dead. It seemed to her that she would be the one getting the short end of that deal.

"I would wish you good luck," Elmer said, "but the faeries would steal the words and use them for their own nefarious purposes."

"Still," Zoe said, "I appreciate the sentiment."

And she did. But she had a feeling that what she was about to do would take more than luck. It would take skill and cunning and a great deal of strength.

But she knew—just like Elmer knew—that the thing she needed the most was the thing the faeries hoarded like gold: a belief that fortune would smile on her in her time of need.

Or in other words—

Luck.

Twenty-seven

Travers paced around the room, careful not to bump into any tables or brush any curio cabinets. The more he walked and peered, the more he saw: little faces smiling back at him; men waving from art deco cigarette cases; women blowing him kisses from World War II recruitment posters.

Now, it seemed, the curtain that Zoe had gone through had disappeared. And Travers couldn't see the back door. He was in a room without exits or windows, filled with stuff he wasn't allowed to touch, in a place that seemed outside reality.

And he also discovered that his cell phone wasn't working. Kyle couldn't reach Travers if he wanted to.

And Travers hated that. It didn't matter how many mental tricks Zoe had taught his son, they didn't compensate for modern wireless communication, done through the wonders of technology.

Travers had just about reached the end of his tolerance. Only he didn't know what to do when he really did reach the end of his tolerance. Would he try to call for Zoe? Or use a modification of one of the new spells she taught him?

Then Zoe appeared in front of him. He almost walked into her, and nearly grabbed an end table to right himself, catching himself at the last minute.

"Zoe?" he asked tentatively, not sure if she was a vision or not.

"Yep," she said. "It's me."

"You didn't come out of the curtain," he said, feeling slightly disoriented.

"Yes, I did." She turned, saw that she was in the center of the room with no curtain in sight, and frowned. "At least, I thought I did."

"Did you get what you wanted?" Travers asked.

She nodded, then extended her hand. On the palm was a very small, fragile piece of paper. Under her left arm, she carried a glowing plastic tube, and under her right, a Cubs baseball cap.

"What're those?" he asked.

"The solutions to the case, I hope," she said. "We need something to put this paper in, though. It has to stay flat."

"Conjure a book," Travers said. He wasn't about to suggest she take one of the books off the shelf he had seen in his pacing. Those books laughed at him—literally laughed—as he walked by. He didn't like them at all, which was something he'd never felt about books before. "You can carry a book flat much more easily than a scrap of paper."

Zoe gave him a wide smile. "You're brilliant," she said, and snapped the fingers of her other hand.

A thick volume appeared in Travers's hands, surprising him. The book weighed as much as a newborn baby.

"Open it," Zoe said.

He did, to a middle page. The writing inside wasn't English.

Neither was the alphabet. He had no idea what language he was looking at.

Zoe put the scrap of paper in the book. "That's page 532," she said. "Can you remember that for me?"

"Easily," he said, using a trick he'd used for memorizing since he was a kid. He made the number into an equation: $5=3+2$. "I didn't see the number on the page."

"Trust me, it was there." Zoe sighed. She took the tube from under her arm, and then the cap from the other arm. "You ready to go?"

"Yeah," he said.

"Good," she said, "because we have a lot to do this afternoon. We—"

"No," he said.

"No?" Zoe leaned back, as if the word had too much force. "What do you mean, *no*?"

Travers looked over his shoulder. He felt like a million eyes were watching them. "Can we have this discussion outside?"

Zoe sighed, and shook her head, but led the way through the maze of tables and cabinets to the door. Travers was amazed she found it. He couldn't see it until they were only a few feet away.

The door looked the same as it had when they entered, and he had no idea why he hadn't been able to find it before. Except, of course, for the magical explanation. He wasn't supposed to leave, so he couldn't find the door.

Travers swallowed his exasperation and followed Zoe outside. The day's heat hit him like a wall. The sun was so bright he had to blink several times before he could see much more than white walls, white concrete, white clouds.

Finally the pale blue of the sky came into focus, and then the black of the iron bars on the windows, and finally the red of Zoe's car.

She opened the small trunk, put her possessions in it, dithered over the book, and finally wedged it against the tire iron and the jack.

"All right," she said, closing the trunk with one hand. "What's so important that we can't finish the case?"

"Kyle," Travers said.

Zoe stopped short, as if she hadn't expected that answer. "Have you heard from him?"

Travers shook his head, then realized he'd better check his cell phone now that he was out of that dungeon. He looked at the LED, saw that he hadn't missed any calls, and slipped the phone back in his pocket.

"Then why are we going to see him?" Zoe asked.

"Because some weird, green-haired woman propositioned me in there," Travers said, "and she knew way too much about my life and what's going on for me to be comfortable. I'm going to check on Kyle. If people are approaching me, then they might be going after Kyle, too."

"Weird, green-haired woman," Zoe repeated, frowning, as if she were trying to place the description.

"With bright green eyes," Travers said. "I saw her in a mirror."

"Hmm," Zoe said. "Could've been anyone from a nature sprite to a faerie. Did she have pointed ears?"

"I couldn't see under all that hair," Travers said, "which is beside the point, anyway. I want to check on Kyle."

"So call him," Zoe said.

"No," Travers said. "We're going back to the hotel. I want to see him for myself."

"He might not be there," Zoe said.

"Then I'll find him."

Zoe studied Travers for a moment. A small smile played at her lips. It was a fond smile, as if she were proud of him for something, but for what, he didn't know.

"All right, then," Zoe said. "We'll check on Kyle. And afterwards, we'll finish the tasks we have for the day."

If Kyle was all right. Travers had the uneasy sense that his son wasn't all right, that something was wrong. But he also knew that if something was seriously wrong, Kyle would have contacted him.

Provided he could.

Travers got into the passenger side of the car. The leather seat was hot. Zoe turned on the air conditioning even though she didn't raise the roof.

Then she peeled out as if she were at the Indy 500 and someone had just waved the checkered flag.

"Maybe you could—um—zap me to Kyle," Travers said, wishing he knew the correct word for that travel-thing he had done.

"Better not to call attention to the magic," Zoe said. "I'll 'zap' you if we run into bad traffic. Otherwise, we're driving. Believe me, I'll get us there fast."

Travers believed her. He just wasn't sure he wanted to be along for the ride. His own driving was scary enough; Zoe's in rush hour terrified him.

Still, he clutched the seat and watched the road, wondering if his nerves about Kyle were just parental jitters because Travers had had a bad experience or if something was really wrong.

Travers guessed he would find out soon enough.

Twenty-eight

Zoe had lied to Travers. She did use magic on their trip back to the hotel; she just didn't "zap" them there. She wanted her car at the hotel for the mobility, in case Travers found some reason not to accompany her on the rest of the trip.

What she did, in addition to driving as fast as she dared, was use a small spell she'd developed when she lived in Los Angeles in the days before the freeways had been built. When she wanted to get from place to place, she visualized the entire route, saw where the traffic was, and wove her way through it, using that special sight to help her.

She knew her passenger was panicked—Travers held onto the armrest as if he were holding the door closed—and she had no idea what he saw. Probably near-misses all along the way, as she froze a car in place so her car could squeeze between it and a nearby truck.

She did that all the way from North Las Vegas to the Strip, the warm wind whistling in her hair, the feeling of freedom tremendous, and the glory of driving more than 70 miles an hour on streets made for 30 even better.

Zoe tried to distract Travers from her driving by getting him to talk about the green-haired woman. He told Zoe the entire story, and she tensed when she heard that the woman offered to give Travers the spinning wheel.

"Why didn't you go for it?" Zoe asked.

"Please," Travers said, sounding just like Kyle. "A scam is a scam is a scam, no matter whether you're trying for magic or money."

Zoe grinned then. She wondered if Travers knew how strong he was or how competent; he worried about a lot of things, but he seemed to handle everything thrown at him with great aplomb.

She admired that. When she had just come into her magic—at a much older age than Travers was now—she was a lot more naïve. Of course, it was a different time, but still. She would probably have fallen for the green-haired woman's scheme and regretted it for the rest of her life.

Zoe wove her way through the Las Vegas Boulevard traffic, finally getting off the main drag and onto the back roads that took her to the hotel. In the midafternoon sunlight, it almost looked seedy, which was odd, considering that the hotels that used to be considered seedy—the ones with gambling—were the ones that looked glamorous now.

As she drove into the hotel's public parking ramp, she thought she saw three men loitering near the front door. They were wearing black leather despite the heat, and they had pointed ears. They also looked familiar.

Her back tensed, and she would have reversed the car, only someone else was following her into the lot. She found a spot quickly, promising to meet Travers upstairs, and hurried down to the front.

But the three men were gone.

Zoe used her magical senses, trying to find a trail, but she saw nothing. Rather than relieve her, it made her even more suspicious.

Were the faeries coming after the Fates? And if so, why? Elmer had hinted there was more to the faeries' and Fates' conflict than met the eye, and Zoe wondered if these three were part of it.

She went in the front lobby of the hotel and asked the manager to alert Travers's room should three men with pointed ears enter wearing black leather.

It was a tribute to Vegas's tolerance—and its reputation for any and all kinds of visitors—that the manager didn't look at Zoe as if she were crazy. He merely nodded, smiled, and promised he would let his employees know.

She didn't feel as reassured as she wanted to. If the three men were faeries, they would know how to slip past any mortals who were looking for them.

The key was, however, that the faeries wouldn't know anyone was looking for them.

Zoe might get lucky.

At least, she hoped so.

Twenty-nine

Kyle rolled over on his bed in the drape-darkened bedroom. Fang tried to curl up next to Kyle, but Kyle was in too much pain. He had the air conditioner on frostbite, but it wasn't doing much for the heat radiating off his skin.

He had forgotten how miserable sunburn could be, how he could stay hot even when he really wasn't. The last time he had a sunburn was the time his dad had taken him to the emergency room, and the staff there had yelled at his dad.

Kyle remembered some cool lotion on his skin, something to make him sleep, and not much else. He wished he could remember a few other things so he could get more comfortable.

Part of his discomfort, though, was his stomach. He couldn't lie on it because it was still too full. He wasn't exactly queasy anymore, but he wasn't exactly not queasy, either. He was kinda bloated, as if he might swell up and explode, which would hurt even more if his skin got tugged.

Outside his bedroom, he could hear canned laughter from the television. The Fates had found him when he had come back from taking Fang out for his walk. They were worried about him, they said: he hadn't acted like himself in the elevator; they thought maybe something was wrong; and they were sure they could help.

Kyle told them all he needed was a nap, but they didn't believe him. Still, they let him go into his room and close the door, but they hovered outside of it, and he could sense their worry.

He would have been better off if they had just gone back to their own room. He was too hot and queasy to think about those three men, and he didn't want to deal with the Fates, either.

So when the phone rang, the first thing Kyle felt was annoyance. If the Fates were real grown-ups, they would answer it. But, of course, they weren't. For a minute, he thought of letting the phone just ring, and then he realized that the call might be from his dad.

Kyle rolled over on his stomach, regretted it as he did so, sat up, and picked up the receiver. He wanted to answer *What?* the way people did on television when they were annoyed, but he'd been raised well.

He said, "Hello," instead.

"Kyle, baby?" The voice belonged to his Aunt Megan She had the most distinctive voice of any woman he'd ever known. It was deep, almost masculine, but it had this female quality that made all men notice when she spoke.

"Aunt Megan," Kyle said, and to his embarrassment, had to blink hard so he wouldn't burst into tears.

"You all right, baby?" she asked. "You sound funny."

"I ate too much," he said, which was true. He didn't want to tell her about all the other strange stuff that was going on.

"That happens when you go on vacation," she said, apparently not noticing that anything else was wrong. "Is your dad there?"

"Nope," Kyle said.

"You're alone?" She sounded alarmed.

"Oh, no," Kyle said. "Some friends are here watching me."

Not that they were true friends of his, even though he liked them, and they weren't technically watching. But he'd heard his Aunt Megan verbally beat up his dad before because his dad didn't follow the prescribed child-rearing fads that Aunt Megan had learned about in school.

"Well, your dad called me and it sounded urgent," she said.

"It is," Kyle said. This was the answer to his prayers. A real grown-up, not a kid in an adult's body like the Fates. "Dad has some business to do here, and he was wondering if he could pay for your trip if you would baby-sit me."

Kyle hated to use the word baby-sit, but he knew his dad would.

"When?" Aunt Megan asked.

"As soon as possible," Kyle said.

"Oh, he always does this to me," she muttered, and Kyle knew she hadn't meant him to hear that. "There's no one else he can ask? Mom, maybe? Or Viv?"

"Grandma and Grandpa say I'm too difficult, remember?" Kyle winced as he spoke those words. His grandparents really loved him, but he'd scared them from the time he was little and he could read their minds.

"And Vivian's on her honeymoon. I'm so ditzy I forgot."

Kyle could almost hear his Aunt Megan's hand hit her forehead as she remembered. She always called herself ditzy but she wasn't. She just thought a lot about a lot of things, and never really focused on the world around her.

In that way, she had a lot in common with the Fates.

"Tell you what," she said, "I'll call back tonight—I'm assuming your dad'll be back by then—and I'll let you know if I can rearrange my schedule. Okay?"

Kyle let out a sigh of relief. He tried not to make it too audible. "Okay," he said.

But she had already hung up. He slid back onto the pillows, which were clammy and too hot, and closed his eyes.

He wished he hadn't had so much ice cream.

He wished he'd remembered his sunscreen.

He wished his dad were here. He wished he was home, in his own bed. He wished he didn't have anything more to wish for, as he finally drifted off to sleep.

Thirty

By the time Zoe made it to Travers's hotel room, she could sense something was wrong. She hurried off the elevator to find Travers's hotel room door open, the TV blaring the Fox News theme to the entire hallway.

Zoe saw no one when she stepped inside. She closed the door, shut off the television, and finally noticed the Fates, huddling in front of Kyle's bedroom door.

"What's going on?" Zoe asked.

Clotho gave Zoe a mournful look. Lachesis sighed, and Atropos leaned her head against the wall.

Their reluctance to speak alarmed Zoe even more. She pushed her way past them and into the bedroom.

The overhead light was on, and so was a lamp beside the bed. The room was so cold it made the Arctic seem like a balmy summer vacation spot.

Bartholomew wiggled his way toward her, his tail at half-mast, his entire body an apology for something she didn't yet understand.

Travers was sitting on the side of the bed, talking softly.

Zoe could see Kyle's bare feet, which looked oddly red and swollen. She hurried to Travers's side.

Kyle was leaning against the pillow, his skin an alarming shade of red. He obviously had the same problem with sunburn that Travers had. Only unlike Travers, Kyle's face beneath the burn was pale. He looked very sick, and Zoe couldn't tell why.

"What's going on?" Zoe asked.

"Don't feel good." For the first time since she'd met him, Kyle sounded like the little boy he was. His face was tear-stained and a teardrop hung on the bottom of his chin like a reluctant skydiver.

"Sunburn?" Zoe asked Travers softly.

"Severe," Travers said. "I'd ask for more of that miracle lotion, but I'm not sure it'll help. I'm going to have to take him to the emergency room."

"Let me try first," Zoe said.

Travers scooted aside to allow Zoe space on the bed. Bartholomew sat at her feet, whining. The Fates still huddled in the doorway.

Kyle moaned.

"That doesn't sound like sunburn," Zoe said, wondering how she knew what sunburn sounded like.

"It isn't," Travers said, apparently understanding her. "It's —what, Kyle?—three milkshakes, a burger, fries, and more things than I want to think about."

"A stomachache and a sunburn?" Zoe asked.

Kyle nodded miserably.

"Yep." Travers's tone was lacerating. "I come home worried that my son is under magical assault and I discover instead that he's just struck by good old-fashioned adult incompetence."

Zoe glanced over her shoulder at the Fates. They bowed their heads, and looked as miserable as Kyle. She didn't try to defend them, even though she could have argued that they wouldn't know better. After all, they weren't used to dealing with mortal children. They were used to dealing with highly temperamental mages.

"It wasn't their fault, Dad," Kyle said. "I forgot the sunblock."

"No," Travers said, "it was mine, and I'm sorry."

His hand hovered over Kyle's arm, as if he were afraid to touch him.

"I've never seen a burn quite this bad," Travers said.

"Here," Zoe said, "let me."

"Zoe, I think we should let doctors take care of this," Travers said.

"And have Kyle be miserable for days?" Zoe leaned against Travers. "Let me, and if it doesn't work, then I'll take him to the emergency room myself. Is that okay?"

She asked this last of Kyle.

He turned those miserable eyes on her. His expression looked so much like Travers's that for a moment, she thought she was seeing double.

"It's okay," Kyle said to Travers.

Travers nodded, and she felt the depth of his worry. Sunburn these days carried more than discomfort with it. People now understood that a few serious sunburns in a lifetime could result in skin cancer later on.

Zoe would reverse any damage, though, and then she'd make extra sunblock for Kyle, with a lot more healing power than she'd used on Travers. Maybe she'd redo his, too. If he had the same kind of skin when he was young, he probably suffered through burns like this, too. He was probably at risk as well for serious side effects.

And that explained his curtness. He understood, better than anyone, how painful such a sunburn was.

"I'm going to have to touch you," Zoe said to Kyle. "It'll be uncomfortable at first, but I promise it'll get better."

"Okay." Kyle's voice was little more than a whisper. He closed his eyes.

Zoe started with Kyle's belly. The poor boy's stomach was distended, probably from gas and discomfort, and it radiated pain. Zoe laid her hand on it, and spelled the pain away.

Kyle's eyes fluttered open. There were tears in the corners. "What'd you do?" he whispered.

"Just eased the stomachache," Zoe said.

"Man, you should bottle that." Kyle smiled at her. "That's a lot better."

"Good," Zoe said. "Now just relax."

She created more skin potion and conjured it in a plastic bottle that looked like Spider-Man, because she knew about Kyle's love of comic book characters. Then she squirted some of the lotion on her fingers.

As she worked the boy's skin, taking the heat and pain and damage out of it, she felt a tenderness that was foreign to her.

Her hand caressed Kyle's face. His eyelids fluttered, and the tears in the corners fell against his skin. She wiped them away, then continued to rub the lotion on his temples, watching the redness recede and his normal light skin tone take its place.

She didn't give him a tan like she had with Travers. A tan left some of the damage, and she didn't want to do that. Not with Kyle.

Travers had no idea how lucky he was. He had a chance to live a normal life, have a family, raise a child—and he had the opportunity to live magically for centuries.

Zoe had never really thought about how good the system that the Fates and the Powers That Be (under the leadership of Aphrodite) had created was. It gave mages a taste of the normal mortal life if they chose to try it, and they also had the chance to live creatively with their powers.

Her fingers slid through Kyle's hair, catching the burned scalp there, too, feeling the raised blisters. If she hadn't been here, Travers would have had to take Kyle to the hospital, and there would have been a week of treatment or more.

She was glad she was here. She was glad she could make Kyle feel better.

"Wow," he whispered. "It doesn't hurt anymore."

Travers was still standing beside her. "It looks better," he said, not willing to say that it was better.

Zoe nodded, then slid her hands out of Kyle's hair. "It *is* better. I think I reversed all the damage. If not, I'll catch the rest when we see it. But he needs something to drink—not a milkshake. Something like Gatorade, and he needs to sleep."

"We'll get the Gatorade," Clotho said.

"No," Zoe said. "I think the three of you need to stay indoors."

"I'll call for it," Travers said. "The hotel can get it for us."

"Dad?" Kyle's eyes fluttered open. They looked clear, less painfilled, but very exhausted.

"What is it, kiddo?" Travers's voice was gentle.

"Aunt Megan called. She's going to call back. She's trying to rearrange her schedule."

Zoe shook her head slightly. What a great kid. He was nearly dead with exhaustion and he still remembered to give his father a message.

"Okay," Travers said. "I'll call her."

"And Dad?"

"Yeah?"

"All day, there's been these three guys, following the Fates." Kyle's eyelids slid closed. The last word almost didn't come out of his mouth. He fell asleep while he was talking.

"Three guys?" Travers asked.

"He's asleep," Zoe said. "Let's get the Gatorade."

"What about these three guys?" Travers asked.

"Let's talk to the Fates." Zoe set the Spider-Man bottle next to the bed. "After we get the Gatorade."

Travers picked up the phone and put in a call to the desk. Then he shut off the light, and headed out of the room.

Bartholomew looked at the bed, then at the door, then at the bed again. He whined.

"It's okay," Travers said softly. "I'll wager that Kyle would love to have you stay."

The dog's tail wagged and he jumped on the bed, careful to stay away from Kyle's skin. Even though Kyle felt better, it was clear that Bartholomew knew what the problem was.

Travers headed for the door. The Fates scurried for the main room as if they saw a tidal wave approaching and were trying to get out of its way.

Zoe took her time leaving Kyle. She had a hunch she needed to go into the living area to moderate the conversation, but she wasn't going to enjoy the role.

Thirty-one

"Those men are nothing to be concerned about," Lachesis said. She was standing behind the couch, her hands resting on it as if it were a shield.

Atropos stood beside her, and Clotho stood on her other side. None of them was sunburned, even though they all seemed to have tanned at some point during the day.

Travers forced himself to relax his clenched fists. "I'm not concerned about the men."

"Good," Atropos said. "Kyle was worried about them, but really, they're not important."

Zoe closed the bedroom door. She walked into the room, and leaned against the armchair near Travers. He was grateful to her, more grateful than he wanted to admit. When she had eased his sunburn, he felt like she had given him a gift, but now, she had done something truly miraculous.

She had made Kyle better. Whenever Kyle was sick, Travers felt completely helpless. Zoe made that helpless feeling go away, and she made Kyle's skin better. The doctors wouldn't have been able to do that. They would have eased his pain, but not reversed the sun damage.

"The men," Travers said, "are welcome to you. I've had enough."

The Fates lowered their heads.

"What docs it take to monitor an eleven-year-old boy? He didn't need any sun and he certainly didn't need that much food. Didn't you realize he was getting sick?" Travers tried to keep his voice down, but the panic he had felt earlier was in every word.

"We have never cared for children before," Clotho said.

"At least, not without magic," Lachesis said.

"He never did say that he was feeling ill," Atropos said.

"He was turning the color of a strawberry. Didn't anyone think that was a problem?" Travers was shaking, he was so angry.

"No," Clotho said. "We used to turn ourselves all sorts of colors."

"Clotho's favorite was purple," Lachesis said. "It made her hair look like the sun."

Travers closed his eyes, biting back the irritation. These women wouldn't understand. They couldn't understand. They had no comprehension of real life and real problems. Their entire world revolved around spinning wheels and magical power struggles, not the health of a little boy.

"Well," Travers said, opening his eyes, "we can't leave him alone with you anymore. I thought the only risk would be some kind of magical attack. I had no idea that you failed to understand the most basic rules of child care. I mean, it didn't bother you that he drank three milkshakes in the space of an hour?"

"He wanted to have fun," Atropos said.

"In your movies, food is always a way to have fun," Clotho said.

Travers let out a small hiss of breath. He whirled away from them, afraid of what he would do if the conversation continued.

"Please, Travers," Lachesis said. "We like Kyle. We meant him no harm."

"Let us continue to take care of him," Atropos said. "We'll do better."

"Our care of Henri's kittens improved, over time," Clotho said, referring to the kittens they'd had at the wedding. "Of course, Henri had left us books on cat care."

"Books!" Travers exclaimed. "Books are no substitute for common sense. Don't you realize that the sunburn alone could have caused Kyle problems for life? I almost had to take him to the hospital. I would have, if it weren't for Zoe."

Lachesis gave Zoe an imploring look, but Zoe didn't move. She watched the entire proceeding as if it didn't concern her.

Perhaps it didn't. After all, she never had to worry about a child and her magic. Travers had no idea what he would do now. He and Kyle straddled two worlds and neither of those worlds was safe.

A knock echoed in the room. At the same time, the phone rang.

"I'll get the door," Zoe said. "You get the phone."

Travers reached for the phone as Zoe hurried across the room. The Fates kept their distance from Travers. The couch remained a barrier between him and them.

Good. At least they understood how angry he was.

"Hello," Travers said, trying hard to be polite.

"What is it with you two?" The voice on the other end of the line was Megan's. "You and Kyle sound so somber. I thought Vegas was Sin City. I thought it was supposed to be fun."

"We've—um—oh, hell, Meg. I've got some problems here." Travers felt relieved to hear his sister's voice. He sank into the armchair that Zoe had been in not moments ago. The cushions were still warm.

"Sounds serious," Megan said.

"Serious and confusing," Travers said. "I almost wish Great-Aunt Eugenia were alive."

"That *is* serious," Megan said. "You always thought she was a flake."

Travers winced. He had had that judgement of everyone who believed in magic. Served him right, he supposed, for his entire life to go topsy-turvy.

"Can you come out here?" he asked. "I have to stay a few days, and I really need someone to watch Kyle."

"I rearranged my schedule," Megan said. "You're lucky you caught me. If this had been two weeks ago, there would've been no way. But I wasn't sure whether I wanted to take a vacation after Viv's wedding, so I booked light this week."

Vivian's wedding seemed so long ago. Travers rubbed the bridge of his nose with his thumb and forefinger. He wasn't sure how he'd manage Megan, the magic, and the Fates, but he'd find a way. Maybe Zoe could help him figure it out.

"When can you get here?" Travers asked.

"Late tonight if you book me a room," Megan said. "I prefer to drive after dark anyway. I avoid the traffic and the heat."

"That would be marvelous," Travers said. It would take the pressure off the next day. Maybe with those things that Zoe had bought at that weird shop, they could settle the Fates' spinning wheel problem, Travers could get some minor training, and he could leave Vegas.

The thought didn't make him as happy as he expected it to.

Zoe was coming back into the main living area now, carrying a bottle of Gatorade and some soda crackers. She nodded toward Kyle's bedroom, apparently wondering if she should give him some Gatorade now. Travers held up a single finger. He wanted the boy to sleep a few minutes longer.

He and Megan finished their plans as Zoe listened. Travers told Megan where he was staying, and promised to book her a room. He also gave her directions to get here. She said she'd meet him for breakfast in his room, and he told her that he'd hold her to that.

Then he hung up, called the front desk, and reserved the room next to his for Megan. He would also get an extra key to his room for her, but he could do that later.

"How will she handle the Fates?" Zoe asked when Travers hung up with the front desk.

Travers looked at the Fates. They were still standing behind the couch, looking very subdued.

"She won't," Travers said. "Her job is to watch Kyle, take him out on the town, and have a good time."

"Don't you think someone should keep an eye on them?" Zoe asked softly.

Travers shook his head. "They're adults. They say there's nothing to worry about. Maybe we should take them at their word."

Zoe turned so she could look at them. She clutched the Gatorade and crackers to her chest. "Who are those three men?"

"We're not sure," Lachesis said.

"They look like people we used to know," Atropos said, "but that was centuries ago."

"So they could be anyone," Zoe said.

The Fates shrugged in unison. Travers suppressed a sigh. He did feel responsible for these women. His anger was dissipating; the mistake had been his, ultimately, not theirs. They had warned him that they knew nothing of this world, of the places without magic.

"We're sure they're from the Faerie Kings," Clotho said quietly.

"Why would the Faerie Kings follow you?" Travers asked.

"We're not sure it's them," Lachesis said.

"We think the Kings sent them," Atropos said.

"They're too young to be the Kings," Clotho said.

"You still look young," Zoe said.

"We haven't wasted as much magic as they have," Lachesis said, and she didn't sound judgemental. It simply sounded like she was speaking fact.

"So we believe they're bodyguards or something," Atropos said.

"Which still begs the question," Travers said. "Why would they follow you?"

"We don't know for sure," Clotho said, "but we think that they want to know if the rumors about us are true."

"Rumors?" Travers asked.

"About the Fates not having powers." This time, Zoe spoke up. "It's all over Vegas now."

"You see," Lachesis said, "if we do have powers, then we're a threat."

"We're on their turf," Atropos said.

"But if we don't, well, we're no different from all the other mortals who come to this city to get lucky," said Clotho.

They were different from all the other mortals. Very different. And Travers had to keep reminding himself of that. If he had thought of that from the beginning, then Kyle wouldn't have had such a difficult day.

"What if they *are* a threat?" Travers asked.

"Neither you nor Zoe could combat them," Lachesis said. "We would be on our own in any case."

They raised their chins—in unison, of course—and looked at Travers. It was as if they were forgiving him, instead of the other way around.

That would have made him angry a day or so ago. Now it just tired him out.

"They might even protect us," Atropos said. "They certainly don't want anything to happen to us here."

"Why not?" Travers asked as Zoe nodded. She clearly understood, but he didn't.

"Because," Clotho said, "the Powers That Be might take any excuse to attack Faerie. And we would be a very good excuse."

Travers put a hand to his forehead. "Even though these Powers took your power away?"

"They didn't take it away," Lachesis said. "We voluntarily let it go."

He knew that. He had forgotten it. "But your job. They took your job away."

"Not permanently," Atropos said. "We're trying to earn it back."

"What Travers is trying to say . . ." Zoe looked at him sideways, asking his permission to continue for him. He nodded. ". . . is that you're not popular with the Powers right now. Why would they defend you?"

"Because they're not real fond of the faeries," Clotho said.

"Very few people are," Lachesis said.

"So they'll take any excuse to fight them," Atropos said.

"Even us." Clotho sounded sad.

This situation was getting worse and worse. Travers was just getting to know this new world, and it was as screwed up as the one he grew up in. Only he was a lot closer to the crazy governments in the magical world than he was in the real—if he dared call it that—world.

It was still hard to take, and he felt just as helpless as he did every night when he watched the news.

So he decided to do something he understood. He slid the soda crackers and Gatorade out of Zoe's hands, and headed for the bedroom. He, at least, knew how to take care of a child.

And at the moment, it seemed infinitely simpler than anything else he could do.

Thirty-two

Zoe understood the Fates' logic a lot better than Travers did. She knew that only because she had had an entire lifetime to get used to the magical world. Travers had been around it for less than a week, and he was understandably overwhelmed.

Still, Zoe felt that the Fates were leaving a few details out, and she felt like they were important details. She was losing patience with the Fates, too. Were they so used to being secretive that they couldn't trust anyone?

Or was something larger going on, something that the Fates didn't want to talk about?

A murmur of voices came from Kyle's room. The Fates were still standing behind the couch. They had used it as a shield against Travers. Apparently they didn't like having anger directed at them—especially not justified anger.

Now they knew how it felt to do something you thought appropriate at the time and to get punished for it. The Fates had done the same thing to countless others. Perhaps, if the Fates ever did get their job back, they would have a little more compassion.

Zoe sighed. She clapped her hands together, and the baseball cap appeared on the table before her.

"This is a protection charm," she said to the Fates. "I got it just for you. It's a minor charm, and it won't last long, but it should take care of you for a few days. Keep it with you, but don't wear it."

She wasn't sure about the wearing part— Elmer hadn't mentioned anything about it—but she decided it was better to be cautious.

The Fates looked at her in surprise.

"You're not going to watch us?" Lachesis asked.

Zoe shook her head. "Not if you want me to find the wheel."

"But we have no magic," Atropos said.

"And you told Travers you'd be perfectly safe," Zoe said.

"From the Faerie Kings, maybe," Clotho said, "but what about everyone else? They're still mad at us."

"The charm will protect you from the others," Zoe said, raising her voice slightly so the Fates could hear her over their low whispers. "At least for a few days. By then, I should at least know where the wheel is."

"All right." Lachesis said, sounding concerned. "But what will we do? Without Kyle—"

"You should probably lay low," Zoe said. "Watch some television, read a few books—"

"We did that at Henri's," Atropos said. "There's a lot to do here."

"Most of it costing money," Zoe said, "and I'm not giving you any. Just relax. You'll be fine."

She picked up the cap and tossed it toward the Fates. Atropos caught it and held it close.

"I'll check on you when I'm done each day," Zoe said. "I'll keep you apprised of what's going on."

Still the Fates didn't leave. They stared at Zoe.

"What?" Zoe asked, knowing they wanted something.

"Did we do that much damage to young Kyle?" Clotho asked.

"Yes," Zoe said.

"Should we have known better?" Lachesis asked.

"Yes," Zoe said, even though she wasn't quite sure how.

"Is there some way we can make this up to him?" Atropos asked.

"I think you might want to stay out of Travers's way for a few days. That would do a lot toward making this better." Zoe wasn't sure what else they could do. They were good-hearted, but they seemed to screw up everything they touched.

All three Fates nodded at her, then filed out of the room like a choir leaving risers. They opened the door and headed down the hall, single-file, their heads bowed.

Zoe closed the door after them and leaned on it for a moment. She couldn't do much more for them. The Fates had made a heck of a choice when they came to the mortal realm without magic.

She pushed off the door and headed toward the murmur of voices from Kyle's room. Travers had left that door open as well, and a soft light played across the bed.

Travers and Kyle were having a serious discussion. Travers held the Gatorade in one hand, and Kyle was holding a half-full glass.

"How are you?" Zoe asked as she stepped into the room.

Kyle smiled at her. His skin was its normal color, and he wasn't flushed or too pale from illness.

"Better," he said. "But Dad's making me go slow on eating. I think I'm okay to have a meal."

He probably was, but better to let Travers fuss.

"I think easy does it is sensible," Zoe said.

"Dad says you don't need him tonight," Kyle said. "Is that true?"

Zoe felt a pang. Travers wasn't looking at her. He was fiddling with the crackers.

He hadn't spoken to her about not helping. He knew she wanted to get a lot done that day. But she understood it. In fact, she didn't want to go back to work, either.

"That's right," Zoe said.

Travers looked at her, his expression open and grateful.

"There's very little to do tonight, mostly Web research," Zoe continued. "I can do that on my own."

"I can help with that," Kyle said, leaning forward.

"You rest," Travers said. "Maybe I'll even order up a movie."

"Pay-per-view?" Kyle asked.

"The hotel has quite a few," Travers said. "I'm sure there's something we haven't seen."

Zoe felt a mixture of two emotions. She loved watching Travers with Kyle. The two of them were quite a team. More than a team, actually. A unit. An impenetrable unit.

And that led to the other feeling. She almost felt jealous. As if she had been thrown over for an evening in a sterile hotel room, watching a bad movie. But she knew it wasn't that exactly which had her uneasy.

Instead, it was the realization that no one would ever get close to Travers. Not while his son was around.

"I need to get going," Zoe said.

"You could stay for the movie," Kyle said.

Zoe shook her head. "I'll be back in the morning."

She walked over to Kyle. She was going to ruffle his hair and tell him to feel better. Instead, she kissed him on the forehead.

"You get well, okay?" she said.

"I'm better already," he said. It would take Travers a lot of work to keep that boy in bed this evening.

"You still need rest," Zoe said, and stood up. She smiled at Travers, about to take her leave.

He stood, too. "Let me walk you out."

She was going to protest, but didn't have the heart. Travers set the Gatorade on the nightstand, and led Zoe out of the bedroom, his hand on her back.

As they stepped into the living room, Travers pulled Kyle's door closed.

"I'm sorry about this," Travers started, but Zoe put a finger on his lips. A little shiver ran through her. She liked to touch him.

She moved her finger away. "It's all right," she said. "Kyle's the most important thing."

"You're good with him," Travers said.

Zoe shrugged. "I like him."

"It's more than that," Travers said. "Most people don't know how to react to him. He's a smart, intuitive kid and he's not exactly what people expect from an eleven-year-old. So they either talk to him like an adult or ignore him. You don't do either. You treat him just like who he is."

Zoe couldn't imagine treating Kyle any other way. "You're lucky to have him."

Travers stuck his hands in his back pockets, and rocked back on his heels. "How come you never had kids?"

"Excuse me?" Zoe asked. No one had ever asked her that question before.

"You're good with Kyle, and that leads me to believe you'd be good with all kinds of kids." Travers shrugged. "From what I understand of all this magic stuff, you could have had children before your powers manifested. What happened? How come you chose not to?"

Zoe stared at him. She wasn't quite sure how to answer him. He was probably the first person she could give the real answer to, the first person who might understand.

"It was the 1850s," Zoe said. "Many of my friends died in childbirth or had their health completely ruined. Medical science wasn't quite the same as it is now, and I had no idea anyone could help me magically."

"You chose not to?" Travers sounded surprised. "I thought it was, like, required of women in those days to have children."

Zoe straightened. So many people were ignorant of the past. It annoyed her. It annoyed her especially coming from Travers.

"We had a budding women's movement in those days," she said. "It came out of the abolitionist movement, in which I was very active. We had meetings, we tried to get women—the word now is 'empowered.' Crap. I can't remember what we called it then—"

She found that mildly embarrassing.

"Anyway, we got women accepted into colleges and law schools and medical schools. We weren't just fighting for the vote. We were fighting for equal rights. Up until that point, women were considered property of their husbands or fathers, and I wasn't about to put up with that. I'm not anyone's property."

Travers's gaze softened. "Indeed you're not."

She drew a breath, forcing herself to think before she spoke next. Was he patronizing her? She couldn't tell.

"Besides," Zoe said, trying to bring the conversation back to the track it had been on before. "I wouldn't have been a good mother."

"You have a lot of empathy," Travers said. "Most people don't realize how important that is."

Zoe tilted her head. She wasn't sure what he was getting at. "I didn't have it a hundred and fifty years ago. I learned how to think about people when I became a private eye. It wouldn't have worked for me. Children, I mean. I'm developing all backwards. Even if I wanted a child now, I couldn't have one."

Travers nodded. He sighed, then nodded again, almost as if he were having a discussion with himself.

And yet, he hadn't said anything about her age. Once again, she'd opened the door, and once again, he hadn't said a word.

Proof, she supposed, that he only saw her as someone to train him, someone who was kind and helpful to him and his son.

"My age doesn't bother you?" she blurted, and then covered her mouth, a gesture she hadn't made since she was a schoolgirl. Where had that come from?

Travers looked as surprised as she felt. "Why would it bother me?" he asked.

"I'm a lot older than you are," she said.

"I'm beginning to realize that a lot of people are," Travers said. "The Fates have made me realize, however, that age and maturity are not the same thing."

"What does that mean?" Zoe asked, again not certain if the offense she felt was a legitimate one.

"The Fates couldn't handle what I consider an everyday task, and I would consider them emotionally immature. Yet they can do—or they could do—things I can't. I guess how you live is a lot more important than how long you live." Travers gave her a sideways smile. "That's all."

"That's all?" Zoe asked.

"That's all," Travers said, and leaned back even farther. Was he trying to get out of the conversation?

"That's all?" Zoe asked again.

"Yep," Travers said. "That's all."

"What she means," Kyle yelled from the bedroom, "is how come it doesn't bother you that she's older than you are."

Zoe felt her face heat up. She rolled her eyes. "I guess we should learn not to have conversations like this around Kyle."

"Only if we're broadcasting," Travers said. He pulled a

key out of his pocket, then took her hand and led her out into the hallway, closing the door behind him.

The hallway was empty, and it seemed to go on forever.

"Now, even if he does hear us," Travers said, "he can't interrupt."

Although Zoe had been grateful for that last interruption. Kyle asked the question she was dancing around.

"So," she said softly, "does it bother you?"

"What?" Travers asked.

"My age," Zoe said.

Travers glanced at the door. "Maybe we should have stayed in there."

"Why?" Zoe asked.

"Because there's no good answer to that question," Travers said. "If I say yes, then you'll think I'm intimidated by your age. If I say no, then you'll think I don't find you mature enough."

"What's the real answer?" Zoe asked.

Travers took a deep breath. He seemed to realize that he wouldn't get out of this conversation until he answered her.

"The real answer?" he said. "It's sometimes."

"Sometimes?" Zoe asked.

He nodded. "When I think about all you've seen and all you've done, I'm fascinated and intimidated. When I think about how easy you are to talk to and how much I enjoy your company, I feel like there's no age difference between us at all."

"But there *is* a difference," Zoe said, resisting the urge to slip her hand in his.

"Besides the obvious and very fun one?" Travers asked. "Yes, there is. Kyle."

Zoe started. She knew that Kyle's presence bothered Travers, but it didn't bother her.

"No," she said. "I meant the magic. I know so much more about it than you do."

"And I know more about corporate tax law," Travers said. "So what?"

"So magic is more useful than corporate tax law," Zoe said.

Travers grinned. "It hasn't been in my life. I've used corporate tax law a lot more than I've used magic. Except this week."

Zoe grinned, too. She couldn't help it. She really did enjoy his company.

"So my age really doesn't bother you?" she asked again.

"Not most of the time," Travers said.

"Wow." And before she realized what she was doing, she stood on her toes, leaned forward, and kissed him.

The kiss was as good as the one they shared in her office. After a moment, Travers's hands slid around her waist. Her hands wrapped around his neck, and pulled him closer.

How had she found this man? And why was he so important to her? And why was she even worrying about any of that when he could kiss so very well?

Down the hall, the elevator doors swooshed open, and both Travers and Zoe jumped back as if they were teenagers caught parking by a cop. Both of them looked down the hall, but the elderly couple getting off the elevator didn't seem to notice them.

Then Travers's gaze met Zoe's.

"Wow is right," he said.

"I know you don't want someone who won't stay," she said, the ideas forming along with the words, "because of Kyle and everything. But I might be the first woman you've met to whom years aren't that important. I mean, if you want to wait because Kyle's eleven, wait until he's out of the house, six years—"

"Seven," Travers said with a bit of a smile.

"Seven years isn't that much to me." Zoe couldn't believe

how forward she was being. And how very vulnerable she felt. She'd never spoken to any man like this. "And I'm willing to—stay away until then, if you're worried, that is. I mean, after we find the wheel and get you mildly trained."

"Zoe—"

She kissed him lightly, stopping him. She didn't want to hear his refusal, not yet. Not when she had just revealed herself like that.

"Think about it," she said against his lips. "I'll see you in the morning. At breakfast. We can talk then."

And then she hurried down the hall, trying not to focus on the fact that he hadn't tried to stop her, and that he wasn't calling after her.

By the time she reached the elevators, she looked back at Travers's door. He wasn't in the hallway any longer.

She was alone.

Thirty-three

"You know, that's a really stupid rule," Kyle said.

He was standing in the living room, his shirt and shorts horribly wrinkled from the bed. Bartholomew Fang was standing near the door to the kitchen, looking expectantly between Travers and Kyle, as if the dog thought it was food time instead of conversation time.

Travers pulled the hotel room door closed. He still felt shaky from that kiss. Zoe may not have followed a traditional marriage-and-family route in the past 150 years, but she sure learned how to kiss.

And that intimidated him. How many men had she kissed and how did he stack up?

"What are you talking about?" Travers asked.

"That rule you're thinking about all the time," Kyle said. "The one about not getting involved with a girl because of me."

"It's not stupid," Travers said. "It's common sense. I don't want you to make attachments and lose them."

"This sounds like something Aunt Meg told you to do," Kyle said.

Travers shook his head. He wasn't going to blame Megan for anything, especially since she was arriving soon. He didn't want her involved with Zoe or the Fates. He would have to explain that to Kyle before she got here.

"I made up my mind about this long before your Aunt Meg finished her degree," Travers said. "I just figured it was best for you."

"Or was it best for you?" Kyle crossed his arms. He looked very adult, and it unnerved Travers. Sometimes Kyle was perceptive, but he was rarely savvy—he was still a boy about some things.

Although that boyhood might not last much longer.

"Come on," Travers said, "let's sit down."

He didn't want his son to keep standing. He knew that Kyle still wasn't a hundred percent, even if Kyle didn't know that.

They both sat on the couch. Travers folded his hands together and leaned forward. He wasn't comfortable talking about this with his son.

"It's true that I was pretty shaken when your mom left," Travers said. "But I didn't swear off women because of her."

"You don't date," Kyle said.

"I don't believe I have time for casual relationships. When you get older—"

"I am older." Kyle was sitting cross-legged in the corner of the couch. Bartholomew Fang had given up his quest for dinner and came toward them, his tail no longer wagging. He jumped on the couch and lay down so his muzzle touched Kyle and his tail touched Travers.

"You may think you're older," Travers said, "but eleven years isn't that long in the scheme of things. I can still remember when you were just a baby."

"So?" Kyle said. "I'm not anymore. I know how things work. And if you want to date Miss Sinclair, I think that's cool, and I promise I won't break down if you can't work it out."

"You can't make promises like that," Travers said.

"Sure I can." Kyle leaned his head back. He was still looking just a bit peaked. The skin around his eyes was hollow and white. "I watch TV and I know what happens to my friends' parents. They all date and those relationships don't last."

Great role models there, Travers thought, and then hoped he hadn't broadcast that thought. However, Kyle didn't show any evidence of having heard it, so maybe Travers was off the hook.

"I thought your friends' parents were married," Travers said.

"Some of them," Kyle said. "Most are divorced and re-married. I can remember when a lot of them were dating. Mike Kimbrough's dad saw a different woman every night."

"And that's precisely the kind of father I don't want to be," Travers said.

Kyle grinned. "You never will be, Dad. You already screwed that up. I mean, you haven't seen anyone. You're just thinking of Miss Sinclair, and she's the first woman I ever knew you were interested in. I can't imagine you seeing a different woman every night."

Travers wasn't sure if he was pleased that his son knew him so well or upset that his son didn't see him as a man who could attract a different woman for every day of the week.

"I think you're just afraid that she's gonna walk out on you like Mom did," Kyle said.

Travers didn't move. He wasn't even breathing. No one seemed to believe that Cheryl's departure didn't bother him. Not even his son.

But he hadn't even been interested in another woman until now.

Maybe he didn't want just any woman.

Zoe Sinclair certainly wasn't just any woman.

"I like her, Dad," Kyle said. "And it's okay if she doesn't stay. I mean, it's not okay, but it's okay, if you know what I mean."

Oddly enough, Travers did know what Kyle meant. He meant that they'd be sad if things didn't work out with Zoe, but they'd be sadder if they didn't try.

"And it doesn't bother you that she's, like, older than Grandma, right?" Kyle asked.

Travers looked at him, stunned. Travers hadn't thought of it that way. Zoe was older than Kyle's grandmother, Travers's grandmother, and his great-grandmother.

"Right?" Kyle asked, looking worried now.

What was the difference anyway? How they looked? Travers didn't want to go there, either. Maybe the difference was that he just couldn't think of Zoe as old.

Experienced, maybe, but not old.

"Dad?" Kyle sounded worried. He leaned forward. "Right?"

"Right," Travers said. He thought about it for a moment more, then nodded. "Her age doesn't bother me the least little bit."

Travers leaned over and pulled his son into a hug. There was one thing he learned that awful week when Cheryl walked out on him, leaving him with an infant who couldn't care for himself.

The best things in life were never easy.

Like Kyle.

Like Zoe.

Like magic.

Thirty-four

Zoe sat in her favorite booth at O'Hasie's, tapping her foot. Herschel and Gaylord were late. She had called them as she left the hotel, and asked them to meet her. They had promised they'd be at O'Hasie's, in their booth, with beer on the table.

She was the one in their booth, and she was the one who had bought the beer, as usual. She had gotten stares from the handful of regulars who filled the bar. The poker players were long gone, and O'Hasie's had gone back to its local bar status, with empty tables, a slow-moving bartender, and no cocktail waitress.

Zoe no longer remembered what she liked about this place. It felt seedy to her suddenly.

Or maybe she was seeing it with Travers's eyes.

Travers. He hadn't called to her, but then he had no reason to. She had set herself up as a teacher to him, as someone much older, not just in years, but in experience. And even though they'd kissed (how had a man with only a few decades of life learned how to kiss like that?), the attraction seemed stronger on her part than on his.

She hadn't realized how very lonely she had been in these last few years. When this thing with the Fates was over, she would have to change the way she was living.

It wasn't good to spend so much time alone.

The dark red upholstered door swung open, and Gaylord entered. He wasn't wearing his usual studded leather jacket— probably in deference to the heat—but he *was* wearing a black t-shirt with the sleeves ripped off. His thin arms were layered in muscle, and the ripped shirt, along with his tight jeans, looked good on him.

When he saw Zoe, he grinned, and crossed the room.

"You got beer already," he said as he slid into the booth.

"I didn't get straws, though," she said, making herself smile at Gaylord. "We've got some serious discussion ahead of us. Where's Herschel?"

"He's parking," Gaylord said, picking up one of the steins.

"Parking?" Zoe hadn't expected them to drive. She figured the last time these two drove was about the last time they bought beer.

"Yeah," Gaylord said. "We got a motorcycle—repossessed from a couple of guys who thought they could sell it on the Internet."

Zoe frowned. "Sell motorcycles on the Internet?"

"To us, you know, our kind," Gaylord said.

"What interest would faeries have in motorcycles?" she asked.

Gaylord made a motion with his hand, meaning that she had spoken too loudly. "You know, we're not all magic and games."

"I know," she said. "I also know that you rarely drive. What's this about?"

"Word was the motorcycle belonged to Evel Knievel," Gaylord said, "so everybody thought it would have lots of superstitious value."

"After all," Zoe said, "it couldn't have been skill that let him jump so far on a simple motorbike."

"Exactly!" Gaylord said, not catching her sarcasm. "Which was what caught everyone by surprise."

"What caught everyone?" Zoe asked, realizing, maybe for the first time, that Gaylord and Herschel had the same circular way of making conversation as the Fates.

"That the bike had no magical power whatsoever. It wasn't totemic. Yet there was proof positive that it'd belonged to Knievel."

"Weird," Zoe said, not thinking it was weird at all.

"Yeah, that was the word," Gaylord said. "Although me and Herschel, we thought it was kinda lucky. We got it for cheap."

"How much?" Zoe asked. Then it was her turn to wave her hand. "Never mind. You probably used faerie money."

Gaylord grinned. "We'd never do that to a pal."

"So you bought from someone who wasn't a pal," she said.

He sipped his beer and raised his already soaring eyebrows. "You are good."

"How long does it take to park a bike?" Zoe asked.

"I dunno," Gaylord said. "I decided to walk. It's a nice night."

Zoe was saved from asking what Gaylord meant by "walk"—it certainly couldn't have been going for a stroll—when Herschel pushed open the door. He was wearing the same ripped-sleeve t-shirt as Gaylord, but he carried a leather bomber jacket over his shoulder.

His face was marked by red lines around his eyes, probably left by goggles, and he carried a helmet that looked like it belonged in a museum of 1940s football collectibles.

Herschel walked over to the table, and slid in beside Zoe. He smelled of exhaust and grease and sweat—all unusual smells for him. Maybe he really had ridden over.

"When did you get your motorcycle license?" Zoe asked.

"You need a license?" Herschel said. "For what? I'm not going to doctor it up."

"To drive it," Zoe said.

"I've never heard of anything so ridiculous." Herschel tossed his coat and helmet on the floor, then grabbed his beer and took a long, long sip. When he set the stein down, he wiped his mouth with the back of his hand. "What's so important that I couldn't drive up to Idaho tonight?"

Zoe looked at Gaylord. "He's not going to the Snake River Canyon, is he?"

"How did you know?" Gaylord asked.

Zoe closed her eyes. "Promise me you'll use magic if you attempt that."

"What, do you think we're stupid?" Herschel sounded offended. Zoe opened her eyes. "Of course we'll use magic. Just like that trickster Knievel did."

"He's not magic," Zoe said. She knew that for a fact. She'd met him a few times, mostly when he came to Vegas between stunts.

"He's got to be," Herschel said. "It's the only explanation."

"For the lack of magic in the bike?" Zoe asked.

Both faeries nodded. She decided not to explain the mortal concept of skill to them.

"So what's going on?" Herschel asked again.

Zoe glanced around the bar. No one was listening to them. "I need your help," she said.

"That's news!" Herschel said brightly, and she realized

she had never asked for their help before. They had asked for hers countless times but she had never reciprocated.

"I figured you'd need help," Gaylord said, putting a hand under his chin. The muscles rippled in his arm with each movement, and Zoe found herself wondering if those muscles were real or magically added to improve the t-shirt's effect.

"The magic has gathered around you," Herschel said, using the condensation on the side of his beer stein to wipe some oil off his finger. "It was obvious from your phone call."

"How can magic be obvious from a phone call?" Zoe asked.

"Sparks," Herschel and Gaylord said in unison. Then Gaylord added, "You have to pay attention to auras and light, Zo."

"You can't see auras over the phone," she said.

"Maybe *you* can't," Gaylord said.

"It's an electronic device," she said. "You're probably seeing some technological change."

"Maybe *you* are," said Herschel.

Zoe sighed. She wouldn't convince them.

Herschel elbowed her. "So, is he cute?"

Zoe immediately thought of Travers. "Cute" wasn't the word. "Amazingly good-looking" might cover it. "Really gorgeous" was better. But she said, "Who?"

"The reason you want to see us," Herschel said. "It's a guy, right? The blond guy? The one we warned you about? You're worried that he's not faithful and you want us to track him down."

She shook her head. She had forgotten about their warning. But it really didn't matter. Travers and Kyle would never hurt her, and it was clear, from Herschel's last comment, that he and Gaylord weren't psychic.

"No," she said, "this isn't about a guy."

She reached under the table and pulled out the tube that Elmer had given her.

"Wipe off the table," she said, "and move your steins."

Gaylord used napkins to wipe off the tabletop. Herschel stood and pulled over another table, setting the steins on top of it. Then he tucked his long, black hair behind his pointed ears.

"A map?" Gaylord asked. "Where'd you get a map?"

"It's got some real power." Herschel had greed in his voice. His canines were showing, looking like little, tiny fangs.

Zoe pulled the map out of the tube and placed the tube beside her. Then she spread the map out on the table.

The map glowed neon blue, red, and green in the bar's dim light. A few of the regular customers looked over at the sudden brightness.

"You want me to zap them?" Gaylord whispered.

"No," Zoe whispered back. "They'll just think it's some new technology they're not familiar with."

Herschel was ignoring the entire conversation. He was staring at the map, his expression cold.

"Where'd you get this?" he asked, and she'd never heard the tone before.

"I have sources," she said.

"Your sources could get in a lot of trouble." Herschel's face reflected green in the light of the map. "You know that it's against the law to have a map of Faerie."

"This is a map of Faerie?" Gaylord looked down, then covered his eyes. "We gotta get out of here."

"Too late," Herschel said. "We've seen it. If we're going to get in trouble, we're going to get in trouble."

"It's not against any mage laws," Zoe said. "Just faerie laws."

"Gee," Herschel said with some force, "guess which laws we follow."

"You don't have the map." Zoe worked at keeping her voice calm. "I own the map. It's my map, and you're just looking at it. I will not give it to you. You don't need it."

Unless they agree to her conditions. Then they might need the map. But she didn't say that.

The map was beautiful. Lots of swirls of light, all variously colored, with drawings that looked like Maxfield Parrish figures painted by Claude Monet.

"Wow," Gaylord said. "It keeps changing."

The figures did move. So did the shapes and the arrows and the writings—all in medieval Faerie, a language that Zoe wasn't fluent in. She could read modern Faerie, and medieval wasn't that different. But it was different enough to make her worry.

"Of course they change," Herschel hissed. "Faerie's always changing. That's why we're not supposed to have a map."

"So that you get lost?" Zoe never did understand faerie rules.

"So that magic is your guide," Herschel said.

Zoe nodded, even though she wondered if her magic would ever be enough of a guide.

"Look," she said, "you know my prophecy. This is as close to Faerie as I want to go. But I was wondering if you would locate something for me."

"Something in Faerie?" Gaylord asked, his tone hushed. Zoe nodded.

"Everything moves, just like Herschel said." Gaylord had leaned back in the booth, his arms crossed. The muscles seemed to have faded away, so they were magical after all.

"Yes, I know everything moves," Zoe said. "But I have to know if something's even in there."

"Why?" Herschel asked. She had never seen this side of him. He wasn't drinking his beer. His expression was serious, and his tone of voice almost frightening.

"For a client," Zoe said.

"We don't let strangers in Faerie," Herschel said.

"My client's not going to go into Faerie," Zoe said.

"You can't, either." Gaylord's eyebrows met in the middle, forming a straight line across his brow—his version of a frown.

"I'm not planning to. Just listen to me for a minute. No questions, okay?"

"Okay." Herschel leaned back and frowned, too, almost as if just looking at the map was bad for him.

"The item I'm looking for was stolen," Zoe said. "Before I venture into Faerie, I want to know that it's even there."

"So you can steal it back?" Gaylord shook his head. "C'mon, Zo. That's so dangerous as to be suicidal."

"I don't steal," Zoe said. "I'm just supposed to locate it. And you weren't supposed to interrupt me."

"Sorry." Gaylord didn't sound sorry. "That doesn't count as an interruption, does it? The sorry?"

"Let her finish," Herschel growled.

Zoe gave him a sideways glance. "The item is a spinning wheel. The Faerie Kings stole it from the Fates—"

"Thousands of years ago," Herschel said. "You don't want to get near it, Zo."

"So it's there?" she asked. "You've seen it?"

"Of course we haven't seen it," Herschel said. "But it's part of legend. It's why Faerie is so great, because we take magic from everyone, even other magical peoples."

Gaylord had a hand over his mouth. "That's not all," he whispered through his fingers.

"What do you mean?" Zoe asked.

"The Faerie Kings guard the wheel. They think it's important, somehow. People say they used it to overthrow the Great Rulers." Gaylord looked at Herschel. "We shouldn't be having this conversation."

"I'd already heard the rumor," Zoe said. "I just need to know if the wheel is in Faerie, and if so, where. I already did a location spell."

She pointed at a red dot that was constantly moving across the three-dimensional surface of the map.

"I just want visual confirmation," Zoe said. "I don't trust magic on magical items."

"Location spells don't work in Faerie." Herschel's tone was so flat that Zoe was convinced he was lying to her.

"They focus on the first magical item," Gaylord said. He had let his hand fall to his lap, his fingers clenched. "And you know, we have a lot of magical items."

She had been afraid of that. Which was why she called them.

"Look," she said, "all I'm asking you to do—and it would be for real money, not faerie money—is go into Faerie, and look for the wheel—"

"I thought you couldn't be bought, Zo," Herschel said. "I thought there were ethics. Didn't you lecture us about ethics all those times?"

"Only about faerie money," she said, trying to remember if she ever said that some things were more valuable than money. Maybe. She might have had too much beer, though.

"Real money," Gaylord whispered. He looked at Herschel. "We could get outta this town, live a quiet life, be our own men."

Herschel rolled his eyes. "We wouldn't live through the day."

He grabbed the edge of the map and rolled it up. Then he shoved it at Zoe.

"It's a death sentence," he said. "The wheel belongs to the Faerie Kings and they're very possessive of it. They have plans for it. They think they can use it to absorb all magic systems into our own. And they might be right."

"We can't do it," Gaylord said. "We'd have our power taken away."

"No one's even seen the wheel, Zo," Herschel said. "They guard it that jealously."

He was lying. She had never had such a clear sense of a falsehood from these two before.

"I thought we were friends," she said. "I thought I could ask you for help and you'd at least consider it."

Herschel grabbed his helmet and jacket. He stood. He hadn't even finished his beer.

"We've been flirting with the mage system for a while," he said. "We like the idea of love and friendship and all those happy, happy thoughts. It's kinda fun, in a hobby sort of way. But we never put ourselves out for other people. Not without real gain—and frankly, real money isn't gain enough. I like you, Zo, but I'm not going to take risks for you."

He stuck the helmet on his head, slung the jacket over his arm, and stomped out of the bar.

Gaylord didn't move. He was still staring at the tabletop as if he could still see the map.

"This is bad stuff, Zo," he whispered, "and Herschel's scared. He didn't mean all of that."

But he had. That time, Zoe had no sense that Herschel was lying. There was a coldness in the center of him, one she had always sensed, but assumed it was just the faerie way. She never thought he would revert to it when things got difficult.

"Is it true," Zoe asked, her voice barely above a whisper, "the whole world becoming like Faerie?"

Gaylord tugged on his shirt collar, as if he were trying to rip the sleeves even further. He shrugged. "There's been talk. But there's always talk. You know how slowly these things can go."

Tricks, coldness, no real affection. It had always been said that faeries had no heart—that they didn't know how to love.

"Even mortals?" Zoe asked.

"Well, we never really cared about mortals before," Gaylord said. "But there's a rift in the power-stream and the Fates aren't taking care of things. So someone's going to have to step in. Instead of love as the highest possibility that mortals can achieve, we'll come up with something else. It'll be a lot more fun than eternal commitment anyway."

"All love would go away?" Zoe asked.

Gaylord shrugged. "Who needs it?"

He glanced at the door. Herschel was standing there, staring at him.

"I've said too much," Gaylord whispered. "I like you, Zo. I wish I'd been born a mage, I really do. But you can't control destiny, right?"

He reached across the table and touched her arm lightly.

"Don't do anything stupid, okay? Faerie really isn't safe. Especially for you."

Then he gave her a sheepish smile, slid out of the booth, and walked away. When he approached the door, Herschel started to yell at him. The door closed on them, Herschel's voice reverberating in the hall.

Zoe leaned back in the booth. Her eyes still saw spots from the neon glow of the map.

No more love. The Fates had left a vacuum that the Interim Fates didn't even understand, let alone know how to fill. And the faeries would step in.

They would change everything.

The world wasn't perfect—there were hundreds of millions of mortals who had no love or didn't take the chances they were given—but at least those mortals had a chance.

And what would happen to other relationships? Not romantic love, but the wonderful bond like the one she'd seen with Travers and Kyle. Would they suddenly hate each other?

What kind of place would this world be?

Certainly not one she wanted to live in.

Zoe grabbed the map and unrolled it on the tabletop again. Faeries were tricksters. She had to remember that. And Herschel was lying to her.

The red dot still showed, right in the center of Faerie. The dot had been in the center of Faerie, even when Faerie changed its shape from circular to rectangular.

She would wager that the wheel was in there, and easy to find.

The prophecy was right: she had met her true love near Faerie. It wasn't just Travers, although she would give almost anything to have him feel about her the way she felt about him. It was what Travers had given her: a way to see this world, a way to understand it, knowing how much she valued life as it was, not as it would be if the Faerie Kings had their way.

She hated prophecies and fixed destinies. They made life seem like it had no choices.

But she could walk away right now, turn her back on everything, and continue for the next thousand years as if nothing were wrong.

Or she could take a chance on not living through the night, and going to Faerie. Maybe she'd find a wheel and maybe she'd take it back.

For Travers and Kyle, and the world that she loved.

Thirty-five

The motorcycle started up, sending a plume of black smoke toward Gaylord. He hovered near the Dumpster, trying to ignore the stench of beer and vomit. The air was cooler than it had been when he arrived; the sun had gone down and so had the temperature, by about 15 degrees.

"Gaylord," Herschel said. "We're leaving."

"You go," Gaylord said. "I hate that infernal machine."

He rubbed his arms, wishing for the muscles back. If he rode on that machine, he'd have to conjure a jacket, too. Even though it was still in the 90s, it felt cold in comparison to the heat of the day.

Herschel looked like an expert on that bike. His legs were spread, one foot on some gadget or another, the other foot braced against the street. His hands hovered over the handlebar squeezy-thingies, as if he knew what he was doing.

"Technology is the wave of the future," he said.

"Technology is already here," Gaylord said.

Herschel rolled his eyes, then pulled his goggles over them. "Our future."

"Not mine," Gaylord said.

"Look, I want to go to the canyon. It'll be fun to drive there at night." Herschel adjusted his helmet. "Don't you want to jump the Snake?"

"Not tonight," Gaylord said. "I have a headache."

Herschel varoom-varoomed the machine. "You're no fun anymore," he said, and drove off.

Gaylord stood in the alley and watched as Herschel disappeared down a side street. Then he felt his shoulders relax. Herschel wouldn't approve of the conversation Gaylord had had with Zoe, and Herschel certainly wouldn't approve of the things Gaylord was going to do now.

He watched the front door of O'Hasie's, waiting for Zoe to exit. It took her a while. He stretched a shred of invisibility over himself and squeezed into her car, in the small space between the driver's seat and the back window.

She got in a moment later, tossed the map on the seat beside her, and started the car. Gaylord was proud of himself for not sitting on the passenger seat. He had been afraid she was going to set the map down there.

She put the car in gear, and he hoped that she would go back to this new man whose sparkles were all over her. But she didn't. She drove down Boulder Highway, and he knew right away that was a bad move.

The faerie casinos clustered along the old stretch of Boulder Highway. The easiest access to Faerie was through one of those casinos.

Gaylord cursed silently, then waved a finger and floated out of the car. He was half a block away from the car when he realized he should have stolen the map.

It was probably too late, anyway. Zoe had a good memory.

He hovered over the highway through two semis and a bus. Then he knew what to do.

He snapped his fingers just once, said a location spell, and vanished.

Thirty-six

They had just reached the point in the second Harry Potter movie where Kenneth Branagh's delightful, scene-stealing professor does a memory-loss spell that backfires. Travers had his feet on the coffee table in the living room of his suite, his head resting on the back of the couch and his arm around Kyle.

Travers finally understood why his son loved these movies and those books so much. He never realized that, in some ways, Kyle saw Harry Potter as the story of his life, and probably wished for a school like Hogwarts where he wouldn't be considered strange.

Travers was going to say something to his son when he realized that Kyle was asleep. Bartholomew Fang had passed out, too, only his tail was twitching and so were his paws. He was probably chasing lunch meat in his sleep.

Travers eased himself out of Kyle's grasp, and moved slowly so his son wouldn't wake up. Then Travers picked up Kyle, trying not to grunt at the boy's weight.

Kyle weighed a lot more than he had the last time Travers

had done this. Travers hugged the boy to him, and carried him
into the bedroom. In five more years, Kyle would probably
be taller than he was. Surly, too. Teenagers usually were.

Travers set Kyle on the bed, then covered him up and
turned out the light. Still, he hovered over the boy for just a
moment. He figured they only had another year or two before the world of girls and adolescent angst would take his
little boy away from him. A year or two of closeness before
the inevitable separation.

Travers sighed and walked out of the bedroom. He pulled
the door closed. The music blared loudly on the television
set. He turned off the movie and wandered into the kitchen
for a late-night snack.

As he stepped into the small kitchen area, a gust of wind
hit him. The wind was warm and smelled faintly of motorcycle exhaust.

Travers stepped back, only to find Bartholomew Fang beside him, growling, famous teeth bared. Travers couldn't see
what Fang did, but he wasn't sure he wanted to.

The wind died down, leaving his hair a mess and grit in
his eyes. He wiped the grit away with his forefinger, then
glanced at it. The grit looked like road dust.

"Show yourself," he said, wondering if any of the training
Zoe had given him earlier that day had stuck.

He was trying to figure out some spell she had given him,
some parlor trick, as she called them, that could be reversed
and maybe make some invisible mage reveal himself, when
a slim teenage boy stepped out from behind the refrigerator.

The boy had long black hair, pointed ears, and delicate
features. He was almost pretty. He compensated for his fragile looks by wearing a black t-shirt with the sleeves ripped
off, black jeans, and black boots that looked one size too
large.

"You know Zoe?" the boy asked and as he did, Travers realized that this wasn't a boy. The voice belonged to a man.

This had to be one of the faeries.

Was it one of the three who had followed the Fates? Travers would have to wait to find out.

Fang was still growling, but he hadn't moved from Travers's side. Travers decided that Fang had the right idea, and staying in one place was it.

"Who're you?" Travers asked.

"My name is Gaylord," the boy said and raised his pointed chin ever so slightly. He seemed to expect Travers to know who he was.

"Gaylord what?" Travers asked.

"What do you mean, *what?*" Gaylord said.

"What's your last name?" Travers asked, a little amazed at himself. He'd been around the Fates for so long that he could now meander his way through a silly conversation like this one.

"Mortals need two names because there's so many of you. We only have one. I am Gaylord."

"You said that," Travers said. "And you also mentioned Zoe."

"You are the soulmate, right?" Gaylord asked.

Travers's stomach twisted. What was this odd boy/man talking about?

"The one she loves? That is you, correct? Because if it isn't, then I need my spells adjusted," Gaylord said. "I asked the winds to bring me to the one that Zoe loves."

And they brought him here. Travers's heart swelled, and he had to work to keep a goofy grin off his face.

"Where is she?" he asked.

"Zoe?" Gaylord said.

"Isn't that who we're talking about?" Travers asked.

"I thought so." Gaylord looked confused. "At least, that's who *I'm* talking about. You never answered my question."

"I hope I'm the one she loves," Travers said.

Gaylord crossed his arms. They were bony and too thin and looked like they had no power at all. Yet somehow he looked fierce. "Do you love her?"

Travers's mouth had gone dry. "What's it to you?"

"If you don't love her, I'll leave," Gaylord said.

"Yes, I love her." The words surprised Travers. He had planned to say that he liked her, maybe even that he was attracted to her. But this love thing caught him by surprise.

And not by surprise. Because the feeling was one he'd been trying to ignore for the last two days, and having more and more trouble doing so.

Even Kyle had noticed.

"Good, because she needs you." Gaylord peered at Travers, as if he were trying to see through him. "You have some magic, right?"

"Some," Travers said.

"Then let's go."

Fang was still growling. Travers wasn't going anywhere with someone his dog didn't like.

His dog. So many changes in the last few days.

"Go where?" Travers asked.

"You have to stop her," Gaylord said.

"Stop her from doing what?" Travers asked.

"Going into Faerie," Gaylord said.

Travers felt his shoulders relax. "She wouldn't do that," he said. "She's afraid of Faerie."

"She got pushed today," Gaylord said, "and now she's on a mission—which, if I had the courage, I would go on, which might be why I mentioned it in the first place, but now I regret it, and we could lose her, and I need your help."

Travers didn't follow any of that except the "lose her" part, which made his stomach twist. "Help with what?"

"The rescue," Gaylord said. "I'd like to figure out a way to do it without getting myself killed."

Thirty-seven

Zoe had always thought that CRAPS, SLOTS AND BEER was a stupid name for a casino, but that was all the neon signs had ever said around the faeries' main casino on Boulder Highway. She was certain there had once been an even larger neon sign, but in all the years she had lived in Vegas, she had never seen it.

The casino parking lot was full, even though this place didn't have specialties like a fake Eiffel Tower or wondrous canals in the middle of a desert. The faerie casinos were no-thrill places, without anything that catered to the clientele.

These places were designed to bilk money from the patrons. No false hope here, no promises of easy wealth. The people who came to these casinos had no illusions and didn't expect any. They came to gamble, and if they came away with money, then they counted themselves mighty fortunate.

She always thought it odd that people expected magic in places run by the non-magical, and in places run by the magical, people didn't expect magic at all. There was some kind of weird truth-in-advertising to that: magic wasn't about great moments and special occasions; it was as mundane as washing your hair, and as exciting as driving around the corner.

She pulled open the heavy double doors that led inside the casino, and immediately got assaulted by fifty-some years worth of unventilated cigarette smoke. The air had long since gone past silver—it was now a grayish purple haze that probably had less oxygen in it than the average exhaust pipe.

Zoe had been prepared, but she still coughed as she stumbled over the rubber mat near the door. That mat looked like it was as old as she was. So did the old man at the corner slot machine—only he looked like he had aged for each decade Zoe had been alive. She thought he had died and mummified there until he moved, pulling down the one-armed bandit and licking his dry lips in anticipation of a jackpot.

The woman beside him lit a new cigarette with the old one, then stubbed the old one out in an ashtray that hadn't been emptied since the Depression. She didn't take her gaze off the slot machine before her, either.

In fact, all of the people in the room seemed mesmerized by their slots. They probably were. The faeries sometimes used magic to addict gamblers to a particular slot.

Zoe made herself focus. She had left the map in her car— no sense calling attention to herself—but she had memorized it, as best she could. She slipped around the outside edges of the slots, listening to the ka-chink! ka-chink! of coins falling into the metal drawers.

The craps tables weren't as full. In fact, only one had a full contingent of players. Most of those players were elderly as well. The faeries were going to have to update their casinos at some point just to attract a younger crowd.

But Zoe wasn't going to tell them that. Like most of the magical, the faeries rarely noticed how quickly mortal time passed. As far as the faeries were concerned, these places were probably considered new.

She hurried past the craps tables, nearly running into a cigarette girl wearing the short skirt, high heels, and carrying a tray around her neck.

Zoe stopped and gawked. She hadn't seen an honest-to-goodness cigarette girl since 1970, and certainly not one this beautiful, ever. Of course, the girl's raven-black hair was cut to hide her pointed ears, and her makeup covered the excesses of her eyebrows, but it was still hard to hide that otherworldly kind of beauty in common clothes.

The girl saw Zoe, smiled, and said, "Cigar? Cigarillo? Cigarette?"

"Ah, um, no, thank you," Zoe said, feeling as if she'd stepped into a bad Bogart film. She hurried on, past the restrooms to the bar.

Slot machines in the corner, video poker on the table, and only hard liquor against the walls. The cocktail waitresses, who cruised the aisles of the casino just like the cigarette girl, wore the same skimpy costume, but not all of them were faerie. A few looked like regular mortals, only a little too thin.

The entrance to Faerie was somewhere in here and, if her map was to be believed, the wheel wasn't far away. She had to be alert to prevent herself from losing time, and she had to be cautious that she wouldn't get lost.

But she figured she had the element of surprise on her side. Herschel was more concerned about his motorcycle; he wouldn't mention her interest in the wheel to anyone. And Gaylord had done his best to warn her away. He wouldn't turn her in now.

She hoped.

She tried not to look too obvious as she rounded a corner, and headed toward the buffet. The buffet smelled like congealed beef broth and week-old cooked carrots. A few patrons sat at the tables, stirring their food into mush. One woman plucked radishes cut in the shape of flowers off the salad bar, while she complained that there were no pickled beets.

Zoe permitted herself one shudder for terrible 1950s meals gone by, and then slipped through the kitchen door, toward the back exit where the entrance to Faeric should be.

She almost walked past it. There was a large closet, housing all of the cleaning equipment for the restaurant, and just beyond that, an ice machine that looked like it hadn't worked since Truman was president.

She touched the metal lid of the ice machine, and found that it was hot. Then she closed her eyes ever so slightly, saw the magical sparks that Gaylord and Herschel liked to talk about, and knew she had found the entrance.

No one on the kitchen staff noticed her. In fact, they hadn't even seen her enter the room, which was just as well. She made a slight invisibility shield around herself as she lifted the lid on the ice machine.

It looked like an empty metal chest. The bottom seemed solid enough. But she leaned over the edge and tried to touch the metal, and found her hand slipping across nothing.

She hoisted herself over the lip, and then slid into the chest, falling down a metal slide like she was at a water park — only worse. She twisted and rolled and spun and the world got very, very dark, and very, very cold.

She could hear laughter and the ka-chink! ka-chink! of slot machines grow louder and louder, and then she realized that no one was speaking English. They were all speaking Faerie.

Her heart nearly stopped. She had to concentrate to keep breathing. She kept falling, feeling more and more lightheaded, and knew that if she passed out, that would be the end of everything.

She had to hold on, and she had to stay awake, and she had to pay attention.

Because she would only get one chance at this, and she had to do it right.

Thirty-eight

Somehow Travers managed to get most of the story out of Gaylord, and it hadn't taken all night. Apparently a week with the Fates had been good for something.

What Travers couldn't understand was why Zoe had decided to go into Faerie at all. She hadn't planned to. She had been adamantly against it.

All Gaylord had said was that she saw some profit in it.

Profit wasn't a major motivation for Zoe, so Travers wasn't exactly sure what was going on. He actually figured he needed the Fates' help. They probably knew a spell or two, which they could explain to him, that might show him where Zoe was.

Or, worst case, prove to him that Gaylord was lying.

Travers picked up the phone, dialed the Fates' room, and asked them to come to his. He had a hunch Zoe wouldn't approve of his methods, but he couldn't think of anything else to do.

The Fates arrived in record time, at least for them. It only took them fifteen minutes from the phone call to their knock on the door. During that time, Travers had to prove to Gaylord that the refrigerator had no beer, and he had to try to convince him that they didn't have time to order any from room service.

Fang never stopped growling, and Travers made certain he never mentioned his precious son, asleep in the next room.

Finally, Gaylord confessed that he hadn't seen either Harry Potter movie, so Travers ordered up the movies again, not certain how long it would take the Fates to arrive.

In the meantime, he paced and thought and paced and thought, and actually wished he knew more about magic than he did. He would be able to know what was going on with Zoe, then, and he wouldn't have to rely on anyone else.

When the Fates knocked, he opened the door, put a finger to his lips, and mouthed, *Don't say who you are.*

Clotho mouthed, *Okay,* but Travers wasn't really sure she understood him.

Then he introduced them to Gaylord as three friends of his and Zoe's.

"Zoe never mentioned any of you," Gaylord said, still staring at the television.

Travers shut off the TV.

"Hey!" Gaylord said. "That's not very fair. Now I'll never know if the kid zaps his aunt and uncle into oblivion."

"Trust me," Lachesis said, "that odious pair shows up in every book."

"At least through number four," Atropos said. "We haven't read number five yet."

Travers looked at them in surprise. He had no idea they were Harry Potter fans. It just went to show that every person on the planet *had* read a J. K. Rowling novel. Every person, that is, except Gaylord.

"You can watch it later," Travers said to Gaylord. "I'll even buy you a copy if your story holds up."

"Holds up?" He gathered his knees against his chest. "What do you mean, *holds up*?"

"I can't go running off to help Zoe without confirmation," Travers said.

"You have magic," Gaylord said. "You should've checked."

Travers looked at the Fates. "I don't know the spell."

Clotho tsk-tsked at him. "Do a simple locate."

"A what?" Travers asked.

"Make a fist," Gaylord said, "then snap up the fingers, and think of the person. You should get a trail of light."

"You faeries do everything backwards," Lachesis said. "You think of the person first, then snap your fingers, and then you'll find yourself wherever that person is."

"Which isn't a really good spell if the person is in trouble," Gaylord said. "Then suddenly you're in the middle of trouble and you're of no use to them."

He scooted to the edge of the couch, and frowned at Travers.

"I don't get it," Gaylord said. "You could've just asked me to prove that she's going off to Faerie."

"But you're the one who told me," Travers said.

"So?" Gaylord said.

"I heard that faeries were tricksters," Travers said. "How could I believe that you'd tell me true?"

"Not all faeries are tricksters," Atropos said. "Some are very nice people."

"Some are even great people," Clotho said.

"Some are even greater than people," Lachesis said.

Gaylord was staring at them. "You know, you ladies look familiar. What did you say your names were?"

All three Fates stiffened, as if they'd been caught being bad. "You know," Atropos said to Travers, "you can try Gaylord's method. Your magic isn't settled yet. You might achieve a fairy spell with great ease."

"And it does make more sense to follow light than to get into the thick of things," Clotho said.

"Although I do believe this boy is telling you true," Lachesis said. "He's always had a mage-like heart."

"What?" Gaylord said. "I could take that as an insult, you know."

Travers was shaking. He didn't want to lose track of Zoe in all of this bickering.

"Okay," he said to Gaylord, "walk me through this."

"He can't," Atropos said. "If he so much as touches you, the spell becomes his, not yours."

"You have a good memory, Travers," Clotho said. "Just do what he told you."

Travers thought of Zoe, made a fist, and opened it quickly, snapping his fingers as he did so. A ray of light beamed across the room, drilled a hole through the wall, and traveled across Las Vegas. The light veered south, down the Boulder Highway, to a group of seedy-looking casinos.

"Stop it!" Gaylord said. "Stop it now!"

"You'd better stop it," Lachesis said. "He's exactly right."

But Travers didn't know how to stop it. The light traveled inside the casino, to the kitchen, and into an ice machine. Travers got a sense of Zoe, and then Gaylord hit his hand.

The light vanished.

"Idiot!" Gaylord said. "You never do mage magic in a faerie building."

"Now they'll change the doorway," Atropos said.

"And they might catch Zoe," Clotho said.

"We have to do something," Lachesis said. "And quickly."

Thirty-nine

Zoe landed with a thud on a carpeted floor. The tube that had deposited her disappeared as quickly as it opened up.

She found herself in the middle of a casino, only one unlike any she'd ever seen.

The lights were brighter, the noise louder, and the people weren't mortal at all. They were all faerie, and they all seemed to be having an excellent time.

She didn't recognize the games, either. Most of them resembled slot machines, but the display panels had actual places on them. It looked like the faeries were betting on real people's lives, on their next actions, on their personal choices.

There were also historical reenactment machines for faeries who wanted to bet on the path of alternate histories (even though they really couldn't change the past—that instruction was on top of the machine in big, bold letters: anyone who monkeyed with the past would be put to death).

And large signs with pointing fingers showed the way to various other parts of the casino—the theater, the comedy club, the bar, the restaurant, and what seemed to be the biggest draw, the collectible pit.

Zoe had no idea where to start.

She was dizzy and sore and very tired. She could feel the energy all around her, and it unnerved her. The magic she felt clearly came from a different place than her own.

She stood, rubbed her backside, and wondered if she should ask directions. More and more faeries were looking at her. Her heart was pounding hard, and she was trying not to think of the prophecy, of losing herself in here.

She was more afraid of getting lost. She couldn't see the signs anymore. They seemed to have shifted, to have moved in different directions.

The slot machines had grown taller, and she felt like Alice in Wonderland. She needed a potion that would make her larger, so she could see over the slots.

But she didn't dare do magic in here. Her kind of magic would call attention to itself, and she was horribly out-numbered. She had to find all of this on her own.

She came to a fork in the bank of slot machines. A new sign, looking like it had been made from sticks, had arrows pointing in all different directions, including up. The instructions told her about various portions of the casino, and then one said quite simply: THE CIRCLE.

The Circle. The Faerie Circle. Where the Great Rulers used to sit and rule the Great Race of Faerie. Where the Faerie Kings overthrew the Great Rulers and started their own customs and traditions.

Where, possibly, the wheel might be.

She tried not to feel too excited about this. The arrow wasn't that clear. It seemed to point past a bank of slots that guided the careers of old Rock 'n Roll stars, but when she looked at the arrow again, it seemed to point toward a sign advertising Vaudeville Night at the Comedy Club.

Some of the names on the sign were vaguely familiar, and she hoped the first two ideas that popped into her head were wrong. She didn't want to see that the old vaudeville stars had been lured down here to perform nearly a century ago, when vaudeville was dying, and they were still doing that or that a lot of faeries were vaudeville stars and hadn't given it up.

Zoe glanced at the Circle arrow again, and it was gone.

She had to think. Either the wheel was in the direction of the Rock 'n Roll slots or it was near the vaudeville performers.

Or it was directly in front of her, and someone was trying to trick her.

Of course they were trying to trick her. She was in Faerie.

She took a deep breath and headed straight forward, down an aisle of video poker machines that when she looked at them, she realized weren't video poker at all. They had the names of credit card companies on the top, and the names of credit card holders on the side, and the faeries set the going interest rate. Every time a consumer paid with plastic the faerie in front of the machine got a small payoff.

Zoe shuddered, and then watched, almost mesmerized, as the rates kept going up and up. She thought she saw the name of someone she recognized, and that pulled her out of the reverie.

She didn't want to be here any longer than necessary.

She had to remember why she was here: it wasn't for the Fates or for the money. It was for Travers and Kyle and the bond between them. It was for love—especially true love, which she might feel but never get to act on.

It was for the world as she knew it, the world that she loved. The last thing she wanted was for these tricksters to have control of the emotions of the people around her. The good emotions.

It seemed that Faerie already had control of some of the baser ones.

She hurried down the aisle toward a glow that rose in the distance. So far, no one in Faerie seemed to notice her.

She had no idea how long that luck would hold.

Forty

Travers drove his SUV along East Tropicana Boulevard, amazed at the speeds he could achieve in the middle of the night. He felt like Zoe, driving well beyond the speed limit. Only she always seemed invulnerable when she did it. He felt like a kid whose father was going to catch him and punish him.

Gaylord didn't help. He was crouched in the passenger seat, his hands over his eyes. He claimed he hated combustion-engine vehicles. If he was going to go more than three miles an hour, he'd do it with his own wings, thank you.

But the Fates convinced him to go with Travers, and they convinced Travers not to use too much magic in arriving at the casino that currently housed Faerie. The Fates were afraid that the entrance might shift, and then where would he be?

He wasn't sure what that meant, and he wasn't sure he wanted to find out. He only knew that for some reason that he didn't fully understand, Zoe had taken it upon herself to go into Faerie. She went without warning anyone and she

went without back-up, and he was afraid that her prophecy
would come true.

He was afraid she wouldn't get out.

Travers had to go around a pickup that was crawling
along the side of the road. That was the only traffic he'd seen
for at least a mile. Theoretically, Gaylord was mentally trolling
for cop cars, but Travers wasn't sure Gaylord knew what a cop
car was. He seemed a lot more knowledgeable about modern
culture than the Fates until you pressed him, and then it became clear that he only cared about the surface and not what
was beneath it.

Before he left, Travers had called Megan and asked her to
hurry, saying he would have to go out on an emergency, and
that three very strange friends of his were baby-sitting Kyle.

Travers also made it clear that he didn't want these friends
baby-sitting Kyle for long, so when Megan arrived, she could
take Travers's bed. Travers left a key for her at the front desk
with more warnings about the Fates (get them out of the
room as fast as possible; try not to wake Kyle; don't answer
most of Kyle's questions—let Travers do that; and remember
that Kyle has been sick, just in case his conversation sounds
a bit . . . disjointed).

Travers didn't know how to cover his butt any other way.
He had wanted to ease his sister into this world slowly, maybe
not expose her to it at all, and now he wouldn't be able to.
She would have too many questions for him to answer, and
he had no idea how to do so.

His palms were sweating on the steering wheel. The lights
along the boulevard seemed bright. The university looked
alive and glowy, despite the late hour. The Liberace Museum
seemed to be the only place that wasn't open—which Liberace
himself would probably have found strange.

Then Gaylord grabbed his arm. The movement was so
quick, and Gaylord's grasp so fierce, that Travers swerved,

nearly lost control, and had to fight to get back to his side of the road.

Fortunately Tropicana was still mostly empty. One other SUV saw his maneuver, and honked as it went by.

"What the hell?" Travers said. "You never grab a driver."

Gaylord didn't seem to notice. He was staring straight ahead. "They switched it."

"Switched what?" Travers asked.

"The entrance."

Travers let out a small breath.

"They probably did it because of the light."

His fault, then. He had no idea if he should trust Gaylord on this. It was Zoe's life on the line. Or Zoe's self. Travers didn't exactly understand the prophecy, but he knew something awful could happen to her.

Which was why he was here, instead of in his hotel room with Kyle, hoping someone else would take care of this—or that Zoe would survive.

Gaylord's fingers dug into Travers's skin. "You've got to turn around."

Travers shot him a quick look. Gaylord had come to him. The Fates believed that Gaylord was right; they believed that Travers's magic had found Zoe and that she was in trouble.

Travers swung the wheel and made a U-turn in the middle of Tropicana. A car zoomed by, its horn blaring. Gaylord squealed and buried his head.

"Where are we going?" Travers shouted.

"The Mirage," Gaylord said.

"Faeries don't own the Mirage," Travers said. Even he knew that.

"No, they don't, but the sidewalk out front by the volcano is sometimes an emergency entrance until a better one opens up."

"By the volcano?" Travers had seen the volcano. It was an amazing sight. "Why there?"

"Because no one looks down there." Gaylord made it sound like Travers was stupid.

"You mean we could've gone there in the first place?" Travers asked.

"No," Gaylord said. "The emergency entrances only open up when the regular entrances close down. You've got to hurry. The next new one could be in the Hoover Dam, for all we know."

Travers turned north on Maryland Parkway, then east on Flamingo Road. The empty streets continued. He drove so fast that the SUV bounced over several ruts in the road, making him feel as if he were flying.

Gaylord had given up looking long ago.

When they finally arrived at the Mirage, Travers tossed his keys at a valet, barely remembered to take the ticket and let Gaylord pay the tip. Travers ran toward the volcano, which was dark. A sign with eruption schedules was posted near the viewing area.

"Where?" Travers asked Gaylord.

Gaylord was stuffing a bulging wallet in the back pocket of his jeans. "I could get in trouble for this," he muttered.

"Where?" Travers asked again.

"There." Gaylord pointed at a scuffed spot on the sidewalk. "It's behind the concrete."

"Lead on," Travers said.

"Are you kidding? I can't bring a civilian into Faerie."

"Then how am I going to get her?" Travers asked.

"She's going for the wheel," Gaylord said. "Just—close your eyes, click your heels together three times, and think of the wheel."

"This isn't a movie," Travers said.

Gaylord blinked at him. "I didn't say it was."

"The Fat—um, my friends said I can't use mage magic in Faerie," Travers said. "It's like a beacon."

"Crap," Gaylord said. "I forgot."

He rubbed his chin, then reached for the concrete himself. He pulled the piece back as if it weighed nothing, revealing a dark and forbidding hole in the ground.

"Okay," Gaylord said. "You've got to trust me."

He reached up with his forefingers and touched Travers's ears. They stretched, aching as they did so, the sound like pulling rubber. Travers blinked, but before he could move away, Gaylord touched his eyebrows. They stretched, too, only no sound accompanied them. Just an ache.

"What're you doing?" Travers asked.

"Giving you a disguise," Gaylord said. "No one'll notice. They're probably focused on the outsider right now."

"Zoe," Travers said.

"You got it. Hurry," Gaylord said. "And don't call attention to yourself."

"Do I get out the way I got in?" Travers asked.

"Yeah, if it's still here," Gaylord said. "Otherwise, I'll be waiting for you at the closest entrance."

Travers didn't like the sound of that. He looked over his shoulder, saw only a few drunken tourists on the sidewalk, staggering toward a different casino.

He grabbed the edges of the hole and swung his legs inside. He got a sense that this was his very last chance to change his mind, his last chance to go back to Kyle and forget that any of this had happened.

But Travers couldn't forget it, and he couldn't leave Zoe alone. Gaylord's words had chilled him.

They were focussed on the outsider.

Focused on Zoe.

And she was down there, all alone.

Forty-one

The glow caught her attention, held her, kept her moving forward, past games like she'd never seen. Clowns making balloon animals that actually mooed, whinnied, and ran off; more faeries grabbing lights out of the sky, and turning them into little winged creatures; a baseball floating above the entire area, like a floating camera.

Zoe hurried. The ground throbbed under her feet, as if she got close to some kind of large machine, something that pulsed and vibrated and kept everything alive. She could hear as well as feel it: the pulse was subsonic and somehow circular.

She knew she was right. She was near the Circle.

The signs had vanished. The farther forward she went, the more the faeries vanished.

Yet she felt like she was not alone. Even though it was hard to hear over that subsonic noise, she thought she heard rustling behind her, but every time she turned, she saw nothing.

The fact that she was all by herself in this section of Faerie was beginning to unnerve her. Everything was unnerving her.

What would she do, exactly, when she found the wheel? Use her magic to get it out of here? Send it to the Fates?

Steal it, like she said she wouldn't?

She wasn't sure. She hoped she would figure it out when she got there.

She hurried forward, and nearly tripped down a flight of stairs. The stairs were clear, lit from below, and nearly blinding.

In fact, the entire floor that she now stood on was a blaze of light. It took a moment for her eyesight to adjust. Then she realized she was in the middle of a round pit.

This pit seemed to be built for gambling. Large tables with dice stood on one section of the floor. Another section seemed dedicated to blackjack, and yet another to poker. A giant roulette wheel dominated the entire area. The wheel shot out lights of red and black that somehow didn't reflect on the all-light floor.

The sound of the giant ball, spinning and ticking in the various holes, filled the room.

Zoe couldn't see anyone else. Then she looked down, and realized that the light had paled her out as well. To anyone whose eyesight hadn't completely adjusted, she would look like a white wall of nothing—maybe even like part of the floor.

Her mouth was dry. She didn't know where to go from here.

And then she looked up at the roulette wheel.

It was huge. Beside it were three chairs, which almost looked like thrones. The chairs were empty. The wheel seemed to be playing itself, and the lights from the red and black sides flared upwards, not down.

Zoe followed the lights, and couldn't see where they led.

But as she looked down, she realized that the wheel looked odd for a roulette wheel. For one thing, it had spokes in the middle, spokes that had been layered over and covered with cloth, but visible all the same. The holes in the wheel weren't carved in its wooden sides, but made special and attached underneath the round part, like they were added later.

And there was more to the wheel—some sort of contraption on which it sat. If she mentally tilted the contraption on its side . . . she had a spinning wheel, with a place for the operator to sit as she created her cloth.

Zoe's breath caught. Somehow she had expected to find the wheel in the collectibles area. She had also thought the wheel would be a lot smaller, not the dominant thing in what seemed like the main part of the casino.

If she took this—if she figured out how to take this—she would be noticed. She wasn't even sure how to get it free without interrupting all of the power to Faerie.

For as far as she could tell, the throbbing, pulsating noise that dominated this area came from the wheel itself.

Zoe took a step toward the wheel, and hoped she would figure out what to do next.

Forty-two

Travers let go of the edges of the entrance to Faerie and fell, straight down, into the hole. He fell for what seemed like forever, and the air around him grew fetid, smelling of earth and mold and damp.

His hair streamed above him, and he knew he was going downward at a furious clip.

He just hoped the landing would be soft.

Then he heard voices, smelled cigarettes, and saw lights. And suddenly he sprawled on top of a silk net, one that had clearly been placed beneath the entrance just recently.

He bounced twice on the net, as if it were a trampoline, and then two women—with ears as pointed as Gaylord's and hair as dark—helped him down.

They smiled at him, then reached up to touch his hair. "Experimenting with the mortals, were you?" someone asked.

Travers made himself grin. Apparently there weren't blond faeries. Gaylord had forgotten about Travers's hair.

And about his height. He was nearly a foot taller than everyone in the room.

Travers made his grin widen. "They like 'em tall and blond these days," he said, and the faerie folk around him laughed.

Most of them were eating—he seemed to land near a buffet of some kind—but he didn't recognize the food. Still, the smells were marvelous, like a mixture of fresh-baked cake and roast beef and a potato dish his grandmother used to make when he was a boy.

Travers's stomach growled. Then he remembered all the stories he'd heard about faeries, how if they got you to eat something, you were trapped by them forever.

Maybe food was one way they made a person lose time. Drink had to be another. Hadn't Rip Van Winkle had a drink of ale with the faeries during the famous bowling match that lasted an entire decade?

Travers now wished he'd been paying attention when they'd taught literature in all of his classes.

He smoothed his hair back, and looked beyond the room. He saw two images: an image made of light that showed various parts of a casino, and a shadowy image, more box-like, like hallways or the mysterious tunnels he'd always heard about that existed behind Disneyland.

He felt slightly lightheaded, like he always did before he played the lottery, and he recognized the shadow-vision as the same thing.

Travers had always convinced himself that he had somehow stumbled on the formula behind random number calculations—that his brain was as swift as a computer and could see the patterns that no one else's could see—but now he knew differently. Maybe he did see the patterns or maybe his magic allowed him an advantage with calculations, but he also had an ability to see things that weren't quite there—or weren't there yet—like the winning numbers on a lottery ticket.

Then the entire room shifted ever so slightly, and the casino spaces filled the shadowy spaces. He felt an odd sense of confirmation that went with his dizziness, and then he saw the shadowy spaces again.

The realization that hit him made him almost as dizzy as the movement of the room—which, he noted, almost no one else seemed to sense. Faerie wasn't constantly changing, not in an illogical way, anyhow. It was a giant fractal, and it created new patterns as it shifted, following some kind of pre-programmed equation deep within its bowels.

Almost as if Faerie were run by a giant computer that kept changing everything.

Travers hadn't moved since he got here, and the faerie women had long since moved off. Maybe this was how people lost time in Faerie—they got thinking and were so wrapped up in their own minds, they couldn't unravel themselves.

He still saw shadowy places, and as he watched them, he saw a lot of faeries move along them, heading in a particular direction.

What had Gaylord said? No one would notice Travers because they would be focused on the outsider.

Focused on Zoe.

But would they actually lead him to her?

Somehow Travers didn't think so.

Still, he moved forward along the shadowy shapes, sensing that there was less to Faerie than met the eye. In fact, if he squinted, he saw that the shadowy shapes hid tubes—long, dark tubes that moved toward a central hub.

He squinted further, let the pattern settle in his brain, and realized he was standing between two spokes of a wheel. The center of the wheel, the hub, the very middle, was straight before him. All he had to do was follow the tubes.

It seemed so simple, but he had to keep squinting. Otherwise, he believed he was walking across carpet, into slot machines, going through walls.

But the walls weren't really there or they had just been there and were leaving or they were coming to that position in a moment. He was walking *between* the casino pattern, *between* the pieces of the fractal just before it rearranged, right to the very heart of the casino, of Faerie, which he could feel.

It pulsed, just like a human heart.

This place had life, and he hoped that the life wouldn't sense him.

At least, not until he found Zoe and made sure she was safe.

Forty-three

The wheel seemed to go forever. Its light dazzled Zoe's eyes, and she could feel the power emanating from it. How had the faeries harnessed it? How had they changed it from a small spinning wheel into this giant roulette wheel? And what was its purpose?

She took another step closer and then felt air on the back of her neck. She turned ever so slightly, and saw a man behind her. He wasn't as tall as she was, and his hair was dark. His eyes glittered.

His hand came up and touched an area just outside her skin. She felt the touch tremble all the way through her.

He was touching her aura, testing her magic with his own.

Another man joined him, and then another and another, and suddenly Zoe was surrounded. She had heard about these situations before—magical theft situations, where a person's magic could be taken, one tiny piece at a time. All the takers had to do was find a chink in the aura, a crack in the light that surrounded her, and they would be able to reach in and steal her magic.

More and more faeries joined the circle around her. She looked up. No one was above her, but she knew better than to use her magic now. Using it would open any gap, would reveal any problem in her aura, and the faeries would use it.

They would use it to destroy her.

She was hemmed in. She couldn't move. She couldn't use her magic.

But she had to find a way out. She had to get out and do something with the wheel.

She was here to steal power, too, only she wanted all of it, and she wanted to return it to the Fates. She didn't want these people to control her world.

She didn't want these people to change Travers or Kyle or anyone she loved.

She had to fight.

If she could only figure out how.

Forty-four

Then Travers saw her. Or more correctly, he saw a crowd gathering near the hub, surrounding someone— that someone just a slight bit taller than everyone else. Zoe's dark hair looked different from the faeries' hair—it had a different texture, a glossiness, and Travers had a sense of her, even from this distance.

She wasn't scared, but she was close. She knew she was trapped, and she didn't know how to break free.

He wasn't sure what to do, either. He just knew he had to do something quickly because if he didn't, they would grab him, too.

He ran down the center of the space between the spokes to the hub, and when he reached it, he shoved his way through the growing crowd around Zoe.

His height helped. His height and his strength, and probably his underlying panic.

"Mine," he said as he moved. "Back off. She's mine. Mine."

And to his surprise, people did. They moved away, as if he were going to hurt them. Then they must have realized that he wasn't, because they closed back in, trapping him just like they had trapped her.

He kept pushing forward with great determination, certain he would get to her.

And suddenly he was there, suddenly she was in his arms, and she was clinging to him, and she *was* scared, which scared him because Zoe wasn't the type to be frightened easily.

Everything shifted around him, and he suddenly saw the room as she saw it—a circular pit, with a roulette wheel in its center. The roulette wheel as the hub.

The roulette wheel—the former spinning wheel of the Fates—was the heart of Faerie.

Travers didn't have a chance to figure out what that meant. He figured he had only one opportunity, and he would take it. He yanked Zoe through the crowd, heading toward the wheel instead of away from it.

The Fates had said the wheel augmented their powers, and unless he missed his guess, it would augment his. And even though he didn't know a lot about magic, he had transported himself once—twice, if you counted getting back, and by gum (was that a phrase?) he would do it again.

Zoe clung to him, moving with him, saying something—although he couldn't hear what with the pounding of the machine here and the murmur of faerie voices, something about not letting her get away.

Then Travers grabbed a corner of the wheel, and it spun him upward, away from the crowd. Zoe came with him, rolling with it, trapped in the red light, making her face look blood-covered.

"We have to take it," she was saying. "The wheel. They're going to use it to destroy the world."

But Travers didn't have enough magic to take the wheel, and he wasn't sure what would happen if he tried, as integrated as it was into Faerie itself.

Instead, he let the power of it burn into his fingers, and then he thought of his hotel and Kyle and safety—

Suddenly Travers shot straight upward in the air. Zoe clung to him, her arms wrapped around his neck as if she were afraid he would drop her.

He held her with one arm. The other was pointed upward—the one that had touched the wheel—and his hand was lost in a large, white light.

Then his hand became a fist, and he pounded through solid ground, but felt no pain.

He burst upward, like a man on top of a geyser, and then fell to the ground, Zoe landing on him, knocking the wind out of him.

They were lying in the middle of Fremont Street, right smack in the middle of the no-driving area, under all the neon lights. The Four Queens was only a few yards away, and their logo blurred so that Travers thought he saw three Fates instead.

Zoe stood before he did, and she helped him up. A few people passed by, giving them sideways looks, but not stopping for any reason. They probably thought Zoe and Travers were drunk.

He wasn't drunk, but he was tired.

The hole in the ground closed, and the concrete reassembled as if it hadn't split. Zoe helped Travers stumble to the sidewalk. His eyes took a moment to adjust to the neon lights, and then he leaned against a support column that held up one of the many signs.

"You saved me," Zoe said.

"I couldn't let you be down there alone," Travers said.

"But you shouldn't have left Kyle." She was running her hands over his face. "What happened to you?"

He touched his upswept eyebrows. "Gaylord."

"Gaylord?"

And then Travers realized that she didn't know any of it—how Gaylord had come for him, how Travers had found her. Or even why he had come.

"I left Kyle," Travers said, "because you needed me."

"It was okay," she said. "I know that he's more important to you. I was going down there for all of us. The faeries want to destroy the world—"

"And you can't stop them, not all alone," Travers said.

"I had to try." Zoe was trembling.

Travers wrapped his arms around her and pulled her close. Then he kissed her. And kissed her, and kissed her one more time.

Finally, he pulled away. He smoothed the hair off her face, touched her cheeks, and said, "You were the world they were going to destroy, and I couldn't let them. I love you, Zoe. I can't imagine life without you."

"But Kyle—"

"Has already told me what an idiot I am for not taking advantage of the situation."

"Situation?" Zoe asked.

"He thinks you like me."

"Oh," she said with a very soft smile. "He's right. I do."

Forty-five

Travers and Zoe caught a cab back to the hotel, and all the way there, Zoe went back and forth between elation—Travers had come for her! She had survived Faerie!—and despair. She hadn't stopped the faeries. She hadn't stolen the wheel. She hadn't changed anything.

She couldn't even save the Fates.

Travers hadn't taken his arm from around her shoulder. They pressed close together, and she didn't mind. She even fantasized that her prophecy might be true—that what he said back on Fremont Street wasn't in the heat of the moment, that it was actually true, that he loved her. That he was her soulmate, and she had found him near Faerie.

She hadn't lost herself inside Faerie because of Travers. Because somehow he figured how to use the wheel to augment his magic, somehow he knew it would protect them from the faeries, and it would get them free.

The cab let them off in front of the hotel. The sun was coming up, sending a golden light over the mountains and into the valley. The city was almost beautiful, and Zoe wished she could hold onto this moment.

Travers took her hand and led her into the hotel.

"Where're we going?" she asked.

"If Kyle's awake, he's worried," Travers said.

"May we see the Fates first?" Zoe asked. She wanted to get that meeting out of the way, to let them know that she failed. "I can go alone if you want."

Travers gave her a warm smile. His face was his own again—no flying Faerie eyebrows, no strange, pointed ears. She had forgotten, just in those few hours, how good-looking he really was.

"I'm sticking with you from now on," he said, and as they got in the elevator, he put his arm around her waist. She slid her arm around him.

None of the men she'd known, or any of the people she'd known, had ever made her feel like this. She had been willing to give up everything, not so she could be with him, but so he could remain happy.

She had never been willing to do that for anyone before.

The elevator doors opened and she walked with Travers to the Fates' room. He knocked.

"You're sure they're there?" Zoe whispered.

"I hope so," he said. "My sister Megan should be with Kyle by now."

At that moment, the door to the suite opened. Clotho was wearing a pink negligée of the Doris Day variety, lots of flowing nylon and feathers.

"You're back!" Clotho said, with a smile. She stepped away from the door. "They're back!"

She called this last to the other Fates, who appeared in the doorways of their rooms like refugees from a 1960s bedroom farce. Lachesis wore a green negligée that matched

Clotho's and Atropos wore a white one. All three women had piled their long hair on top of their heads.

Zoe stepped inside, followed by Travers. He pulled the door closed.

"You're safe," Lachesis said.

"We were worried," Atropos said.

"But not that worried," Clotho said.

"We did have faith in you," Lachesis said.

Zoe held up her hand. She couldn't listen to this anymore. "I didn't get it."

"Get what, darling?" Atropos asked as she stepped into the suite's main room.

"The spinning wheel," Zoe said. "I didn't get it."

"It's the heart of Faerie," Travers said. "Removing it might be impossible."

"Nothing's impossible," Clotho said, but Lachesis smiled.

"Did you hear what he said?" she asked. "It's the heart."

Atropos tapped her chin with one polished fingernail. "Interesting."

They didn't seem upset at all. But Zoe was. She was trembling.

"Don't you understand?" she said. "I didn't get it, and the faeries plan to use it to change the power structure in the whole world. Gaylord said—"

"Where is Gaylord?" Clotho asked.

"I left him at the Mirage," Travers said.

"The Mirage?" Lachesis asked. "Why?"

Travers shook his head. "It's a long story."

Which Zoe heard only a part of on the cab ride back. She had been thinking too hard to concentrate.

"We know about the power structure," Atropos said to Zoe. "We know all about the possible changes. That's why we sent you in."

"But I didn't get it," Zoe said. "I left it down there."

Clotho shrugged. "Ah, well."

She didn't seem upset at all.

"You need it," Zoe said. "You said you need it. Gaylord said the world needs it. We could lose everything—"

"Calm down," Lachesis said. "You should be happy."

"What?" Zoe looked at all three of them. They were still smiling. Travers stood beside her. At least he was as confused as she was. "Why should I be happy?"

"Didn't your prophecy come true?" Atropos asked.

Zoe flushed. "Yes, but—"

"No buts," Clotho said. "People should be both happy and grateful when they find true love."

Travers slipped his arm around Zoe again. She leaned into him. She couldn't help it.

"But the wheel—"

"Forget the wheel," Lachesis said. "You were just supposed to find it. If you couldn't get it out, we had a back-up plan."

"You did?" Travers asked.

"Why didn't you tell us?" Zoe said.

"It's not that important," Atropos said.

"If the fate of the world rests on it, it is," Travers said.

"The fate of *your* world is decided," Clotho said. "You're going to live happily ever after, right?"

Travers frowned. "If Zoe'll have me."

"Then we've done our duty," Lachesis said.

Atropos grinned. "Even without magic."

"But the wheel," Zoe said.

"We've already put out feelers," Clotho said. "We're going to get Robin Hood to get the wheel."

"*The* Robin Hood?" Travers asked.

"Why do people ask that question?" Lachesis said.

"Yes, *the* Robin Hood." Zoe sighed. She knew him. He had

been to a few Vegas conferences over the decades. "Are you sure he's right for the job?"

"Can't think of anyone better," Atropos said. "Now, go on with your lives and let us worry about the future."

"What about you?" Travers asked, with typical concern. "Who'll take care of you?"

Clotho's smile was mysterious. "Why, darling, if you don't mind funding the hotel room, we can take care of the rest."

Lachesis tapped the Cubs baseball cap. "After all, we are protected."

"Go get some sleep," Atropos said. "When you get up, you can tell us all about your adventure. But for now, we think you two lovebirds should be alone."

The three Fates ushered Zoe and Travers out of the hotel room. Zoe had never left a conversation with the three of them so fast. The next thing she knew, she was in the hallway with the door closed.

Travers was staring at the door. "Did that seem odd to you?"

"Yes," Zoe said. "Which frightens me. We are talking about the Fates, here. Odd for them is truly strange."

He ran a finger along her chin. "You never answered me," he said softly. "Will you have me?"

"Is that a marriage offer?" she asked.

He smiled. "Yes."

"Travers, marriage among our people, it's for life."

"That's how I was raised, too."

"Life means thousands of years," Zoe said.

"I doubt that'll be long enough," Travers said. Then he blinked. "You don't have hesitations, do you? I know you didn't want children—"

"How can anyone fail to love Kyle?" Zoe asked. "He's perfect."

Travers bit his lower lip. He was studying her, and she

realized she had never told him her reasons for going into Faerie, her reasons for protecting this place.

Even when they popped back onto Fremont Street, she hadn't told him that she loved him.

She slipped her arms around his neck. "You're perfect, too," she said. "Amazing and strong and brilliant. Do you think you can put up with the chaos that is my life?"

"Looks like that's mine, too," he said, bending down to kiss her.

But she put a finger on his lips, stopping him. "One more thing before I say anything else."

She could feel his muscles tense. "Yes?" he asked.

"I have to tell you how I feel, not how the Fates think I should feel."

His muscles got even tenser. Apparently he had noticed, too, that she hadn't said she loved him.

"You're the most spectacular person I've ever met," she said, "and I love you. I'll love you forever if you let me."

"Let you?" he whispered. "I'd never dream of stopping you."

And then he kissed her, and the kiss was just as amazing as the first kiss. Even more amazing, really, and she had thought that first one was pretty outrageous.

The kiss became another kiss, and then another, and as the kisses continued, she realized that even though he was younger, and they had differences, and they had to make a lot of adjustments to have a life together, they would be able to.

Together, they would be able to do anything.